# Stealing Sorcery

## By Andrew Rowe

# DEDICATION

For my brother, Aaron Rowe, for always being a fantastic role model.

# TABLE OF CONTENTS

ANDREW ROWE

# ACKNOWLEDGEMENTS

The earliest of my development of the setting for these books came from gaming in the IFGS, as well as Dungeons and Dragons campaigns. I'd like to thank both the founders of the IFGS and the creators of Dungeons and Dragons for helping me bring my fantasy worlds to life.

I'd also like to thank the gamers who put up with me while I carved out this world, such as Kai Connick, Joshua Noel, Rachel Noel, Anthony Scopatz, Mallory Reaves, Carly Thomas, and Andrew Warren.

When I moved from Dungeons and Dragons into running my own game system, I had lots of help from other Game Masters. Thanks to Andrew Bice, Kari Brewer, Danielle Collins, Edward Fox, Rachel Noel, Ian Sorrensen, Eric Maloof, Mallory Reaves, and Andrew Warren, for assisting with running events.

Thank you to my beta readers, including Chris Avellone, Danielle Collins, Jessica Richards, and Christine L. Rowe.

Thanks to the community on /r/fantasy for providing me with awesome feedback and discussion about my first book.

# PROLOGUE – JONAN – HEARTLANCE

The evening chill was Jonan's only company as he traversed the unfamiliar streets of Velthryn. The map burned into his memories had proven accurate thus far, but uncertainty always weighed heavily on his shoulders during clandestine operations.

He had arrived in the city only hours before, but his orders had insisted upon haste. Upon reaching the gates, he had briefly considered delaying his report until after he had slept for a few hours – but Symphony would have discovered his lapse. She always did.

Upon catching sight of his destination, the sorcerer retreated into a nearby alley, pressing two fingers from his left hand to his forehead in the Velryan sign for "safety". Among the Thornguard and their allies, it was used as a signal meaning "I am safe" or "I can be trusted".

To an outsider, he would have immediately vanished from sight, although he retained the ability to perceive his own body. The gesture was a nervous habit - he had long ago learned to hide his image without strictly needing to resort to gestures or words.

His vision was already poor, so he barely noticed when the spell extracted its cost. Sight sorcery was among the least obtrusive forms of sorcery – vision was a small price to pay for the freedom that his skills provided.

With his spell in effect, Jonan moved toward the building, a towering three-story housing complex with the dubious distinction of standing next to the local Perfect Stranger Tavern. Such establishments were frequently used as fronts for the Thieves' Guild of Velrya, an organization with deep ties to his own. Arranging for a room there would have been easy, given his connections, but he disliked the idea of finding housing so close to his rendezvous point. His contact could most likely discover where he stayed regardless of the location, but he liked to have at least some pretense of security.

Invisibly opening doors often attracted undue attention, so Jonan chose the more awkward route of making his ascent via a series of stairs on the outside of the building designed to be a fire escape. At the top of the final stairway was a ladder that led the rest of the way to the roof. Gripping the rungs while holding his staff proved difficult, but after a few moments of awkwardness, he approached the roof.

A figure enshrouded in shimmering cloth loomed over him from above, reaching down with a hand. Her body had feminine curves, but any details were washed away by the voluminous sashes that draped her form.

Jonan grit his teeth and accepted the hand. He was pulled to the roof in a disorienting instant, after which he took a breath and steadied himself, planting his staff on the flat stone rooftop.

"Loyalty is like a crystal sword," came a feminine voice from within the layers of fabric.

"Sharp and beautiful, but easily shattered," Jonan finished the phrase as he had been instructed. He barely managed to restrain himself from rolling his eyes. Aayara's methods were effective, but often bordered on the theatrical.

"Not bad," the enshrouded figure mused. "I can't see you at all. What do they call you? Stealth, maybe?"

He scratched his head, giving a sheepish grin, only realizing a moment later that she wouldn't be able to see it. "Scribe, actually." With a thought, he let his invisibility fade. Maintaining the spell wasn't particularly taxing, but now that he had reached his destination he didn't see any point to it. "You're Silk, I take it?"

"No," came a deep voice, echoing from behind him. "I am."

Jonan spun, finding nothing behind him. And then the figure gave an unladylike snort of amusement.

"I've always wanted to do that – you should have seen your face."

Jonan sighed, turning back around. "Sound sorcery? I suppose I should have expected that."

Silk gave a melodious laugh that echoed much like her false voice had. "Maybe, but it was more fun for me this way. I haven't had a partner to practice with for months."

He frowned. "I'm afraid I'm just here for a delivery."

Silk folded her arms and tilted her head to the side. "A delivery? And no new orders, then?"

Jonan shook his head. "No, but I've been told I can make use of you, if I need to."

"Make use of me?" There was a hint of amusement in her voice. "I suppose there might be some entertainment after all. So, what kind of present did you bring me?"

Jonan extended his hand holding the quarterstaff. There was no longer any sight sorcery concealing the weapon within – instead, an actual branch had been hollowed out, and the metallic core was concealed inside and held in place with an adhesive. Someone holding it might notice the staff's unusual weight, but the camouflage worked well against a casual glance, at least.

Silk tilted her head to the side dubiously for a moment, then snatched the staff out of his hands. "Oh," she mumbled, turning the weapon over in her hands. "This...this will do."

*That's a bit of an understatement.*

"What will do you do with it?"

"That," she replied, "You'll find out very, very soon."

# CHAPTER I – VELAS I – JUST A SMALL FAVOR

Velas Jaldin strode through the halls of the Citadel of Blades with her back straight and her head held high. She had long ago learned to conceal her anxiety behind layers of outward walls; in this case, professionalism was her first line of defense.

"You sure you want to do this?" Landen was walking in pace with her, a couple steps to her right. His incessant worrying over her was endearing at times, irritating at others. This was one of the latter cases, but she wouldn't let that show. There could be no cracks in her mask when so much was at stake.

She glanced at him, beaming a smile in his direction. "No worries, Lan. It's just Lydia."

Her companion twisted his lips. "Right. Just Lydia."

Velas chuckled as she continued to walk. *Poor Lan, still swooning over sorceresses. He never changes.*

The Citadel of Blades was the central structure for the Keldrian Crossing Holy Grounds, a parcel of land that had been owned by the Priesthood of Tae'os for centuries. As the priesthood expanded and developed a military branch – the Paladins of Tae'os – the Holy Grounds had shifted from its initial purpose as a center of worship into a permanent military base.

The Citadel of Blades itself was now one part temple, one part fortress, and about five parts administrative center. Ringed with dozens of other buildings, the citadel housed the offices of most of the officers of the Paladins of Tae'os – the newly promoted Major Lydia Hastings among them.

It had been eight months since Lydia had discredited Edon, the leader of the supposed "gods" of the city of Orlyn. Eight months since Prince Byron had been crowned king of Orlyn. And eight months since Velas and Landen had been "relieved" from the Queensguard.

Normally, she would have expected to transition directly into being a member of the new Kingsguard, but Byron did not trust that anyone who had served his mother would be loyal to him above her. Frankly, he had probably been right.

It had been Landen's idea to chase Lydia's skirt all the way back to her home in Velthryn. She had rolled her eyes at the idea outwardly, but she had agreed – not just to support her friend, but also because she had business of her own to pursue in Velthryn. Business that was long overdue.

They had arrived in Velthryn just under six months ago and immediately met with Lydia to discuss the possibility of joining the Paladins of Tae'os.

She pushed the errant thought from her mind, arriving at Lydia's door. She didn't know the paladin particularly well, but they had met a few times in Orlyn and several more since coming to Velthryn. It had, of course, been Landen's idea to offer to join the Paladins of Tae'os. Velas thought they were hideously overqualified to sign up as fresh recruits, but fortunately, the paladins apparently had plenty of other applicants with prior experience as soldiers, mercenaries, and even members of other military orders.

People like Landen and herself were given the option to participate in an accelerated training program, culminating in a series of proficiency tests to see if they were a match for any of the seven suborders. The training had been tedious, but relatively easy by her standards. The hardest parts were the history lessons – they were boring and completely impractical, as far as she was concerned.

The combat training, on the other hand – now that was fun.

Velas glanced over at Landen, who just shrugged unhelpfully at her, and knocked on Lydia's door. The exasperated sigh that came from the other side was loud enough that she could have heard it easily, even without her own particular talents.

"Come in."

Velas turned the knob, giving one last look to her brown-haired companion, who leaned up against a nearby wall. He was trying to look natural. It was half-surprising that he had even accompanied her this far, given his reservations about her plan.

Velas opened the door, stepped in, and closed the door behind her. Afterward, she turned to see Lydia sitting at a desk stacked with an implausible number of papers. The paladin leaned against her left hand, rubbing her temple. Her right hand rested on the table, her fingers blackened with ink and grasped around a quill.

The former Queensguard wasn't wearing a sword, so she simply raised her right hand to her chest as a salute. Lydia sat up a little straighter, abandoning her quill to mirror the gesture.

"At ease, Velas. What can I help you with?"

Velas relaxed her stance a bit, taking a moment to look Lydia over. Several errant threads of crimson hair had slipped out of Lydia's traditional bun, and her spectacles served to magnify the bags under her eyes. Nevertheless, her uniform was immaculate.

"Was hoping you could do me a favor. You got a few?"

Lydia nodded sleepily, standing and retrieving a rag from a nearby shelf. She wrapped the rag around her ink-stained hand, and the black liquid seeping into the cloth reminded Velas of binding a wound.

"I could use a break from all this paperwork. Apparently coming home a hero makes you uniquely qualified to be a secretary. Who knew?"

Velas frowned in something she hoped resembled sympathy. "Sorry, Lydia. Anything I can help with?"

She didn't want to help Lydia with anything, but she was also pretty sure Lydia wouldn't agree.

"Actually—"

*Shit. Platitude gamble failed.*

"—I saw something on your application about sorcery resistance. That's intriguing – what did you mean?"

*Oh, that.* "Got a knack for shaking off anything that tries to get into my head. Always had it, far as I can tell. My aunt figured it out when she was trying to teach me something. Had me try it with a bunch of people."

Lydia finished wiping off her hand, setting the blackened cloth down on a far corner of the table. "I'd like to see that."

*Oh, that's not so bad.* She never minded a good chance to show off. "Okay, Red. Hit me with whatever you've got."

"You'd better sit down first." Lydia pointed to a chair on the side of the desk near the entrance. She had a mischievous glint in her eyes, which Velas had to admit was kind of cute. *Maybe Landen's taste isn't complete resh after all.*

Velas sat down, folding her arms behind her head. "What's on the bombardment agenda?"

Lydia sauntered up to her, put a finger on her bicep, and said, "Sleep."

Velas' eyes closed. Purple threads appeared in her mind, spreading through the veins at the point of contact in her arm to spread throughout her body. Velas felt a momentary chill as she pulled on the threads with her mind, syphoning them away from her arm and into a central point in her right hand.

*Expel,* she silently commanded the threads, envisioning them surging out her fingertips into the empty air.

The chill faded and Velas opened her eyes, grinning.

"Gotta do better than that, Red. Unless your spell was meant to knock me out for about ten seconds."

Lydia frowned, shaking her head. "I'm afraid you've been asleep for several hours, Velas."

Velas blinked, opening her mouth and then closing it again as words failed to emerge. The faintest hint of a smile crept its way to Lydia's lips.

The former Queensguard narrowed her eyes at Lydia, and then burst out laughing. "Okay, that was pretty good. You actually had me there for a second, and I'll tell you, that's not easy to do."

"I know – it was a rare opportunity, so I had to take it. Your ability is extraordinary. How did you do that?"

Velas scoffed. "After you pulled that little trick on me? Forget it. You can keep guessing. It's a trade secret."

The paladin rolled her eyes. "Fine. I'll figure it out one way or another. Now, what brings you to my secluded cavern?"

*Oh, that.* "Put my preferred team on my application. Which, given that you just grilled me about my talents, you've already seen."

Lydia nodded, leaning back against her desk, a hint of exhaustion returning to her expression. "Yeah. You want me to make sure you're placed with your friends, I take it?"

Velas nodded.

"Easy enough. Anything else?"

*Really, that's it?* "Was expecting you to require convincing."

The paladin shrugged. "It's hardly a surprising request. Anyone with connections is going to try to utilize them. I'm a Sytiran – pre-planning for your success is something I encourage. Besides that, it's not like there are many local candidates this year. Putting you with two other heavy melee fighters makes perfect sense. Although I was somewhat tempted to pair you and Landen with Keldyn Andys."

"That guy? He's all flash. Granted, he's got a lot of flash – but you take his trick away and there's no substance beneath."

Lydia raised an eyebrow. "I have it on good authority he was an accomplished swordsman even before he earned his gifts. But if you've got that strong of an opinion about him, maybe I should put him on your team. You might both learn a few things from each other."

"You're kidding. What am I going to learn from him, arrogance and condescension? I'd rather take those lessons from Salaris – at least he can back it up."

"Fine, fine. But you're going to have to train with some people outside of your own little circle. The three of you will be slotted into a larger platoon, and I don't expect you to ignore the rest of the platoon in favor of each other. From what I hear, some of the foreign candidates might even be a match for you or Landen in a duel."

Velas smirked. "Good. Give me the best of them. Unless we're fighting the other platoons – in which case, give me some raw material to work with. I could use a challenge."

"Don't worry, Velas. We'll make sure you're more than adequately challenged."

*If you're putting me on a team with Lan and Salaris, I sincerely doubt that. Unless these other applicants are legendary heroes and demigods, I'll wager we're going to come out on top.*

Velas felt the knock before she heard it. She deliberately slowed her reaction – turning too fast could be startling to others.

The door swung open before Lydia even had a chance to respond. A younger paladin was standing at the entrance, his forehead drenched with sweat, his breath ragged. He barely managed to raise his hand into a salute before beginning to speak. "Major Hastings! Please come with me, there's been an incident."

*An incident? What the resh does that mean?*

"What happened?" Lydia stood up straight, adjusting her sword belt.

"House Theas. There's been an assassination attempt —"

Lydia pushed past Velas and broke into a run.

## CHAPTER II – LYDIA I – A TASTE OF POISON

Lydia shoved her way through the heavy doors to House Theas' manor, racing down the halls toward the fevered sounds of Aladir's incantations.

"Let Lissari's light live within your body, and let the spark of her love —"

*Gods and monsters, he's casting a Spark of Life. The victim must be...*

Her steps carried her faster, ignoring the startled looks of servants and the numerous signs of wealth that lined the building's floors and walls.

"—renew you, and let your heart beat once again!"

A flash of green illuminated a distant hall, and Aladir's voice rose again.

"Let Lissari's light live within your body..."

Lydia came into view of her companion sitting with a corpse laid across his lap, a pool of blood beneath the pair. Not all of it belonged to the victim.

"Aladir, stop," Lydia commanded, only noticing the other figures standing nearby a moment later. The two women watching over Aladir were similar in visage, albeit separated by many years, but their demeanor could not have been more distinct.

The elder woman had been shattered by panic and anguish, her makeup smeared by freely-flowing tears. In another circumstance, she might have been quite beautiful. In this, her image was that of grief itself.

The younger stared downward at Aladir and the deceased man with a hawkish glare, scrutinizing with a mixture of inquisitiveness and anger.

"...and let the spark of her love..."

Lydia ignored both of the women, grabbing Aladir's hand and pulling it away from the dead man's torso. Aladir raised his head, seeming to notice Lydia for the first time. The Rethri's once-brilliant green eyes were the dullest she had ever seen them, and a stream of blood ran from his nose down his chin.

"Aladir, you need to stop. It's too late for him, and you're going to kill yourself if you continue." She wiped a line of blood out from under his nose, showing it to the Rethri to emphasize her point.

"The healer will stop when I tell him to." The tear-stained woman hugged herself, shivering as she spoke. "If he dies, at least it will even the scales."

The younger woman – just a teenager, Lydia realized at a second glance – turned to the elder, folding her arms. "I told you it was too late, mother. Putting another grave beside Kae's will not comfort his spirit."

The mother took a step closer to her daughter, raising her hand – and then her eyes narrowed as she spun on her heels, retreating from the room.

Left alone with Lydia and Aladir, the younger girl knelt down, putting a hand on the victim's forehead.

"Kae was always fragile," the girl explained, moving her fingers to close the deceased man's eyes. "Father sheltered him, pampered him. As the eldest – and the boy – he was the only heir."

The girl moved her fingers to the man's hair, straightening it with careful motions. She moved her gaze upward to Lydia. "He will be furious when he returns. You are the other paladin, yes?"

Lydia nodded.

"My name is Nakane Theas. My brother was fragile, yes, but not fatally so. He seemed so happy this morning – he just wanted a breath of fresh air. And then when he pricked his finger on that thorn – no, a single wound would not kill a man. Not even poor Kae."

"I tried to save him," Aladir muttered, his voice weak. "I tried everything."

"Your everything, it would seem, was insufficient," Nakane replied. "But you can still be useful. You both can, in fact."

"You think your brother was murdered," Lydia surmised, glancing around the room.

Nakane tilted her head down, giving Lydia a cold look. "Oh, I am certain my brother was murdered. The only questions are who and how."

*Not why? I suppose there are some obvious potential motives – the man was Edrick Theas' son, after all.*

Edrick Theas was among the most famous sorcerers on the continent – and one of the few publicly known for having found a method to extend his life. He was certain to have many enemies, both among the inherently long-lived Rethri – who might fear a human with a lifespan comparable to their own – and other scholars that were envious of his discoveries.

Lydia stood up. "I'm going to look around. Aladir, can you stand up and come with me?"

The man nodded weakly, pausing for a moment set the body gently on the ground.

"May Lissari guide your spirit to its rest," the Rethri muttered, bringing a bloodstained fist to his heart.

"May Lissari guide your spirit to its rest," Lydia echoed, closing her eyes. When she opened them, she found Aladir and Nakane standing, both looking at her expectantly.

"You should wait with your brother," Lydia instructed the young woman, who quirked an eyebrow in reply.

"Why? He's dead. He's not going to get any less comfortable."

"I just thought it would be respectful—"

The younger woman shook her head at Lydia. "I don't think you fully comprehend the situation. When my father hears of this, someone – possibly several someones – are going to find their heads separated from their bodies. Unless, of course, we find and deal with the culprit before he returns." She folded her hands together in front of her. "Surely, as an agent of justice, you would rather handle this matter expediently and cleanly?"

*That's a strange way to react to the death of your brother, but I suppose she's not wrong. If my brother died—*

She shook her head, dismissing the thought before it could progress any further.

"All right, fine. First, can you give me any more details on what happened? When your servant arrived at the Citadel, all he said was to come quickly because your brother had been badly injured."

Nakane disentangled her hands, raising one of them to her chin. "Well, Kae had just gotten out of bed, and he was in such a golden mood... Normally, we would have spent much of the day reading, but it was lovely outside. He wanted to feel the dawnfire's rays on his skin."

The young woman paused, sealing her eyes shut. "I'm not giving you anything useful." She took a deep breath. "He pricked his finger on a plant. We should start there."

"Just a moment, before we do that."

Lydia leaned down, putting a hand against the dead man's skin. "Dominion of Knowledge, I invoke you."

*Dominion of Life.*
*Dominion of Poison.*
*Dominion of Water.*
*Dominion of Protection.*

The words that appeared in her mind were unsurprising, but she grit her teeth nonetheless. Poison. Aladir's attempts at using life sorcery would have been useless – in fact, depending on the type of poison, they may have expedited the victim's death by spreading the poison faster. Water sorcery was better for treating poison, but if that had been Aladir's work, it hadn't been strong enough to neutralize the toxin.

Lydia decided to omit telling Aladir that the life spells may have worsened the victim's situation– the Rethri paladin was undoubtedly suffering enough. She could reveal that information later if necessary.

"What are you seeing?" Aladir tilted his head downward, brushing an errant lock of hair out of his eyes.

Jarred out of her introspection, Lydia hesitated for a moment before answering. "Evidence of the healing attempts. He also has an aura of protection sorcery."

Nakane pointed to the ring on her brother's hand. "His signet. Father makes them for us. They protect against physical attacks and direct sorcerous attacks."

Lydia nodded. *It probably works similarly to my shield spells, then. That would imply the poison was administered through something the ring wouldn't stop – ingesting food, perhaps, or contact with an everyday object coated with a toxin.*

The female paladin stood, glancing around the room. "Dominion of Knowledge, illuminate your sources."

Green auras manifested around Aladir and Nakane. Neither was surprising – she had known Aladir's sorcerous capabilities, and a daughter of House Theas being a sorcerer was hardly unexpected.

The glowing trail across the room's white tiled floor was somewhat startling, however. She reached up to adjust her glasses, deliberately extending the spell beyond the moment it normally lasted.

Inspecting the boy, Lydia noted a light glow around the ring Nakane had mentioned. There was no evidence of other enchanted items on his person. She looked away, turning her gaze back to the sorcerous path.

"There's something odd here." Lydia could not detect the form of sorcery in the glowing path she saw without casting another spell, but it was intense enough that she could discern the directions that it led. "An aura of sorcery that does not belong. We can investigate the flower you mentioned in a moment, Nakane, but I need to follow this."

Lydia moved toward the source of the aura, and as she drew closer, she was able to distinguish more detail. The path consisted of glowing footprints with additional splotches of green, like droplets of paint, falling beside them. She knelt down for a moment, hearing Aladir and Nakane following quietly behind her. She measured the size of the footprint – more accurately a boot print, she realized – and decided it belonged to a large man.

A backward glance showed that both Aladir and the corpse of Kae Theas were wearing shoes. Probably not their trails, then.

Sorcerous auras normally faded quickly – she had never seen footprints leave a mark of this kind. The level of power it would have taken to mark the floor with every step was staggering, and she briefly debated methods by which it could be accomplished.

*Deliberately dipping one's boots in dominion essence doesn't sound like a very likely tactic, but I don't like the idea of something powerful enough to leave this kind of trail on its own.*

The trail led in two directions, and she followed it first to the left. The path led up a circular stairway draped with red carpet and past a series of paintings – one of which seemed to depict a younger version of the murder victim, a bright smile on his pale face.

They arrived at a closed door shortly thereafter. "My brother's bedroom," Nakane explained. "What are we doing here?"

"I'm following a trail of sorcerous energy that is visible to me," Lydia explained, only realizing in that moment that she had failed to provide the others with any information.

Aladir slumped against a wall, using a sleeve to brush blood off his face, and Lydia gave him a concerned look.

"I'll be fine," he insisted. "Find the bastard that did this."

Lydia nodded, opening the door to the room.

The bedroom was surprisingly plain for the residence of the heir to a famous noble house.

*A moderate sized bed with immaculate covers. There's a small desk near the wall with a glass of water on it, half-consumed. Opposite the bed, there's a bookshelf and a table. At the table, a chair, tucked in.*

The room's large window was open, and the light that streamed inside somewhat obscured the glow from the trail. After a moment, she discerned that there were footsteps leading to two places – the bedside table and the open window.

And the liquid in the cup next to the bed was glowing.

*Touching the cup should be sufficient for this, given the strength of the aura.*

Lydia moved beside the bed, touched the glass, and incanted again. "Dominion of Knowledge, I invoke you."

*Dominion of Poison.*

She winced, in spite of the words providing exactly what she had anticipated.

She turned to the others, noticing that her concentration had failed as she processed the latest spell, and the trail had faded from her view.

"There's poison in the water." Lydia raised a hand to indicate a glass.

Nakane let out a low hiss. "Poison is a coward's tool. Exactly the sort of thing Hartigan would use."

Hartigan. Blake Hartigan. Edrick Theas' rival. The pair argued sorcerous theory and philosophy in every possible format – letters, books, and even public gatherings. While Theas was primarily famous for defensive sorcery, Hartigan was the city's foremost expert on flame sorcery – one of the deadliest dominions for attack spells.

Like Edrick, Hartigan was one of the few sorcerers who had discovered a method of prolonging his lifespan. Aside from flame sorcery, Hartigan was well-respected for his mastery of alchemy – and it

STEALING SORCERY

was broadly speculated that he had discovered some sort of potion or elixir to stop his aging process.

Alchemy, of course, was also famous for producing deadly poisons.

"Hartigan hasn't been in the city for years," Aladir offered, breaking into a fit of coughing a moment later.

"You think that he couldn't hire a travel sorcerer to move him from place to place? Please, Aladir, don't be foolish." Nakane waved a hand at the Rethri dismissively. Her expression softened a moment later, even as she folded her arms across her chest. "You should stop following us. You're clearly too weak to continue."

Aladir raised a hand in a gesture for them to wait, finishing his fit of coughing before he spoke again. "Doesn't matter. Kae was my friend."

*That's news to me. I didn't realize they knew each other – although I suppose it shouldn't be that surprising. Edrick himself is a life sorcerer, and Aladir is the best of our generation. Maybe Aladir was one of Edrick's students.*

Lydia rubbed her temples in frustration. Murder was never an easy thing to trace, especially when sorcery was involved. As potent as her information gathering spells were, a competent enemy sorcerer often had concealment abilities that were on-par or superior to them. She had spells designed to counter nearly every type of direct obfuscation, but certain types of sorcery could inhibit an investigation without involving direct concealment. Levitation spells, for example, were an easy way to hide tracks – and they left too small of a trace for her own spells to discern.

"We can speculate about the culprit later. There's still a trail to follow, and it's fading. I need to gather as much information as I can before that happens."

Nakane nodded in agreement. "Proceed, paladin."

*She could call me by my name...except that I never offered it.*

"It's Lydia, by the way. Lydia Hastings," she added awkwardly. "May Lissari give your family comfort."

"Yes. Now, go ahead with the detection spell."

Lydia turned back toward the window, and then repeated the spell that had detected the trail. "Dominion of Knowledge, illuminate your sources."

The footprints reappeared, leading out the window. She moved to the window, looked outward, and discovered a sheer three-story fall to

24

the ground below. The glow of additional footprints was faintly visible outdoors.

"We're going to follow the path the other way," Lydia declared, turning to move along the trail in the opposite direction. She continued after reaching the point where they had started, tracing the footsteps as they headed to another door – which led outside.

"He pricked his finger not far from here." Nakane's voice was quiet, barely above a whisper. "And then he collapsed in the fountain."

"Show me."

Nakane led Lydia to – and then past – a large series of hedges. They might have been at the entrance to a maze, but Nakane did not lead her inside. Instead, she took the paladin to a simple rose bush, pointing at a spot where a drop of blood highlighted one of the thorns.

"No additional sorcery here," Lydia explained. "The thorn was not the cause."

Nakane nodded somberly. "The glow – is it over here?"

Lydia shook her head. "No, it was back near the door."

"Let's head back that way, then."

They returned to the doorway, and then followed the path further, finding that it led around the side of the house – and intersected with the path that led out from the window. The footsteps were going opposite directions, meaning that whoever had infiltrated the house had done so through the path they were following, and then retreated through Kae's window and returned to their starting point.

*The path they chose was hardly concealed,* Lydia realized. *They had to have opened a door, crossed several well-traveled rooms, gone up a flight of stairs, and opened Kae's door – all without being noticed. Could the assailant have had access to some sort of invisibility spell, like what Jonan uses?*

She briefly considered the possibility that Jonan was the killer, but that was ridiculous. He wasn't even in the city, and he had no motive.

The path moved deeper into the grounds outside House Theas, leading into a large forested area. The trees were thick enough that she could barely see any buildings in the distance. For the first time, Lydia felt a pang of concern that they might actually stumble upon the killer – it had been well over an hour since the attack, but it was plausible that the assailant was still nearby.

Lydia shifted her belt to allow for an easy draw of her saber. Her own protective sorcery was already in place, but she paused to extend a hand to Aladir. When he accepted her hand, she spoke familiar words. "Dominion of Protection, fold against his skin."

Her partner nodded in appreciation, withdrawing his hand, and Lydia looked to Nakane next.

"I am already shielded." The dark haired woman raised a hand to display a ring similar to the one her brother had worn, confirming one of Lydia's earlier suspicions. The knowledge sorceress nodded, returning to the hunt.

Aladir's breath grew heavier as they walked. After a few minutes, Lydia glanced over her shoulder, finding Nakane assisting the Rethri paladin with walking. In spite of the girl's brusque words, her face was showing a hint of obvious concern.

It took several more minutes before the path terminated, and her sorcerous sight was not necessary when they found their destination. A hexagon lined with tiny script had been carved into a large grey stone, and atop the stone was a yellow crystal sphere, shimmering with inner light.

*Dominion essence of poison*, Lydia realized, *and a very powerful source of it.* The sphere was the size of her fist, which would have been impressive enough for a dominion that was generally in a solid state. The Dominion of Poison was gaseous, and manipulating that much essence into a solid would be a tremendously difficult process.

Nakane brushed past Lydia, examining the tiny lettering. "A summoning ritual," she said immediately, turning back to Lydia. "And also an exit portal. Is this the end of the glowing region?"

Lydia nodded.

"I suspected as much. So, someone came here, summoned an entity tied to the Dominion of Poison – and then commanded it to kill my brother. They left a return path through the same location the creature was summoned from." Nakane's lips tightened and she turned her head, examining the area.

Lydia stepped closer, dismissing her spell and examining the script. The lettering was difficult to read, but it had been scribed by a professional hand. The quality of the lettering wasn't important to the efficacy of the ritual – in fact, the words weren't relevant at all – but words were a useful tool for focusing, and the quality of the lettering could be a useful clue to the culprit.

*Visage of venom, herein lies your prison and your escape. With your essence you are bound; complete your task and you shall be free.*

After a moment of examination, Lydia reached up adjusted her spectacles. "You could be right, Lady Theas, but nothing here explicitly states that the creature is from the Dominion of Poison. In fact, I doubt it was – natives of other dominions rarely have access to sorcery aside from the plane they are native to. Whatever was summoned was both powerful enough at poison sorcery to leave a trail, and talented enough at another form of sorcery to remain undetected in your home long enough to poison your brother."

Nakane tightened her jaw. "That's even worse, then. What else could it have been? A powerful Esharen?"

Lydia shook her head. "I doubt that. A sorcerer trying to control an Esharen would be very foolish – Esharen adapt to sorcery too quickly."

The ritual circle appeared to be inert, most likely having ceased to function after the summoned creature returned to it. *Interesting that the sorcerer didn't retrieve the dominion essence. Did he want someone to find it? It could be a signature for an assassin – or something left behind to obfuscate the real trail. Alternatively, the sorcerer may not have had time to retrieve it.*

Slowly, the sorceress reached a gloved hand into the ritual area. No defensive measures were triggered by the intrusion, so she picked up the yellow orb. A flicker of blue on her hand indicated the activation of her Comprehensive Barrier spell reacting to the foreign essence. *Dominion Essence of Poison,* the spell reported, confirming her earlier hypothesis.

"Dominion of Knowledge, show me the path to the creature who shares essence with this orb."

Nothing happened.

Nakane and Aladir looked at her expectantly, but Lydia shook her head. "Nothing. The summoned creature must have moved outside of the range of my tracking spell – perhaps back to its home dominion."

"Well, regardless of what the creature was, it isn't the real problem – the summoner is. This is travel sorcery of the highest possible magnitude. It's cross-planar in scale. Not many people could manage that," Aladir pointed out. "Can you track the summoner with your spell?"

Lydia frowned. "No, it doesn't work like that. It only traces connections between essence. Some of the caster's essence would have been in the ritual area while it was active, but there wouldn't be enough left to trace now that it's inert. This sphere shares essence with the summoned creature, not the sorcerer. If we could find the summoned creature and it still has an active spell effect from the sorcerer, I could potentially trace that – but finding the summoned creature could be as or more difficult. As you said, there are only a limited number of people who could have accomplished this. We should investigate them directly first."

"Hartigan has the resources for something on this scale." Nakane raised a finger to her chin. "Or Shalvinar Vorinthal, maybe. Or Erik Tarren, if the old coot is even alive. Or," she turned her head toward Aladir, "Ulandir Ta'thyriel."

The Rethri paladin returned Nakane's gaze, and then looked away into the distance.

"Yes," he replied. "My father could have done this."

# CHAPTER III – TAELIEN I – CUTTING IN

Blades flashed in the morning light. Taelien caught the first two against the edge of his own weapon, knocking them out of the way with a forceful parry, even as he side-stepped to dodge the third incoming sword.

There was no time for a riposte – not even a moment to increase his distance. His first attacker's two short swords moved in fluid union, tracing unrelenting lines toward any spot he left vulnerable. His second opponent had a longer blade, matching his own, and she skillfully harried him with probing strikes to prevent any counter attacks.

It was an unfair fight. Exactly the type of fight he preferred.

*Shift.* At his command, his weapon's mass shifted toward the tip, even as he swung it directly toward the female fighter's torso. She parried, just as he had anticipated, but the altered weapon carried a harder impact than she had been prepared for. She fell back a step – not much, but maybe enough...

Taelien swept his sword in a downward arc at the man with two swords, meeting another parry, but shoving with enough strength to push the shorter blade backward and impact the man's arm. The swordsman grunted, dropping the sword he had been carrying in that hand.

A blade swept in front of Taelien's face, almost too fast to register. He took a step back reflexively, raising his sword to defend against the follow through.

"Stop," instructed a gruff voice. "Rotate."

Taelien sighed, lowering his blade and turning to where Herod was sitting in the otherwise empty stands. The older man sat with his right hand settled near his hip, near where a sword's grip might have once been. In spite of being many years retired, he still sat with his back perfectly straight, his grey hair cropped close to his head and his beard trimmed short enough to make him look refined, rather than aged. His civilian garb never seemed to quite fit his well-muscled form.

The metal sorcerer wasn't sure what rank Herod had held as a paladin while he served, but based on the way the other paladins looked at him, Taelien assumed it must have once been substantial. While most retired paladins found a civilian occupation or settled down with their families, Herod was omnipresent on the training fields, haunting them like a spirit of the past age. When Herod issued an order, even full paladins were quick to comply.

"Why?" Taelien asked the older man. "I didn't get hit."

"Only because I checked my swing, silly. Wouldn't want to ruin that pretty face of yours." Velas stepped closer and tapped a gauntleted hand against his helmet, her blue eyes somehow managing to display her smirk even with the rest of her face obscured.

Taelien batted her hand away playfully, shaking his head. "You never could have gotten that close if I wasn't wearing this stupid helmet. It ruins my peripheral vision."

Herod stood up, folding his arms. "If you want to take idiotic risks on the battlefield, I can't stop you. While you're training, however, I have an obligation to keep your 'pretty face' intact. Now, you did have a pretty good defense there for a while, but you have a tendency to trade hits as soon as you see an opening. That's not acceptable in general, and it's an even worse strategy in a two versus one scenario."

"Trading hits is fine when one hit from me is like five hits from anyone else," Taelien mumbled, quiet enough for his sparring partners to hear, but hopefully not loud enough for Herod.

"So you keep telling us." Velas lifted her sword in one hand, leaning it against her shoulder, and cracked the fingers of her other hand against her armor. "Let's take that theory to a barrier bout some time and see if you can back it up."

"He can." Landen had picked up his second sword and wandered close enough to chat, stretching out the arm that Taelien had hit. Their swords were metal, but with blunted edges, and a heavy layer of padding wrapped around the blades for training purposes. Even with the padding, the swords still had the potential for deadly swings, so each of them was wearing a full suit of armor for their practice. "He beat Myros in the arena, remember?"

Velas scoffed. "Not quite how I remember it."

"Quit flirting down there, otherwise I'll reset all three of you the hard way," Herod snapped. Taelien glanced at his companions, and the three of them quickly retreated. The other trainees referred to Herod as 'old as the city walls and twice as strong'. While the retired paladin didn't look quite three thousand years old, Taelien had seen enough demonstrations of the man's skill to consider the latter claim to be a possibility.

Their starting positions were the three points of a chalk-drawn triangle within a larger circle. It allowed the three to start at equal distances, and the circle represented the full bounds of their fighting area. The current activity was a two versus one exercise. A single hit to a non-vital location was treated as a wound to that body part – thus, Landen had dropped his sword when Taelien had managed to tap his arm. A strike to the torso or head was a kill, and the killer would be the target for the next round.

Taelien raised his sword over his heart, offering Velas the traditional salute of the Paladins of Tae'os. Velas returned his gesture.

"Begin."

Taelien charged. Hardly a surprise, given his proclivity for utilizing that strategy, but his sword was still weighted toward the blade and that favored an offensive strategy.

Velas took the Teris Low-Blade stance, a low stance designed for defense. A sound strategy against two opponents, but Taelien considered it a delaying tactic. The only way to "win" was to eliminate all opposition.

He raised his blade above his head into the Sae'lien Slaying Form. This would theoretically force Velas to move further to block, since her sword was starting out in a low position.

Taelien swept his sword toward her head just as he came into range. She ducked the swing, quickly stepping forward and slamming a shoulder into his chest, knocking him backward. Startled, Taelien barely raised his arm quickly enough to block the dagger she had drawn with her left hand, and it glanced off his bracer – a hit.

He grudgingly released his "wounded" right hand from his sword, then kicked Velas in the chest and sent her stumbling backward, nearly out of the ring. Before his sword hit the ground, he kicked the hilt back upward, catching it with his left hand.

Then something hit Velas in the chest, and toppled to the floor.

There was a moment of silence.

"A throwing dagger, Landen?" Velas turned to the other swordsman, who removed his helmet, shrugged, and gave her a sheepish grin.

"Gotta have some way of evening the odds against monsters like you two."

*Monsters?* Taelien frowned, shaking his head. *Bah, he didn't mean anything by it.*

He sheathed his sword, removing his own helmet brushing a lock of sweat-drenched black hair out of his eyes. "Water break?"

"Only if you can get it on the way to your class," Herod projected from the stands. "You've got ten minutes until history lessons start."

"Gods, why didn't you warn us?" Velas complained, removing her own helmet. She was off and sprinting the next moment and Herod emitted a thunderous belly laugh.

"Guess we'd better follow her," Taelien mumbled, taking off into a run.

"Don't we always," Landen murmured in reply.

*\*\*\**

Eight months had passed since Taelien had made the trek to Velthryn. Lydia had set the pair of them up as caravan guards, which had helped Taelien replenish his sorely wounded funds. The sorceress had also finally retrieved the meager belongings that Taelien had carried when he had been arrested in Orlyn, but those didn't amount to much, anyway.

By the time they had reached the legendary city, the swordsman felt like he had learned its entire history. Lydia practically glowed whenever she talked about her home, regaling him with tales of the city withstanding assaults from the Xixian Empire, the armies of Daesmodin, and numerous other foes.

As it turned out, Lydia was a more entertaining way to learn about the city than history class. Unfortunately, she also hadn't covered every detail a prospective Paladin of Tae'os was expected to know.

And thus, three days a week, Taelien Salaris, who had battled false gods and sorcerers in their own domains, sat among children in the mandatory study of Velthryn's past.

"And so, when the tides of Vyrek Sul's armies pressed close against our gates, Edrick Theas deployed a final defense. Can anyone tell me what that defense was?"

Taelien was pretty certain he knew the answer to that particular question, but he remained seated out of habit. A Rethri teenager a few seats to his left stood first.

"The Kalsiris Barrier, sir," the boy said, a slight nervous stammer in his tone. "A spell that protects the whole city, powered by three towers built just outside. It's named after his son."

"Very good, Tirith."

The class continued much as many others had, with Taelien paying as close of attention as he could to the mostly dry material. Velas and Landen sat nearby, the former writing something – or, more likely, drawing something – in her journal.

At first, he was mildly bothered by her constant displays of wealth, but he eventually discovered that paper just wasn't as rare or expensive in Velthryn as he was used to. He wasn't quite sure why – he suspected some sorcerer had discovered a spell for conjuring paper directly from the Plane of Nature, but he hadn't had sufficient interest to investigate the issue directly.

"Now, how many of you are planning to take the Trials of Unyielding Steel next week?"

The question snapped Taelien out of his wandering thoughts. Landen and Velas stood up, so he did the same.

Landen and Velas had arrived in Velthryn a few months after Taelien had, the former having come at Lydia's invitation. They were both former members of the Queensguard of Orlyn, and Lydia had correctly guessed that they would be robbed of their jobs after the coronation of the new king, Byron. The sorceress had explained to Taelien that Byron had (potentially legitimate) concerns that the Queensguard might have been compromised by Donovan Tailor, his political enemy, and that they would most likely all be dismissed and replaced.

Regardless, Taelien had been thrilled when Landen had arrived. The two had developed a fast friendship during their time in Orlyn, and Landen was one of the few trainees that could keep up with him.

Velas had been a pleasant surprise. A close friend of Landen's from the Queensguard, Taelien had expected her to be competent in a fight, comparable to the other Queensguard he had fought with. She was nearly as tall as Taelien, with long blonde hair and an athletic physique.

Velas had quickly corrected two of these misconceptions.

She was not merely "competent" in a fight. Their first match had been a near-disaster from Taelien's perspective, where she had literally thrown him out of the ring when he lowered his guard. After that, he had looked at the young woman in a very different light.

Second, she threw herself into combat with a manic joy that he had only seen in one other place – his mirror image.

A few other students stood along with them.

The first were a pair of Rethri twins, one male and one female, but largely indistinct from one another in appearance due to their voluminous robes. The most obvious difference between the pair was their eyes – the female, Terras, had burning red eyes, and Lysen's eyes were ice blue. Taelien would have guessed them at a couple years his junior by their appearance, but they both had gone through their Dominion Bonding ritual, which made it near impossible to tell.

Finally, the last man stood slowly, not out of apathy, but rather out of what Taelien had quickly learned was a form of calculated drama. He stretched his well-muscled arms over his head, yawning lightly enough to border between tiredness and mockery.

Taelien was well acquainted with pride – he possessed a fair bit of it himself – but Keldyn Andys was a merchant of the stuff. The first in generations to possess the Gifts of Aendaryn, Keldyn was well-known to be a prodigy with a blade and capable of utilizing techniques long relegated to fanciful Tarren tales. He never lowered himself to direct challenges, of course – his displays were almost always against stationary targets, and in front of a large and endearing audience.

Keldyn was also notable for looking at Taelien with nearly palpable detest. It was clear from every glance, every interaction. The reasons why seemed obvious; Keldyn seemed to have formed his self-image around being chosen by Aendaryn himself to be a symbol for their generation. This probably was working wonderfully until Taelien arrived at the city gates, wearing the sacred sword of the gods on his hip and accompanied by a returning hero – Lydia Scryer – who sang praises about how Taelien had triumphed over a pantheon of false gods.

Taelien wished Lydia would tone down her rhetoric a bit, but he understood her reasoning. By making him look like a child of the Tae'os Pantheon, she was practically assuring him a quick rise through the ranks – and her prestige would grow along with his. It was a practical strategy, if somewhat distasteful.

"Six of you? That's good, because you'll be organized into teams of three once the others arrive," the teacher explained. He was an older priest of Sytira, his gray beard nearly the length of his cane.

"The others?" Landen asked.

"Oh, yes, you're new. Candidates come from around the continent for the paladin tests. We hold them twice a year here, and only rarely elsewhere."

Taelien and the others already knew these tests were their fastest way to join the Paladins of Tae'os. The usual method was joining as a squire, where you would train under an established paladin until you were deemed ready – which typically took years. A final option was the direct request of an officer, which had to be approved by several other officers before it was granted.

The last case was rare outside of war, and while Lydia had recently been promoted to Lieutenant Commander for her exceptional work in Orlyn, it would have looked bad if one of her first actions was to request to have Taelien entered into the paladins without any training or taking the traditional test. She might have done it if he had pushed, but he didn't like the idea of special treatment.

Thus he would take the tests – seven reportedly grueling examinations, one corresponding to each of the Tae'os deities.

"The testing period begins in one week," the teacher continued. "Use that time wisely. I can't advise you about the individual challenges – they change every year. No test will be impossible, and most will offer multiple solutions. Think before you act."

That last bit of advice was bordering on breaking the rules – the tests were notoriously secretive, and veterans were sworn to avoid revealing details about the challenges.

Taelien knew that with Lydia's practical mind, she probably would have found a way to sneak him information if she thought it would help – but she had never taken the test, having taken the longer road from squire to paladin status. The tests were designed for people like him –

men and women who were already adults with combat experience. They would gauge if he had the right mentality to be a paladin – the right amount of knowledge, dedication, and faith.

*I'd better hope two out of three is good enough.*

# CHAPTER IV – JONAN I – A LITTLE WELL-DESERVED VACATION

Jonan flicked a finger at the candle next to his simple tavern bed, igniting the wick. It flickered weakly, but anything brighter would have been intolerable for his already vicious headache.

*I'm a complete failure at the concept of vacation.*

His visit to Velthryn was ostensibly a rare instance of taking leave from his work for the Thornguard. Like all of his previous instances of "vacation", this meant that he had been given orders that could not be disseminated through the standard chain of command.

His first task had been to deliver the Heartlance to Silk. In the few weeks since then, he had done his best to prepare himself for whatever Aayara's next assignment would be. Today, that had meant a particularly daunting challenge – socializing.

Velthryn was one of the few cities south of Orlyn that held a significant - and legally recognized – Thornguard presence. He had spent most of his day at the local base, drinking and carousing with the soldiers posted there, gathering what little information he could about the local chain of command and any resources he might be able to make use of.

The results were somewhat disappointing – without any kind of official requisition, he wasn't going to be getting much out of the local base. Not even lodgings, even though they appeared to have ample space. He caught a hint of subtext that the local officers didn't trust him – frankly, he couldn't blame them. His personnel files were classified at a level where even the local commander probably wouldn't be able to get more than a few lines – a fact that Jonan found both amusing and inconvenient.

He wouldn't have trusted himself, either.

Fortunately, a scribe didn't need any form of special permission just to get access to the libraries, and he far preferred those to the company of most members of the Thornguard. Now that he knew where they were, he resolved to return to them the next time he could tolerate the presence of people in his vicinity.

Seating himself carefully on the bed, the sight sorcerer opened his belt pouches, removing the four hand mirrors that he carried at all times. They were not his entire supply, but represented the four he checked the most frequently – ones linked to mirrors carried by Thornguard Commander Madrigan Ferrous, Rialla Dianis, Lydia Hastings, and of course Vae'kes Aayara.

It was Rialla's that contained a message, surprising him. Rialla had accompanied him when he left the city of Orlyn, traveling to Selyr to seek help for her ailing brother, Elias. Elias was a rare Rethri born without a bond to a specific dominion. Typically, these children swiftly died, but Rialla had sustained her brother's life with powerful sorcery and searched for many years for a cure.

During their time in Selyr, Jonan had introduced Rialla to several other sorcerers, but most offered little more than condolences. He had advised her to be patient, but they both knew that Rialla's best hope was to go to one of the most powerful beings on the continent.

*Scribe,*
*I have a delivery for you. Meet me at the Southway Manor. It's located at the eastern end of Aldwyn Street in the High Quarter. Soon.*
*-Shiver*

Jonan's headache worsened just parsing through the message.
*She's taken on an "ess" name. I warned her…but I suppose it doesn't matter.*
Jonan lay back on the bed, closing his eyes.
*The name suits her, but any name that begins in that way is short for slave.*
His jaw tightened and he clenched his fists in the air, trembling.
*One more soul sold to the Vae'kes. One more spirit destined to be bled dry.*
The scribe sat up, shaking his head. *And this time, I'm the one squeezing the vein.*
*I'd better not keep her waiting. We are friends, after all.*

Jonan reached under his bed, pulling out the large backpack he had stowed beneath. Searching within, he retrieved two objects. The first was a sheathed dagger, which he attached to his belt on the left side, opposite his pouch. Digging deeper, he found his selection of cases for his glasses, taking one wrapped in purple-dyed leather and opening it.

The lenses within were bonded to the Dominion of Clarity. They had cost a small fortune, but Jonan had little else to spend his income on. The bond would do nothing to aid his vision – in fact, his vision was notably blurrier when he switched pairs, which was always frustrating.

The Dominion of Clarity was formidable at blocking mental compulsion – such as the Dominion of Deception, one of Rialla's favored forms of sorcery. She tended to cast by locking eyes with her victim, and he had been on the receiving end of her talents in the past.

Friends, in his experience, were the people you knew well enough to prepare countermeasures for.

***

While Jonan had been tempted to dress as a beggar for old time's sake, he ultimately decided that the joke would require too much effort. Thus, he simply headed to the High Quarter immediately upon packing his mirrors back in his bag. He didn't know when Rialla had sent the message, but it had been within the last few hours, based on when he had last checked his mirrors. That meant she was likely still at the rendezvous point – if he waited until the next day, she might choose to try to find him instead. Given how things had gone last time she had sought him out, he decided that tracking her down immediately was the safer approach.

The High Quarter was because of its association with nobility. Rather, it had developed that name for having the tallest buildings within the city. Many were sprawling complexes that housed dozens of homes, but the quarter also housed a number of the homes of ancient families. It was one of the oldest parts of the city, but well-maintained.

The dawnfire had retreated from the sky by the time Jonan reached the location that Rialla's note had mentioned. A pristine manor awaited him, the blackened iron gates wide open and inviting. Walls of rose bushes lined the path to the door. Undisguised and visible, Jonan felt positively naked when he knocked on the thick wooden doors.

The door swung open.

Rialla appeared in the doorway, reaching out to grab him and pull him inside. "In, quickly."

He allowed her to drag him within, watching as she slammed the door shut behind him. "You weren't followed?"

Jonan shook his head. "I can be relatively confident of that, at least."

The Rethri woman peered at him with those ominous indigo eyes for several moments before nodding and running a finger across an etched rune in the wooden doorframe. A hint of frost appeared on her fingertip and glowing blue vines spread out from it, weaving across the door.

*A ritual shielding effect of some kind, triggered by her ice sorcery. Interesting — and expensive.*

"Should I be expecting an assault at any moment?"

"You should always be expecting an assault at any moment." She pulled her hand away from the door, folding her arms. "That's the business we're in."

*Actually, you're the only person who's ever broken into my home. But I suppose mentioning that might not be the best way to initiate a friendly conversation.*

Jonan settled for nodding sagely.

"Follow." She turned and began walking without waiting for an answer.

The manor was enormous.

Blue carpets covered the marble floors, and a rack of glittering weapons was prominently displayed above a central fireplace. From the entrance, he could see multiple rooms to each side and a spiral stairway leading upward.

Even more impressive, however, were the sheer number of brightly shining mirrors on the walls.

Rialla seemed to notice his gaze immediately, tugging on his arm again and bringing him over to one of the mirrors. It was nearly as tall as he was, bronze rimmed and demonstrating a flawless luster. It was, however, not displaying a reflection of the room.

Instead, he saw a familiar jail cell, long abandoned, within the city of Orlyn. He felt an odd welling of emotion at the sight.

"You...brought my mirrors." Jonan gave her a quizzical look. "These were destroyed."

She paused in her step, giving the slightest hint of a frown. "I had the ones that weren't beyond salvage repaired, since I was somewhat responsible for the damage. There are a few new ones as well."

*Somewhat? You broke them yourself.*

"New mirrors? You mean just regular mirrors, then?"

Vorain shook her head. "No, more like yours. When I told Lady Aayara I was having your mirrors fixed, she insisted on sending a few more she prepared herself. Claimed they were an 'improved design' that she was sending as a gift."

Jonan closed his eyes, taking a deep breath.

"Yes. A gift." He paused for a moment. "Thank you, Vorain – I mean, sorry, Rialla."

She shrugged. "I don't mind the old name. It's probably better not to call me Rialla in this city. I wouldn't want my father to find out I'm here."

*Right, this is where she grew up. I suppose she could still be recognized.*

"That makes sense, but Vorain is clearly somewhat conspicuous as well. We'll have to come up with something else for you to use later."

"That would be a good idea, yes. So, I'm sure you're wondering why I brought you here."

Jonan nodded fervently.

"We've got a new assignment. A rather important one, in fact."

Jonan quirked a brow.

*We?*

"What sort of assignment?"

"Come sit down first. There's a great couch back here – it's very comfortable." She finally released his arm, but continued to lead the way. He followed her into another room. There were three long sofas, laid out as three lines of a square.

Rialla sat on one of the couches, folded her legs, and gestured toward the one across from her. Jonan dutifully followed, taking a seat.

"What do you think of our new home?"

He scratched his chin. "It's...big. What's this about a mission?"

"I meant in terms of security. But yes, I suppose it is 'comfortable'. In terms of our mission, we're going to be tracking someone."

"Who?"

"Cassius Morn. A former Thornguard. He was a member of the Bladebreakers."

Jonan whistled appreciatively. The Bladebreakers were one of the most famous Thornguard units, generally working under one of the Vae'kes to eliminate high profile enemy targets. They were, in part, why the Thornguard were often confused for being assassins.

"He's missing? What happened?"

Rialla lifted a hand and ran it through her hair. "He failed to check in after a mission."

*Seems like a good reason to find him.* "How long ago?"

"Three and a half years."

Jonan groaned. "And they're just sending someone to look for him now?"

"Oh, no. They've sent people before. Six times, in fact."

He was pretty sure he knew where this was going. "What happened to the first six squads?"

"Well," Rialla replied, "The four and a half squads they've found so far were dead."

Jonan closed his eyes, taking a deep breath.

*Why does this always hap- oh, right. I'm expendable.*

"Great. What kind of sorcery does he specialize in?"

Rialla grinned brightly. "That's the fun part. None."

Jonan narrowed his eyes. "None?"

"He's not a sorcerer. To date, he's killed more than thirty of our agents. Without a single spell."

# CHAPTER V – VELAS II – MURDER IS SUCH A STRONG WORD

Some nights, sleep could be as elusive as Symphony herself. Velas Jaldin was having one of those nights.

Sitting up in her bed, the former member of the Queensguard of Orlyn massaged her own shoulders, working at unrelenting knots. Asking someone else to help occurred to her, but it invited more complications than she was willing to deal with.

*Gods, what's wrong with me?*

She sprung from the bed with more energy than necessary, snatching her sword belt down from where it hung on the wall. She pulled on her trousers and a light green vest, slipped her feet into ill-fitting boots she'd never bothered to replace, and strode out of the apartment.

Velthryn had, thus far, not been what she had expected. She had grown up on stories of towering spires flashing with sorcerous light and legendary warriors dueling in the streets. The city had towers, but their radiance had been somewhat... overstated. There were no mighty battles being fought, and the 'heroes' she had once idolized were relics of a former age, more likely to be found drunk on the street than displaying their talents in an arena.

Herod, at least, had some faint spark of his former glory. Though he had retired after the fall of Xixis, she never saw him far from the training grounds, his failing eyes always searching for someone who could measure up to the memories of his long deceased companions.

*I will not disappoint you in the days to come, Master Herod.*

43

The nightfrost had just begun to recede from the sky when Velas arrived at the training ground. She was not the first one to arrive. This was not surprising in itself, but the sight that greeted her was unexpected.

Taelien knelt in the center of a raised wooden platform near the center of the field, tracing his fingers across the surface of a red-bladed sword. Velas had seen the unusual weapon before, but not for several months, and she had never seen him with it on the training ground.

Pausing in curiosity, she observed the swordsman from a distance. *Is he praying? I didn't think he was the type.*

It was more likely he was focusing on something, but he didn't seem like the meditative type, either.

As she observed, she noted a hint of light on his fingertips as he brought them across the blade – the light of a flame. As he reached the hilt, he brought his hand back upward – and a glow lingered on the edge.

A brilliant flame manifested as Taelien's fingers reached the tip of the sword, bathing the area in orange light. He quickly dragged his fingers downward, causing the flame to spread across the surface of the blade. When he reached the hilt, the fire flared brighter. Taelien winced and withdrew his glowing hand, shaking it in the air. The flames dissipated.

Velas gave a slow clap, smirking as she walked closer. Taelien looked up, a startled expression on his face.

"Knew you had one dominion bonded sword – you carry the thing everywhere – but I had no idea you've been hoarding more of them. You've been holding out on me." She put her hands on her hips, giving him a playful grin.

He sheathed the weapon in a scabbard on his right hip – the opposite side from where he wore the Sae'kes – and stood up, grimacing.

"It's not a dominion bonded weapon, it's just some kind of strange metal. How long have you been watching me?"

"Long enough to get a pretty show, but not long enough to figure out the details. You're practicing, obviously, but for what?"

"Trying to make this thing useful." He tapped his fingers on the now-sheathed sword, shaking his head. "When Lydia and I determined how it worked, it sounded like the type of thing that could be quite potent. 'Absorbing dominion energy' sounds great in theory, but it doesn't work fast enough to block offensive spells."

Velas absently flicked a strand of hair out of her eyes. "So you're trying to figure out how to light the blade on fire. Flashy, but not very practical."

He shrugged a shoulder. "I've run into some monsters that wouldn't be vulnerable to conventional attacks. A Harvester of Shadow, for instance."

She raised an eyebrow. Harvesters were creatures native to other planes that had a reputation for being horrendously dangerous. She had seen Taelien perform some impressive feats in combat, but facing a Harvester seemed a bit implausible, even for him.

*Was that in the Paths of Ascension?*

Months before, Taelien had supposedly gone to a place called the Paths of Ascension in the city of Orlyn. The Paths were rumored to be a way to ascend to godhood, but Taelien had learned that they were actually some sort of ancient vault left behind by the Xixian Empire. After he had traversed the depths of the Paths, he had confronted one of the city's false gods along with a group of allies.

The swordsman had shared the broad strokes of his story with Velas and Landen, but neither he nor Lydia – the paladin of Sytira that had encouraged him and Landen to come to Velthryn – had been willing to share the details of what had happened to Taelien while he was on the Paths. He had definitely found some treasure in there – Velas had seen some of it, including the sword – but he had also been severely injured while exploring the depths.

Velas suspected that they were keeping the details private so that they could monopolize any remaining treasure inside the Paths. *Lydia is probably just waiting for Taelien to earn his paladin status, and then she can take him on as a partner and go back to Orlyn.*

*Not that Taelien needs any more treasure.* "Why bother figuring out new tricks with a mundane sword when you have the Sae'kes? Pretty sure that thing would be more useful, even against a Harvester."

He turned his head away from Velas. "I wish it was that simple."

With surprising intensity, Taelien spun back around to face her, closing his eyes and drawing the Sae'kes from its scabbard. She had seen the blade before – but he never drew it without purpose.

The blade shined like the purest of silver, with the seven runes upon the legendary blade representing each of the gods of the Tae'os

Pantheon. Of the seven runes, five of them blazed with brilliant azure light.

She understood the problem immediately.

"You can't control it."

Taelien nodded.

"Nearly my entire life, I've trained to use this weapon. Day after day, year after year." He opened his eyes to gaze at the surface of the blade with a longing expression. "No amount of willpower, of focus, or training has proven sufficient."

She shrugged. "So try harder."

He laughed, turning to the side and swinging the blade in place. A note carried through the wind as the blade parted the air, as if the weapon mirrored the swordsman's laughter.

The two sounds made her heart race in a way she had not anticipated.

"I knew there was a reason I liked you," he said, returning the weapon to its metal-lined scabbard.

"You talking to me or the sword?" She teased, folding her arms.

"Both." He turned back to face her. "Anyway, I haven't given up. I still train with the Sae'kes every day, and I won't stop until I'm ready to use it. But even then, it won't be the right weapon for every situation."

She raised an eyebrow. "How so? If it was good enough for the god of swords..."

"It's too destructive. Even with all seven runes lit, I doubt I'll have enough control to render it non-lethal."

"Ah." The Paladins of Tae'os placed the preservation of life as one of their highest values. Velas considered the idea of sparing her enemies nonsensical, but like Taelien, she had learned to say the right words to serve her goals.

Unlike Taelien, she had learned to be convincing about it.

"So, I take it you couldn't sleep either?" Taelien asked.

*Trying to change the subject? Alright, fair enough.*

"Yeah, I'm nervous about the tests. I take it you're feeling the same?"

He nodded. "I wish we had more of an idea about what we're up against."

She shrugged, and then stretched her left shoulder again, grimacing at the stiffness in her muscles. "Shouldn't be too complicated. There are only so many tests they could come up with. You heard anything from Red? You're always following her around like a duckling."

He rolled his eyes. "I'm not a duck."

*Didn't deny following her around, though,* Velas noted in wry victory.

"And no, Lydia never took the test," he added. "And even if she did, she wouldn't help me cheat."

Velas waved a hand dismissively. "Gathering information is hardly cheating. These paladins look all bright and shiny, but Lydia was a spy for years, wasn't she? Her and half the Eratar branch."

Each of the Paladins of Tae'os was assigned to a specific branch dedicated to a certain deity. Typically, each branch had different responsibilities. The Paladins of Eratar – the god of travel – were reputed to be the branch dealing with espionage, information gathering, and similar activities. Publicly, they served as scouts, advisors to nobles, and other functions that could easily cover their more clandestine activities.

Teasing aside, Velas had nothing but respect for Lydia's years of successful infiltration into Orlyn's government. Her successes were worthy of praise, even if Taelien did idolize the girl a little more than Velas considered healthy. She wasn't even any older than they were.

"Well, if you want to end up in the Eratar branch, they'd probably approve. But I doubt the rest of the orders would be quite so tolerant. Our instructions were explicit."

"Sometimes what someone says and what they mean are different things." Velas rubbed her shoulder. "But in this case, I suppose you're probably right."

"So, what were you coming out here for? Not just to spy on me, I assume."

"No that was just a pleasant surprise. I was planning to warm up on some sword work until Landen arrived. Oh, and when you arrived about two hours later."

"I prefer to do most of my training at night, right before they close up the armory."

"Uh-huh. When no one else is around to verify it."

"When it's cool enough to wear a suit of armor without feeling like I'm courting death."

She took a breath, bending down to stretch her legs. "All right, fair argument. It's still pretty cool right now, though. Up for a match?"

"The armory is locked up at this hour. We wouldn't be able to get armor or training weapons."

"I know." Velas drew her long sword from her hip, giving Taelien a wink. "That's why I'm excited."

Taelien folded his arms. "I shouldn't have to tell you how dangerous that would be."

"You can't tell me you never trained with real blades when you were working with the Thornguard."

He frowned. "This is different. You're not—"

"I spent four years in the Queensguard of Orlyn. The *actual* Queensguard, not like your little pre-Thornguard training group. You don't think I can keep up with you?"

The swordsman sighed. "I don't have any ordinary weapons on me."

"Use the Sae'kes, then. I'd love to see what it's like fighting against that thing."

Her pulse quickened as she pictured having to snake her own sword around his to prevent the artifact from tearing her weapon apart.

*Please.*

He reluctantly drew the red-bladed sword. Her eyes continued to focus on the winged hilt of the Sae'kes at his side.

"I'll spar with you, but I'm not going to use an unfair advantage." He moved to the back of the wooden platform, taking the Teris-Low Blade form, a defensive stance. His feet weren't aligned properly, showing how rarely he used that particular form.

"Ready?" He asked.

"Let's find out."

Velas raised her blade and charged. If he wasn't going to use the Sae'kes, she'd have to find another way to make some fun.

Her sword flashed diagonally downward from a high stance, aiming for his shoulder.

The parry she expected came, and Velas stepped back for another strike – only to find her blade stuck to his.

By the time she realized what had happened, Taelien was already stepping to her right and shoving forward on his weapon. Velas stumbled back, her left foot brushing the edge of the platform, letting out a hiss as she realized he was trying to push her off the platform.

She let go of the hilt of her sword, stepping left and sweeping her foot to try to hook his right knee. He stepped back, taking the kick in the front of the leg and wincing.

Then he tossed the two connected blades aside, right off the platform.

Velas grinned.

"Thought you said you weren't going to use any unfair advantages. Metal sorcery? Really?"

"Using my own personal skills is hardly unfair."

She circled around to his right, and Taelien stepped back, raising his arms into a typical blocking position near his face. His expression was calm, his stance cleaner than it had been with the Teris Low-Blade stance. She had sparred with him dozens of times before, and she knew he preferred grappling to striking when unarmed. This was unsurprising, given his background with the Thornguard, who wore heavy armor and trained for fighting other people in heavy armor.

Traditional Velryan dueling had bored Velas as she came into her adolescence, so she hired tutors. When she had exhausted the limits of their talents, she traveled to Orlyn, trained with the Queensguard and fought in the arena. When she had been dismissed from the Queensguard, it had been almost a relief – she had learned all she could from the meager competition in Orlyn.

Herod had proven a competent sword instructor, and Orin Dyr was an excellent unarmed combat teacher. Dyr was a lieutenant colonel for the Paladins of Koranir, the God of Strength. The former Queensguard relished the opportunity to learn from his experience – and to show off what she had picked up.

"Suppose I'll do the same, then."

She opened with a half-hearted jump kick toward his face, which he brushed aside just as she had expected. As she landed, she ducked his follow-through punch and kicked at his left knee. As he backed away, avoiding the kick entirely, she grinned and took a step back.

He stepped back as well, quirking an eyebrow.

She charged forward, jumping again – higher this time. And she landed on top of his shoulders.

Velas hopped down before he could react, kicking backwards as she descended and hitting him square in the back. The swordsman staggered, spinning around just in time for Velas' fist to catch him in the gut. Her knuckles stung from the impact.

*Gods, it's like punching a breastplate. Stone sorcery, maybe?*

Taelien reeled back from the strike, moving his left hand to cover his stomach.

*A mistake.*

She had already hit that spot once.

Instead, Velas shot a fist out toward his jaw. He grabbed at her hand, but the attack had been a feint, blocking his field of vision while she kicked at his right thigh. The kick knocked him back a step, preventing him from snatching her arm out of the air.

Taelien let out a low growl, shifting into a sideways stance that she was unfamiliar with. She paused. It looked like an unarmed version of something a duelist might use to keep as little of their body exposed as possible.

Velas' grin broadened. *That stance isn't as suited to grappling – maybe he'll actually try to punch me for a change.*

"Not bad," he mumbled. He extended his right fist in front of him, taking a deep breath. His eyes caught hers, his growing smirk offering a challenge.

She was more than happy to oblige.

He would be ready for a jump this time, so when she rushed forward, she ducked instead.

*Surge.*

A burst of kinetic energy carried her across the platform as she twisted her hips into a punch at his solar plexus. Taelien twisted to the side, causing her fist to brush against his ribs rather than connecting directly, and he slammed his forearm down against her right shoulder.

Pain surged through her as his arm impacted, but her left arm was already moving, her open palm slapping him across the back.

*Push.*

Essence surged through her hand, sending Taelien skidding across the platform. The swordsman dug his boots into the wood, slowing his movement until he could spin around and reset his stance.

Taelien used his off-hand to rub at his ribs. "What, precisely, was that?"

Velas folded her hands in front of her. "Trade secret. Feel like surrendering yet?"

"Oh, not by any means. Things are just getting interesting."

She rushed forward. Taelien broke from his stance and charged to meet her, ducking her first punch and raising his right leg to block her incoming kick.

Taelien's palm shot out toward her face and she stepped backward to avoid it. She realized too late that the hand had never been intended to connect – just as a flash of blinding flame manifested in his hand.

It was gone in an instant, but her vision swam, and his left hand slammed into her shoulder.

*That wasn't very fair.* She gritted her teeth and closed her momentarily useless eyes. Guided by sound, Velas side-stepped an open hand aimed at her ribs and grabbed his arm with both of her hands.

She heard a telltale gasp of surprise, which was sufficient information for her to pull him forward and bring a knee up toward the general location of his groin. She felt her shin connect with his, indicating that he had managed to raise his own leg to block, and then something caught her under the chin with enough force to separate the pair.

Velas staggered back, blinking her still-recovering eyes, and seeing Taelien bearing down on her again. Ignoring the pain in her jaw and shoulder, she lowered her stance and braced herself. As Taelien brought his arms around in a hugging motion, she launched a quick jab toward his ribs, which he caught with his left arm. She feigned disappointment, making a second strike that mirrored the first. As expected, he grabbed her right arm as well.

She hopped upward, kicking both legs out toward his chest.

Rather than reeling back as she had expected, he grit his teeth and pulled on her arms. She pushed back with her legs, but he somehow maintained his grip, visibly straining from the force she was exerting.

*Enough.* She pulled one foot away and then brought it back down against his chest. *Push.*

The sorcerous force sent the pair flying apart, Taelien hitting the wooden floor and Velas soaring momentarily skyward before hitting the dirt just outside the platform. She landed in a roll, pushing herself back into a kneeling position near-instantly.

Whereupon she saw a familiar pair of legs standing in front of her. She looked up with a sheepish grin as Landen reached down to offer her a hand.

"No helping, I'm not done," she said breathlessly, still blinking to get the spots out of her vision.

"I think I am." By the time her watering eyes focused on Taelien, he was sitting on the platform, fiddling with his right hand. "I hate splinters."

There was a hint of disappointment in his tone. Had he wanted to continue the fight as much as she had?

"Splinters? Try falling on rocks," she mumbled in complaint, patting the ground beneath her. Sighing, she grabbed at Landen's offered hand, and he pulled her to her feet. She shook her head, disoriented, both from the state of her eyes and her use of sorcery.

"So, why are you two trying to murder each other this morning?" Landen reached a hand toward her head, which she almost ducked instinctively, but she managed to still her reflex from years of training. He plucked a leaf out of her hair and handed it to her.

"Murder is such a strong word." She brushed the dirt off her pants. "We were only sparring."

Taelien approached the pair, cradling his stomach with his left hand. "Velas, as usual, is amending the definition of sparring to her tastes. But it was fun."

"Herod would have murdered you if he saw you throwing sorcery around in a practice match like that," Landen pointed out.

"We were careful," Taelien insisted, drawing a bit of surprise from Velas. She hadn't expected him to defend the potentially dangerous fighting, given how hesitant he seemed to be to engage in it in the first place.

Then again, he had very deliberately removed both of their swords from the fight immediately. Perhaps the weaponry had been his only real concern.

"Now that we're done, you mind letting me in on how you were throwing me around like a five year old?" Taelien asked.

"A girl has to have her secrets," Velas said, fluttering her eyelashes at him.

"It's motion sorcery," Landen said, deadpan. "I didn't see most of your 'sparring', but I saw the end of it. That was definitely motion sorcery."

She elbowed Landen lightly in the ribs. "Why'd you have to ruin all my fun? I could have kept him guessing for weeks."

"That was my first guess anyway," Taelien said. "I've seen someone use it before. Why'd you use it today? I've never seen you use sorcery before, although you clearly have practice."

*You haven't seen it because I'm usually subtler about it.* "You don't normally use your metal sorcery, so I assumed it wouldn't be fair. But since you decided to show off that trick, I had to even the field."

*"Always have another secret to reveal,"* she remembered her mentor saying. *"Every layer can be used to obfuscate the next."*

"Well, if you're both done ruining my secrets, can we get back to the fun part?" She pointed at the two swords that were lying near the other side of the platform, still intertwined by Taelien's metal sorcery.

"Dawnfire is up," Taelien said. "Armory should be open. We can go get practice gear."

"I was enjoying this more." Velas stretched her arms. "How about you, Landen? Up for something a little more...exciting, than what we've been doing lately?"

He leaned his face into his fist. "Your idea of exciting is, unfortunately, somewhat different from mine. Don't get me wrong, I enjoy putting you in the dirt as much as the next guy, but—"

"Oh, if you want to talk like that, I'll—"

"Actually," Taelien cut in. "I think I have a better idea for all of us for the day. Something even you might appreciate, Velas."

"Oh?" She turned away from Landen, quirking a brow at Taelien.

"You wanted to gather information earlier – we can do that right now. Just not the kind of information you were talking about."

"Go on."

\*\*\*

"I'm not sure how looking at paperwork would be considered exciting, Taelien."

The swordsman retracted his hand, pulling the stack of papers to his chest and giving her a hurt look.

The three of them were sitting in the commissary, and they were not the first to arrive. She saw a few other recruits with bags under their eyes – including that pompous blade sorcerer, Keldyn Andys. As big as he talked, he must have been just as nervous as they were. That soothed her ego a bit, which simultaneously made her feel a little bit like a horrible person for reviling in someone else sharing her misery.

Emotions were such nuisances sometimes.

"You could at least look at them." Taelien frowned.

Velas sighed. "You're such a baby sometimes."

She stuck her spoon into the nondescript gruel that served as "breakfast" in here. *This paste is so thick I'll probably develop my arm muscles just by stirring it.*

Taelien handed the papers to Landen.

The brown haired former Queensguard scanned over the first page, then raised an eyebrow. "Where'd you get these?"

"I have friends in high places." Taelien smirked.

"Okay, so what did Lydia give you that's so impressive?" Velas continued stirring her food, although she glanced toward the doorway and noticed a trio of unfamiliar figures wandering into the room.

The first was an androgynous looking brunette with a long scar that curved from beneath her right ear to the center of her chin. While she had no visible weapons, Velas noted that the newcomer moved with the kind of confidence that came with being prepared for instant violence. She wore an immaculate red tunic embroidered with the symbol of a rose with a dagger blade in the place of a stem.

The second was a clean-shaven man in glistening plate armor, the same symbol on his breastplate. Velas rarely saw anyone wearing armor in the commissary, but it wasn't strictly unheard of. The matching heraldry was more interesting – it wasn't uncommon for multiple members of the same family or organization to try to enter the paladin examinations together, but she hadn't seen other groups like that yet.

Finally, a towering figure ducked through the doorway, nearly his entire form concealed within a voluminous red cloak. As he walked, she saw a glint of matching armor beneath, and a pair of weapon hilts on his hips. His face was concealed by a veil of similar material to the cloak and his eyes were a darker red than his garb. He had no sclera in his eyes.

*Wearing a cloak and veil into the mess hall? That's a little bit pretentious. I suppose he wants to cultivate a "mysterious" image, but he's trying far too hard.*

It was none of those three that truly intrigued Velas, however. A lone man entered several minutes later, quickly taking a seat in a far side of the mess hall, his back to the wall. He was tall, with an athletic build, and cleanly cut short blond hair. His form-fitting black shirt helped emphasize the musculature in his arms, while a cerulean vest and a darker blue hat displayed a hint of style that she rarely found amongst the other paladin recruits. A bronze-hilted rapier sat on his left hip. The complete image struck her as the ideal of a traditional Velryan duelist, but the way his eyes scanned the room instantly upon his entry indicated a degree of caution that usually came from more covert work.

For an instant, his eyes locked on hers, and his expression twisted into a grin. He tilted his hat down toward her in a form of acknowledgement, and she nodded her head and pressed two fingers from her left hand against her forehead. If he recognized the gesture, he made no sign.

"Think those three are here for the trials?" Velas waved a hand to indicate the newcomers.

"Yeah," Landen said, "Because they're described right here."

That got her attention.

"What?"

Landen leaned over the table, whispering to her. "These are dossiers on all the applicants."

Velas gave a low whistle. "Okay, Sal. I take it all back. That does sound interesting."

"Sal?" Taelien raised an eyebrow. "Never heard that one."

"I think it'll stick. Taelien is too pretentious, and Salaris is a mouthful. Sal is cute, though."

"Uh, thanks, I suppose." He blinked, looking uncharacteristically stymied. She flashed him one of her usual grins, then turned back to Landen.

"So, when do I get to see?"

"When I'm finished," Landen replied. "After all, you told 'Sal' they sounded boring."

She sighed. "You could at least read me the highlights."

"I'm not sure we're even supposed to have these."

Taelien shrugged. "I already asked the trainers."

Both Landen and Velas turned to stare at him.

"What? I didn't want to get in trouble later. And they said something about information gathering being a useful skill, so it was fine."

*You are so naïve sometimes, Sal. I'm not sure if it should be infuriating or just adorable.*

From Landen's expression, she could tell he was thinking along similar lines.

"Never mind. If you want to discuss this, we should do it elsewhere," Landen said. "You two done eating?"

Velas thrust her spoon deep into the gruel, and then pulled upward, lifting the bowl. "Yeah, I think I'm done."

***

Landen's apartment was much better furnished than Velas'. She never understood why people needed fancy things like rugs, tapestries, and the like – even though her family had always had them when she had grown up. Practical things she could understand; additional colors and artistic flourishes were just noise.

Nevertheless, she had long ago learned to pretend. "Nice painting, Lan. That new?"

She pointed at a random portrait on the wall. It was a depiction of General Therin, white-bladed sword in hand, looming over a vanquished Vyrek Sul, the former ruler of the Xixian Empire. Therin was bare-chested and looked more like a sculptor's model than a swordsman.

"Yeah, it's my new favorite. You like it?"

Velas nodded. "Yeah, it's a good one." She could appreciate the male form, at least, and the detail on the ancient sword that Therin carried was impressive. The artist had put some work into researching the artifact, at least.

She took a perch on the side of Landen's bed, cracking her neck to the left and right while the others sat down at the nearby kitchen table.

"Okay, so who are we up against?" she inquired.

"Well, it's not really that kind of test," Landen pointed out. "There are teams, but it's not a direct competition."

"Aww, that's bullshit and you know it. The judges are definitely going to compare the performance between different teams, even if we're not literally fighting each other. And, by the end, I fully expect we will be literally fighting each other. We've got a god of swords, remember?"

"Don't get my hopes up," Taelien said with a grin.

*Couldn't be any higher than mine.* She squirmed a little on the edge of the bed.

"Are we all even on the same team?" she asked.

Landen shrugged. "Not sure yet. We need to make it through the preliminary rounds first. We're likely to end up in the same platoon if we make it through, though, since we're all classified as melee combat specialists. Also, I'm anticipated to have the highest score."

"What? Let me see those!" Velas sprang to her feet and reached for the stack of papers, which Landen deftly swept out of the way.

"When I'm done," he said. He pointed at the bed. She sat back down, folding her arms.

"He's telling the truth," Taelien said. "I skimmed them last night. I'm projected to have the lowest scores of the three of us." He sighed. "Apparently I 'lack discipline'."

"That's true," Velas said.

"Definitely true," Landen echoed.

Taelien glanced at Landen, smacking him playfully on the shoulder. "Hey, whose side are you on here?"

"Oh, picking sides now, are we?" Velas grabbed a pillow from the bed, glancing at the two swordsmen with a menacing expression.

"Just read, Landen," Taelien said with a sigh. "I want to hear your assessment on the biggest threats to our group."

"You can read these," Landen passed a smaller stack to Velas. "I've already read them."

The next hour passed with minimal conversation as they each devoured the details about their potential competitors. There were hundreds of candidates, but Taelien only had paperwork for the locals and a few others that had arrived and registered early enough for Lydia to make copies of their dossiers.

After finding one particular dossier, Landen frowned and handed it to Velas. "What's a 'Bladecaller'?"

Velas glanced over the sheet detailing the capabilities of Keldyn Andys, the local swordsman reported to be blessed by the god of blades.

*Keldyn Andys*

*Human Male Age 23; Hair: Blond, Eyes: Hazel*

*Height 178 cm, Weight: 76 kg*

*Experience: Priesthood of Tae'os 14 yrs., Tournament Duelist 1 yr.*

*Languages: Velthryn*

*Weapon Proficiencies: Sword (Teris, Velthryn, Aayaran), Dagger, Bow (Velthryn)*

*Sorcerous Proficiencies: Gifts of Aendaryn; Bladecaller*

*Expected Performance Rating: 88*

*Description: A third generation paladin. His mother, Sarellia Andys, was one of the Arms of Therin and deployed in the final push at Xixis. She was killed in action along with the rest of her unit in the aftermath of the battle. Keldyn was raised by his father, a blacksmith, and sent to train as an acolyte at 8 yrs.*

*At 16 yrs., Keldyn applied for a transfer from the priesthood to the Paladins of Tae'os. At the time, his application was denied due to his lack of experience.*

*Applicant Andys employed a private fencing trainer while continuing with his normal responsibilities as a priest, entering private tournaments and displaying progressively improved skills. He continued to serve in the priesthood until 22 yrs., at which point he manifested the Gifts of Aendaryn during a duel.*

*With Aendaryn's favor clearly displayed, he was permitted to begin accelerated paladin training to prepare for the Trials of Unyielding Steel.*

Finished with reading the document, she looked back at Landen. "A 'caller' is the local term for a sorcerer who specializes in summoning raw material. We'd call it a dominion sorcerer back home. They'd call me a Motioncaller, for instance."

Taelien chimed in a moment later. "The other side of it is a 'shaper', which means someone who specializes in changing the properties of a material. Most sorcerers have some ability at both shaping and calling, but many of us specialize. They'd call me a Metalshaper here, for example."

Velas nodded. "Or a core sorcerer of metal in Orlyn."

Landen scratched his chin, glancing at Taelien. "What can you do with that? I've seen you magnetize things in Orlyn, or shift the mass of your sword. Can you turn copper into gold and make a fortune?"

Taelien shrugged. "Haven't figured that out yet. I can only switch one or two things about an object at a time – and the appearance of a metal is derived from other characteristics, which makes that sort of thing tricky. I've heard it's possible, but I'd imagine it would be very taxing on the body. Reshaping something into a material that has vastly different properties – like my magnetism trick – costs my body more than just redistributing the mass. Magnetism is tied to lightning, for example, so it's like casting both a metal spell with a little bit of lightning involved."

Landen tapped a hand on his leg. "But you can't cast lightning spells, right?"

"Unfortunately, no. Not strong enough – but everyone has hints of every single dominion, and some spells can draw subtly from dominions that you're not actually strong enough to cast from."

Velas passed the dossier back to Landen, who handed it to Taelien. "Anyway, about Keldyn. There's no known Dominion of Blades – no plane that's just made up of a bunch of floating swords. Being a Bladecaller means that Keldyn somehow manifested the ability to summon swords out of…something. People think it's tied to the god of swords somehow, since that's something Aendaryn did a lot of in the old stories."

Landen raised an eyebrow. "Isn't that something Sal could do?"

Taelien shook his head. "I'm no good at calling metal – but even if I was, I'd just be making a normal metal sword appear in my hand. This guy apparently makes floating, glowing swords that can fight on their own."

Velas' former Queensguard partner nodded appreciatively. "Okay, that does sound pretty impressive. Guess the god of swords *does* like him, then."

"Maybe," Velas shrugged. "Maybe he's just picked up a neat trick. Anyway, enough about Keldyn. I want to see what some of the newcomers look like."

The details on most of the foreigners were sparse, but Velas quickly found the ones she was most interested in.

*Susan Crimson*
*Human Female Age 22; Hair: Brown, Eyes: Brown*
*Height 166 cm, Weight: 54 kg*
*Experience: Pre-Thornguard 4 yrs, Thornguard, 6 yrs.*
*Languages: Veltrhyn, Isendri*

*Weapon Proficiencies: Sword (Sae'lien), Spear (Sae'lien), Dagger, Lance, Bow (Isendri)*

*Sorcerous Proficiencies: None Declared*

*Expected Performance Rating: 52*

*Description: The third daughter of House Crimson, a lesser noble house in Selyr. Sent to Thornguard training at 12 yrs., most likely due to the family lacking sufficient lands to allocate to all children. Served 6 yrs. in the Selyr region and on deployment to the Lissec region. Combat experience in multiple encounters with Xixian forces while on deployment. Disillusioned with Thornguard politics, she chose to leave them after serving her mandatory years.*

Velas put that dossier back in the pile, skipping the rest of the information. The question of the unusual heraldry solved, she didn't find anything of particular interest about the young woman. She skimmed over the file on the armored man who had followed Susan into the mess hall next.

*Bertram Colt*

*Human Male Age 24; Hair: Brown, Eyes: Hazel*

*Height 182 cm, Weight: 79 kg*

*Experience: Pre-Thornguard 4 yrs, Thornguard, 8 yrs.*

*Languages: Veltrhyn, Isendri*

*Weapon Proficiencies: Sword (Sae'lien), Spear (Sae'lien), Dagger, Lance, Bow (Isendri)*

*Sorcerous Proficiencies: None Declared*

*Expected Performance Rating: 43*

*Description: A former servant to House Crimson, Bertram Colt entered Thornguard training at age 12 yrs. After completing his training, he served for several years before being reunited with Susan Crimson, who he had known in his childhood. The pair left the Thornguard together after serving on deployment in the Lissec region.*

Slipping that paper back into the file, she tapped her fingers on the table, considering. *These are awfully vague. Not enough to really evaluate their motives or weaknesses. Still, neither of them sounds like much of a threat. Let's see about Mr. Cloaky.*

*The Wandering War*

*Classified Species Male Age Classified; Hair: Copper, Eyes: Crimson*
*Height 194 cm, Weight: 85 kg*
*Experience: Details Restricted*
*Languages: Veltrhyn*
*Weapon Proficiencies: All conventional weapons*
*Sorcerous Proficiencies: Details Restricted*
*Expected Performance Rating: 100*
*Description: Bound servant of House Crimson. File restricted on the authority of Arbiter Stone. Observe with extreme caution.*

Velas raised an eyebrow at the page. *Expected performance of 100? All right, that one is far more interesting than I gave him credit for. "Classified Male?" Does that imply he's not Rethri? If so, what is he? I finally find something amusing and all the details are locked away. Figures. Going to need to see if I can get some better data on him later.*

She frowned, passing that dossier over to Taelien, and began searching through the pile for the one she was most interested in.

*Jonathan Sterling*
*Human Male Age 25; Hair: Blond, Eyes: Blue*
*Height 185 cm, Weight: 74 kg*
*Experience: Soldier 4 yrs., Bodyguard, 2 yrs., Haven Knights 5 yrs.*
*Languages: Veltrhyn, Teris, Old Velryan*
*Weapon Proficiencies: Sword (Sae'lien), Spear (Sae'lien), Dagger, Lance, Bow (Isendri)*
*Sorcerous Proficiencies: None Declared*
*Expected Performance Rating: 71*
*Description: Born in Velrya, Jonathan Sterling served in the local military for the standard four yrs. After this, he spent two yrs. as a professional bodyguard to the Stalwart family. After saving the life of the family heir, he was offered a position in the Haven Knights, a prominent local knightly order. Several years later, he chose to apply to the Paladins of Tae'os following the departure of his grandfather, a former paladin.*

*After passing his basic qualifications, Jonathan indicated that he preferred to take the expedited examinations rather than serve as a squire due to his age and prior experience. His application was approved by Paladin Lieutenant Shaw on 4th Era'dae 3208 VC...*

She skimmed the rest – she had already read the most important details. *A Haven Knight, eh? I didn't realize the Havens were sending their enforcers this far south. It'll be interesting to try to figure out why he's really here.*

"Woah, look at this one," Landen said, passing Velas another sheet. She only had to glance at the second line to see what he was talking about.

"A Delaren? That's gotta be a joke." She parsed through the rest of the page rapidly, shaking her head in disbelief.

The Delaren were a species of humanoids that were supposedly created in the earliest days of the world, much like the Esharen. After a war between their two races brought the Delaren to the brink of extinction, the Delaren went into hiding.

"I didn't even realize there were still any alive," Taelien said. "But the description is interesting. Apparently she brought two human 'attendants' with her, and they're all applying to join the Paladins of Tae'os together."

"So, it's a political thing?" Velas asked. "I can't imagine the Delaren have the same religions we do."

Taelien shrugged. "No idea. If she's here as some sort of political move, it's a strange way to do it. Wouldn't it make more sense to marry her off to a prince or something?"

"Most women don't like being 'married off' like they're objects, Sal."

He frowned. "Sorry, I didn't mean to imply that. I just thought that, you know, traditionally—"

"Yeah, I get what you meant. Anyway, from the description, it sounds like she came here of her own accord. And if she has human guards with her, they already have some integration with human culture."

"Why come here now, though?" Landen asked. "And taking the trials to join the Paladins of Tae'os – I mean, that implies she must have at least known when they were happening and how they work."

"Well, why don't we just ask her when we see her?" Velas set the paper aside. "Shouldn't be easy to miss the girl with purple crystals for hair."

"The paper said she doesn't have any transformations yet, so she must be pretty young," Taelien added.

Delaren were well-known for being born with the ability to reconstruct their bodies. According to legend, Delaren were born with a humanoid appearance and could only grow larger over time – once they had added something to their bodies, they couldn't get rid of it. Amir Orin, a legendary Delaren king, was often described as having a layer of bony armor and tremendous wings.

The transformation abilities of the Delaren were supposedly fueled by dominion essence contained in their crystalline hair. This essence was reportedly essential to the Delaren's survival, making a Delaren's hair a major point of vulnerability.

It was also one of the most stable sources of dominion essence, since it naturally grew into a crystalline state, and each hair-like strand contained a mixture of essence of several different dominions. That made it an extraordinarily valuable commodity to sorcerers – valuable enough that the Xixian Empire had captured and bred Delaren slaves for centuries, purely to harvest their hair.

Aside from transforming their bodies, Delaren could supposedly use their hair to enhance their physical or sorcerous abilities – but at the cost of years of their lifespan.

"I suppose she'll be able to blend in somewhat if she hasn't transformed at all yet," Landen remarked. "As long as she keeps her head covered."

"Yeah, at least she'll be able to fit through doorways," Velas added. "A fully grown Delaren could barely move around in a city like this."

"A good point. I wonder what their cities are like," Taelien mused.

"This is interesting, too." Landen lifted a few other pieces of paper, passing them to Velas. "Valerians. You know any of them?"

Velas glanced over names on the papers. "No one I recognize in specific. This gal is from House Laurent, which I've heard of, but I don't know her specifically."

"Unfortunate. Well, nothing else in here seems quite as exciting as that creature of legend."

"Asphodel," Taelien noted, drawing looks from the other two. "Her name is Asphodel."

Landen nudged Taelien. "I didn't know purple was your color."

Taelien shook his head. "It's not that. I'm just tired of people thinking of me as 'the man with the Sae'kes' rather than Taelien or Salaris. I'd say she's probably going to be dealing with a similar problem."

"Suppose that's fair," Velas noted, "But if you feel that way, you really shouldn't be calling yourself Taelien. It invites people to think about you that way. And, as I said, Sal is a much cuter name."

Taelien sighed.

"You're not going to let that go, are you?"

## CHAPTER VI – LYDIA II – SUBOPTIMAL MOVES

Lydia navigated the citadel's halls by rote, reading while she walked. The book was the latest in a series on protection sorcery by Edrick Theas, the father of the murder victim. Reading the book served to both enhance her sorcerous techniques and to try to glean more information about the writer. If his daughter's assessment was accurate, Kalsiris Theas – apparently called "Kae" by his friends – was likely murdered for political reasons connected to his father.

*It was during the third year of the western campaign that I began to favor the use of spells that simulated the creation of a suit of armor. I did not invent the Sorcerous Armor spell, of course, but conventional wisdom had long held that it was better to completely stop an attack with the ubiquitous Sorcerous Shield or Essence Barrier spells.*

*My logic for the switch in methodology came down to two factors. First, since the Sorcerous Armor spell only served to deflect a portion of an attack, the amount of essence expended for any given strike was far less than attempting to stop an attack entirely. This meant that an armor spell with the same amount of essence invested could diminish the impact of a much larger number of attacks. Since the armor's protection was often sufficient to prevent weaker attacks – such as arrows or ordinary swings of a sword – from causing harm, the extra essence expended by a more potent defense was essentially wasted.*

*Second, I found that soldiers and sorcerers alike were more cautious when they felt the impact of attacks. Someone who knows that they are likely to be completely unharmed by a certain number of strikes is far more likely to take risks, and much less likely to realize when their defensive spells have been worn away. The more granular nature of the armor spell allows the recipient to continue to feel the force of each impact increase as the armor weakens, giving him or her a chance to react appropriately.*

*While I have primarily switched to using armor spells for protecting the troops under my command, I do still utilize the more traditional defenses in specific cases. Armor spells provide minimal defense against mental incursion, and thus, I typically protect myself and others with Sorcerous Shields when confronting Esharen sorcerers. Similarly, armor spells are insufficient against attacks with a level of force that would crush an ordinary suit of armor – and thus, Sorcerous Shields are also necessary protection against siege engines and war sorcerers.*

*Of course, the best defense against a siege engine is still to avoid being hit by a siege engine. No amount of sorcery can provide certain protection in the face of sufficient force.*

The writing was sufficiently enrapturing that she didn't notice Taelien standing outside the door of her office until she had nearly wandered into him. Blinking, she looked up to meet his grin. "Oh, Salaris. I don't think I have time to give you any advice on the tests today."

Calling him *Salaris* still sounded awkward on her tongue. Using *Taelien* in Velthryn would drag them both into more politics than she was prepared to deal with – at least for now. Once Taelien was established as a paladin…then things would be very different. She needed to wait for the right time to strike.

He stepped out of the way of the door, motioning toward the handle for her to open it. "I'm not here to bother you about that. It's the eighth."

She quirked an eyebrow, searching her mind and failing to find the connection. *Looks like one of my spells must have eaten that memory. Either that, or I'm just getting old.* "The eighth?"

"Sorcery measurements."

"Ahh, right." She found a bookmark in her pouch, shoved it into the book, and then dug deeper into the pouch for the key to her office. After a few more moments of fumbling, she opened the door and gestured for Taelien to go inside. "I suppose we'll have to do it now, then, or the tests will be invalid. We'll have to be quick, though. I have some rather important business to attend to."

"Anything I can help with?" Taelien tilted his head to the side.

She shook her head. "Not at the moment, unfortunately. Once I've concluded the preliminary investigation, perhaps."

Once they were within, she locked the door. This wasn't the kind of business she wanted someone walking in on.

Taelien took a seat in nearest chair, unrolling his sleeve. Lydia walked around to the opposite side of the table, lifting up her own chair and dragging it over to set it down next to Taelien.

The swordsman took a deep breath. "Before we start, have you heard anything from Colonel Dyr?"

Lydia shook her head. Back in Orlyn, Taelien had been advised to ask Orin Dyr about Erik Tarren – the man who had handed an infant Taelien to his adoptive parents. Lydia had asked Orin on Taelien's behalf, but Orin hadn't seen Tarren in years.

At Lydia's urging, Orin had sent letters to a few locations he knew Tarren visited – but it was not uncommon for Erik to disappear for years at a time. An expert on travel sorcery, Erik wandered the countryside to learn its features, which enabled him to teleport to a broader variety of locations.

"Nothing. He sent a letter to Erik's family in Velrya to ask if they know anything, but it will be weeks before we hear a reply."

Taelien nodded sadly. "Thank you for looking into it, at least."

"It's nothing. Any other questions before we begin?"

Taelien shook his head.

"Alright, then. Anything unusual to report?" It was her standard opening question, but she didn't expect much of a reply.

"*Apparently*, Velas is a motion sorcerer. Explains how she throws me around like a rag doll."

Lydia rolled her eyes. "I already knew that. Anything about your own abilities?"

He shrugged. "Still stuck at four runes most of the time. Occasionally, I can get up to five, but it's extraordinarily difficult. I'm not sure why. In the past, whenever I managed to reach a certain degree of control over the sword, repeating the process got easier – that doesn't seem to be the case anymore."

"I'm pretty sure I know why, but we're going to gather more information today. If it agrees with my previous findings, I'll let you know about my hypothesis."

Taelien raised an eyebrow. "Finally filling me in? You must be pretty confident, then."

*I was pretty confident five months ago, but I hate being wrong.*

"Yeah, I'm getting there." She put a hand on his exposed arm. "Okay, you know the process. Anything else before I start?"

"Don't think so. Ready as I'm going to be." He took a deep breath. "Go."

Lydia closed her eyes, picturing an outline of Taelien's body in her mind. "Dominion of Knowledge, measure the flow of essence within his body."

Within her mind, Taelien's body began to glow. Networks of lines illuminated a multitude of sorcerous connections. The brightness made it difficult to examine any individual line, but she knew that the spell was attempting to illustrate each of the dominions within his body in a form that she could comprehend. Each line was a different color, allowing her to distinguish between the dominions they represented.

Most humans had about two dozen visible lines of color within their bodies, representing each of the prime dominions and a series of deep dominions that were essential for the functions of the body. In an ordinary human, these lines typically displayed similar levels of brightness, although there were exceptions. Athletes often had strong lines of motion or stone, scholars often had powerful lines of knowledge, and artists frequently had brilliant lines of deception.

Sorcerers displayed stronger lines for any dominion they practiced, and spells similar to Lydia's were often used to evaluate the potential for talent among students at sorcerous academies. These lines would grow stronger through use, like working a muscle – but, much like with muscles, they could be torn and ruptured, damaging both the ability to use that form of sorcery and other bodily functions.

Rethri typically had a single dominion that was particularly dominant, and their other dominions were frequently less pronounced than those in humans. After a Rethri received their dominion bond during their coming of age ceremony, they developed a visible pool of dominion essence of that type near their eyes. If Lydia's measurements on Aladir were any indication, this pool grew stronger over time even when the dominion was not being actively used – making Rethri extremely potent at their own particular sorcerous specialties.

When Lydia had first examined Taelien's dominions while he had been jailed in Orlyn, she had detected what appeared to be two dominion bonds. Initially, she had assumed this meant that he had been bonded with a ritual similar or identical to the ones the Rethri used. Having two bonds was rare, but not entirely without precedent – she had heard of cases of powerful Rethri developing bonds to a prime dominion and one or more of the deep dominions connected to the prime.

A more thorough examination had displayed problems with that hypothesis.

His dominion bond to metal was easy to examine with this more advanced spell, but the form it took was perplexing. A Rethri bond looked like a single lake feeding into tiny streams. Taelien's was a broad river that began at his right hand and traveled down the length of his right arm before splitting off into the smaller streams. His focused source of essence made it easier to draw on if he was touching something directly.

The essence source she had assumed was a second dominion bond was even more perplexing. When visualized, it did not look like veins of light at all – rather, it looked like his body contained several tiny stars, each of which emanated essence that permeated everything nearby. The auras from the stars saturated his entire body, growing brighter every time she observed them.

The brightest stars were within his hands, and these were what she observed as Taelien began to draw the Sae'kes.

As soon as the first rune was visible, Lydia watched the lights in Taelien's body flicker and redirect essence toward his right hand. From there, she could sense it flowing directly into the Sae'kes to power the rune.

"Stop there for a measurement. Dominion of Knowledge, measure the rate of essence flow into the Sae'kes."

*Three point two domini per minute,* the spell registered. *Almost exactly what I estimated. We'll see if the trend holds.*

The sorceress had developed this particular spell specifically for the purpose of this test, since most knowledge spells directed at the Sae'kes showed useless results. She had made some progress with identifying the functions of the gemstones in the hilt and pommel, but the blade itself offered no answers.

"Go ahead and power the next rune," she instructed. She kept her eyes shut, watching the star on his right hand intensify.

Most dominion lines dimmed when in use, rather than growing brighter. Even Rethri dominion bonds were no exception.

Metal scraped against metal as Taelien continued to draw out the blade until the second rune was exposed. He let out a deep breath as he infused the second rune.

"Dominion of Knowledge, measure the rate of essence flow into the Sae'kes," she repeated.

*Ten point two four domini per minute,* the spell reported to her. Lydia nodded absently. "Continue."

She repeated the process for the third and fourth runes, mentally recording the results.

*Thirty two point seven eight domini per minute.*

*One hundred four point eight five seven six domini per minute.*

The star in his right hand was blinding, its aura extending beyond his arm and half way across his chest. The other stars within his body pulsed independently, seemingly unaffected by this process. The lines representing his other dominions were gradually fading. They were slowly being drained.

She paused, debating if she wanted to push him to continue. The amount of essence he was burning through was absurd by a normal sorcerer's standards, but his breathing seemed normal, and his results were matching what she expected.

*Do I need another data point? Not really.*

"I need to keep my eyes closed. Keep your sword out, but put your left hand in my left hand," Lydia instructed. It was a non-standard test, but potentially useful. "Dominion of Knowledge, measure the uncategorized essence within his left hand."

This spell required two adjustments – one to only measure within his hand, another to measure the unusual essence within the 'star'. She used the term "uncategorized" because she still had no idea which dominion it represented – any effort to identify the sorcery type had provided her with nonsensical results.

*Two hundred fifty-five point nine domini.*

Lydia frowned at the number. *Disconcerting how much essence he can hold. With that amount of essence, he could power several spells without needing to draw on dominions at all. That would probably kill him, of course.*

"Keep your right hand on the sword, but put your hand in contact with mine."

"That's going to be tricky to do without cutting you, give me a minute."

Taelien pulled his left hand away, shifted in his seat, and she felt the brush of his skin against her fingers a moment later.

"Okay, you're touching me."

Lydia nodded once. "Dominion of Knowledge, measure the uncategorized essence within his right hand."

Numbers flickered in Lydia's mind, flickering as they rapidly shifted. One thing was clear in the chaos of digits, however.

*He's drawing essence from somewhere else just as rapidly as he's using it.*

"All right, Tae – Salaris. That's enough. You can sheathe the sword."

She opened her eyes, blinking. She could feel a burning in her temples and at the back of her neck – the first signs of a mild overuse of her own sorcery.

Taelien carefully pulled his hand away from hers, allowing the runes to fade one at a time as he slowly lowered the blade back into the sheath.

"I heard some new incants in there. What'd you figure out?"

Lydia lowered her head into her hands, rubbing at her temples. "Well, to begin with, you're completely unnatural."

"We knew that. Anything with a bit more substance? You've been keeping me in suspense for months." He slid his chair closer, putting his hand on the back of her neck and beginning to slowly rub the soreness away. She let out a soft hum of appreciation.

"Thanks," she mumbled. She knew it wasn't a romantic gesture – Taelien just seemed unusually comfortable with being physical with people he was close to. When she had asked him about it before, he had attributed it to his upbringing among the Rethri, but none of the Rethri she knew were as tactile as he was. Perhaps the Rethri in the Forest of Blades were more culturally accustomed to physical contact, but she suspected it was more of a personal characteristic of his – possibly even tied to his unusual dominion allocations.

Either way, Lydia wasn't going to complain, as long as the door was closed. If someone saw them, rumors would be spreading within hours.

Which wouldn't be bad, once he was more established. In fact, it might be useful — but she wasn't quite ready for that stage yet.

"Right." She paused, focusing her thoughts. "I have a hypothesis about why you're having such a hard time igniting that fifth rune. Or, a component of the problem, anyway."

"Really?" He sounded excited, which was unfortunately rare these days. His happiness level had steeply diminished as the stress of nearing the tests had approached, but she expected that he'd acclimate to the challenges and improve his mood when the testing was over.

"So, each time we've been doing this, I've been recording the amount of essence you expend on igniting each rune. It goes up every time."

Taelien lifted his other hand and scratched at his chin. "That's strange. What do you think it means?"

"At first, I considered the possibility that the development of other dominions in your body was making the transfer of essence less efficient. I postulated that if some dominions are more compatible with the runes than others, and your dominion balance was shifting in an opposite direction —"

"The total amount of essence needed to accomplish the same result would increase. Yes, that makes sense."

*He's sharper than I give him credit for sometimes. If he actually bothered to try thinking about his problems instead of brute forcing them, he'd be even more of a force to be reckoned with...which could be dangerous, in the long run.*

"It does. But, unfortunately, it doesn't hold up to scrutiny. I've measured the changes in your body's dominions over time, too, and while some of them have increased in measurable quantities — notably metal and flame, which I know you practice regularly — none of them have increased in an amount to scale with the increasing costs. None with the exception of the one I can't measure properly, that is."

"Ah, my mystery dominion. So, you think that it is getting stronger at the same rate at which my efficiency is decreasing?"

She nodded. He shifted his chair, moving to rub her shoulders with both of his hands. She let herself sigh audibly as he continued to work. "Essentially yes, but it appears to be more complex than that. In addition to that dominion growing more dominant in your body over time, I'm seeing something even more unusual. When you are igniting the runes, that particular dominion seems to draw in more essence from an external source."

"That doesn't sound that strange. Don't normal dominion sorcery spells use your essence to call something from a dominion?"

"Yes, but that's to conjure something outside of yourself – like a ball of flame or one of my barriers. Dominion sorcery doesn't summon anything directly into the body's systems for storing and manipulating essence. Even spells that directly interact with the body do so by changing the body's physical form – they don't put more raw essence into it. The body isn't designed to handle much more essence than it has while at rest. There are a few spells that sorcerers can use to transfer essence to one another, but they're dangerous, especially if the target is already near their essence capacity."

Taelien slowed his massaging, apparently distracted by his thoughts. "So, I'm pulling in foreign essence, which is both unusual and dangerous. Wonderful. I'm getting less efficient at using the sword because of this strange dominion essence, I take it?"

"In a sense, but I don't think it's working the way you're thinking." She paused for a moment, contemplating how best to explain her hypothesis. "You know how Esharen are supposed to adapt to a dominion the more they're exposed to it, developing a resistance over time?"

Taelien went still, his jaw tensing. "Yeah, that's common knowledge."

*He still hasn't forgiven himself for that Esharen he killed,* she realized. *I need to be more sensitive about that.*

"Well, my second hypothesis was that the sword was adapting and developing a resistance. But that didn't make sense – as unusual as your sword might be, I'm relatively certain it isn't sentient, and I've never picked up the Dominion of Adaptation on it. Nor can I even think of a good reason for someone to build in an autonomous mechanism for it to be resistant to the user's attempts to control it. Granted, your own dominions do grow stronger from the strain, but building an unnecessary essence cost into a weapon is a horrific risk. This sword wasn't made for training. As you've pointed out to me before, it was clearly made for destroying things."

The swordsman pulled his hands away from her back, folding them in his lap. "At first, I thought the runes were a test – something the gods put on the weapon to see if someone was worthy to wield it. If it only gets harder over time, however, that doesn't seem to serve much of a purpose."

"Right. So, if it's not something philosophical, there must be a practical reason behind it. I thought about that a lot, and I went back and questioned our assumptions about the runes. We've never been able to identify the runestones directly, but we know the pommel's gemstone has something to do with the Dominion of Travel, and the hilt gem has to do with the Dominion of Insight. The blade's only obvious function is the cutting aura – nothing to do with teleportation or the manipulation of essence like those dominions would imply. I tried looking at the picture holistically, rather than just the disparate component parts."

"Don't keep me in suspense, Lydia."

"I believe that every time you try to use your essence to control the sword, some of the sword's essence is bleeding back into you in the process. Your own essence is gradually becoming more like that of the sword, especially near your right hand. It's not that the dominions in your body are opposing the sword now – it's that they're too similar."

She paused, contemplating how to explain the problem. "When you attempt to control the sword, it's like trying to dilute a liquid – say, mixing water into wine. But every time you do it, some of the wine is getting into your water supply. Now you're trying to dilute wine with something with wine already in it, which is less efficient."

Taelien was silent for several moments, glancing down at the sword. "That's…it doesn't make sense. It means that every time I train with the sword, I make it harder to use next time."

He shook his head, resting his left hand on the hilt of the weapon. His expression was grim. "You're saying that my training with the sword has been worthless. Years and years of training."

*Maybe I shouldn't have told him about this.* Impulsively, she leaned over and put a hand on his. Taelien took a deep breath, closing his eyes.

"No, I don't think so. You're building up some kind of dominion in your body – that's something you could learn to control."

"But it's possible that my training is going to make it harder to use the sword – I might never be able to control it completely if I keep mingling my own essence with it. And that unknown dominion might have no useful function – we have no way of knowing at this point."

She frowned, but she had to concede the point. "You're not wrong. I'm sorry, Taelien."

"It's fine. I've managed to ignite more and more runes over time – which means not all of my training was a waste. Just the training focused on the sword itself, it seems."

"That wouldn't be a waste, either. Just because training with the sword isn't going to make the number of lit runes increase doesn't mean it doesn't have a purpose – it's still strengthening the other dominions in your body, even if you don't value the improvements to the unclassified one."

He lowered his head. "I guess you have a point. I've just been so focused on the runes for so long – it's been my only sign of progress. Why would someone make a sword that gets harder to control over time? That seems like madness."

"Well," she said in a tender tone, knowing that this point might be making things worse, "It was probably forged for someone strong enough to use all seven runes from the first time he picked it up. With sufficient control, the essence might not have bled back into the wielder at all."

"Oh." Taelien released his grip on the sword's handle, folding his hands in his lap. "The god of blades. Of course. If he could wield it at full strength immediately, he'd never have to worry about training with it." Taelien gave a hollow laugh. "I've been looking at this the wrong way the whole time. The runes were my way of trying to earn the right to use the sword. To prove that I was somehow worthy of having the blade of a god left in my care. How hilariously misguided."

Taelien stood up. "Thanks for telling me the truth, Lydia. I know you've probably been keeping this from me to protect me, but it's better that I know. Now I can try to plan around it."

The sorceress nodded, uncertain of what to say. "I'm sorry if the knowledge disappointed you, Taelien." She used the title deliberately, and he seemed to notice the gesture, giving her a half-smile. "For what it's worth, I don't think you need the sword to prove if you're worthy. You've proven it to me, at least. I hope you can prove it to yourself."

"Thanks, Lydia. I'll see what I can do."

Still bearing an expression of pain, Taelien turned and left the office.

\*\*\*

It was midday by the time Lydia found her way back to the grounds of House Theas. The house guards swiftly escorted her to Nedelya, who she found seated at a small table on a patio on the second floor of the manor. The baroness wore a fine red dress trimmed with gold, her hair raised into an elegant display. She looked less like a woman in mourning and more like a lady prepared to attend a courtly ball.

In her right hand, Baroness Theas held a mostly full glass of wine by the stem. The bottle on the table next to her, however, was quite nearly empty.

Nedelya did not turn toward Lydia as the sorceress approached. Instead, she silently stared out over the nearby railing. The sorceress glanced at the nearby house guard, but he simply shrugged. Lydia stepped closer, looking over the railing and finding the source of Nedelya's distraction – a familiar pair sitting at a similar table in the gardens below.

Aladir and Nakane seemed oblivious to their observation, staring in rapt concentration at the game board in front of them. Lydia squinted, trying to make out the details of the individual pieces. The game was Crowns, a popular war game among the local nobility. It was asymmetrical, with each player selecting an army that represented a particular faction, such as the armies of a city or an organization like the Paladins of Tae'os.

"She must like him," Nedelya noted without shifting her gaze. "Nakane almost never lets anyone win."

Lydia tilted her head to the side, trying to get a better angle to look at the board. Aladir's pieces were bright blue, and she noted several archers on his side of the board. Nakane's pieces were red, but with orange highlights rather than the gold of House Theas. They appeared to have an equal number of troops still in play, but Aladir's archers had the high ground, giving them the range they needed to fire on Nakane's sorcerers.

"Perhaps she's just distracted, given everything your family has been going through."

Nedelya just shook her head. "Nakane is never distracted, my dear. Do you see how she clenches her jaw as she moves that paladin? She knows she is making the wrong move, extending herself needlessly. Aladir knows this as well – that is why he is smiling."

Lydia leaned out over the railing, watching the pair play. It was only after several minutes of watching that she grew certain of what she suspected.

*Aladir is deliberately making suboptimal moves, too.*

But, unlike Nakane, he never stopped smiling.

"Do you play, dear?"

Lydia glanced to her right and saw that Nedelya was finally looking directly at her.

"No, Baroness. It's not an accurate depiction of military tactics, and thus I've never found it useful."

The baroness took another sip of her wine, frowning. "I don't believe most people play because they are making a study of tactics, Miss Hastings. I believe they find it enjoyable."

"Hm." Lydia pushed up her glasses, which had been slipping down her nose while she leaned against the railing. "Do you play, then, baroness?"

Nedelya chuckled lightly, raising two fingers to her lips. "Of course not, darling. Crowns is not a lady's game."

The baroness turned her head, looking back over the railing. "Nakane, unfortunately, has never been much of a lady. She has always taken more after her father."

*I'm not sure how to respond to that in a way that would not be insulting to someone.* "She seems to be very talented."

"Yes," the baroness nodded. "She plays each game on several different levels."

"What do you mean?"

Baroness Theas momentarily shut her eyes, and then waved her wine glass over the railing. "She plays a friendly game with the son of a man who may have murdered her brother. In playing, she chooses the armies of Blake Hartigan, her father's greatest rival – and then allows herself to lose to the pieces of House Dianis, skillfully chosen by Aladir as a logical army to counter her own."

*Lydia frowned. Is she testing Aladir somehow?* "Why is she playing the game that way?"

Nedelya fluttered her eyes, forming a slight smile. "I haven't the faintest idea, my dear. I don't play Crowns."

\*\*\*

It was hours past nightfall when Lydia finally found an opportunity to meet with her partner alone. The pair patrolled the grounds, searching for any sign of intruders, as they had each night since the attack. Pairs of guards were placed outside Nakane's and Nedelya's chambers, rotating every four hours. Initially, Lydia had pushed for the guards to wait inside the rooms, but the noblewomen both scoffed at the idea.

"Any luck at the citadel today?" Aladir asked, his hands tucked into the pockets of his trousers. It wasn't particularly cold by Lydia's standards, but she was wearing a long sleeved robe, and Aladir almost always wore sleeveless tunics. They were both wearing standard issue single-handed paladin swords on their belts, and Lydia noted that Aladir also had a dagger sheathed on the opposite side of his own belt.

"None. Arbiter Stone remains as implacable as his name implies. He won't even give me a single squad. He said he's lucky we're being allowed to pursue this at all, given that it's not officially in paladin jurisdiction."

Her partner shook his head, his green eyes the brightest thing in the night. "I could try talking to Arbiter Lyselia. She's a friend of the family."

"Going to another arbiter after being denied is a good way to get both of us demoted, Aladir."

Aladir paused in his step, lowering his head. "Kae is dead, Lydia. You think I care about politics?"

"Of course not, but you should care about practicality. If House Theas wasn't so influential, I don't think they'd even be letting the two of us look into this."

The life sorcerer balled his hands into fists. "I hear your words, Lydia, but how can our order turn their gaze aside when an innocent is dead?"

The sorceress sighed, putting a hand on his shoulder. "I'm sorry for your loss. Truly. But any breach of protocol is only going to hurt us when we catch the bastard who did this."

"If. If we catch him." Aladir looked up, turning his gaze to Lydia's eyes. She met his stare. "You're more confident than I am at this point. With each passing day, our chances diminish. We guard when we should hunt."

"The city guard is investigating, and they have more manpower than we do. If we find anything that warrants additional resources, I'll ask again —"

"We're not getting help, Lydia. And we're not helping here." He jerked a thumb toward the tower where Nedelya slept. "What are we going to do if the assassin returns, using the same methodology as last time? Presume that it was a Harvester of Poison that was summoned."

"I —"

"I'll tell you what we'd do — die messily." Aladir withdrew his hands from his pockets, folding his arms in front of him. "We can't fight a Harvester, Lydia. But we can fight someone who can summon a Harvester — and you're our best chance of finding him."

Lydia folded her own arms. "You're wrong. About the first part, at least." She reached into the pouch on her left side, withdrawing a large crystal — the Dominion Essence of Poison that they had found in the ritual area. "If we encounter a Harvester of Poison, I would throw this at it and run. Then, while it's busy absorbing this lovely crystal, I would gather Nakane and Nedelya and flee to the citadel. Two paladins may not be able to fight a Harvester, but you can rest assured that two thousand would be more than sufficient."

Aladir sighed, unfolding his arms and rubbing the back of his head. "I'm sorry for being so negative, Lydia. But it's been weeks with no sign of progress. I'm sure the city guards are doing all they can, but…"

"Protecting the most likely targets for a second attack is more important than catching the assassin. And we're the best chance the remainder of the Theas family has to survive."

Her partner turned his gaze away, clenching his jaw. "Fine. We can stay here, for now. But isn't there anyone we can trust to investigate? I'd ask my family, but of course, that wouldn't quite work."

Lydia leaned her head against her hand, considering. *Taelien is still in training — and he wouldn't even know where to start looking. Landen and Velas are in the same position…but I suppose there is someone.*

"I have someone I can ask, but you're not going to like it."

***

Hours later, Lydia pressed a letter against a mirror.

*Dear Jonan,*

*I know you've been looking for a good opportunity to visit Velthryn. As it turns out, now would be a good time.*

*-Lydia*

# CHAPTER VII – VELAS III – EXCESSIVE DAMAGE

Velas sat in the stands of the Korinval Coliseum, overlooking the setup of the contest in the arena below. The stadium was the largest in the city and dedicated to Koranir, the God of Strength. During sporting events and war games, the coliseum could seat nearly twenty thousand citizens. At the moment, it held a smaller but still intimidating number – more than a thousand full paladins, several hundred squires and priests, and nearly five hundred paladin applicants.

*Must be more than half of the paladins in the city here. This is going to be embarrassing if I mess it up.*

She noted a few boxes of private citizens in the stands as well – the majority of whom were probably close friends of high ranking paladins or nobles who donated significant amounts of money. She saw the banners of House Korvis, the owners of the coliseum itself, in one of the larger boxes – although not the largest. To the left of House Korvis she noted another box flying the banners of House Glaid, the house of the city's current champion swordmaster, Dreas Glaid. She couldn't quite see into the box from her angle – it was too high up – but she wondered if the swordmaster himself would be watching the contest below.

"You're thinking. That's dangerous." Landen poked a finger into her ribs and she playfully smacked his hand. He was dressed in full armor; a look she thought suited him. Freshly shaved and with his hair trimmed short, he was the very image of the perfect knight. In times like this, his persona glittered just as brightly as his mail and served just as well for deflecting threats. Velas knew how to exploit the weaknesses in both of his forms of armor, but she hoped she'd never have to make use of them.

"Oh, you know, just looking for any actual competition since there isn't any close by."

Landen raised a hand to his heart, fluttering his eyes. "I am wounded by your dismissal, my lady. Is that any way to treat a man with a higher estimated performance score than yours?"

Velas folded her arms, which were just as well armored as Landen's. She wasn't wearing her full armor today – just a mail shirt with bracers and greaves – because they didn't know the details of the test and she wanted a mix of protection and mobility. If their qualifying event was a footrace she suspected Landen was doomed. "Oh, you know those scores are bullshit. And you're only six points higher than me anyway."

"If they're bullshit, why do you remember our exact scores?"

"Sometimes it's important to quantify the exact values of bullshit. In this case, the delta between my test scores and reality is about thirty points."

"So, you're saying they should have put you at a forty instead of a seventy. That's very humble of you, I'll make sure to let the testers—"

She smacked his arm playfully, then raised her fists and shook them in the air in challenge.

"Okay, okay, I surrender." Landen held up his palms in a defensive gesture. "And I think they're about to announce something."

"Finally. We've been waiting for hours and I'm starving."

On the opposite side of the coliseum, a portly man stood on a raised platform dressed in ostentatious robes trimmed with silver. He was flanked by a pair of paladins, but wore no indications of any affiliation with the paladins or priests himself. Velas didn't recognize him.

*Most likely one of the people from House Korvis, then.*

It took her several moments to realize that he was speaking – and then another moment before a wave of sound sorcery washed over her, carrying his voice along with it.

"Good day, friends, and welcome to our arena! Today, by the grace of Koranir, we will witness a fearsome contest. More than four hundred men and women, eager to prove themselves in the eyes of gods and men. Behold, the first of the Trials of Unyielding Steel!"

He clapped his hands, which with the benefits of sound sorcery felt like a thunderclap. Velas grit her teeth at the impact.

*The man doesn't have a tenth of the presence that Edon did, but at least he's excited to be here.*

The speaker looked around, grinning from ear to ear, and then continued. "I, Orellas of House Korvis, have the great esteem to preside over this contest. In a few moments, you will see the nature of the challenge."

Velas watched as numerous attendants entered the arena below, beginning to prepare the field for the event. She tightened her jaw when she caught a glimpse of a straw dummy used for archery practice. All of the paladin trainees had some degree of archery training, but it was hardly her area of expertise.

When she saw the distance between the targets and where the attendants began to set up the stations with bows and standing quivers, she exhaled deeply.

"Don't be nervous, Vel. You've got this." Landen patted her on the hand.

She let out a light laugh. "Me, worry? Never."

Velas pulled her hand away, clenching her fists in her lap.

"As you can see, this will be a medium distance archery contest. With a few extra rules to keep things interesting." Orellas made a sweeping gesture with his hand, indicating where a second group of attendants were entering the arena. A stream of dozens of people carried armor and helmets, dressing the straw dummies in them.

Landen let out a groan, and Velas let herself crack a grin.

"Who's nervous now?"

"Quiet. I'm thinking." Landen folded his arms.

A group of uniformed paladins lined up behind the dummies, placing their hands on the shoulders of the straw men. Velas and Landen watched as the paladins spoke in unison – although their voices were too distant to hear – and blue auras flickered and disappeared around the figures. The paladins retreated from the arena shortly thereafter.

"As you can see, these archery targets are quite thoroughly protected. Armored and helmed like real soldiers, they have few vulnerable points – and even then, they are guarded by a layer of protective sorcery."

The announcer pointed his hand toward an area in front of the archers where a group of attendants was measuring out a line in chalk. "Applicants will line up at these bows and pick a target. They will be given twelve arrows to fire. After each applicant has shot his or her arrows, they may all cross the line to retrieve them – this is the only time the applicants may walk across the chalk line."

The representative of House Korvis grinned, gesticulating at the dummies. "But merely firing your arrows will not be enough – you must cause grievous harm to your formidable foes. Each applicant will be allowed a total of three flights of arrows. No more! When you have shot each of your arrows, the paladin judges," he gestured to a nearby box where Velas could see a few armored figures, "will score you from zero to one hundred points. When all of the applicants have finished the test, we'll reveal the scores. Of four hundred and eighty six candidates, only forty will pass on to the next stage of your tests."

Velas heard a series of groans and gasps from the other applicants in the crowd, but she wasn't surprised. These tests took considerable resources to run, and she knew the paladins only wanted the best of the best.

*At archery, at least. Bah. At least I don't have to go first.*

On their way in, the paladin applicants had pulled numbered wooden wedges out of a jar to determine when they would participate in the contest. Taelien had been unlucky enough to pull a "1" – meaning he was going to be in the first group below. Landen and Velas had both pulled group "3", so they would be taking the test together.

"One more thing, before you get too clever! No damaging the dummies while you collect your arrows."

Another series of groans.

"And now, before we begin, I would like to lead you in the warrior's prayer."

Velas and Landen stood automatically, having heard and spoken the prayer hundreds of times. It was one of the most traditional Tae'os prayers, often being used before contests of battle, as well as most sports. They each raised a fist over their hearts, symbolizing carrying a sword.

As Orellas began, over a thousand voices spoke with him, nearly in unison.

*Sytira, grant us the wisdom to see the path to victory,*
*Aendaryn, give us the skill to fight without equal,*
*Eratar, shelter us from the arrows of our enemies,*
*And Lysandri, give us the strength to shelter our friends.*

*Lissari, let your light wash over our wounds,*
*Koranir, give us the strength to fight again,*
*And Xerasilis, let our battles always be just.*

Velas closed her eyes as she spoke the prayer. She did not believe the gods would hear them – that was not why she prayed. Even the most fervent of paladins didn't literally believe that the gods listened to words spoken into the wind. She prayed, as each of them did, to reinforce those values within her – and to give her the inner strength to persevere.

There was a brief silence as the prayers concluded and many eyes reopened.

"First contestants, you may enter the arena!"

Velas watched as the first group of twenty-five applicants entered, still holding a hand over her chest. It was only as Taelien entered the arena, sheathed swords swinging on each of his hips, that she allowed herself to grin and return to her seat.

Keldyn Andys marched right behind Taelien, head held high. Rather than armor, he was dressed in a gilded tunic, like he was attending a formal party. His only visible weapon was a long dagger on his left hip. He waved to the crowd as he approached his arrow stand.

Keldyn leaned toward Taelien and whispered something as the pair approached their bows. The latter just shook his head. Velas thought she could see a grin on his face.

Very few of the other contestants looked familiar – which was unsurprising, given that there were hundreds of total applicants. Most were visitors from outside the city, but she also knew there were a few classes of paladin applicants that had trained separately from her own. She was looking forward to seeing what they were capable of.

But, more importantly, she was looking forward to seeing what Taelien managed to score.

"Contestants, bows ready!"

The archers lined up, drew their bows and knocked their first arrows.

"Aaaand...fire!"

Nearly all of the archers missed. Taelien and Keldyn both missed badly.

Velas lowered her forehead to her hand as she heard hooting and jeering from the crowd.

*This could be embarrassing.*

Eleven arrows later, Orellas called, "Cease fire!"

Taelien's target sprouted a single arrow, barely piercing the right elbow, which was only covered with light mail. Three of his earlier arrows had struck the target, but two had been deflected by the sorcerous barrier around it and a third had deflected off the helmet.

Keldyn was faring just slightly better, with one of his arrows having pierced the target under the shoulder – a deadlier shot, but still not likely to be instantly fatal to his straw opponent.

The pair glanced at each other, and then at their other contestants. At least two of the other applicants had done considerably better. One of them was a young boy, looking like he had barely reached his teenage years. His target sprouted two arrows that had pierced through the chain mail around the neck.

*Tirith,* she remembered from seeing him in the history class. *I had just assumed he was planning to be a squire. Would they allow someone his age to become a full paladin?*

*I suppose I'll find out soon enough.*

"Contestants, retrieve your arrows!"

Velas watched closely as Taelien braced his hand against his target's neck, twisting his single arrow to safely retrieve it without breaking off the head. Unconsciously, she rubbed her own arm as the arrow slipped free.

After the contestants retrieved their arrows, there was a brief pause as a line of paladins emerged from the opposite arena entrance. They stood behind the dummies and, in perfect sync with one another, recast the protective spells to shield the targets from harm.

Velas let out another groan along with dozens of other members of the audience.

The announcer laughed. "You didn't think we were going to let you wear the barriers down between volleys, did you? This needs to be a challenge! Now, archers, raise your bows!"

*This is bad. At least Taelien landed an arrow – I don't even know if I can do that much. Landen is going to be fine – he's a good shot. Better than anyone down there right now, and easily good enough to get into the top forty. Sal and I, though…we're going to need help.*

"You may fire when ready!"

Taelien didn't fire at all. At first, Keldyn didn't fire either, turning to watch Taelien curiously. As the others loosed their arrows, however,

Taelien simply grinned and folded his arms, watching. Eventually, Keldyn lost his patience and began to fire as well.

When Keldyn and the other archers finished, Taelien still hadn't taken a single shot. Keldyn's target had three new arrows embedded within – two in the less-protected lower body and one glancing hit on the neck. He grinned, saying something to Taelien.

Taelien set down his bow, grabbing all twelve of the arrows from his quiver and lifting them together. Then, as the audience watched, he ran his hand across the arrowheads.

And then he opened his hand.

The arrows shot straight toward his target as a cluster, slamming into the barrier and piercing through it. A cheer erupted from the crowd as the handful of arrows impacted the target, half a dozen of them embedding into the neck. Only one deflected to the ground – the remaining five simply stuck to the bits of metal they impacted with.

Taelien turned toward her and Landen and winked.

Velas rolled her eyes.

"Well, wasn't that exciting? Well done, young man, quite the spectacle. You all still have one round left, however! Go retrieve your arrows!"

The contestants moved to pick up their arrows, Taelien walking with renewed swagger. Velas was pretty sure she saw him blow Keldyn a kiss.

Taelien pulled his arrows away one at a time, tapping the arrowheads, which seemed to remove the magnetic effect he had placed on them.

*Interesting. Is he going to try the same trick twice?*

Once again, the applicants returned to their bows, and the paladins returned to the arena and restored the barriers around the targets.

Taelien readied his bow this time, but Keldyn did not.

"Begin!"

The archers loosed their arrows again, several of which performed better than in the previous rounds. Taelien's archery was still sub-par; his sole face hit deflecting off the barrier spell.

Keldyn had closed his eyes, pressing his hands together in front of him in concentration. As the last of the other archers finished, Keldyn raised his right hand – and a glowing golden sword appeared in the air above him. Velas heard a series of murmurs and gasps from the crowd.

*The Gift of Aendaryn. The Dominion of Blades.*

Keldyn lowered his hand. The sword shot forward, gold sparks flickering as it tore through the barrier around the target and paused, floating in the air.

The blond-haired swordsman smiled and slashed his hand through the air.

The straw dummy's head fell, severed by the golden blade.

As the crowd stood and cheered, Keldyn opened and closed his hand, causing the golden blade to vanish. Then, he grasped all of his arrows in a hand as Taelien had – turned around, and carelessly tossed them over his shoulder and past the chalk line.

"With all of the arrows past the line, I do believe our first test –"

Taelien was drawing the sword on his right hip.

The sword's vermillion blade reflected in the dawnfire's light, drawing the eyes of the crowd. Taelien raised it reverently, kissing the blade, and took a step back.

Then, he reversed his grip on the hilt and dragged two fingers from his other hand across the blade.

The sword's blade ignited with brilliant blue fire. Taelien took two more steps back, adjusted his grip, then stepped forward and hurled the sword like a javelin.

The crowd fell deathly silent as the flaming blade soared through the air. As it struck, the flaming sword penetrated the barrier and continued forward, piecing straight through the dummy's breastplate and all the way through the back. The flames surged and spread, quickly engulfing the entire body.

Once again, the crowd rose and cheered.

"Wonderful! This is wonderful! I must give my commendations to both of the sword-throwers below." The announcer's gleeful laughter echoed throughout the stadium, amplified by sorcery. "Goodness, I've rarely seen such things, and it's only the first group! Well, the stage has certainly been set. First group, well done, all of you. You may return and let the second group come forward."

*Not bad, Sal. Not bad at all.*

*How can I do better?*

"Um, so, that was interesting," Landen mumbled.

"Yeah, we're kind of screwed, aren't we?" Velas chuckled, watching the second group of applicants come forward. She recognized the Rethri twins, Terras and Lysen, in the group.

*Sorcerers have a huge advantage here. A shame my dominions aren't really ideal for the situation – and Landen isn't a sorcerer at all. A burst of motion sorcery would add a lot of punch to one of my arrows, but I couldn't guide it accurately that way. And there's no way I could throw something that distance – Taelien must have guided his sword with magnetism, like he did with the arrows.*

When the order to fire was given, Terras and Lysen didn't pick up their bows – apparently Taelien had started a trend.

Terras lifted her hands, pressing her forefingers and thumbs together and creating a triangular shape. After several seconds of no apparent effect, a bolt of lightning arced from the cloudless sky and smashed into her target, melting the armor to slag and setting the dummy ablaze.

To add to the effect, she launched each of her arrows into the flaming wreckage. She didn't miss a single shot.

Lysen, conversely, pressed his palms together, his fingers crossing each other and making a "V" shape. Mist rose from below his dummy, growing thicker with every passing moment. By the time the other archers had ceased firing, his dummy was completely obscured.

He launched a single arrow into the mist, and then discarded his remaining arrows as Keldyn had.

As the mists lifted, the audience saw the remains of his dummy – frozen solid and shattered into pieces by his arrow.

More cheering for Terras and Lysen. Velas joined half-heartedly, feeling more nervous by the minute.

The remainder of the round passed largely uneventfully – there wasn't even enough left of Terras and Lysen's targets for them to bother continuing to fire. While several of the archers in this group were talented, none of them directly attracted Velas' attention.

And then it was her turn.

Velas and Landen moved to the staging grounds, where they lined up with the twenty-three other applicants who would be going at the same time they were. Velas recognized Bertram Colt, one of the somewhat suspicious applicants from Selyr, among her group.

Landen brightened as soon as they walked into the arena – he loved a crowd, regardless of the odds. She let his enthusiasm wash over her, and the pair of them waved as they approached the archery stands.

*We've beaten worse odds together in the arena before.*

*Wait. Together.*

*I'm an idiot.*

"Archers, bows at the ready!"

She grabbed Landen's arm as he was preparing to raise his bow. "Don't fire yet."

Landen blinked at her. "Okay?"

"Archers, fire when ready!"

Landen lowered his arm, raising an eyebrow at Velas.

Velas gestured at the quiver. "Arrows aren't going to hit hard enough to guarantee we win this. And, let's be serious here – I can't shoot for shit."

"No need to be so hard on yourself, Vel." He glanced from side to side. Some of the other archers were watching them, but most were already firing.

"I'm not being hard on myself. I'm being realistic. Hand me your first arrow."

Landen reached into his quiver and retrieved an arrow, handing it to her gingerly.

She tapped a finger on the tip. *You're not the only one who can play this game, Sal.*

"Don't touch the tip. Be very careful. Go ahead and fire it."

The swordsman took the arrow from her carefully, still looking dubious, and assumed a firing stance. Then, after a few moments of aiming, he loosed the arrow.

The resulting explosion of concussive force rippled across the barrier, putting visible cracks in the shield and shattering the ground around the dummy.

"Ooh, nice. Let's do that again."

The next arrow shattered the remains of the barrier.

The third slammed into the dummy's center, bursting through the mail and embedding in the straw man's chest.

The fourth hit the post that was holding the dummy, the explosion shattering the post and knocking the dummy to the ground.

The fifth hit the fallen dummy and carried it back another dozen yards, tossing it like a doll.

Velas didn't use sorcery for the rest – Landen just shot his remaining arrows at the fallen target.

Then, the pair moved to where Velas' bow and arrows awaited – and again, Landen raised the bow.

Velas smirked. "Let's repeat that, shall we?"

Landen's arrows each struck true, the first two shattering the barrier and the third piercing the dummy's shoulder. The fourth shattered the post, sending the dummy to the arena floor. After that, Landen laughed and handed her the bow. She only managed to hit the fallen target once, but the crowd laughed and cheered when she did.

"Contestants, retrieve your arrows!"

After the arrows were retrieved, the paladins moved Velas and Landen's fallen dummies back into line with the others. Since the posts that held them up were shattered, they simply left the targets on the ground, but once again reinforced them with protective sorcery.

Landen walked over to her this time while the other archers opened fire. "Okay, Vel, that was fun. Any clever ideas for this round?"

*Nothing that wouldn't give away more of my abilities than I want to demonstrate this early.*

"Not really. If I thought we could throw our swords accurately, I'd put the same kind of effect on our blades, but…"

"Yeah, I don't think we can get that kind of distance, either. And you can't control a throw that well with your sorcery, right?"

She shook her head. "I can try to shoot something straight ahead, but I wouldn't even be confident about hitting my target with that while it was standing. Now that it's on the ground…"

"Guess I could just fire off each of our quivers and hope to land a few more hits, then. I think our targets are probably in bad shape at this point, but a little more damage wouldn't hurt."

She chuckled at his terrible joke, offering him an arrow. "After you, then."

Landen launched another dozen arrows at each target, but with the dummies on the ground, not many of them hit any particularly vulnerable spots. He did manage to put a couple arrows into the area just underneath the breastplates for each dummy, but Velas doubted those were worth many points.

As they retrieved their arrows for the last time, Velas glanced at the other targets. One target had been incinerated by a flame sorcerer, and a pair of skilled archers had reduced their targets to pincushions. Bertram, it seemed, was not one of them. His dummy was all but unscratched and his expression was of shame. Velas felt for him – if she hadn't had Landen with her, she might have been in the same situation.

*And,* she considered, *we still might not have done enough. Landen hit the chest on his dummy, which probably counts as a kill – but mine is still relatively intact.*

Landen seemed confident – this time he started firing as soon as the order was given, successfully planting a few more arrows in his fallen target. None of them hit vital spots, but she was convinced the judges would consider his target killed from attrition, if nothing else.

When he turned to her, however, she shook her head.

"I've got this one."

He grinned warmly at her, giving her an old Queensguard salute with his left hand.

*This is going to be really embarrassing if it doesn't work,* she considered, snatching her arrows from her quiver. *But here I go.*

Velas stepped back away from the line, further and further, keeping her quiver of arrows in her left hand. Then, with her right hand, she drew her sword – and charged.

She heard gasps from the crowd – and she grinned. Just before she reached the chalk line, she jumped.

*Surge.*

She focused the burst of motion into launching her further into the air, carrying her higher and further – but it wasn't enough. So, as she began to descend, she did it again.

*Surge!*

The essence slammed into her legs, carrying her back upward before she touched the ground, sending her in a soaring arc toward her target – and in a trajectory that would carry her over it.

*Fuckthisisgoinghurt.*

*Surge.*

Velas called the last blast of force to push down on her, smashing her downward, her sword pointing downward. As she plummeted, she called on the Dominion of Motion to slowly apply upward force to control the speed of her descent.

She landed with a crushing impact, plunging her sword into the dummy's neck as she fell. The force of the fall threw her off her feet, sending her tumbling to the ground in a roll, never losing her grip on the sword.

As the crowd cheered, she shuddered on the arena floor, pulling the dummy closer to her by tugging on her sword. When the straw man rolled close enough, she plunged all dozen arrows into its face.

And, with the dummy slain, she wobbled slowly back to her feet.

***

After Velas' scrapes and bruises from her encounter with the arena floor had been patched up, she returned to the stands to observe the remaining teams. Taelien was sitting next to Landen. He had stolen her seat.

She sighed and sat on Landen's lap. He grinned and affectionately tousled her hair.

"That was pretty impressive back there, Vel." Taelien nudged her arm. "I mean, not as impressive as what I –"

"Oh, shut it, Sal." Velas folded her arms, leaning back against Landen. "Not everyone has metal sorcery and sorcerous swords to lean on."

"I told you, this one isn't dominion bonded, it's just –"

"Yeah, yeah, a ridiculously rare metal that happens to perfectly compliment your already extraordinarily useful skill set."

"Yeah, you both did all right. I mean, it would have been better if you had tried some archery in the archery contest." Landen chuckled, and Velas stood up, walking to the edge of the stands in front of them and turning around.

"Oh, sure, keep teasing. See if you get anyone else sitting on your lap."

"I'm pretty sure I could get Sal to sit on my lap." Landen nudged the swordsman sitting next to him.

Taelien sighed. "You can have my seat, Vel."

Velas put her hand to her forehead. "It was my seat in the first place. But fine."

Taelien stood up, making a sweeping gesture of benevolence with his arm. "Please, my lady. Forgive me for presuming upon your property."

"Gods, I leave you two alone together for five minutes and suddenly you're both impossible."

Nevertheless, she sat back down in her old chair. The ministrations of the medics had helped with her scratches and bruises, but they could do nothing for the shooting pain in her ankles from landing too hard, or the creeping ache in her shoulders from overusing her motion sorcery.

Still, the crowd had cheered for her. Everything had been worth it.

Taelien walked over to the railing to lean against it, staring into the arena below. Velas caught the source of his staring almost immediately – a woman with brilliant purple plumage rather than hair.

*Asphodel*, she remembered. The Delaren.

Like her description in the files had indicated, she looked young – maybe a few years younger than they were. Unlike most of the files, Asphodel's hadn't given many specifics about her age or background. She had no prior connections with the Paladins of Tae'os, and the Delaren were notoriously secretive and xenophobic – Velas hadn't even heard of any Delaren applying to join the paladins in the past.

*If the legends are true, her abilities involve changing her shape – but I don't think she'd bother doing that for a little contest like this. The alterations are supposed to be semi-permanent. It'll be interesting to see what else she could do.*

The answer to that proved to be remarkably simple. Asphodel closed her eyes each time she nocked an arrow, and each time, the arrow hit perfectly on target.

By the end of the first round, her target had two arrows where its eyes should have been. Six more were in the neck, and another two in the shoulders – and the remainder had been used to break the barrier.

*She's even more accurate than Landen or that Terras girl. Air sorcery when she closes her eyes, maybe? It wouldn't be impossible.*

Two more rounds of a dozen arrows left Asphodel's target thoroughly torn apart. No other applicants in her round showed similar promise.

The next round, however, was far more intriguing.

On the far left side of the group was Jonathan Sterling, the bright-haired "Haven Knight". He still wore a dueling sword on his left hip. As he approached his shooting position, he scanned the crowd. Velas thought his gaze slowed for a moment when it passed over her, but she couldn't be certain.

Toward the middle of the group was Susan Crimson, the former Thornguard from Selyr. Given Bertram's performance, Velas didn't have particularly high expectations for Susan, but the House Crimson woman was wearing a belt with a pair of throwing knives and half a dozen small pouches. That offered her some options.

Sterling's first round of arrows was accurate, but uninspiring. His archery skills seemed similar to Landen's, with several hits landing on target, but without any sorcery to augment the strikes he only managed to pierce the target twice. One of those hits was to the neck, however, which Velas judged to be likely to count as a kill.

Crimson removed her first arrow from her quiver before lifting her bow, reaching into a pouch and retrieving a vial. She unstoppered the vial, pouring a few drops on the tip of the arrow, and then replaced the cap.

*Poison? Really? In a competition to join a paladin order?*

Velas shook her head, continuing to watch. Crimson's first arrow flew true – and never encountered a barrier.

It sunk directly into the target's face.

There was a brief murmur from the crowd. Susan grinned, applied a few drops to the next arrow, and repeated the process. Of her twelve arrows, seven hit the target, and none of them suffered any interference from the sorcerous shield.

After a paladin visibly checked the target and renewed the barrier, the crowd watched in anticipation for her next volley.

She didn't apply the liquid this time – and the barrier stopped her first four arrows.

*That's a very, very dangerous trick. I'm going to need to figure out how to copy it.*

Sterling put another few arrows in his target, but Velas barely noticed. Susan had all her attention now. *What's she keeping in those other pouches? How many interesting tricks does she have?*

The House Crimson woman didn't open any of her other pouches in the final round, nor did she throw her throwing daggers. Throwing daggers that distance would be difficult, but not as hard as throwing a sword – and she had been somewhat hoping that Crimson would try it.

Nevertheless, as she watched the young woman leave the arena, Velas raised a hand to her lips. *I'm going to have to keep two eyes on that one.*

Other rounds came and went, with none offering the spectacle that the first few had. Velas suspected that the local candidates were deliberately sorted into the first four rounds, most likely to give them a better chance at higher scores – she suspected the judges would get progressively harsher with later candidates.

Of course, she considered the possibility of the opposite – later applicants would have the chance to observe the earlier rounds and learn any tricks that others used. That advantage diminished rapidly after the first few rounds, however, and she suspected the judges would be more lenient with people they were already familiar with.

Only two contestants were disqualified outright – one for running across the line early, and the second for damaging his dummy deliberately while he was retrieving his arrows. One candidate doused his target in alcohol while retrieving his arrows – which was allowed, apparently – and then set one of his arrows on fire and succeeded in setting his target ablaze.

By the time of the final round, the audience seemed to have lost most of its enthusiasm. Resetting the targets for each contest was a time consuming process and the dawnfire was quickly retreating from the horizon.

As the last group approached, Velas only recognized one person among them – the monstrously tall man who called himself "The Wandering War". He was still wearing his hood and cloak, which Velas was starting to suspect was more than just pretentiousness. *If those documents are accurate, he's not human – and probably not Rethri, either. Esharen, maybe? Would the paladins allow an Esharen candidate?*

"And – open fire!"

Velas watched as The Wandering War lifted his bow, drawing back the string. An aura of orange light formed at the arrowhead, twisting and swirling as it grew. He released the arrow.

The streak of orange flashed forward across the arena, ripping not only through the barrier, but all the way through the target. It continued to fly until reaching the outer wall of the arena, smashing into the stone and triggering a flicker of blue and orange sparks – the marks of the arrow striking a powerful defensive spell on the arena itself.

The hole in the center of the straw man was larger than Velas' fist, and irregular in shape, like a massive screw had been drilled into the dummy's chest.

As the other archers finished firing their arrows, The Wandering War raised his hands – and each and every arrow tore free from the other targets, soaring through the air toward his. His own eleven arrows rose, seemingly of their own volition, and joined other arrows in flight, burying themselves in the dummy. Fallen arrows that had missed their targets initially rose again, each striking The Wandering War's target from another angle.

When the round ended, all three hundred arrows had pierced The Wandering War's target.

The audience sat in silence.

## CHAPTER VIII – TAELIEN II – PROBABLE SUICIDE

Taelien stood at parade rest in the second row of paladin candidates. His position in the group had been determined based on his arrival time at the meeting grounds, not on any sort of merit. Velas was positioned to his right, and Landen to his left, since the three of them had arrived together. With great effort, Taelien restrained himself from making any nervous movements.

The meeting ground was a grassless oval field large enough to fit hundreds of people. Taelien had been there twice before to observe large scale tactical exercises, but he had never participated in any activities there himself.

Most rows consisted of twelve candidates, and there were two rows behind Taelien. Oddly, the final row had a thirteenth member. The candidates had stood in their positions for several minutes while a group of three paladins – some of whom Taelien had seen, but none of whom he precisely recognized – spoke several yards in front of them. Eventually, the discussions ceased, and the three paladins turned to face their audience.

*Three rows of twelve – and one row of thirteen - make forty-nine of us, which is nine more than the number that passed the preliminary exams. Some candidates that skipped the preliminaries somehow are possible, but it's also possible there are some full paladins in here with us as plants to observe our behavior.*

Two of the paladins were wearing a dress uniform in the colors of their order. The paladin on the left was male, looked to be in his thirties, and wore the green and brown of Lissari. The emblems on his tunic indicated that he was a Lieutenant. The two other paladins were female.

At the center was a woman who had a young face, but more gray than brown in her hair. Her immaculate dark blue uniform was accented with silver, indicating that she served Sytira, much like Lydia did. Her eyes swept across the candidates, searching, but she gave no obvious tell if she found who or what she was looking for. The addition of two bars and a triangular emblem above pins similar to the Lieutenant's indicated that she was a full Colonel – a considerably higher rank than Taelien had expected to observe the instruction of mere cadets.

On the right was another woman, the tallest of the three paladins, wearing full armor with a steel grey tabard with the symbol of Koranir emblazoned on the front. Unlike the other two paladins, the Koranir follower took a stance of rigid attention. Her tabard had no symbols of rank, indicating that she was either a rank-and-file paladin or had some reason she preferred not to show her rank.

"At ease," spoke the woman in the center. One of the candidates to Taelien's left took an audible breath of relief as the group adjusted into more relaxed positions, but remained in their formation. The speaker's eyes shifted, seeming to note the lapse, but she made no comment on it. Taelien noted as he adjusted his own stance that the paladin of Koranir remained at attention, even while the candidates did not. He wasn't clear if that was normal behavior. "I am Colonel Wyndam, and I will be overseeing your tests. Lieutenant Morris will explain the structure of your examinations."

She gestured to the man at her side, and he nodded and stepped forward.

"For the next three months, you will be tested. You will not always be aware of when you are participating in a test. There are seven primary tests that you will participate in during this time period, each of which corresponds to one of our gods. If at any time your score on one of these tests falls below the acceptable threshold, you will be disqualified from the examinations. If at any time your cumulative score falls below the acceptable threshold, you will also be disqualified. If you are discovered attempting to cheat in the examinations in any way, you will be disqualified and lose any opportunity to retake the examinations in the future."

Lieutenant Morris paused, examining the crowd, and then spoke again. "If your performance on a test is unsatisfactory, but not low enough to disqualify you completely, you will be issued a red flag. If you are issued two red flags, you will be disqualified. Most candidates that are issued even a single red flag will not have a high enough cumulative score to complete the examination process."

The lieutenant took a breath, and then continued. "During the course of the examinations, each of you will be assigned to a barracks. An experienced paladin will be overseeing each of the barracks to ensure proper conduct. You will be assigned a uniform, which you will be required to properly maintain and wear for your examinations. You will also be assigned other tasks and responsibilities during the testing time frame. Failure to complete these tasks, or demonstrate proper conduct, will result in being disqualified from the examinations."

"There are forty-nine of you now. Tradition dictates that of the forty-nine candidates that begin the tests, only seven among you will be selected to join the Paladins of Tae'os during this test. The Arbiter of each branch of paladins will be presented with results of each test and personally select one applicant to honor with a chance to join our order. Those of you who perform well, but are not selected, will be given a chance to skip the preliminary examinations in future years."

"A schedule of examinations will be posted in your barracks. You will arrive in uniform and on time for each of your examinations, or you will be disqualified. Second Lieutenant Banks will take each of your groups to your new barracks. First row, attention."

The first row of cadets snapped to attention, although some handled the transition more smoothly than others. Taelien noted that Keldyn Andys was in the first group, along with the Rethri twins Terras and Lysen. Next to them was the tall man in the billowing cloak who called himself "The Wandering War". Susan Crimson was in the first group as well, but a few people separated her from the others that he recognized.

The paladin of Koranir wordlessly stepped forward, and then gestured with a hand. "First platoon, follow me." She unceremoniously turned around and began to walk, not waiting for the cadets to respond. They quickly turned and followed her.

Taelien let his mind wander as the group stood waiting for Second Lieutenant Banks to return. The Colonel had turned back to conversation with Lieutenant Morris, and many of the candidates near him seemed to be getting nervous. Velas glanced toward him and raised her eyebrows, but he just gave her a slight shrug, uncertain what she was asking.

*Maybe she's wondering if we're at a disadvantage for being in the second group? Possible, I suppose, but I doubt it. Have the tests already started? What Colonel Wyndam said was pretty vague.*

A quarter of an hour later, Lieutenant Banks returned and ordered Taelien's group to fall in behind her. They dutifully did so, and Taelien suspected they felt just as grateful to finally be moving as he did.

The walk to the barracks wasn't far. A uniformed paladin – this one wearing the light gray and blue of Eratar – leaned lazily against the wall next to the barracks door. A rapier and a main gauche sat sheathed against his hips, their brilliantly polished steel pommels standing as a contrast to the obvious creases in his uniform.

"Platoon 2, halt," Lieutenant Banks called, and Taelien's group ceased their march and fell into resting at attention. "You could at least try to look professional for the cadets, Lieutenant Torrent."

The paladin at the door gave an unapologetic shrug and a slight smile. "I keep telling you, call me Garrick. So, I take it these are my new puppies?"

Banks' lips twitched. "This is Platoon Two. If they are not properly prepared, I am holding you personally responsible."

With that, she briskly turned ninety degrees to the right and marched off. Lieutenant Torrent shook his head at her as she departed, and then stepped away from the wall.

"Welcome," he said, gesturing broadly with both hands. "You kids are the lucky ones. You get to work for me."

In spite of his use of the term 'kids', Taelien suspected that Garrick was at least a year or two his junior. *And a fan of theatrics. I shouldn't be surprised, given which branch he belongs to.*

"Be at ease. I'm going to take you for a tour of our lovely new home," he said, gesturing to the door. As the candidates fell out of their marching formation, Garrick turned around and opened the door, stepping into the barracks. The candidates followed him shortly thereafter.

Taelien had lived in other barracks before, during his training under the Thornguard, and this one was little different. There were six sets of bunk beds, each with two large trunks stacked in front of them. It struck him for the first time that there were a mixture of men and women in his platoon – they had been separated during his earlier training. He realized that might have been because of differences between the paladins and the Thornguard, or it might have just been because he had been so much younger the last time he had gone through similar training.

Also, unlike the other barracks he was familiar with, this one had two doors toward the back. Garrick was already walking toward the one on the left. "This is my room. I'm a fairly sound sleeper. If you wake me up and the barracks isn't on fire, I'll disqualify you immediately," he informed the group cheerfully.

*First hint of an edge I've seen to him,* Taelien considered. *Guess he might not be quite as much of a pushover as he sounded like initially.*

"Oh, and with that in mind, pick any beds you want. You each get a trunk. Once we issue your uniforms, you'll be responsible for keeping those in your trunks when they're not being used, and keeping them in good condition. If you don't, well, disqualified!"

He walked over to the second door at the back, knocking on the door. "Chamber pot is in there. Remember to knock."

He folded his arms, glancing from side to side. "For the next several weeks – assuming you puppies last that long – your first obligation is to each other. Sure, you'll have individual test scores, but platoon averages will hit all of you. I'm happy to disqualify you one at a time, but when we get to the team tests, you're going to want as many friends as you can get."

A moment of silence followed as the candidates looked each other over, most bearing grim expressions.

"Questions? Didn't think so. Find yourself a bed. Get to know each other."

Garrick immediately turned and retreated into his own quarters, leaving the second platoon standing around awkwardly by themselves.

Landen immediately sat down on one of the beds closest to the entrance – and thus furthest from the Lieutenant. "You heard the man. We wake him up, we're done."

"Yup." Velas brushed past Taelien and grabbed onto the ladder connected to the bunk bed that Landen was sitting on, hoisting herself up onto the top bunk. She sat with her boots hanging over the side, looking down. "Better find yourself a bunk quick, Sal. Hope you get a good bedmate."

She gave him an overly obvious wink, and Taelien just sighed and shook his head.

*Great. I don't really know anyone else here.*

The other local paladin candidates had ended up in other platoons. He glanced around at the other candidates, who were quickly following Landen's lead and taking beds as close to the entrance as possible.

The lone Rethri candidate in his group looked marginally familiar, so Taelien approached him first, extending his hand in greeting. "I'm Salaris. Is the other bunk here taken?"

The Rethri hesitated for a moment before clasping him on the wrist, turning his gaze away. "Eridus. Sorry, bed's taken."

The swordsman nodded as Eridus swiftly retracted his hand. "No problem. You look a little familiar – you from Selyr or thereabouts?"

"No, sorry. Don't think I know you." Eridus took a step back, waving a hand toward the other beds. "Better get one of those before they disappear."

"Right - thanks anyway. Pleasure to meet you."

*Wonder why he looks so familiar. Blue eyes, which makes him a water sorcerer, I think. Maybe he's one of Aladir's friends or relatives? There are so many Ta'thyriels it's hard to keep track of them all.*

By the time Taelien glanced around again, there were only two beds left, and a group of three people standing near the back and discussing them.

Two of the three looked relatively ordinary, a male and a female that looked a few years younger than Taelien, each wearing matching leather armor and a pair of curved short swords. The matching swords and armor might have made Taelien suspect they were related, but they didn't share any obvious physical characteristics. The girl was a few inches taller than her male counterpart, and she had short, wavy black hair and matching dark eyes. The male was brown skinned and shaved bald, with broad shoulders and thick biceps.

And standing in a sheltered position between the pair was a girl with a cascade of shimmering crystalline strands – each about the width of a finger - that reached from her head down to her knees. She wore a simple grey tunic and pants and observed the other candidates with eyes wide with curiosity.

Taelien approached the group, reaching out to extend a hand to the closer of the two armored figures.

"Stop," the armored female said. "Do not come so close to the oracle." Her eyes shifted to Taelien's sword, narrowing. "You are armed."

*Oracle? That's an odd title. And why would a Delaren need bodyguards? And human ones, no less?*

Taelien carefully took a step back, lifting his open hands. "Sure am. Looks like you're pretty well equipped, too. I don't mean you any harm. The name is Salaris."

"I am Asphodel," the Delaren girl said, stepping toward him and extending a thin hand as her guards looked on with horrified expressions.

Taelien reached out with his own hand, clasping hers at the wrist. *Her skin is cold,* he realized. He gave her a warm smile. "Pleasure to meet you. I'll look forward to working with all three of you."

He released her wrist, and she smiled brightly in reply. "Thank you. Please forgive my friends, they are unaccustomed to being so close to so many people."

"Oracle," the male guard said, "You should remember what your father told you. You expose yourself to danger when you are within weapon reach of a stranger."

Asphodel turned around, which Taelien absently noted had actually made her more vulnerable – a deliberate gesture? – and stepped back behind the two guards.

"You two are Asphodel's guards, I take it? You've got nothing to worry about from me. I can't stand hurting people."

"You should not refer to the oracle in such a familiar fashion," the female guard said. "You are merely a human."

"And your words are suspect. One with such disdain for harm would have little motivation to join a military organization," the male pointed out.

Taelien raised an eyebrow. "You know the paladins of Tae'os emphasize protecting life at all costs, right? That's one of the core tenants of the religion."

The guards looked at each other uncertainly. "Words such as those are little solace to the dead, one-called-Salaris," the female guard said.

*Well, that was remarkably foreboding and vague.*

"Well, your skepticism about my motives aside, we've got two beds left here. We're going to have to split them up."

"We were just discussing that," Asphodel explained, folding her hands behind her back and looking at the floor. "Would you share your bunk with me?"

"Sure. You want the top or the bottom bed?"

The male guard took a step toward Taelien, and then turned toward Asphodel. "Oracle, I must insist, you should not be so close to an outsider. He is not –"

"He is the Taelien. I would wish to know him better." She stepped over to the last bed on the left, the closest to Garrick's door, and sat down on it. "I will take the bottom."

*Taelien?* He hadn't mentioned that name – but he was wearing the Sae'kes on his hip. *Did she hear that I used to go by that name from someone, or is she just associating the name with the sword in the way some of the people back home did?*

"Sounds good." Taelien turned to the guards. "We're going to be working closely with one another. Do you mind if I ask your names?"

"Teshvol," the man said, not extending his hand.

"Kolask." The female guard hesitated for a moment, then glanced at Asphodel, and finally offered Taelien her hand. He grasped her wrist and gave her a firm nod before releasing it.

"Thank you," Taelien replied.

"If you harm her—" Teshvol began.

"Teshvol, that is enough," Asphodel commanded. He lowered his head and fell silent. "Taelien, we will have much to discuss."

Taelien turned to Asphodel and raised an eyebrow. "Such as?"

"That," she said, "Will best be discussed in private."

***

Taelien arrived at his assigned testing area ten minutes early, stopping at the door to the three-story training facility. The building had several rooms on each floor, and during the rest of the year, each room was assigned to a specific form of practice. While the outdoor training grounds were more commonly used for direct combat training, the indoor facilities were specifically equipped for handling sorcery training and specific forms of armed combat.

Since the tests had started, the entire building had been made off-limits to recruits. He assumed that meant that the rooms inside were being repurposed for the specific tests they would be undergoing, and when he had been handed his testing schedule, that hypothesis had quickly been validated.

Nervously, he adjusted his uniform, attempting to ensure everything was immaculate. Fortunately, the candidates had been allowed to wear their own weapons of choice – he would have felt naked without the Sae'kes on his hip. He had not let it escape his sight since his battle with Myros in the arena in Orlyn, more than eight months before.

He snapped to attention as the door opened. A uniformed Paladin of Sytira exited the training structure, and Taelien delivered an immediate salute. The paladin was a stocky blond man with a wicked flanged mace hanging from a cord on his left side. The cord seemed to be looped directly through the pommel of the mace, which looked impractical.

*Some kind of trick knot that he can quickly pull free to ready the weapon?* After a moment, he shook his thoughts free. *Can't think about that right now. Focus on the test.*

The paladin glanced Taelien over for a moment, and then returned his salute. "At ease."

Taelien nodded and shifted his stance. "Sir."

"You're cadet Salaris, I take it?"

"Yes, sir."

The paladin frowned. "I was picturing someone taller."

Taelien barely resisted the urge to note that the paladin was at least half a head shorter than he was. He had an odd scar that ran diagonally across his nose, hooking around to meet the right side of his lips. "Sorry if I've disappointed you, sir."

The paladin made a dismissive gesture. "Nothing to worry about. I'm Lieutenant Trace. I'll be explaining the details of your first test."

"Yes, sir. Thank you, sir."

The paladin paused, glancing at the Sae'kes, and then looked up to meet Taelien's gaze for just a moment before turning away. "Right. So, this first test will be a simulation. You will be taking on the role of a paladin serving as an advisor to an influential military leader during a major battle. For the sake of this scenario, assume that you are a newly assigned paladin lieutenant, and that no higher ranking paladins were available to provide support. For the sake of convenience's sake, you may use your real name. Every person you encounter will be playing a simulated role.

"If you encounter anyone you recognize, treat them as a stranger, and in accordance to their simulated role. For example, if you recognize an actual paladin officer playing the role of a servant, ignore his or her actual rank for the purposes of the scenario. Instead, act upon the information that you can glean from the setting of the scenario itself."

Taelien nodded. During his training under the Thornguard, he had participated in other types of simulations. While he had never taken on the role of a military advisor, he had observed similar tests and studied several texts on historical battles. He wasn't precisely relieved by the scenario, but it certainly could have been far worse.

"The scenario you will be participating in is a high stakes battle, and it will require careful judgment on your part. Are you prepared?"

"May I ask you questions about the scenario in advance, sir?"

The paladin shook his head. "It will be your responsibility to ascertain the details of the situation when you arrive. You may safely assume that the military leaders have requested an advisor from the Paladins of Tae'os, and that you are the advisor that was sent. Your orders are to provide any and all assistance you can to the military leaders."

"Understood, sir. In that case, I am ready."

"Very well. Remember, once you step inside that room, treat everything in the simulation as if it is your new reality."

Lieutenant Trace opened the door to the room. "You may step inside and begin the test."

***

Upon entering the room, Taelien's path was immediately barred by a pair of oddly dressed soldiers. As they maneuvered their halberds to block his path, Taelien scanned their white and red uniforms for anything he could recognize.

*An antiquated style, and I don't recognize most of the symbology. I think that pin might be an older version of Koranir's shield, but I'm not sure.*

He took a stance of attention, raising his right arm to his chest in a paladin salute.

"Paladin Lieutenant Salaris, reporting as requested," he droned, examining the situation beyond the two soldiers as he spoke.

The room was at least thirty feet across, and toward the center, three uniformed officers stood around a table. Laid out across the table was a map, and atop the map were numerous different figures. *About as traditional of a depiction of a war room as I've ever seen.*

"Come in," said one of the men around the table, making a dismissive wave at the guards. The two soldiers retracted their polearms, giving a brief salute to the speaker before taking a restful stance.

Taelien lowered his salute, advancing toward the table and pausing a few feet away. "Hello, I'm Paladin—"

"Yes, yes, we heard," said a clean-cut older man at the opposite side of the table. His uniform was the most decorated of the three people standing around it, with dozens of pins and sigils that Taelien didn't quite recognize. Fortunately, he did recognize the four bars on the right side, signifying a specific military ranking – a lieutenant general. This man was, presumably, the army's leader.

It took Taelien a moment of paralyzing shock to recover from the realization that the man standing in front of him was Herod, the retired paladin who had been observing his training. *He looks...impressive like this. The uniform fits him far better than civilian garb ever did.*

"There's no need to be rude, Ravellan. We did send for an advisor," spoke the lone female officer at the table, an older woman with bright white hair. She wore a pair of short swords on each of her hips, a choice that Taelien approved of. If he hadn't spent most of his career training with the Sae'kes, he might have preferred a similar style.

"You sent for the advisor." Ravellan sighed. "But he's here, so I suppose we should let the boy tell us how we're waging war all wrong." The lieutenant general waved at the map. "Please, enlighten us, servant of the gods."

Taelien glanced over the table, noting soldiers in several different colors on the map. There were several types of pieces representing soldiers, and fortunately Taelien had seen similar ones used in other war games in the past. He quickly recognized spearman, swordsman, archer, catapult, and commander pieces. There were, however, three types of pieces he did not recognize.

There was a city near the center, and black markers for soldiers all throughout. Outside the walls, there were a larger number of white pieces and red pieces. Some of the red pieces were interspersed among the white ones, others were separated into smaller units.

The black pieces inside the walls of the city were almost exclusively archers and catapults. The majority of the city did not have any pieces within – which implied that the black force's swordsmen, spearmen, and other pieces were most likely still within the walls and that they did not have enough information on their locations and numbers.

This in turn meant that the white and red forces were most likely his forces – and the ones attacking the city. The white and red uniforms matched that hypothesis nicely.

*That's…not good at all. Being the attacker in a scenario with an unknown number of enemy forces inside a city is a terrible situation.*

Glancing at the white and red pieces, Taelien estimated at least one hundred of them. The archers on the inside were far fewer, at least – only about twenty pieces. Each side had four visible catapults. He assumed each piece represented either ten or a hundred troops, but he wasn't sure of which, and it clearly would make a significant difference.

"I'm afraid my briefing on the situation was…well, brief, if you'll excuse the pun." Taelien chuckled, but no one else laughed. "Can you clarify for me how many troops each of these represents?" He pointed at one of the red spearmen.

"One hundred of our best," the third officer said. "The Ember Legion has never been defeated in battle."

*Ember Legion…I've heard that name before.*

"We're being quite rude to the poor boy." The female officer extended a hand toward Taelien. Realizing that they appeared to be simulating some sort of older siege, Taelien took her hand and shook it, rather than clasping her wrist in a modern fashion. She smiled. "Lieutenant, I'm Colonel Morningway. This is Colonel Laurent," she said, releasing Taelien's hand to point to the last officer who had spoken, "And our leader, Lieutenant General Ravellan."

"A pleasure to meet all of you." Taelien exchanged handshakes with the other two men. "You'll have to forgive my questions. I would prefer to have as much context as possible before offering any advice."

"Of course," Laurent replied. Ravellan simply sighed again.

*So, one hundred troops per piece. That means we have roughly ten thousand troops total. I'm sure the commander pieces don't represent one hundred commanders, but even accounting for that, we have a lot of troops. We clearly appear to outnumber the enemy, but even just their archers represent about a fifth of our numbers. That's four times our number of archers – implying that if the ratio is maintained, they have four times our number of troops. Fortunately, they probably don't have quite that same ratio – as defenders, they probably gave bows to as many people as possible, possibly depriving them of other forces. Hard to know for certain.*

Just having walls gives the defenders a tremendous advantage.

Taelien quickly scanned across the map, noting two water sources flowing into the city walls. Controlling those points would be important – water was not only necessary for the people inside to survive, it was also a potential method for infiltration or for the enemy to send troops out, depending on who controlled it.

"I fear I don't recognize all these types of pieces. I see spears, swords, bows, catapults, and commanding officers, which I'm familiar with. I'm not certain what this one," he pointed at a piece, "or these two types of pieces represent."

"Those," Laurent pointed to a unit of unique red pieces, "Are my pride and joy."

"Sorcerers," Morningway clarified.

Laurent scoffed. "The Cinders are no mere 'sorcerers'. Once you see what they can do…"

*'Cinders' appears to be a division name within this Ember Legion. I know I've heard those names.* He scratched at his chin. *Weren't those the war sorcerers who died during the siege of – oh.*

*Am I fighting the final battle against the Xixian Empire?*

The fall of Xixis was legendary, but details were scarce. The capital city of the Esharen had withstood numerous assaults throughout the millennia of its existence, with most invading armies unceremoniously crushed. While Xixis did eventually fall, the circumstances behind the final battle were known to few – mostly because so few survived it.

Something so terrible had happened there that Xixis was no longer even drawn on maps. Some claimed that Vyrek Sul, the final emperor, had cast a ritual that had immolated the entire city and burned most of the invading army alive. Others spoke of a plague that spread through the survivors, claiming their lives before they could return home in victory. Still others claimed that the desperate Xixian sorcerers had discovered a way to force the dead to stand and fight again, controlling both former friends and foes like deadly puppets, forcing friends to cut their former comrades apart to keep them from rising again.

*This could be one interpretation of how the battle may have been waged,* Taelien realized. *There are books detailing how many troops were sent to the battle, and analysis of the claims of the survivors. I even read a few of them back when I was in my early days of training. A shame that was so long ago — those details might have been useful.*

"The Cinders have a reputation that precedes them, Colonel Morningway. I'm certain they will be instrumental in our success," Taelien offered respectfully. It was not a mere platitude — he suspected that the sorcerers would be necessary to offer any form of fighting chance against the capitol city of Xixis.

Laurent grinned in reply. "Glad someone around here takes my men seriously."

"What of these other figures?" Taelien pointed at the other two types he had failed to identify.

"These first ones are infiltrators. I'm not surprised a paladin wouldn't be familiar with them." Ravellan folded his arms.

*A light jab, but one intended to make it clear he doesn't have much respect for my organization. I'm probably not supposed to stand for the paladins being insulted, I suppose. Either that or I'm supposed to grin and bear it, since he outranks me and I want to influence him. Not sure on which.* "On the contrary, General. We make judicious use of scouts and infiltrators. We simply do not give them different pieces on our war maps, because our enemies tend to use them, too."

Herod flushed, gritting his teeth. "Of course."

*That might have been a poor move, but it felt great.* "And the final pieces?"

"Anything not covered by the other categories." Morningway pointed at one of the white pieces close to the back of the army. "These ones here represent medics, for example. Others represent messengers, squires, and other miscellaneous support troops."

Taelien nodded. *That takes about eight hundred 'troops' out of my calculations, since these would not be direct combatants.* "Excellent, thank you for the clarifications. I assume the grid squares on the map represent one kilometer?"

"Yes." Morningway picked up an archer piece that was near the front lines. "Meaning our forward troops are currently outside of the range of their archers and just approaching the range of their siege."

"And I assume they are aware of us already?" Taelien folded his arms, squinting at the organization of the troops. He already saw elements he wanted to reorganize – spearmen that needed to be moved in front of swords, archers that were uselessly out of range, and sorcerers with no protection – but he suspected those issues were less important than the basics of the first engagement.

"Yes, we sent a messenger ahead with our demands days ago. He never returned, of course. We've spent the intervening time taking positions and evaluating their movements. We currently plan to engage at nightfall." Morningway walked over to a stack of soldiers that were off the board. "These additional troops represent reinforcements we are expecting from Velrya. They should arrive within a few days. We were expecting them by now, but we no longer feel we can wait. Even a few more days could cost the prince his life."

*Prince? What's this now? I probably should already know this, and I've already been asking a lot of questions. Maybe I should try to figure this out on my own.*

"I would advise against attacking at nightfall," Taelien offered.

"Oh? And why is that?" Ravellan leaned across the table, looking unamused. Taelien felt his lip twitch when the larger man knocked over a soldier piece with his movement.

*Herod sure does a good job of pretending to be an asshole. I hope he wasn't actually like this when he was a paladin officer.*

"Infiltration at night might offer some slim benefits, but the Esharen have better night vision than we do. Their archers will be better shots at night."

The old general rolled his eyes. "Of course they will. We're not idiots, boy. We're going to open up with sorcerers and burn their siege. Once we do that, we can start pounding their walls from a distance without opposition."

Taelien scratched at his chin. *Not a bad idea, actually, at least on the surface. Am I supposed to find flaws in that plan?*

"We'd be playing our best hand early," Taelien hazarded. "It's a sound plan, but we'd have to be prepared for the consequences. Any Esharen that are directly exposed to the bombardment will adapt to it. At this distance, our sorcerers won't have any degree of precision – they might destroy the siege engines, but the enemy troops will barely be touched. And if the Esharen withdraw after absorbing sorcerous energy from the attacks –"

"They'll be immune to it next time." Laurent tapped his fingers on the table. "That's only true if our sorcerers use the same dominion each time, however."

"How versatile are these 'Cinders'? I recall hearing they're primarily trained in Velryan War Sorcery, utilizing the dominion of flame across broad areas." He couldn't keep himself from smirking a little. If they were going to be testing him on history, he'd have to drop as many little facts like that as possible.

"Actually, no."

Taelien frowned.

"You're not entirely wrong – they do focus on broad-area bombardment, using the Velryan school. The name 'Cinders' doesn't come from using the Dominion of Flame, contrary to popular belief. It's just derived from the name Ember Legion. We have a broad variety of different types of sorcery at our disposal. Stone sorcery is actually the most common, followed by lightning."

*Huh.* "The versatility of your sorcerers does them credit, Colonel."

Taelien pondered that for a moment. "Do we know anything about the enemy sorcerers? Bringing our own sorcerers into engagement range might be dangerous if we don't know how many sorcerers they have, or how powerful they are."

Laurent gave a helpless shrug. "Our best men have been trying to break through the divination shield around the city since we arrived, but we've had no success."

"What about mundane scouts?" Taelien pointed at a lake that fed water into the city. "Could we send some of our infiltrators up one of the waterways to gather some intelligence?"

"It's a city, not a single fortress," Ravellan noted, reaching a hand up to straighten his hair. "They could have sorcerers dispersed throughout the entire area. We can't know for certain until we attack, and our sorcerers have the longest range, so they offer the lowest risk."

*Excellent points. Maybe they're supposed to be right about this part of the strategy, and the key is that I'm supposed to know when not to argue?*

He argued anyway.

"What about sending in some infiltrators during daylight, while we still have some time, with the intent of capturing an enemy officer? Or even just a single enemy sorcerer? Either could potentially provide us with useful information."

The three officers glanced at each other, but Ravellan shook his head.

"I don't like the odds of a group of our scouts being able to get in there and out before nightfall. And infiltration during daylight hours wouldn't be easy."

Taelien turned to Laurent. "Do you have any Sight Sorcerers, by any chance?"

Laurent nodded. "Of course. We have the largest collection of sorcerers here on the continent. What did you have in mind?"

"Even in daylight, a small team accompanied by a sight sorcerer could most likely get inside the city. Do we know where any key points in the city are located? Their central government building, perhaps, or their military headquarters?"

The officers shook their heads. "No, the city has been significantly renovated since the last time we attacked. We don't even know where they're keeping the prince..."

*There's that mention of the prince again. I'm clearly supposed to know who that is, but why? Maybe I'm being too stubborn about asking.*

"What can you tell me about the prince's situation?" He was purposefully vague, since he didn't want to openly display his complete ignorance.

"Prince Adellan is the foundation of our alliance. If he dies, everything we've worked for could fall apart," Morningway offered. "His capture was a tremendous blow to morale, but it also served to unite us like never before. Velthryn's forces, Belyr's Ember Legion, and even Velrya working together – it's unprecedented. But his death could splinter this frail alliance before it firmly takes root."

*Prince Adellan?...*

*I've been looking at this whole scenario the wrong way. This isn't the siege of Xixis. This is an attack on Orlyn – the same city I just returned from.*

*And it's an attack that's destined to fail.*

The swordsman bit his lip. Prince Adellan had thrown himself from the tower chamber he had been locked away in. The attempt at escape had been a futile gesture – the "water" below his tower was just painted tiles, and he had died from the impact. The whole setup of his prison tower had been a cruel joke – a "room fit for a prince" that he had been unable to reach while he had been chained to the wall.

Taelien knew this well because he had been imprisoned in the same chamber, hundreds of years after Adellan's death. While this assault on the city would fail, and Adellan would die, the city would be successfully claimed by human armies many years in the future – and humans would prove to have just as depraved senses of humor as the Esharen had.

"I might know where the prince is being held," Taelien offered, his mind swimming with new information.

"Oh? And how is that?" Ravellan tilted his head to the side, looking more curious than imposing this time.

*I'm pretty sure telling them that I've been sent back in time is out of the question. Not only does even the most elementary education in sorcerous theory indicate that time sorcery of that nature is impossible, it would sound rather absurd.*

"This is their palace, correct?" Taelien pointed at a large building on the south side of the city. He hadn't recognized Orlyn previously because of the massive renovations that had occurred in the intervening centuries – even the walls were in different locations – but the place he knew as the 'low palace' was still in the same location relative where Lake Evershine flowed into the city.

*Answering questions with questions is a tried and true tactic,* Taelien assured himself.

"Yes, we believe so," Morningway offered, leaning her elbows on the table. "Why would the prince be there?"

"Well, from what little I was told before being sent here, the message sent upon the prince's capture indicated he would be treated with 'all of the accoutrements deserved of a prince', or something along those lines. Korvax, the local ruler, is known for his twisted sense of humor. Rather than keeping Prince Adellan in a prison, why not keep him right inside the palace?"

"It's possible," Ravellan admitted in a drawn-out tone, "But guesswork at best. And the palace will be better defended than any other location in the city. Even if we think he's in there, what does that gain us? We'd still have to take the entire city to have a chance at cracking the palace open."

"Not necessarily." Taelien folded his hands together, finally feeling like a plan was coming together. "The hardest part is getting inside the city itself – even the waterways are likely to be guarded."

Taelien glanced around the room. "Has this chamber been thoroughly checked for any sort of divination?"

Laurent nodded. "Yes, we've already taken that precaution. What's your plan?"

"Send them another messenger. I want to challenge their leader to a duel."

\*\*\*

After several minutes of waiting, a "scout" reported that Taelien's challenge had been accepted. The officers had been skeptical about the duel idea, but the other elements of his plan had convinced them to make the attempt.

If he failed, the bombardment of the city would begin at nightfall, just as the officers had initially planned. Taelien had taken the last few minutes to suggest some rearrangements of the troops, but he suspected that the minute details wouldn't matter. He was gambling nearly everything on this infiltration plan.

*I wish I knew if Prince Adellan's death had already occurred at this point in history. If he's already dead, this whole strategy might be a waste. A potential hit to enemy morale, certainly, but not enough to turn the tide.*

*Maybe this whole scenario was intended for me to recognize an impossible fight and withdraw...but I'd rather turn an impossible fight into a possible one.*

The "scout" escorted Taelien into the next room a few minutes later. The new chamber was largely unadorned, with several people standing around and talking in hushed tones. The immersion of the scenario was temporarily broken, as Taelien saw several people sitting at a table in paladin garb – a few of them marked with officer signets – toward the back of the room.

*The judges,* Taelien guessed. *Am I already done?*

"Wait here," the man dressed as a scout said. "We'll need to prepare the next part of your scenario."

*I suppose not, then.*

Taelien waited near the door for a few minutes, leaning back against the wall, before Lieutenant Trace emerged from a door on the opposite side of the room.

"A duel, huh?" Trace offered Taelien a smirk. "We haven't had anyone try that in years."

*Probably because it's suicide,* Taelien considered grimly. *And because there's no chance the Esharen will deliver on the terms, even if they lose.*

"The duel isn't really the key part," Taelien offered, feeling a bit defensive about his plan.

"Oh, I know. I actually rather like your idea. I'm looking forward to seeing how it plays out."

*Plays out? Are they actually going to have me duel something...? They can't possibly have any Esharen costumes around here, can they?*

"Uh, thanks," Taelien offered, suddenly self-conscious.

Another man emerged from the next room, nodded at Trace once, and then stepped back inside.

"Looks like they're almost ready." Trace grinned. "Huh. You look nervous. You sounded much more confident in the first part of the scenario."

*Could he hear me? I didn't see him in there at all.*

*Is that a picture frame on the table with the judges? Maybe it works like one of Jonan's mirrors. With sound, apparently.*

"I'm perfectly confident about my part," Taelien said, although it was a little less truthful than usual. Just fighting an actual Esharen might have been easier, although he tried not to think about what happened the last time he had encountered one. Even being observed during combat was nothing new. Testing his knowledge of history – and tactics – was infinitely more intimidating. He felt like the lives of thousands of soldiers were in his hands, even if they weren't real.

"Right." Trace gave him a friendly slap on the shoulder. "Okay, you're going to need to know a few things for this next part." The paladin lieutenant straightened up, taking a more formal tone. "The next part of the scenario will take place in Orlyn. You can safely assume that the other plans you set in motion are in progress, and that time will be passing while you head to the city for your duel."

*So, they probably won't actually be sending actors to play the infiltrators I asked for. That probably will make the logistics easier.*

"As for the duel," Trace continued, "We have arranged for a simulated duel opponent for you. You may feel free to attack the target as if it is a real Esharen. The same is true for any other enemies that attack you in the next stage of the scenario. Before you head into the next room, you'll be given a protective barrier to prevent you from suffering any serious bodily harm. If you get hit, though, you're still going to feel it, and there's a chance of actual injuries. If we feel that you've suffered enough damage that you would actually be incapacitated, the scenario will be paused and advance as if that occurred."

The swordsman nodded. "Will I arrive within the city before nightfall?"

"It will be two hours before nightfall when you arrive."

Taelien tensed his jaw. That wasn't a lot of time for his plans to work – but it could offer benefits, too. If the bombardment started while he was still inside, that could offer a valuable distraction – but it could also force the Esharen to move or even execute the prince. Assuming he was even alive at the outset of the scenario.

The paladin candidate tapped the sword on his belt. "If you're going to have me engage in combat with anyone, I really shouldn't be using this. It could cause significant, actual collateral damage, even if you're using barriers. I tend to cut right through most protective spells."

"Oh." Trace's eyes widened, as if he was noticing the Sae'kes for the first time. "Oh, yes, um, of course. I'll need to confer with some people."

Lieutenant Trace moved over to the area that Taelien had identified as the judge's table, exchanging whispered words with a few of the men and women sitting there.

*Six judges,* Taelien noted. *I would have expected seven.*

Trace returned after a couple minutes, looking strangely nervous. The judges had looked away from the portrait, and now they were all looking in Taelien's direction. "I know this is an odd request, but would you mind drawing the sword for a moment?"

*They probably want to see if I can actually use it,* he realized. "Not a problem. You might want to step back."

Trace nodded hastily, taking several steps away. The swordsman placed his hand on the Sae'kes' grip, closing his eyes in concentration. The gesture was unnecessary, but he knew it lent a look of seriousness to the idea of drawing the weapon, which the paladins always seemed to consider to be a religious matter.

*Release,* he commanded the scabbard, sensing it through the metal that connected the sword to the sheath's metal lining. The lining separated from the sword, allowing Taelien to cleanly draw the sword from the scabbard. The simple metal sorcery trick he used to lock the blade in place had lent an air of mysticism to the weapon, and it doubled as an excellent precaution to prevent anyone else from using the sword.

As the sword exited the sheath, the first five runes on the blade flared to life. *Five,* he considered. *That's better than usual. If I didn't know any better, I'd say it was pleased by the occasion.*

Lighting each of the runes took years of practice. Each of the lit runes continuously drew away some of his strength in order to focus the destructive waves that surrounded the blade. Igniting each had proven more difficult than the last, and he had only succeeded at lighting the fifth – signifying Eratar, the god of travel – during the confrontation with Edon in Orlyn. It was fitting, then, that he was displaying the same level of control when going to a simulated version of the city.

When he opened his eyes, he noted that Trace's were closed.

And several of the people in the room were kneeling.

*Right. Sacred weapon.* He held the sword awkwardly for a moment, and then brought it over his heart in a traditional paladin salute. Those paladins that still had their eyes open returned the salute immediately.

He lowered the sword, and the paladins rose.

*That was a little eerie.*

Trace reopened his eyes, smiled, and turned around. "Wait right there!"

*The swordsman frowned as a creeping numbness began to make its way across his fingers. I'm not sure they realize how much this thing takes out of me, especially with five of the runes lit. I can't imagine how bad it's going to feel when I've mastered six or all seven of them.*

His body had gradually acclimated to using the sword each time he managed to activate one of the runes, but the first time he ignited a new one was always worse than the last. He had barely remained conscious the first time he had activated that fifth rune, but he knew that was at least in part because of the injuries and fatigue he had already accumulated.

The paladin lieutenant rushed into the next room, returning a few agonizing minutes later with a man in the blue and silver robes of a priest of Sytira. He looked to be about Taelien's age, but he was almost painfully thin, and had a streak of gray in his otherwise well-trimmed blond hair.

"Hold that aloft, would you?" The skinny man asked. "And keep it still."

Taelien frowned, acquiescing to the request.

"Dominion of Knowledge, evaluate the intensity of this effect." The follower of Sytira reached forward to touch the glowing aura around Taelien's sword, and the swordsman instinctively recoiled, drawing the weapon away. The priest's eyes narrowed.

"You're going to burn your fingers off if you touch that."

"I very much doubt that. I'm well-protected by a sorcerous shield."

*Didn't Lydia tell them anything about her own measurements? I suppose not – she's been pretty secretive about the details of her findings, even to me. I'm going to have to bother her more about that after this is over.*

"Last time I used this, I cut a couple pieces out of an artifact. I'm sure your shield is very potent, but –"

The thin priest shook his head. "Fine, fine. I can do it through an implement." The shorter man reached into a pouch, retrieving a small metallic rod. "Now, don't interrupt me this time."

Taelien resisted the urge to roll his eyes. He was pretty certain he knew how this was going to end.

"Dominion of Knowledge, I invoke you to extend my senses into this wand."

Taelien raised an eyebrow appreciatively. He hadn't heard that spell before – but it sounded useful. He already was capable of extending his detection of metal through metallic objects he was holding, but this sounded like a much more general version of that. Unfortunately, he had proven useless at attempting to cast knowledge sorcery, but maybe Lydia could make some use of the spell if she didn't already know it.

Realizing he was still holding the sword away from the priest, he carefully extended it again for examination.

"Thank you. Dominion of Knowledge, evaluate the intensity of this effect."

The priest extended the wand into the sword's aura – and, as Taelien had anticipated, a flash of blue sparks erupted on contact. When the skinny man instinctively withdrew the metallic rod, the once-rounded end of the rod had been shorn off into a flat edge. There was no sign of the missing metal – it had been cleanly disintegrated.

"By all the gods," the priest mumbled. "The…I don't even understand what that was."

Taelien nodded sagely. "Can I sheath this now?"

The knowledge sorcerer nodded absently, still staring at the wand.

"Get anything useful?"

The priest of Sytira bit his lip. "The spell measures the intensity of other spell effects in standardized units, which we call domini, after the word dominion. A typical offensive spell effect has an intensity of between thirty and eighty domini. An expert sorcerer or a specialist in a particular dominion might manage two to three times that. People claim to have measured Hartigan's fire spells at over six hundred domini."

"I take it the aura measured higher than you expected?"

"Er, well, I didn't see a number at all. More like a string of incomprehensible letters. I have to assume that the measuring spell didn't function properly, since the rod suffered catastrophic damage when it came into contact with the aura…"

Taelien chuckled. "No, letters instead of numbers sounds about right to me."

The priest frowned. "I, um, don't really know what to say to that. We can't …Well, hrm. I'll have to bring you a prop to serve as a functional replacement for the scenario, but it won't be anywhere near as potent as your sword, ah, probably is?"

"That's probably for the best. Thank you."

The priest nodded absently and retreated from the room.

"That was amazing," Trace offered. "It really is the real thing, isn't it? Who else besides the Tae'os Pantheon could forge something so great?"

"Right," Taelien patted the hilt of the sword, feeling uncertain. *It's powerful, certainly, but I don't think that necessarily says anything about who made it. Or, perhaps more importantly, about why it was forged in the first place. Their legends say this was a sword forged for an alliance between gods – but all it does is destroy. There's a secret there, and I don't have even a hint on where to begin to unravel it.*

The priest returned a few minutes later, gingerly carrying what appeared to be an exact duplicate of his sword, scabbard and all.

*Huh.*

"I'm sorry, it won't perform quite like the real thing. But it'll be as powerful as I could manage."

Taelien accepted the false sword, noting that the weapon was significantly lighter than the real thing. *A training sword, probably reshaped with metal sorcery.* Interestingly, when he withdrew the blade, runes flared to life on the surface – all seven of them. Frowning, Taelien sheathed the false sword.

Realizing he was still being observed by most of the people in the room, Taelien unfastened his belt and removed the scabbard containing the actual Sae'kes. He was loathe to part with it, but if he was only going into the next room, he suspected the paladins here could keep watch over it for a few moments. He carefully laid it against the wall, fastening the fake sword on in its place. The minute difference in weight scratched at the back of his mind, but he offered a friendly smile to the priest regardless. It wasn't the other man's fault that sacred weapons were hard to perfectly copy on a moment's notice.

"Thanks for arranging this for me."

"Of course," the priest said. "It was an honor to have a chance to inspect the real Sae'kes. Would you mind if I take another look at it while—"

"Not now, Halwell," Trace instructed in a stern tone. "We need you to finish setting up the scenario."

"Right, right. Well, good luck in there," the priest offered. Taelien gave him a nod of thanks as the shorter man rushed back out of the room.

The other people within the room gradually went back to their own conversations, and it was several more minutes before Trace left and finally returned once again.

"It's time. Assume for the scenario that you are being escorted by Esharen who met you at the gate to meet with your opponent in the duel."

*Korvax. Even when Orlyn finally fell, Korvax was never defeated – in fact, the invaders picked a time when he wasn't in the city to strike. He's still alive today, as far as anyone knows – unless he died during the fall of Xixis. Which, somehow, I find unlikely.*

*The stories say that he killed hundreds of men with his bare hands. Now that I think about it, that might have been at this very battle. Blades broke against the plates on his skin, and arrows bounced off any part of him they struck. Only sorcery had any effect at all, so he slaughtered sorcerers as soon as he found them.*

*My false blade,* he considered, awkwardly reaching for the grip of the fake sword, *might not be strong enough.*

***

Taelien was escorted by four bulky Esharen, each at least a head taller than he was. Unlike the one real Esharen he had met, these looked almost human, with ordinary skin visible between their obsidian-like plates.

*I wonder what these Esharen are,* he considered. *People in extensive costumes are unlikely on such short notice. Perhaps they're under illusions?*

While he was supposedly outdoors for the scenario, the bounds of the room were still clear – if there was a sight sorcerer making the Esharen, he hadn't bothered to make the walls or ceiling invisible. It wasn't a real problem, of course – the goal of the scenario wasn't complete immersion. They were testing his strategic abilities, and possibly his combat prowess, not his ability to act.

"Stand here, human," one of the Esharen said, leading him into a marked circle on the ground. *A fighting ring. I can deal with that. But where's my opponent?*

The door on the opposite side of the room exploded.

Taelien shielded his eyes from the wood splinters as smoke cleared away from the doorway, revealing a figure tall enough to brush the room's ceiling. His skin was like polished obsidian, although the lower half of his body was covered by thick mail. He had no weapons on his belt – instead, strands of string draped small objects, that Taelien recognized after a moment to be human ears.

*Well, someone's feeling theatrical.*

"It is a pleasure to meet the current bearer of the Sae'kes," the huge Esharen spoke, his tone rich and full of mirth. "I've been anxious to have an artifact of my own for quite some time."

Taelien gritted his teeth, stepping into his side of the circle. "I'm sorry to disappoint you, but your exposure to the weapon will be brief, and probably uncomfortable. Korvax, I assume?"

The big Esharen grinned, shaking his head. "Oh, no, he's presently busy dealing with your little invisible friends. Clever, having them stand by the gates while we opened it to meet you. I wasn't expecting a human to be so canny."

Taelien shrugged a shoulder. *Well, there goes that part of the plan. Maybe. He said they knew about the spies, not that they had caught them.* "I appreciate the compliment. For what it's worth, I'm impressed by your defenses. What name should I remember you by when you're gone?"

The Xixian brought back his head and gave deep, bellowing laugh. "You're an amusing one. I think I'll keep you around for a while, once you've been sufficiently tamed. But I'm being rude – I didn't answer your question. Kyrzon Dek, Crown Prince of Xixis."

*Oh, resh.*

The prince appeared in front of him a moment later, leaving a burst of smoke at his previous location. Taelien didn't have time to draw his sword, he just barely managed to raise his right arm in time to block the prince slamming a fist forward with immense force, catapulting Taelien across the room. He slammed into the back wall, the protective spell that had been cast on him in the preparation chamber only serving to somewhat dampen the force of the impact.

A wheezing breath escaped his lungs, and then Kyrzon Dek was above him, bringing a fist downward.

Taelien pushed off of the wall, throwing himself into a roll. He had hoped to bring himself back to his feet in a single motion, but the impact had thrown him off balance, and he found himself awkwardly pushing himself from a kneeling position back to his feet.

Something wrapped around his neck from behind, and Taelien slammed an elbow backward. He met solid resistance, but the grip on his neck loosened, and he raised his right hand and pointed it backward.

*Blast.*

The burst of flame that emerged from his hand was largely cosmetic – he had never managed a flame spell that dealt any real damage at range. As he expected, however, the force around his neck vanished, and Kyrzon appeared across the room a moment later. His opponent hadn't risked being hit by the attack, as weak as it was.

"Oh, a sorcerer, too! Delightful." The Xixian prince knelt down, his previously human-looking fingers visibly shifting into claws.

*Transformation sorcery,* Taelien noted. *That's unusual for a Xixian – it's more common for Delaren – but not unheard of. More importantly, it's really bad that he can do that. And also teleport.*

*Fortunately,* Taelien stood up, *he also gave me a chance to breathe.*

The false Sae'kes sang as the blade scraped against the metal inside of the sheath, seven runes flaring to life on the surface of the weapon.

"The last time I fought an Esharen," Taelien said, wheezing slightly as he attempted to buy a moment of time to recover, "I beat him with my bare hands. You seem to be slightly stronger, though, so I'll offer you the respect of meeting my blade."

"You beat an Esharen barehanded?" The prince brought a clawed hand to his chest, looking strangely like a mockery of the paladin salute. "Was this a baby, fresh from drinking mother's milk?"

*Do Esharen drink milk?*

He had never considered that before.

"No, fully grown, I'm afraid. Sadly, he lacked your skill at using sorcery to compensate for physical weakness."

"Oh, you wound me, dear human. Tell me, what name shall I inscribe upon the slave-band that I will place upon your neck?"

Taelien grinned, cracking his neck. "Well, the name is Salaris. But, to you, the name Taelien might be more appropriate. After all, that's the name of a legend that you stand no chance to defeat."

The prince vanished again, but this time Taelien was ready. He swept the blade out in a gleaming arc in front of him, sundering the air.

Unfortunately, "ready" did not account for all possible positions.

Kyrzon Dek descended from the sky.

Taelien fell backward a moment before the Xixian impacted with him, which saved him from being eviscerated by the creature's newly-formed claws. Instead, he felt a burning sensation as the sorcery-altered fingers ripped through his uniform and impacted his right shoulder, just before the creature's full weight landed atop him and slammed him into the floor.

His head swam, but Kyrzon Dek didn't slow. Taelien barely managed to raise his left arm in time to block the next claw's swipe, and he felt a surge of agony as the barrier along his arm flickered and faltered.

The Esharen grabbed at his arms next, and while Taelien was nearly able to match the creature's strength, its superior leverage kept him pinned to the ground. So, unable to move his arms, Taelien slammed his forehead into the Esharen's nose.

Kyrzon recoiled immediately, and that moment was all he needed. Taelien didn't have much room to maneuver the false Sae'kes, but he didn't need much, either. An ordinary sword's edge would have had no effect on Kyrzon's scales, but when Taelien ran the Sae'kes along the huge Esharen's chest, the aura shredded plates and the tender flesh beneath. The demon prince shoved himself off the floor, and Taelien slashed as the larger man retreated, taking a gouge out of the creature's leg.

The Xixian prince vanished, reappearing near the door where he had entered.

"Kill him," the prince ordered, vanishing again.

Taelien spun and rolled as he left the floor, bisecting the first Esharen in an instant. The other three froze as the two halves of the first fell to the ground. Taelien brandished the glowing blade, and then pointed it downward at the creature he had just slain.

"I will allow you to flee," Taelien offered the three remaining guards.

They fled, exiting through the door that Kyrzon had entered.

After a moment, he processed what had just happened. *I really hope I didn't just cut an actor in half. That had to be an illusion...*

Taelien took a deep breath, glancing around the room, and realizing that he had been left alone.

After a moment of checking himself for real injuries, Taelien determined that he was fully intact – although his uniform's shoulder had been badly damaged. He wasn't sure if that would get him into trouble or not.

Uncertain of how to proceed with the scenario, he headed for the area where Kyrzon had appeared, walking to the gap where the Xixian prince had entered – and slammed straight into an invisible wooden wall.

*Of course they didn't actually blow up the door,* Taelien realized, shaking his head. *It's just an illusion.*

He heard the sound of the door he had entered from opening, and Trace walked into the room.

"You've completed this part of the scenario." He had only the slightest hint of emotion in his tone, but he was grinning broadly. "Come back into the waiting area."

Taelien sheathed the false Sae'kes and followed Trace back into the previous room. Most of the judges looked up at him as he entered, giving him varying looks. He couldn't read most of them, but one of them – a younger man – gave him a nod.

*That's a good sign, right?*

"Well, that was, um, unusual," Trace offered. "I'm afraid we're not prepared to simulate the entire city, so if you'll let me know what your next plans are, I'll relay them to the judges."

"Before that. Those four guards – they were just sight and sound sorcery effects, right?" The swordsman's right hand twitched when he thought about the possibility that he had actually just cut someone in half.

"Of course they were. Only the demon prince was solid." Trace gave him a quizzical look. "Is something wrong?"

Taelien shook his head. "I was just disturbed by the thought that I might have just hurt an actor in a costume."

"Oh, we wouldn't take that kind of risk. Don't worry about it. Are you injured at all? Looked like you took a few serious hits back there."

"Doing just fine. Can I have a minute to think about the next steps in my plan?"

"Sure. I think it would be at least a few minutes before the Esharen sent someone else to kill you."

"Right." A few main options at this point. *I could try to sync up with the infiltrators and help rescue the prince. They might need the help. On the other hand, I might make things worse by attracting more attention to them – I'm not very good at stealth.*

*I could try to go rescue the prince separately. I know the city layout relatively well, and I know the palace layout even better.*

*I could try to follow Kyrzon Dek. Killing him would be a tremendous blow to the Xixian Empire as a whole – but I think I've lost my window to do that. He won't make the mistake of fighting me in melee combat again, now that I've cut him.*

*I could try to find Korvax, but he could be practically anywhere, so that option wouldn't really work.*

*Or I could probably get out of the city intact and report back that our infiltrators are being hunted. Maybe someone outside the walls could send help.*

*Or maybe I'm fixating too much on taking immediate action.*

"I'm going to go find an empty house and hide."

Trace blinked. "What do you mean?"

"Given that the city is about to come under siege, they've probably evacuated some of the locations near the walls. Even if they haven't formally evacuated anything, I can probably just find a place to hide somewhere. I'd regret having to fight civilians if I run into any, but I could probably scare them off. I'd hide until the bombardment starts, and then once the battle is going in earnest, I'll go for the prince. If the infiltration squad already saved him, great. If not, I'll do it myself."

"Okay. How long would you wait after the bombardment starts before heading to the palace?"

"Only a few minutes. There's the possibility that they might try to move or execute Adellan once the battle begins, especially since they know we sent in spies. It's possible he's already dead. If I find evidence of that, I'll try to take one of the Xixian royals as my own prisoner and extract him or her from the city."

"Huh. I, well, wouldn't have considered that. I'll go tell the judges." Trace ran off to the judge's table, leaning down and exchanging more hushed conversation with them. He returned to Taelien after several minutes.

"You've given us enough to begin evaluating your test results."

Taelien blinked. "Really? That's it?"

Trace laughed. "Usually it's over a lot faster than that, actually. But you didn't hear that from me. And remember, no talking to any of the candidates about this until you're all done."

"So...did I pass?"

Trace shrugged. "No idea. The judges will need time to make a decision. But either way, you gave us a pretty impressive show."

# CHAPTER IX – JONAN II – OLD FRIENDS

Velthryn's winding streets were somewhat easier to navigate in the dawnfire's light, but only slightly. The city had grown rapidly from its founding until a mere fifty years ago, when Edrick Theas had laid the city's famous boundary wards – a series of protection rituals that made the walls nearly impervious to harm. The wards were broadly believed to have other functions, such as preventing teleportation into the city from outside, but Jonan didn't know the details.

He did, however, notice one of the consequences. When the wards were built, the city could no longer be built outward, otherwise the wards would lose their function. From that point on, the citizens had been forced to build in other directions – upward and down.

Selyr had its share of tall towers and majestic keeps, but they were few and reserved for the wealthy. Nearly every structure in Velthryn, however, was several floors tall. Individual houses were practically nonexistent outside of the wealthiest areas. Those wealthy areas were easy to discern visually, but the city didn't seem to follow the same structure of clear districts that Selyr and Orlyn did, at least so far as Jonan could tell.

Tall housing complexes sat directly adjacent to warehouses, restaurants, and shops. The civilians seemed to know their way around instinctively, but the servant of Vaelien often found himself frowning at his map, pondering what sort of madness could have led to a city so lacking in organization.

It was midday before he found Orison Park, one of the few spots of green in a city of cobblestones and grey masonry. He paused to take a breath of the air nearer to the trees, hoping that the scent would remind him of the familiar forest air of home, but that effort ended in failure. The wood here had a sweet scent that struck him as unnatural, far unlike the sharpness of pine that he had grown accustomed to.

He found the twisting trails within the park easier to navigate – these, at least, appeared to lead specifically to or past points of interest. He passed a large statue of Lorain Valere, one of the city's founders, and smiled at the children that were attempting to climb up the base. Past that, the trail led him to a pond. A group of young men were running circles around it, while a couple took turns tossing something – food, perhaps? – near a group of birds in the water.

Passing these people by, Jonan trekked onward, finally finding his destination – a lone bench, a familiar figure sitting atop it, a book pressed close against her face.

Jonan paused for a moment, uncertain what to say in spite of the hours he had spent aware of his destination.

Lydia spoke first, without even looking up from the pages. "Good morning, Jonan. Join me?"

He silently took a seat by her side, and she set the book down on her lap a moment later. Instinctively, his eyes shifted to the cover of the tome as she moved.

"Reading more of Tarren's work? Don't you ever get tired of it?" Jonan had read several of Tarren's works – they were practically a mandatory part of any sorcerer's education – but he found the scholar's style too informal and whimsical for his tastes.

"He's the expert on something I've been needing to study. But we'll get to that."

He nodded, glancing around. "Beautiful morning."

"Is it?" Lydia followed his gaze, and then shook her head. "I hadn't noticed."

Truthfully, he hadn't really, either – but someone else had mentioned it to him earlier, and he had long ago learned to mimic platitudes to mask his own awkwardness.

"So, uh, it's been a while."

"It certainly has. Thank you for coming on such short notice. I wouldn't have asked if there wasn't a good reason."

*A good reason? I suppose just wanting to see me wasn't good enough.*

"I suspected as much," he replied. *And I was already in Velthryn, but she can't know that.* "What do you need my help with?"

She tilted her head to the side, allowing a free strand of red to fall in front of her eyes. "A couple things, actually. First, I was hoping you'd be willing to share the results of your studies of Donovan's sorcerous experiments."

Several months earlier, Jonan and Lydia had worked together to investigate Donovan Tailor, a former Priest of Sytira who had set himself up as a "god" in the city of Orlyn. They had found evidence that Donovan had discovered a new way of applying ancient sorcerous techniques, which the sorcerer had used to fake his divine status.

Their work had resulted in Donovan's arrest, and Jonan had managed to hold on to Donovan's cryptic research notes when they had left the city. Throughout the intervening time period, studying those notes had occupied the vast majority of Jonan's time. He had sent Lydia several messages about his progress – via a dominion bonded hand mirror that shared images with her own matching mirror – but he had kept the notes deliberately vague, just in case Lydia had somehow lost her mirror.

"I suppose I could, but I'm not sure this is really the right place." He looked around again, not seeing any civilians in the immediate vicinity, but knowing that he had seen people no more than a few minutes away.

"I thought of that, and there isn't really a much better location. I can't exactly bring you to the paladin headquarters, and I sincerely doubt that wherever you're staying is secure."

*That's an understatement.*

"All right, fair enough. But I'll keep it in broad terms. I don't want anyone overhearing us and piecing together secrets of world-shaking scale."

Lydia gave a scoffing chuckle. "There's no need to be so dramatic. No one is going to be able to do anything with that information without the sufficient context to know what we're talking about."

"You're more right than you realize." He took a breath. "We had only scratched the surface of understanding Donovan's research when we confronted him."

She reached upward with a slender hand, pushing her glasses further up her nose. "Go on."

"Well, you remember those strange words that Edon was using for his spells? I think each word – possibly each syllable, really – corresponds to some sort of function. I don't want to go so far as to say the sounds have intrinsic meaning, although they might, but something is capable of interpreting them and producing results."

This explanation wasn't completely new – they had speculated the possibility when they had confronted Donovan, even though it sounded completely contrary to typical sorcerous theory.

"Right, but we've both tried using the same words he did. Repeatedly, in my case." Her lips contorted in frustration. "They don't do anything on their own."

"That's where I've made a bit of progress. Do you still have the ring he was wearing, and that gemstone?"

The question was a probe for information, but it was only fair – what she was asking him about was even more valuable.

The knowledge sorceress nodded. "Yes, and I've spent some time studying them. Initially, I thought the ring was the power source for those unusual flame spells both he and Veruden were capable of using, but the phrase he used doesn't activate the ring like I expected it would."

"That," Jonan smirked, "Is because he was changing the function of the ring."

Lydia raised an eyebrow. "Go on."

"So, remember when we talked about the marks on artifacts potentially corresponding to different words or concepts? Edon realized that if he could connect with an artifact, he could add additional words to change or activate a specific function."

"Like adding keys to a dominion sorcery spell..." Lydia nodded, a thoughtful expression on her face.

"That's the point of all those dominion marks he was putting on Veruden – and, presumably, on himself. When one of them activated a dominion mark, it would send a command to an artifact the mark was linked to. Their words would determine the exact function. It's possible the marks even sent some sort of default message if they were silent - the notes in the journal were not that specific."

Lydia turned her eyes skyward. "So, if we wanted to create the same effects, we'd need to be able to create identical bonds to the ones he did – meaning we'd need access to the same artifacts, and to know exactly how the marks were constructed – and then use the exact same words. That sounds somewhat challenging."

He was tempted to tell her about the freshly-burned mark on his right bicep, currently concealed beneath his nondescript brown tunic, but he decided against it. She had probably been bright enough to guess that he had stolen the Heartlance after their confrontation with Donovan, but she didn't need to know that he was able to tap into its abilities. She already knew far more of his secrets than he was comfortable with.

"Yes," he said after a moment of hesitation. "But not impossible. I believe I have sufficient notes to attempt making a mark corresponding to the ring you have, but I do not have the resources."

"Dominion essence corresponding to the dominion of the artifact, I assume?" Lydia asked in a rhetorical tone. "I could probably arrange for that. Provided you're putting the mark on me, of course."

He nodded affirmatively. "That would be acceptable. I think we could gain some valuable information from testing the interactions between a mark and that ring. Donovan's notes were impressive, but not exhaustive. And, as you suspected when we last discussed this, I believe he was expanding his vocabulary of terms that the artifacts recognized with each one that he studied. If you could convince Taelien to let us study the Sae'kes—"

Lydia folded her arms, tilting her head downward with a frustrated expression.

Jonan raised his hands defensively. "Hey, I had to ask. You Sytirans do love knowledge, so I thought..."

"Studying a sacred artifact amongst our own is one thing. I like you, Jonan, but you are literally a spy for a foreign government."

He rolled his eyes. "Well, when you put it that way..."

"If I asked you to loan me Vaelien's personal weapon for some research, how would you react?"

Jonan scratched at his chin. "With amusement, really. I mean, do you really think I'd have any access to that? It's not really a comparable scenario."

"Fine, fine. But it does sound ridiculous, right?"

"Well, if I did have access to it, I would try to at least entertain the idea."

Lydia sighed. "Ultimately, it's up to Salaris, but I'd advise him against it."

Jonan furrowed his brow. "Salaris? I've never heard you call Taelien that before."

"I've had to get into the habit. Calling himself Taelien was one thing in Orlyn, but here, it's more than a little presumptuous."

Their mutual friend had always referred to himself as Taelien, as long as Jonan could remember – it was the title of the sacred weapon he carried. Taking a title as a personal name wasn't exactly uncommon, but since the sword was a key element of the Tae'os religion, using the name in a Tae'os worshipping city was essentially telling people he was a messenger of the gods.

Which, given the swordsman's capabilities, Jonan suspected might actually be the case. He had watched bouts between some of the most skilled fighters in Selyr, and less than a handful of them came close to Taelien's raw speed or strength. And that wasn't even accounting for his ability to manipulate metal, which was so useful in a sword fight it seemed almost unfair.

He had only heard the name "Salaris" – which was apparently Taelien's actual birth name – thrown around once or twice. The swordsman didn't seem particularly fond of it.

"I guess I'll keep that in mind if I run into him. Is he going to be in on whatever you called me here for? I'm sure you didn't ask me to come out to Velthryn just to discuss Donovan's notes, as interesting as they might be."

"You're right, I did have another reason for talking to you. A more immediate concern than the notes, although I don't think you should underestimate my interest in them. An entirely new method of casting spells could have the potential to reshape our society."

Jonan waved his hand dismissively. He was well aware of the vast potential behind this Donovan's discovery – a concept he was calling 'artifact sorcery' in his mind – and that potential was exactly why he didn't intend to share the full extent of what he knew with anyone, even Lydia.

More dreadfully, he also knew that Donovan's research partner – a sorceress named Morella – most likely understood the concepts even more intimately than he did, and that she was more than likely currently plotting her revenge against everyone who had been involved in Donovan's downfall. Taelien, Lydia, and Jonan were probably among the top entries in that list.

"Yes, yes, sorcery is important. What's this more immediate concern?"

"Well," her lips twisted into a frown, "A young man was murdered."

*Murders happen all the time. Normal people should look disturbed at a revelation like this, however.*

Jonan gave his best simulation of a sympathetic frown.

"Go on."

"About a week ago, a young woman came to the Paladins of Tae'os asking for a healer. She said her brother was bleeding from several places, and she suspected a sorcerous cause. My partner, Aladir Ta'thyriel, was the first to make it to the scene. I can say without exaggeration that Aladir is the most powerful life sorcerer I have ever encountered. His ministrations – up to and including multiple Spark of Life spells - had no effect."

Spark of Life was one of the most powerful known spells in all of dominion sorcery. It was a way of forcing a mortally injured body to restart its essential functions. Laymen often confused it for being a resurrection spell, but Jonan knew it was merely a potent measure for treating life-threatening injuries.

If administered quickly enough, it could reportedly even restart the beating of a failed heart, but Jonan had never personally confirmed that. He had never met a life sorcerer even remotely close to powerful enough to cast it, let alone more than once.

"Did your partner survive the attempt?" He asked without thinking, contemplating the costs on the body of such an effort.

Lydia nodded. "Yes, but he's still recovering. I arrived to find him still trying, but the victim was clearly beyond saving. To save you a longer story, I investigated the scene and discovered a trail of dominion essence of poison."

"Ah, yes. Life sorcery wouldn't do much for poison. Water would be better for that." He realized after speaking that his commentary might have come across as rude or dismissive of the efforts of Lydia's partner, but she simply nodded to acknowledge the point.

"I followed the trail and found a ritually-marked area. It was designed as a two-way portal, marked with the largest piece of dominion essence of poison I've ever seen. I say 'piece' in the literal sense – it was solid, like a stone."

Jonan quirked a brow at that. Dominion essence usually was conjured in the natural state of the plane it originated from – for example, dominion essence of stone was solid, and dominion essence of water was liquid. The Dominion of Poison had both liquid and gaseous locations that sorcerers could draw from, but no locations that were solid. That meant that someone had to convert gaseous or liquid essence into a solid, which was tricky business.

Converting dominion essence from one state to another was something of a hobby of his – which helped explain at least part of why Lydia had called on him. She probably didn't think he was a suspect – she hadn't known he was already in the city.

*Or had she? Could she have discovered me somehow? Perhaps she made a spell to measure the current distance between our mirrors – it wouldn't be impossible...*

*Gods, I'm getting paranoid in my old age.*

In Jonan's case, "old age" meant almost twenty-two.

"So, you want me to take a look at the stone for you?"

She shook her head. "No, that wasn't the idea, although if you could glean something from it we can look into that. I'm going to be very busy between trying to investigate this murder and protecting the remaining members of the family."

"You think the killer might strike again?"

Lydia shrugged. "We don't know anything about the killer's motives – except the identity of the victim. Kalsiris Theas."

"Theas? Like, as in, related to Edrick Theas?"

"His son."

Jonan let out a string of curses. Lydia blinked rapidly, appearing confused by the display.

"You're sure you want to get involved in this, Lydia? Edrick Theas – he's a powerful man. He probably has the resources to handle this himself."

And, more importantly, anyone willing to pick a fight with Edrick Theas is either colossally stupid or extraordinarily powerful. Given Jonan's luck, it was more likely to be the latter.

"That's precisely the problem. Edrick isn't in the city right now. And Nakane – that's his daughter – is fairly certain that this will end badly if he returns before we find the culprit."

Jonan tightened his jaw. "Well, that's just lovely."

"Will you help me?"

*An assassin killing high profile targets? That could be the same man that Rialla wants me to look for. Or we could just have two extremely dangerous assassins loose in Velthryn – that'd be even better.*

The scribe pressed two fingers of his left hand against his forehead, anticipating the beginnings of a murderous headache. "Of course. Where do we start?"

# CHAPTER X – VELAS IV – THE SUBTLETIES OF CONVERSATION

On the morning after Velas completed her first test, she found a note in her bed. This was more than slightly disconcerting, given that whoever had placed it had been subtle enough to avoid waking her.

The contents of the note were more worrisome.

*Fellow soldier,*

*I saw your signal. Your presence here was not anticipated. Cannot make open contact; on discreet assignment. Expect significant collateral damage. Advise you to withdraw from paladin trials; potentially lethal danger if you remain active.*

*Apologies; will not contact again.*

*-S*

Velas carefully destroyed the note, keeping a single shred of it - a section marked with a few letters – for the possibility of using it with tracking spells or attempting to match the writing. Landen had the easiest access to drop something in her bed, since he shared her bunk, but she doubted he had written the note. Neither the shape of the letters nor the terse style matched his writing.

The obvious answer was Sterling, since she had sent him a signal before – but that didn't mean he had been the one that had actually seen it. Given that the writer was insistent on not making open contact, she would have to investigate discretely or risk angering her new contact.

The letter referred to her simply as a "soldier", which implied the writer didn't know who she was. That was potentially a positive sign.

Unfortunately, the signature itself was too vague to give her any additional hints toward the identity of the writer.

The overt warning within the letter was a dangerous sign. Whoever had recognized her sign was most likely affiliated with either the Thieves Guild of Velrya or the Thornguard. Both organizations had a history of small conflicts with the Paladins of Tae'os, but she was not aware of any recent changes that would trigger "lethal danger" to paladin candidates.

*Can I warn an officer somehow without making myself a suspect?*

*Probably not. And I won't be in any position to help my friends if I'm arrested – or if I leave.*

Velas bit her lower lip, frustrated. *I need to figure out who sent this and pry for more information. I can't protect anyone with so little knowledge of whatever this impending doom might be.*

She didn't even consider dropping out of the exams – it wasn't an option. She did, however, spend some time during the following week making preparations for several potential scenarios.

*If I see any hints of danger, I'll tell Lan and Sal immediately. One of them can convey the message to an officer if necessary without referencing me as a source. Lan knows how to keep his mouth shut, at least. Sal …maybe less so. Shame, since putting Lydia on this might actually be a good idea, if it wasn't so likely to get me into trouble.*

For the next week, each of other the cadets underwent their first test, sworn to secrecy until the final applicant had completed it. They quickly fell into a routine of physical training in the mornings, classes in the afternoons, and combat exercises in the early evenings. It was relatively light training by Velas' standards, containing little of the psychological conditioning that most traditional military training entailed.

The former Queensguard guessed that this was most likely because, like her, most of the other candidates already had some degree of existing military training. The conditioning exercises seemed to be more about gauging the current condition of the candidates than molding them into shape, and the combat exercises were more about team building than general discipline. The most important step of the process was clearly the testing, which was geared toward disqualifying anyone who didn't fit with the organization.

And thus, by the end of the first week, the twelve original platoon members in Platoon 2 had dwindled to nine. Unsurprisingly, Taelien and

Landen had made the cut, as had the strange Delaren girl. In spite of the restrictions on discussing test results, rumors were already rapidly spreading that Taelien had come a hand's breadth away from failure.

With the first week completed and the tests finally done, the applicants had finally been given permission to discuss the details of their own tests. A score sheet had been posted on the wall of each of the Platoon Barracks, and Velas had been amused by the results. She mentally noted the rankings of the people who interested her.

The public rankings used a letter code, although she suspected that the paladin candidates were actually being given a numeric ranking that was being kept hidden to help foster more speculation and competition. The key indicated that the passing rankings normally went from "A" to "C", with "S" being a rarer notation for exceptional performance. Rank "D" represented a failing grade for a particular test. There were no listings of "D" at this stage – anyone who scored that low early on was simply disqualified outright. She suspected that "D" ranks might be allowed to progress in later exams if their aggregate score was sufficiently high, but she wasn't certain.

*Keldyn Andys – Rank A. Unsurprising, given his reputation.*

*Susan Crimson – Rank C. Apparently military strategy isn't her strength.*

*Asphodel – Rank A. Apparently she's got a good head on her shoulders.*

*The Wandering War – Rank A. Apparently his name is applicable to wartime strategy.*

*Jonathan Sterling – Rank B. Interesting. I expected him to perform better.*

*Velas Jaldin – Rank A. That's a relief. Looks like I evaluated the situation correctly.*

*Salaris – Rank C. Ouch. Sal is going to need to pick up the pace.*

*Terras – Rank B. Not bad. B is probably a pretty typical passing score.*

*Lysen – Rank B. Same as the twin. Guess they think alike, too.*

*Kolash – Rank B. I would have expected the warriors to be better at tactics than their "oracle". Hrm.*

*Landen – Rank S. Now that's very interesting. Going to have to ask Lan how he managed that. I don't see any other "S" ranks on here at all.*

*Teshvol – Rank C. Barely passed. I'll need to look into that as well.*

After gathering a bit of information from other cadets, Velas headed to the mess hall to discuss what she had heard.

Velas took a seat next to Landen, putting her tray down and leaning across it toward Taelien.

"Heard you got your ass kicked by an illusion." She grinned brightly. "That takes talent." Taelien rolled his eyes.

"The 'illusion' was covering something that was solid. I'm still not sure how they managed it – whatever that thing was, it was heavy, strong, and capable of teleportation."

"Something made from construction sorcery, maybe?" Landen took a bite out of a chicken leg, shaking his head and setting it back down on his plate. "They wouldn't have to actually teleport it, the sorcerer could just dematerialize and move the construct."

"Possible, given that I didn't actually have any way of telling what was real." Taelien cracked his knuckles. "Anyway, I won that fight. Construct or not, it ran away."

"Oh, so you scared off the illusionary monster?" Velas gave a mock clap, smirking. "As always, your heroism is without equal."

"Hey, at least I actually went for the objective. I hear you didn't even attack the city." Taelien pointed a finger at her accusingly, while simultaneously lifting a cup with his other hand and taking a drink.

Velas shook her head. *Of course I didn't attack the city. I lived there for years – I knew all about how the Battle of the Three Fords went. There was no chance of success in a direct conflict – the Esharen had the human army outnumbered, had better training, and had defensive walls.*

"Yeah. Instead of beating my head against a wall, I looked at the broader picture. I think that's what they were looking for – the ability to identify when the odds are against you and how best to deal with that situation." She shifted her weight, leaning against her left hand. "I took Fort Lysen to the north of Orlyn, had my army wall up there and took prisoners. We offered a prisoner exchange for the prince. They turned it down, but our close proximity forced their army to take the field to try to recapture the fortress. That gave us the defensive advantage, making the battle vastly more plausible. I think we might have won, given enough time."

"You might have won by attrition; I might have actually saved the prince." Taelien sat up straighter in his chair. "I think you're right about what the instructors wanted, but that doesn't mean the instructors have the right answer to the scenario."

Velas chuckled at that. "It's a test, Taelien. Part of the test is figuring out what the instructors want you to do. Fail at that and it doesn't matter how creative your ideas are."

The swordsman lowered his head, frowning. "Maybe."

Velas felt an unexpected – and uncharacteristic - pang of guilt at seeing his expression. "Hey, now. I didn't mean to—"

"No, you're right. You just gave me something to think about."

Velas turned toward Landen, who was still eating with a mildly amused expression. "You're looking smug."

He raised another chicken leg, making a circular gesture with it. "Well, I just find your lecturing a little silly, given that I out-scored both of you."

Velas shrugged. "I figured you probably did the same thing I did, but with a little better micromanagement, or with judges who liked you better."

Landen made a scoffing noise. "Not even close, Vel. I won the scenario."

She raised an eyebrow. "Won? I talked to half a dozen other people before I came here, including some full paladins. That scenario doesn't have a win condition."

"It didn't until I made one."

She rolled her eyes. "Okay, Lan, I can tell you want to regale us with your epic story of struggle and triumph."

"Actually," he pointed downward at his tray, "It was remarkably simple. What am I pointing at?"

"A tray with food, dinnerware, and a drink," she replied, trying to sort through his logic. "What, you sieged them until they starved?"

He shook his head. "I considered that, but it's even simpler."

Taelien seemed to have cheered up, his expression having shifted from sad contemplation to a look of intent focus. "You could be pointing at any of the component parts that Velas mentioned. The food on the plate might represent destroying supplies. The knife could represent assassinating key targets. The drink…gods, did you poison their water supply?"

Landen's expression brightened. "And we have a winner."

Velas leaned back, folding her arms. "That doesn't sound like the type of strategy paladins would typically approve of. They would have had human and Rethri slaves in Orlyn at that point in history – you would have doomed them as well."

"That's why I used lysinium toxin. Deadly to Esharen, but it has almost no effect on humans and Rethri, aside from the possibility of rashes or some stomach problems. They didn't know about it at that point in history, of course, so using my knowledge might not have been considered fair. Apparently, the judges deemed it a legitimate solution."

"Still, isn't poison something they would consider dishonorable?" Velas tightened her jaw. *I might have been reading this whole organization wrong.*

"Oh, I didn't use it to kill the whole city. First, we encircled the city, like we would in a traditional siege. Then we gathered both the necessary supplies to poison the water supply – and, this was the tricky part – the supplies necessary for a ritual to neutralize it. Then we sent them a messenger and told them about it, and demanded that they surrender the prince, as well as all their human and Rethri slaves and hostages. In exchange, we would neutralize the poison and withdraw."

"Couldn't they just neutralize the poison themselves if they knew about it?"

"They didn't know the materials necessary for the cure, and I made sure we kept the supply trains far away from our base camp and under extraordinarily heavy guard. Battle sorcerers, anti-scrying fields on the area, the works. They could have taken the time to test the water and try to formulate their own cure, but that would have meant dehydrating their city and risking panic until they had a solution. And while they might have had one or two water sorcerers as slaves, Esharen sorcerers almost never learn water sorcery – they considered it one of the 'weaker' sorcery types. So, they wouldn't have enough sorcerers to make water for the city, or to attempt a ritual to purify the water."

"I'm a little surprised they didn't just attack your forces directly, given that they apparently had overwhelming numbers." Taelien tapped the bottom of his knife on the table, looking slightly perplexed.

"That wouldn't fix their problem – in fact, it might have made it worse. Esharen are extremely tough, but they still dehydrate just like we do. Engaging in battle would have sped that process up. We tainted our own water supplies with the poison, too, so even if they seized our resources, they'd just end up killing themselves with it."

"That's...uncharacteristically devious of you, Landen." She gave him a nudge. "I'm rather proud of you."

"Thanks," he said, setting down the chicken leg. "I don't know if it would have worked in reality, but the judges seemed to like the core idea. Even gave me this blue flag." He reached into a pouch on his side and retrieved a cobalt ribbon, about a foot in length. "It's supposed to cancel out a red flag if I get one of those in another test."

Velas pulled her lips into a pout. "I didn't get one of those."

"Well, you didn't get ranked with an 'S'. I don't even know what exactly that means, but apparently I'm exceptional."

She groaned. "You're exceptionally full of yourself, at least."

"You turned what was supposed to be a no win situation for you into a no win situation for the enemy. That's pretty brilliant." Taelien set down his knife on his tray. "That's what I should have done. Instead, I took a serious gamble, risking our success on my own proficiency."

"To be fair," Velas scratched at her chin, "I think your plan had some merit, too, Taelien. The team you brought in with you might have rescued the prince even if you had lost that duel. I think the reason that you barely passed was because you risked the Sae'kes. Some of the judges might have considered that sword more valuable than the mission."

"It's just a sword," Taelien mumbled, almost in a whisper. "It cuts well, but so do a hundred others."

"It's a symbol to people," Landen gestured at the sword, which was sheathed on Taelien's hip. "Like the Heartlance was back in Orlyn."

"Sure, I know that, but I don't think it's fair to treat it that way for a test about military tactics. The people in that army were not particularly religious, so losing it wouldn't have been a tremendous impact to morale. There were no other paladins there, and the sword itself was a minor tactical asset at best." Taelien frowned.

"This goes back to what we were saying before, Taelien. The tester is as or more important than the test itself. You have to get into the heads of the people running the exam." She pursed her lips. "Although apparently I didn't do quite as good of a job as I thought I did, given that Lan managed to show me up."

"You should be used to that by now." Landen winked at her.

Velas resisted the urge to stick out her tongue, settling for just staring at him for a moment before replying. "Only because I don't use my sorcery when we spar."

"Usually."

"Usually," she agreed. "Gotta keep you on your toes."

Her former Queensguard partner rolled his eyes, and then looked back to Taelien. "Anyway, we all passed. That's the important part. We should do something to celebrate."

"Drinks? I like drinks. You could buy me said drinks." She gave Landen another affectionate nudge.

"I think I've bought you enough drinks to last a lifetime, Vel. I was thinking maybe we'd go out to the city and do some sight-seeing. I've heard they're going to give us a day off to do whatever we want during the Cleansing Festival."

"You want to go sight-seeing during the festival? Festivals are about eating and drinking, Lan. Possibly a few other things that you'll learn about when you're an adult." She gave him an exaggerated wink.

Landen sighed. "How about you, Taelien? Any plans for the Cleansing Festival?"

The swordsman shook his head. "Not really, but I might try to visit Lydia. I haven't seen her in a while."

Landen grinned. "I wouldn't mind seeing a bit more of Lydia—"

Velas finally picked up her knife, cutting into her rapidly cooling chicken. "Well, maybe when the two of you are done courting the fair maiden, we can do something that's actually fun."

"It's not like that with Lydia," Taelien jabbed a piece of fruit with his fork. "She's just a friend. A mentor, really, in some respects."

"Uh-huh. Maybe for you."

Landen visibly blushed, as she knew he would. It was all too easy sometimes.

"—anyway, I'm sure we can find time to do something as a group for the festival," Landen stammered, rapidly taking a drink from his cup afterward.

"Great. I'll think of something. You two are going to love it." Velas cut off a strip of her chicken, grinning to herself. "Trust me."

Velas turned at the sound of footsteps approaching her from the right. Lieutenant Torrent paused, folding his arms across his chest and

144

tilting his head to the side. "Better finish that food fast, Jaldin. You're due in the briefing room at six bells."

*Six bells? That's less than an hour.*

"Yes, Sir." She gave him a crisp salute, which he lazily returned.

"And pack your bags before you go to briefing. You've got a trip ahead of you."

***

*Pack my bags? Was I just disqualified?*

Velas frowned as she opened the door to the barracks. It was dinner hour, so she didn't expect anyone else to be there.

Asphodel was in the center of the room, sitting cross-legged on the floor, a large piece of parchment spread out in front of her. She let out a mild gasp when Velas walked in, hastily grabbing the parchment and beginning to fold it up.

"You aren't supposed to be here," Asphodel mumbled, sounding more confused than accusatory. "No one is supposed to be here."

"Finished dinner early," Velas explained, heading over to the large trunk next to her bed to begin gathering her things. "That a map for the next test?"

Velas caught Asphodel shaking her head out of the corner of her eye.

"Not for the next test."

*Well, now that's interesting. She's got a map for a future test?*

"No need to be shy," Velas offered, "Your secret is safe with me. And if you wouldn't mind sharing…"

"No," Asphodel said. "I cannot."

Velas raised an eyebrow as she laid out supplies on her bed. A backpack, two uniforms, a bedroll to attach to the backpack, a waterskin, flint and steel, a coil of rope with a grappling hook, an extensive medical kit, a packet of herbs for water purification, and a few other miscellaneous supplies. And, of course, a scabbarded longsword and an eating knife. She was already wearing her good boots, and she had her quarterstaff leaning against the nearby wall.

Once her supplies had been organized, Velas attached the bedroll to her backpack and began to change into one of her uniforms.

"Why? I won't tell anyone. It'll be just between us."

"You are not supposed to be here. I didn't see you coming."

Velas frowned. "This have something to do with that 'oracle' thing Teshvol keeps calling you?"

"Yes."

*Not much for words, this one.*

"Okay, so you didn't predict me walking into the room. Why is that significant?" She glanced over to Asphodel. The purple-haired Delaren had folded up her map, and she was now standing straight up, gazing directly at – or perhaps through – Velas.

"I can't see you properly."

Velas paused, half-dressed, and turned to Asphodel, tilting her head to the side. "You're saying I'm invisible?"

"Not in the way you mean. I can't see your path. Your potential future." The Delaren frowned. "It is disconcerting."

*She can see potential futures? That's…disturbing, if it's true. I'm not sure if it's more disturbing that such an ability exists, or that I don't show up on it.*

"Has this happened before?"

"Yes."

*Again, lovely answers.*

"Right. How does your ability work? Should I be worried about your inability to see me?"

Asphodel frowned slightly. "I'm not sure. If you should be worried, that is. My ability – I am an oracle. Your people might call it the sorcery of destiny."

She raised an eyebrow. "Destiny sorcery? That's one of Sytira's gifts or somesuch, isn't it?"

"Your people believe it to be so. It is a rare and special gift. My people believe the power of foresight – the gift of the oracle – comes from Kelryssia, the Maiden of the Stars."

She'd never heard that name before. *Some ancient, mostly forgotten goddess, perhaps? Or just an alternate name for Sytira from another culture?* "Is that what you believe?"

"No."

*Helpful. Real helpful.*

"All right. Well, what does your lack of ability to see me say to you?"

Asphodel moved back toward her own bed, slipping the map under her mattress, and then returning to look at Velas. "I cannot predict your

146

actions – at least not in the long-term. When I gaze at you directly, I can see a few moments, but no more."

*Interesting. I need to do some research on this destiny sorcery – if it's real, that could be a tremendous asset, or an incredible liability to my plans. I need to make her mine.*

"Well, that should make things more fun, won't it?" Velas gave a grin. "It must get tiresome being able to predict everyone else's actions in advance."

"Not everyone else," Asphodel corrected. "But yes."

"Seems like you might benefit from having a friend to talk to that won't give you answers you already have. Maybe we can play some tactics games sometime. Might be useful to you to practice against someone you can't read as easily."

Asphodel nodded. "Yes."

*Well, the hook is in her. We'll see if I can reel her in later.*

"I have to hurry for now. I think I have another test to take. But we should talk again soon."

Asphodel tilted her head quizzically. "Very well."

Velas finished changing, belted on her sword and knife, and put on her backpack to prepare for travel. "Any ideas where I'm going to be headed?"

"Telling you would be cheating," Asphodel said, giving the slightest smile.

"Right. Cheating. Wouldn't want to do that."

"No."

Velas just shook her head.

*I'm really going have to keep an eye on this one.*

\*\*\*

Velas arrived at the briefing room a few minutes early, and stood outside as patiently as she could. *I wasn't expecting them to send us out of the city so soon. Am I going to be set up with a squad? If so, wouldn't it logically be Taelien and Landen?*

*They eliminated more than three people – we can't be evenly distributed into squads of three now. I wonder if they're going to break us up into different sized groups for different tasks.*

Second Lieutenant Banks emerged from the briefing room a few moments later wearing a dour expression. "You're early." She slammed the door shut behind her.

Startled by the lieutenant's attitude, Velas still managed to raise a hand in a weak salute.

"At ease. Your next test is another simulation. Assume that you are just about to walk into the briefing room for an assignment – just like you were – but that you hear something unusual inside."

Banks snapped her fingers, and Velas *felt* a wave of sound sorcery pass her. She barely resisted the urge to interact with it during the instant of contact.

"Stop, right there!" The voice was unmistakably Landen's, and it was coming from inside the room. "Drop your weapon!"

"Remember, this is a simulation," the Second Lieutenant assured her. "Dominion of Protection, form a layer of armor around Applicant Velas."

Banks pressed a hand against Velas' shoulder, and the former Queensguard felt the familiar sensation of a suit of incorporeal armor wrapping around her. She knew from experience that the spell would dampen, but not completely absorb, any attacks that struck her – at least until the armor was destroyed.

"The people inside will be shielded as well?" Velas asked.

The Second Lieutenant nodded, and Velas heard the clash of steel on steel. "You may begin."

Velas snapped into focus, immediately playing into the simulation. "Sir, I believe I hear combat in the briefing room!"

Banks frowned, which Velas took as a sign that she wasn't expecting to be included in the simulation. "Go see what it is. I'll seek out help."

"Yes, Sir!"

Velas spun around, drawing her sword and rushing to the door. She heard a thump inside, followed by a groan. She grabbed the door handle and turned it, immediately taking a defensive stance while she scanned the room.

A black-cloaked figure was standing over Landen, who was lying face-upward on the floor, his twin swords both lying out of his reach. He had visible cuts – real or fake? – on both of his arms, and his uniform was cut over his chest, but she couldn't see any injury to his torso from the current angle.

The figure that loomed above him was dressed in all black, wearing a white neutral mask and a voluminous black cloak. The gender of the figure was indeterminate, but he or she was carrying a single long sword – paladin standard issue – and looked to be about ready to plunge it into Landen's chest.

*A stereotypical assassin. Not a thing like the reality, but I get the point.*

"Stop!" Velas shouted, drawing the figure's attention. "I've already called for help. This place will be swarming with paladins in minutes. Landen there is a low-value target. He's just a cadet. Killing him will accomplish nothing for you. Surrender now and we will give you a chance to explain yourself."

Somehow, in spite of the mask, she thought she could see the assassin's eyes narrowing in scrutiny.

Then he turned and ran, throwing something at the floor behind him as he moved.

Landen was roughly in the center of the room. Velas judged that that the other door – which led deeper into the building – was about five meters away from the assassin. A glance at the floor quickly identified what the assassin had thrown – caltrops, designed to slow down pursuit. With motion sorcery, she normally could have quickly covered the distance between them, but the caltrops would make that trickier. If she jumped, and then used a burst of motion to push herself across the room—

*But maybe I'm thinking about this the wrong way. Maybe catching the assassin isn't the most important part of this test.*

She rushed to Landen's side, throwing off her backpack, eyes following the assassin while he rushed into the next room.

"What're you doing, Vel? Get after him!" Landen coughed, clutching at his chest. It was a fake wound – she could see that clearly now that she was up close – but he was putting up a good performance.

"That's not my priority right now. I already raised the alarm – he's not getting away. Now, how do you feel?"

She examined the injuries, noting something that looked sickly greenish mixed with his blood.

"I feel like I just got sliced open a few times. Should be fairly evident, yeah?"

"Don't smart talk me. Can you raise your right arm?"

His arm shuddered slightly, but didn't move.

"Resh. Okay." She opened her backpack, swiftly finding her medical kit. "How much pain would you say you're in?"

"Quite a lot, actually. More than these little cuts should be. Listen, Vel, he got the drop on me –"

"I don't need excuses, I need to diagnose you. Remain calm and keep your breathing stable."

Landen frowned. "All right."

"Are you feeling any tingling in your extremities?"

"Yeah, a little, now that you mention it. And a buzzing in my left ear."

Velas let out a curse, grabbing a coil of rope from her bag. It was the best thing she could think of. "Bite down on this."

He blinked, but complied when she shoved the coil in his mouth.

"This is going to hurt. A lot."

She retrieved an empty flask from the medical kit, as well as two vials, and poured in some of each vial. "Three quarters adenas root extract, one quarter vespas leaf," giving the ingredients out loud for the benefit of whatever judges were obviously watching the exchange. It was the specific antidote to Sythus viper venom, which was the poison his symptoms seemed to indicate he was suffering from. Normally, his eyes would also be dilated, but she expected that they didn't go to the extreme of faking that for the test.

Once the liquid was mixed, she poured it on the chest wound. It sizzled on contact, causing Velas' eyes to widen briefly. That was supposed to happen if it was real poison – she hadn't expected a reaction to occur.

*Whoever faked the alchemical portion of this took it very seriously. I wonder if I was supposed to test his blood for the poison somehow…but I don't have a way to do that quickly. I suppose if it's always the same test regardless of who is participating, they might have put some real venom on his uniform in case a knowledge sorcerer decided to test it.*

"It should be working," she said. Landen gritted his teeth against the rope, twitching on the floor and moaning slightly. His acting was pretty good, considering he probably wasn't in any actual discomfort. Hopefully.

Next, she mixed another batch of the antidote, pouring it on his other two wounds. It reacted similarly. She had worried briefly that he might have been exposed to multiple poisons, but the attacker only had a single visible weapon, and mixing poisons on a single blade was rare.

"You feeling any better?" Velas asked. Landen weakly shook his head. "Fair enough. Probably will take you a few hours to feel any better. If you said you were, I'd think you were lying to get me to chase the assassin." She grinned.

Landen spat out the rope. "You should go after him now, regardless."

She shook her head. "Nope. He could loop back around to finish the job. My work isn't finished until you're on your feet."

He moved a hand to try to push himself up, and she grabbed his wrist. "Don't even think about it. You need a few hours, at a minimum. And you're still bleeding, even if the poison is most likely neutralized. You still feeling the tingling in your hands?"

Landen shook his head. "No."

"All right, let's get you cleaned up."

She tore the cut in his uniform wider, distributing a little bit more of the antivenom across the surface of his skin, and then retrieved a roll of bandages from her medical kit and began to wrap his chest. "Just relax. We're going to get you better."

"Sorry, Vel. I messed up," he coughed, wincing afterward.

"Nonsense. I assume he cut you before you even saw him?"

Landen nodded weakly. He was sweating profusely, which was a little odd, given that he probably hadn't actually been poisoned. "Yeah. Came here for my mission briefing, but no one was here – not anyone I could see, anyway. Heard something and turned around. The guy had sliced my left arm open before I could draw. Tried to talk him down, but I got weaker and weaker. Had to drop my left sword, then he found an opening."

"Did you get a good look at him?"

Landen shook his head. "No. Did you see anything?"

*Might be part of the test.* "He's carrying a paladin issue sword, so he could be one of us." She thought back, finishing the wrapping on his chest and beginning to bandage his arms. "His garb was unusual. Concealed his appearance, sure, but wearing a cloak like that is impractical. He looked more like a caricature than a real assassin. Not to say he wasn't dangerous, of course. Throwing those caltrops means he was pretty well prepared. You've got good eyes and reflexes – if he got the drop on you, he's probably a sight or shadow sorcerer."

"You're just saying that to make me feel better." Landen gave a brief grin, but it faltered when she tightened the bandages around his left arm. "Don't take these off. If the tingling returns, inform me immediately. Are you injured anywhere else?

He frowned. "Well, it's a little embarrassing, but—"

"Nothing I haven't seen before, I assure you." She folded her arms. "Just treat me like a doctor."

"Well, he hit me in the leg, but just below my—"

"Left leg or right leg?"

"Right," he said, grimacing.

She leaned over, finding a slit in his pants that had been concealed by his position, cursing. She removed a pair of scissors from her pack, methodically snipping off the pant leg at just above the point of the cut. There was a thin line across his skin – just a graze. She mixed more of the antidote.

"This one's not too bad, but this is still going to sting. Bite the rope."

She offered the rope back to him, and he grudgingly bit down.

She was washing the wound when the door behind her burst open. Three armed and armored paladins – Banks in the lead – swarmed into the room.

"Jaldin, report!" Banks ordered.

Velas continued washing the wound, not pausing to salute. "A would-be assassin attacked Landen moments ago. He is carrying a paladin-issue long sword laced with Sythus viper venom. He is wearing a mask and a heavy cloak, and potentially carrying other weapons concealed within. He threw caltrops on the other side of the room to slow pursuit. Cadet Landen is poisoned and injured. He fought bravely, but the assassin had the element of surprise. Given that Landen did not immediately see anyone in the briefing room, the assassin may be a sight or shadow sorcerer, and whoever was supposed to be briefing Landen may be injured as well."

"Good work, Cadet." She gestured to the other two paladins with her. "Peters, Valoran, pursue the assassin. I'll see if I can locate whoever was supposed to give the briefing."

The two paladins swiftly moved past Landen and Velas. She watched them carefully, just in case one of them was going to make any sudden actions that would indicate betrayal.

When the two other paladins had made it to the other side of the room, one of them opened the door.

"And that concludes the test," Banks said. "Cadet Jaldin, Cadet Landen, you may return to your quarters."

Landen grinned and raised an arm to wipe off his forehead, his pained expression fading immediately. "Nice work there, Vel. Thanks for saving me."

She reached down and offered him a hand to help him stand, which he accepted. "Sure. Sorry about your pants, though."

He shrugged. "Hey, if I'm going to have my pants cut off, you're the first person I'd want to do it."

"Charmer." She grinned, turning back to Second Lieutenant Banks. "How'd I do?"

The second lieutenant's expression was neutral. "You'll find out when everyone's tests are completed. Dismissed."

She's no fun at all.

*Velas saluted, and Landen quickly mirrored the gesture.*

"C'mon. Let's get you some new pants."

# CHAPTER XI – LYDIA III – HINTS OF A BROADER GAME

Lydia stared at her pieces on the board, inching a hand toward one of the mounted knights on the right side. Across the table, Nakane sat with her hands folded in her lap, her expression neutral.

*I probably should have asked Aladir for advice before letting Nakane convince me to play. I expected her go easy on a beginner. I apparently expected wrong.*

Her deliberations were interrupted by the sound of one of the house guards approaching. He bowed to Nakane, who gestured for the man to speak.

"M'lady, there are visitors at the gate. They claim to be acquaintances of Miss Hastings."

Nakane turned her head toward Lydia, quirking an eyebrow. "Expecting visitors, Lydia?"

She nodded, though she couldn't keep her expression completely neutral. *Yes, but not so soon.* "I believe those visitors will be the Thornguard contacts I mentioned."

"Ah, of course. Elden, please bring them in. I will be quite interested to meet Lydia's friends." Nakane turned back toward Lydia as the guard moved to comply. "But don't think this gets you out of our match."

"Of course not." The sorceress pushed up her glasses. "I was just warming up."

Nakane cracked a grin – a rare sight, in Lydia's experience. Perhaps she had smiled more when her brother was alive, but Lydia did not know the young woman well enough to judge.

Lydia stood up from the table and stretched, straightening out her tunic. Nakane stood as well, running fingers through her hair, and then turning her head toward the sound of approaching footsteps.

Jonan was better dressed than usual, indicating an unusual level of awareness of social conventions on his part. His red tunic matched one of the colors of House Theas, indicating a degree of respect and solidarity. He wore grey trousers with knee-high black boots, which Lydia noted to be common among higher class citizens this year. He was cleanly shaven for what was, as far as Lydia could guess, probably the first time ever. His brown hair also looked to have been trimmed short and slicked back.

*Not bad, Jonan. You could probably pass for a Thornguard — which is probably your intention.*

Seeing his companion lent a degree of context to his unusually pristine appearance. Her indigo eyes, completely lacking sclera, were just as striking as Lydia remembered from their days in Orlyn's courts. She had rarely encountered the so-called goddess Vorain, but the woman was unmistakable in spite of her own change in garb. Gone were the flowing rune-etched robes of office, replaced by a simple Thornguard tabard over a mail hauberk. The armor covered to just below her waist and was cinched by a belt carrying a long, thin-bladed dueling sword. Her trousers and boots were a perfect match for Jonan's.

"My lady Nakane," Jonan offered, stopping several feet away and bowing at the waist. "It's my utmost pleasure to meet you. I am Jonan Kestrian, scribe to the Thornguard, and this is my companion V—"

"Vorianna, m'lady," the Rethri woman cut in, bowing as well. "Also with 'te Thornguard. Pleasure."

*Vorianna? Really? That's the best they could come up with?*

"You are both welcome guests in my home, Thornguards. What brings you here?" Nakane looked at Vorain, openly appraising the young woman. If she had any knowledge of Vorain's other identity, she didn't betray it in her expression — just a degree of curiosity and interest.

Lydia took the moment to shoot Jonan a quizzical look, which he replied to with an exaggerated wink.

"Well, Jonan heard from your Lydia," Vorain pointed helpfully at the sorceress, "That you'd be needing a couple extra sets of hands. I've got me some time to kill, bein' on leave an all, and lost a bet to this bastard besides. So, here we are."

"Here you are, indeed." Nakane turned her gaze toward Jonan, "Lydia spoke quite kindly of you, but she did not indicate that you were a simple scribe. I was under the impression she had contacted you to see if the Thornguard could provide me with additional protection, given the absence of a response from her own organization."

Jonan nodded. "Yes, that's right. Lydia and I are old friends, you see. We go way back."

*Eight months and change*, Lydia noted.

"And?" Nakane prompted.

Jonan shrugged a shoulder. "And here we are. Oh, if you're worried that we're not a sufficient force, don't be. Vorianna here is one of our best, and if you need to be defended against any sort of paperwork, I'm your man."

"Intriguing. And what sort of paperwork defense do you provide?"

"Well," Jonan lifted his right hand, opening his palm, "I find it best to be thorough."

A sphere of orange flame flickered to life in his hand. Even from a distance, Lydia could feel the heat emanating from the orb – which meant something important.

*That's real fire. That's…new. Either that, or he just never shared the talent with me before. Strange that he'd choose this moment to demonstrate the skill if he was deliberately hiding it in the past, however. What would that imply?*

"Ah, a fire sorcerer. Very well, I suppose you have an applicable skill after all." Nakane nodded appreciatively. "You can dismiss that now."

Jonan closed his hand, the flame disappearing as he made the gesture. "I've heard you're quite the talented sorceress yourself, Miss Theas. Perhaps we could trade some tricks while I'm here."

"I doubt that. Your assassin's sorcery leaves a poor taste in my mouth." She hesitated for a moment, her eyes narrowing, and then added, "But I won't discount the idea entirely."

"Excellent," Jonan said. "And if the thought appeals to you more, I can certainly share my limited experiences with the local methods."

Nakane waved a hand dismissively, turning to Vorain. "And you, Thornguard? What can you do?"

"Quite good with a sword, miss. Quite good." The former goddess tapped the hilt of her sword appreciatively.

"Very well." Nakane turned to Lydia. "I suppose they'll be sufficient for now, but I'd feel more comfortable if you or Aladir remain present as well. My mother has grown accustomed to your presence, and I suspect your departure would make her uncomfortable."

Lydia nodded. "I'll make sure at least one of us checks in on you periodically. You can trust these two, however. They're being quite humble about their skills, I assure you."

"I should hope so. Well, if you're satisfied with the protection these two can provide, what will your next move be?"

Lydia reached down, moving her knight forward in a daring charge into enemy lines. "Confronting the assassin, of course."

*** 

"What, precisely, do you mean that Ulandir Ta'thyriel is unavailable?"

Lydia stood outside the grounds of Ulandir's manor, only one of several on House Ta'thyriel's grounds within the city. The three guards – Rethri homes generally had three guards, she had never learned why – were all offering her apologetic looks with varying degrees of sincerity.

The guards were dressed extravagantly, with their blue tunics embroidered with the symbol of a bird - also blue, but with green highlights – on a purple shield. They wore green trousers with golden trim, all pristine in quality. Each wore a short sword on their hip, and the two in back carried iron-tipped spears.

Lydia knew House Ta'thyriel wasn't the wealthiest house in the city, but she had a hard time believing it looking at their servants – and their perfect gardens, or the marble statues that dotted the grounds of the complex. The sorceress had never had the occasion to visit the few families that reportedly commanded even greater resources – she imagined they would have to line their paths with solid gold to look any more opulent.

Aladir wasn't with her, which was probably for the best. His relationship with his father had been strained for years, and even if the two had been on good terms, he couldn't have been expected to be objective in an investigation.

That didn't stop her from using Aladir's name to improve her odds of getting quick access to Ulandir, of course, but she had been stopped by something far more mundane.

"Forgive me, Dame Hastings. He is not currently in the city." The guard bowed slightly at the waist, putting his hand over his heart and closing his eyes in a demonstration of sincerity.

The title caught her slightly off-guard – "Sir" and "Dame" were generally considered antiquated titles. Either the man was trained to be extremely formal, or he was simply trying to let her down as lightly as possible.

The reason was irrelevant, of course – she needed results, not platitudes.

"Where is he, then?" She crossed her arms, then uncrossed them quickly, reminding herself not to look as impatient as she was feeling. She didn't realize that she had unconsciously been tapping her foot as well.

"I'm afraid that's not something we're aware of," the same guard said. She watched the other guards to see if they had any reactions to his statement, but their expressions were completely taciturn.

*Gods, I wish I had about ten guards this disciplined to keep an eye on Nakane.* Her request for additional help had been met with the usual reluctance, followed by an assurance that she would be given additional manpower just "as soon as possible". Which meant never, in all likelihood.

For the last three days, Lydia and Aladir had taken shifts protecting both Nakane and her mother, Nedelya. House Theas had their own guards, but they had proven insufficient once already, and Lydia was convinced that there was still the threat of another attack.

*I just don't have enough information. I need to try to discern the motive, at least.*

It had occurred to Lydia that Nakane was a suspect – she was a sorceress, and as the younger child, she had just potentially won an inheritance with the death of her brother. Her behavior was strangely detached, at least by comparison to the obvious grief of her mother.

The main reason she doubted Nakane was responsible was that she was almost certain that Edrick would be able to determine Nakane's innocence or guilt when he returned to the city – the man's resourcefulness was legendary, and he was almost certain to expend all his efforts in attempting to find his son's killer.

*Which could be why Nakane is so desperate to find someone else to pin this on,* Lydia reminded herself. *It's plausible she could feel the brunt of the investigation – or just the blame – if no one else is available to be Edrick's target.*

"Very well," she said, mirroring the formal tone of the guard. "In that case, I will need access to his home."

The lead guard quirked an eyebrow. "I am certain we could arrange a tour. May I inquire as to the nature of your business?"

"Aladir and I are in the midst of a criminal investigation, and we had hoped to utilize Ulandir as a resource." *Partially true. The elder Ta'thyriel's sorcerous expertise would be quite useful if he is not the culprit.* "In the absence of Aladir's father, I might be able to find something useful in his library. He's known for having an impressive collection, and some of the books may be relevant to our needs."

"I see."

The lead guard hesitated for a few moments, took a breath, and then turned and waved a hand at one of the other uniformed men. "Aloras, please escort the paladin to the library. She is to be given access to any of the books, provided of course that she reads them within the library." He turned back to Lydia. "My apologies, but as much as I would like to, I cannot allow you to remove any of the books without the lord's permission. Unless, of course, you have a writ—"

She waved a hand dismissively. "I'm not putting Ulandir under arrest. This should be quite satisfactory. If I need to withdraw anything, I'm sure I can send Aladir to retrieve it."

"Ah, yes, of course." The elder guard gave a strained smile. "If you require nothing else of me..."

*Hrm, guess I wore him out.* "You've been very helpful. I'll be off to the library now."

\*\*\*

Ulandir's library was as extensive as Lydia had suspected, and searching through it in detail would have taken a considerable amount of time. She contented herself to looking for anything overtly suspicious. The sorceress did not expect to find anything as conspicuous as a book on murder – although she did find a rather fanciful novel supposedly written by the Blackstone Assassin. Instead, she hoped to find anything related to the Dominion of Poison.

House Ta'thyriel was famous for their study of healing – both mundane and sorcerous – and just finding a book on poison would not have been suspicious in itself. She found several scrolls and a few books detailing mundane poisons, their symptoms, and their treatments. They certainly could have justified having a book on the Dominion of Poison, but she didn't find any. With some hesitation, she eventually asked the librarian if they had any, and received a negative in response.

Lydia did find multiple books on the Dominion of Travel – one of the necessary prerequisites for the summoning ritual she had discovered. That was, unfortunately, also nothing that could be used as evidence by itself. Travel sorcery was notoriously difficult, but relatively well-studied due to the utility that it provided. She had even spent a bit of time studying it herself, but only the theory behind it. She had never actually cast any spells of the kind.

During her time in Orlyn, her former friend Veruden had been a practitioner of travel sorcery. He had explained that it was relatively easy to use travel sorcery to enhance your own movement, and much more challenging to use it for its most famous applications – teleportation and summoning.

Teleportation could be used to move from one place to another in an instant. From what Lydia understood about the theory, the spell was actually moving the target into the Plane of Travel, then to another point on the Plane of Travel that corresponded to your destination, and then back out into the Core Plane. Distances on the Plane of Travel differed from distances on the Core Plane, but she was not aware of any published equation with a conversion ratio. Instead, it was more popularly accepted that locations were linked between the planes through concentrations of energy, rather than distance.

There were two main limiting factors on teleportation – conceptualization and strain. The first meant that the caster needed to have a clear concept of the destination for their spell to function – typically, this involved having visited the location before. The easiest form of teleportation was to go somewhere else that was currently in sight, since conceptualizing the movement between those locations was simple.

Travel sorcerers often used objects or locations infused with travel sorcery as beacons for teleporting long distances. Lydia knew that

Veruden had concealed jars of dominion essence in several locations in the low palace to have convenient locations to teleport to, but she found the idea terrifying. Anyone who knew about the jars could have moved them, changing the destination of Veruden's teleportation spells.

The second limitation, strain, was comparatively simple. The further you traveled with a single spell, the more strain the teleportation put on the body. The amount was not directly equivalent to the amount of stress on the body from physically walking the entire distance, but it was considered conventional wisdom that teleporting more than a day's walk was unwise. Physical conditioning helped to tolerate teleportation strain – an experienced long-distance runner could teleport long-distances much more easily than someone without similar conditioning. Similarly, children and the elderly suffered more from teleportation strain.

Interestingly, travel sorcery could be used to cross planar boundaries without exponentially greater strain. Most sorcerers believed that this meant that the planes were not physically distant from one another, but somehow overlapped. The analogy that Lydia had heard was that two planes were like two pieces of parchment in a stack. When standing atop the top piece of paper, the bottom piece is invisible, even though it is a minute distance away. If she wanted to reach the other piece of paper, she did not have to traverse the entire length of the paper to get to the next, she merely needed to find a path through the top paper to the bottom page.

That analogy made traveling to other planes sound simple, but while studying the sorcery books, Lydia realized there were several problems with it. First, the conceptualization limitation – someone who had never been to another plane had no destination to focus on. Without a familiar location, moving to another plane meant going to either a place at random or whatever spot on the other plane was "closest" to where the caster was currently located. In either case, the destination was very probable to be unsafe.

Any given plane was primarily constructed from its namesake dominion, although every plane would have some energy and materials from other adjacent planes. Traveling to the plane of water in a random location meant that you were probably going to appear underwater. Even a sorcerer prepared with spells for breathing underwater might not be safe, however, since the water could be in any possible state, depending on where the sorcerer ended up. The travel sorcerer could appear inside a block of ice larger than a planet, or in a similar sized cloud of water vapor. And water was one of the safest planes – many of the others offered instant death for an unprepared visitor.

Thus, sorcerers typically used other forms of sorcery, such as knowledge and sight sorcery, to scout out possible destinations on other planes well in advance. Existing research could be helpful, but most sorcerers would take the time to verify it to the best of their own ability. From there, the sorcerer would have to research any of the necessary forms of protection to survive on the other plane. Since having access to more than two or three types of sorcery was rare, that typically meant a single sorcerer could not do all of the research, preparations for survival, and teleportation all on their own.

The books that Lydia found were similar to the ones that she had read in the past - mostly containing theory and the application of basic spells. Summoning was advanced enough that she only found a single paragraph on the subject.

*In 2884, a group of Thornguard experimented with the concept of using a "reverse teleportation" spell, referred to as a "summoning" spell in modern nomenclature, for the purpose of bringing a native creature from another plane to the Core Plane. The project garnered the attention and subsequent sponsorship of one of the Vae'kes, whom provided the resources necessary for dozens of attempts. After over a hundred trials, only a single entity was successfully summoned – a creature that resembled one of the Esharen, but with green and brown skin and deer-like horns. The creature reportedly survived the teleportation process, but details are scarce. The project was abandoned shortly thereafter, and all participants sworn to secrecy.*

In the more than two hundred years since the date cited in the book, the study of summoning had advanced significantly, but the paragraph did help to reinforce how difficult and expensive the process was. That only helped to reinforce Lydia's belief that this murder could not have been committed without a strong motive – the cost and level of difficulty was simply too high.

More importantly, the story reminded Lydia that there were many distinct types of life on other planes. Comparatively simple creatures like Fragments, Gatherers, and Harvesters, were well-documented, but every plane had their own types of unique forms of life – and even communicating with the best-known types of extra-planar creatures was difficult. Convincing such an entity to go to the Core Plane to kill someone seemed like more trouble than it was worth.

*Is that even what happened, then? I've been assuming that someone summoned something like a Harvester of Poison and sent it to kill Nakane's brother, but what other options are there?*

She bit her lower lip, considering what other possibilities she could think of.

*Maybe the sorcerer has some kind of home on the Plane of Poison. Rather than summoning a creature from there, he or she simply teleported from the Plane of Poison to the Core Plane, committed the murder, and then returned to that home. Creating a safe location on another plane would be difficult, especially on a plane like that – but not impossible.*

*That ritual we found definitely did look like a summoning ritual, though. Someone could have set it up deliberately to look like a summoning ritual had been used as a form of deflection from their actual methodology, but that's a little unlikely.*

*...but we assumed the exit portal was leading to the same place as the entity was initially summoned from. The sorcerer could have summoned the assassin from anywhere, and then placed the dominion essence of poison in the circle afterward, making the destination different from where it initially came from. Given how strong of a connection to the Dominion of Poison the creature had, however, a native to that plane – or something attuned to it – would still be the most likely case.*

*An Esharen, or another creature that is capable of adapting to dominion energy, could have survived being exposed to powerful poison and taken on an aura like that. Another option to consider, but even more complex than summoning something native to that plane.*

Lydia flipped through another several books before coming to the frustrating realization that she was broadening the possibilities of how the crime had occurred, not narrowing down the culprit. While the information she had gathered would be useful for eliminating subjects that lacked the resources to succeed at the rituals she had witnessed, she needed more definitive evidence to know who to focus her investigation on.

For that, she was going to need a bit more help. She offered her sincere gratitude to the librarian and the guards, and then left to meet with one of the most dangerous men in the world.

\*\*\*

The town of Edgelake was more commonly referred to simply as Hartigan, the surname of the local ruler. It took two days of riding for Lydia to reach the town, but it would have been remiss of her to dismiss Nakane's first suspect simply because of the distance. As the Theas daughter had pointed out, Blake Hartigan was one of few who had the necessary wealth and power to arrange to be teleported back and forth from the city.

*Although,* Lydia considered, *the city's walls are supposed to prevent teleporting directly into the city from outside. Wouldn't that apply to summoning an entity from another plane?*

She frowned at the incongruity and decided that she'd have to investigate the wards to determine exactly how they functioned. Several possibilities occurred to her immediately, but the most concerning was that the summoner might have been powerful enough to bypass the wards with brute power. It was an unlikely possibility, but disconcerting to say the least.

It was more likely that the protection simply did not apply to spells that originated from within the city, which the summoning spell would have – or that something had been built into the defenses to allow them to be bypassed through specific means.

While she didn't find it likely that Hartigan was the culprit, she was well-prepared for a possible confrontation. She wore a saber on her left hip and a dagger on her right, the latter balanced for throwing rather than parrying. The sorceress was also wearing Edon's ring, and though she hadn't been able to activate it yet, she had some ideas on how to force it to function in an emergency situation.

Finally, she had surrounded herself with a Comprehensive Barrier spell – her own personal invention, and practically a second skin during any operation that she considered dangerous. The spell utilized the Dominion of Protection to block attacks, while simultaneously using a Key from the Dominion of Knowledge to identify any offensive spells that struck the barrier. The combination allowed her to make tactical decisions on how to counter the abilities of enemy sorcerers – although she had a pretty good idea of what she'd be facing if she antagonized Hartigan. His reputation for incinerating dozens of enemies at a time had earned him the moniker "The Ember Lord".

The paladin wasn't exactly sure how she'd approach Hartigan, even after two days to think about it. The man was a notorious recluse, even more so than most sorcerers. At least finding him would not be difficult – his residence was a colossal stone tower, standing vigilant over the comparatively minuscule homes of the town's other residents.

The tower itself made sense to Lydia – after all, the vast majority of spells were easier to cast with the target within sight, and the top of a tower was a fantastic vantage point. Hartigan's habits were strange even by the standards of sorcerers, however. Rumors indicated that he spent months isolated in his tower, only to emerge to purchase – or requisition – broad varieties of strange goods from the townsfolk. She had heard stories of the sorcerer levitating a dozen live goats onto the top of his tower before thanking the previous owners and returning to his work.

While stabling her horse at the local inn, Lydia asked a few questions of the other patrons, learning that Hartigan was well-liked in spite of his odd habits. He would respond quickly if the village faced any large problems, and often gave generous gifts with seemingly no concern for their value. And while he had a reputation for being fiercely dangerous, he had apparently never turned his dangerous powers against any of his own people – in fact, they felt safer when he was around.

There didn't appear to be any particular customs for greeting the local lord. While she absently considered bringing some live goats, Lydia settled for simply knocking on the tower's wooden doors.

*I wonder if he can even hear me if he's all the way up there,* Lydia considered, looking upward at the dozen or more floors of the tower looming above her. *Maybe if he marked the door with sound sorcery of some kind to project the noise from knocking—*

The door opened.

Beyond the door stood a woman that looked to be in her forties, folding her arms over a lightly stained apron. "What you want, girl?"

Lydia blinked. "I'm, um, looking for Lord Hartigan."

"'Course you are. Ain't got anyone looking that fancy come calling for me. What you here for?"

Lydia didn't think her travel-worn outfit looked all that fancy, even with her Paladins of Tae'os tabard worn over it, but clearly this woman had different standards. "I'm Lydia Hastings, with the Paladins of Tae'os. I'd like to speak to the lord as part of an investigation."

The older woman sighed, turning around and facing toward a spiral stairway within the tower. "Blake! There's a paladin here to see you!" The older woman turned back around, rubbing her hands on the apron. "Guess you'd better come on in, then."

"Thank you...miss...?"

"Hartigan, dear. Sara Hartigan." She waved a hand, beckoning for Lydia to come in. The paladin took the cue, stepping inside, and Sara closed the door behind them.

"You must be Lord Hartigan's...granddaughter?"

The older woman made a scoffing noise. "You're too kind, dear. I'm his wife. Spare him the judgments for marrying a woman a century his junior. Once you get past around thirty, the years mean less and less."

Lydia nodded uncertainly, doing her best not to show her embarrassment. A man descended the spiral stairway nearby a few moments later, and Lydia raised her head to examine him. A few strands of brown were still visible amongst his graying hair, and his face was deeply lined with the wrinkles of many years of mirth. He was barefoot, wearing plain trousers and a simple linen tunic. The only obvious signs of his wealth were the half-dozen rings on his hands. His age seemed similarly concealed – he walked with a straight back, and without the assistance of a cane. If she had not heard Sara call for Blake, she would have guessed she was seeing someone else entirely – a man in his fifties, perhaps, rather than a sorcerer of over a hundred.

She hadn't been certain what a man who had preserved his own life through sorcery would look like, but she hadn't expected the answer to be "completely normal".

"What's this all about, hm?" The man finally seemed to notice Lydia when he reached the bottom of the steps. "Oh, we have a guest. How can I help you, young lady?"

Lydia glanced at Sara, who seemed to be watching her expectantly. *Well, this is awkward. I'd rather talk to him alone, but I can hardly dismiss the woman in her own home.*

"Well, I suppose I should start by introducing myself. I'm Lydia Hastings, a Major for the Paladins of Tae'os." She didn't typically like to open a conversation with her rank, but when dealing with nobles, it often served to help them take her more seriously. This was especially true when dealing with the older nobles, who didn't tend to give female paladins much respect.

"Been awhile since I've had a visit from a paladin. Blake Hartigan." He approached and extended a hand cordially, and she returned the gesture by clasping his wrist. The sorcerer froze for a moment as she did so, and as she pulled her hand away, he raised his own hand to his chin.

"That ring you're wearing. Are you one of Donovan's students?"

*Oh, resh. Hartigan practically invented the process of enchanting rings. Of course he recognizes it.*

*Better be honest. He'll probably figure it out eventually one way or another.*

Lydia shook her head. "No, I'm afraid not."

"How'd you come about that ring, then?" He shook his head. "You'll have to forgive me, I've been terribly rude. Please, come sit with me."

He turned around without another word, waving a hand for her to follow.

"I suppose I'll go make some tea," Sara said, rolling her eyes.

"Thank you, Miss Hartigan," Lydia said. "Sorry to trouble you."

"Oh, you're fine, dear." The older woman disappeared into a smaller room on the left, humming to herself.

Blake Hartigan led Lydia up the spiral stairway, passing a single door before stopping at the next and waving his hand across a sigil above the door knob. The sigil flickered and vanished, leading Lydia to quirk an eyebrow.

*Most ritual protections require a more complex action for deactivation. How did it detect his wave? Something with the Dominion of Sight, perhaps? Or maybe it isn't actually seeing him — the ward could be triggered by proximity to him...or to one of the rings. It's probably one of the rings.*

He turned the knob, leading Lydia into a sitting room. A single table sat in the center, littered with books and surrounded by plush chairs. A footstool accompanied each chair, an accoutrement that Lydia could appreciate. Tall bookshelves lined the walls, housing an impressive collection of tomes, scrolls, and what looked like vials of liquid on one of the shelves. A single window, sealed with heavy bars, let in light from the outside.

Hartigan patted the back of one of the chairs. "Please, sit," and moved on to sit in the opposite chair. Lydia dutifully followed his instructions. While she was still nervous that he could react poorly to an explanation about how she had obtained the ring – or about why she was there – she didn't see any reason to be discourteous.

Also, the chair was pretty comfortable.

"So," Hartigan began, propping up his feet on the stool next to his chair. "You've got quite an interesting object there, Miss Scryer."

Lydia noted that he had used the name "Scryer", which was not the name she had given him. "Scryer" was the name she had used when she had attended the sorcery academy in Velthryn – it was her adoptive father's surname. It was, notably, also the surname she had used in Orlyn when she had been investigating the local "gods" – one of whom was Donovan, the man Hartigan had mentioned.

*Okay, so he knows something about who I am, and he wants me to know that. Interesting, but not necessarily a threat. Not yet, anyway. He might just have heard my name sometime at the academy – he did teach classes there, even if I never took any of them.*

"Yes, thank you. You have some exceptionally fine rings yourself. Is one of those the legendary Hartigan's Star? I've always wanted to see it."

The older man leaned his chin into the knuckles of his left hand, smirking slightly. "No, these are lesser trinkets, I'm afraid. Perhaps I can show you the ring later. Is that why you're here?"

She shook her head. "No, I'm afraid I have some official business to discuss."

Hartigan nodded, leaning back. "I suspected as much. Indulge my curiosity, however. How did you come upon Donovan's ring?"

*Well, nothing to do but gamble at this point, one way or another.*

"Several months ago, Donovan Tailor was masquerading as a god in the city of Orlyn. I was involved in his arrest, and confiscated this ring in the process."

Hartigan chuckled lightly, shaking his head. "Oh, that boy. Too smart for his own good. I knew he'd get himself into trouble. I hoped the ring might help keep him out of it, but that was too much to hope for, I suppose."

Lydia wasn't sure what to say next, so she remained silent and as still as possible.

"Pretending to be a god. Such ridiculousness. He always had delusions of grandeur, but I had hoped I had taught him to have the sense not to act on them. He was an idealist, though. Still is, I imagine, if he's alive. Did you kill him?"

The sorceress shook her head. "No, I assisted in his arrest, and he was turned in to the queen for a trial. As far as I'm aware, he was not executed."

"How were you able to apprehend him? Donovan was no amateur sorcerer, and one of the most paranoid men I've ever met."

Lydia tensed her jaw, not sure how much to say. "I investigated his capabilities to the best of my ability. When an opportunity presented itself, I incapacitated him using sorcery. I also had help."

Hartigan scratched at his chin. "Interesting. Incapacitated him how? He was fairly good at protection sorcery, if I recall."

*He's trying to gauge my abilities,* she realized. *Which could mean he's planning for a fight. It could just be honest curiosity, I suppose. Sorcerers do tend to love hearing about fights between other sorcerers. Still, I should be careful what I say.*

"One of my allies was able to disable Donovan's barrier. From there, I knocked him out with a simple sleep spell."

*After intercepting an attack on Taelien, hitting Donovan's barrier repeatedly, faking my death when I was enveloped by one of Donovan's spells, and enhancing one of Jonan's illusions with a protective barrier to make it appear to be corporeal. But Hartigan doesn't need to know about those little details.*

"A sleep spell." Hartigan covered his mouth, laughing deeply into it. "That has to be the most ignominious way a deity – fake or not - has ever been defeated." The man made a circular gesture with his hand, taking a tiny bow at the waist. "And you managed to walk off with his ring. 'Confiscated for the paladins of Tae'os', or somesuch, I imagine? You have my commendations, miss."

The sorceress wasn't quite sure, but she was fairly confident she was blushing. "Thank you, sir."

"You wouldn't happen to know what happened after you…," he snorted, "put Donovan to sleep, would you?"

Lydia shrugged at that. "I don't know much, to be honest. I doubt he'd be executed. He was the leader of the local 'gods' for years, after all – that might make too much of an uproar. As far as I'm aware, he's still imprisoned."

"Imprisonment may be a harsher fate for a man such as him. I doubt he'll ever stop searching for ways to escape – but never mind that."

He lifted a hand, pointing it at the ring. "I made that, you know. And no, that isn't Hartigan's Star, either, if you were wondering." He smiled softly. "It was an earlier version. The seventeenth of them. I scrapped most of them, using the materials for the next copy, but a few I gave to especially promising apprentices – such as Donovan."

Lydia quirked a brow, genuinely surprised. "Donovan was your apprentice? I never read anything about that in his files."

"No, just like no one will read about this visit in your file, unless you choose to tell them about it." She saw a hint of mirth in the older man's eye. "Most people who come to me for training do so discretely, especially paladins and priests. I have a bit of a reputation, you see."

Lydia let herself chuckle at that remark, while playing over the implications in her head. *So, he's trained paladins and priests before? How many, aside from Donovan? And what does he teach them?*

*Is he how Donovan learned how to extend his life?*

That was a loose end she had never completely tied up. She had figured out how Donovan was making his "miracles" and imbuing others with sorcery – but the man had also appeared too young for his physical age, much like Hartigan himself did. Powerful sorcerers like Edrick Theas and Blake Hartigan were so notoriously secretive that she had assumed that Donovan had found a new method.

*And Jonan hypothesized that Donovan was extending his life through sacrificing the Rethri,* she recalled. *But we determined that he wasn't doing that – he was experimenting with Rethri dominion bonds. And I never investigated Donovan's agelessness afterward; it just didn't seem important, once we had the details of how he was doing everything else.*

*Interesting.*

"Are you implying that you'd be willing to train me?" Lydia asked, intrigued in spite of herself. This wasn't what she was there for, and her professional instincts were inwardly kicking her, but she had to ask.

"I'd be willing to entertain the possibility. I could use an assistant around the lab, and good help is hard to come by. But I've already delayed your own inquiries quite enough. I've been quite rude, forgive me. If you're here on paladin business, please, tell me what it pertains to."

Resh, he was good. She already hadn't wanted to antagonize him, since he was tremendously dangerous. Now she also wanted to stay on his good side so she could try to take advantage of the possibility of training under him. If anyone knew how to figure out how to make the ring work, it would be the man who made it – and Hartigan undoubtedly had far greater secrets. Like immortality, for example.

His manipulations were impressive, but loyalty, unfortunately, came first.

"I'm here as part of a murder investigation. Kalsiris Theas was killed six days ago. You are one of the possible suspects."

Hartigan's expression darkened immediately.

"Kae was murdered? The poor boy. His father must be crushed. How did this happen?"

Lydia sat up in her chair. *Hartigan's use of the nickname 'Kae' certainly implies he knew the victim. And he didn't even address the fact that I just mentioned he was a suspect.*

"I'm afraid I can't give you too many details until I've ruled you out as a possible suspect. I apologize. I can say honestly that I find it unlikely that you were responsible, given your remote location, but—"

"But I have a well-documented rivalry with Edrick, yes. Of course. When two men know each other for over a hundred years, there are bound to be conflicts of interest from time to time. I assure you that my disagreements with Edrick were – and still are – philosophical and academic in nature. I would never commit violence toward him, and certainly not to his family."

Lydia nodded. "Where were you on the evening of the seventh, around – no, let's just say the whole evening."

The man shrugged his shoulders. "I don't keep that close of track... I mean, I was here, that much is certain. I haven't been out of the tower in a month. I don't remember specifics. I could go check my alchemical notes, I suppose."

"Alchemical notes?"

"As I'm sure you're aware, I make potions, salves, and elixirs of all sorts. Many of them require adding ingredients at specific intervals. After singing off my eyebrows the first few times, I learned to take extensive notes."

"I would be interested in seeing those notes. If they include anything that occurred during the time of the attack, that could be some slim evidence in your favor, although obviously such notes could be easily faked if you had committed the attack and planned on being investigated."

Hartigan nodded. "Yes, of course. I'll retrieve the notes. Please wait here."

He stood up and retreated from the room. Lydia absently felt for the comforting presence of her barrier spell, which remained intact.

*If he's going to try to kill me, now would probably be the time to do it.*

The sorceress sat facing the doorway, glancing from side to side periodically, and keeping her hand near the hilt of her saber. She resisted the urge to search the room while Hartigan was absent – it would be somewhat rude if he wasn't intending to murder her.

The older man returned a few minutes later with a thick stack of parchment, setting it down on the table a moment later. "You'll have to forgive me, I just grabbed a whole section. I haven't had a chance to parse through it and find the night you spoke of yet. If you wouldn't mind..."

"I'll take half the stack," she offered with only a slight grimace, taking his cue.

Parsing through the notes was dull work. They were exhaustive, just as he had claimed, but not in any obvious order. Usually, two or three adjacent pages corresponded to the same date, but papers didn't always sit next to the ones from the next date. By the time she found the night of the attack, she suspected that he organized the papers based on the components used in the potions, presumably so he could keep track of any unusual results or his current stocks of each.

"I found something," she noted, slipping out a few pieces from the pile. There were, in fact, notes that seemed to cover the entire evening of Kalsiris' death – but with at least two notable gaps of a few hours.

"It looks like you were not working on any potions for about three hours here," she noted.

"Hardly enough time to travel to Velthryn, wouldn't you say?" The older man set down his stack of papers, shrugging. "I was probably having dinner."

"It could be enough time if you teleported," Lydia pointed out.

"Ah, was teleportation involved in the crime?" Hartigan scratched at his chin.

*Still prying for more information.* "It might have been. I assume your wife would vouch for your presence, but frankly, that doesn't amount to much, either."

"Well, it's dreadfully hard to prove a negative, as I'm sure you know. What would you need to rule out my involvement?"

*What, indeed?* It was an excellent question. She hadn't been directly involved in a murder investigation before – her research on Donovan was probably the most similar situation, although she had also traced smaller crimes back to specific sorcerers in the past. She had a spell for identifying which specific dominions a sorcerer had access to, and that was typically quite useful, especially for finding obscure dominions.

She had considered using the same methodology for this case, but most of the spells she could cast on Hartigan wouldn't provide any sort of certainty, since he was famous for utilizing enchanted items and potions. Even if he wasn't personally capable of casting travel or poison sorcery, he could have an item – or even an apprentice, since apparently he had those – capable of casting the spell.

"It would be difficult to prove your innocence definitively without evidence you were here at the time of the crime. At the moment, I'm more interested in finding evidence that could potentially indicate that you are the killer – and, in the absence of that, I can move on to look into other culprits."

"Very well." Hartigan clapped his hands together. "I will give you full access to the tower for your investigation. I'll be interested to see your process, in fact."

That latter sentence added an unstated restriction, and one that could be potentially frustrating – he would be watching her progress. Granted, it was fairly reasonable for him to make sure she was escorted while she was rifling through his possessions…especially since, embarrassingly enough, he already knew that she had "confiscated" Donovan's ring. He also appeared to have protective wards, and his presence might be necessary to deactivate them.

All in all, it wasn't ideal, but she couldn't see a way to avoid letting him follow her around while she investigated the tower.

It was going to be a long day.

# CHAPTER XII – TAELIEN III – THERE ARE ALWAYS MORE ASSASSINS

Second Lieutenant Banks was standing outside the briefing room when Taelien arrived.

"You're almost late." She leaned forward slightly as she spoke, lending an extra edge to her monotone voice.

Taelien paused in his step and saluted. "Yes, ma'am. Sorry, ma'am."

He had taken an extra few minutes to prepare his equipment, but he was relatively certain he had arrived at least ten minutes before he had been instructed to. He knew that arriving earlier might have given him more of a chance to gather information about the test, but he felt that being better supplied would be even more important. His message had implied that he was about to be sent on a mission immediately, so he had packed for potentially leaving the city. That meant food supplies, water, and miscellaneous camping equipment. Fortunately, he had most of those supplies readily available in his storage chest – he simply needed to organize them and throw them into a backpack.

The lieutenant crisply returned his salute, allowing Taelien to lower his own hand.

"Since time is short, I will be brief. You will be participating in another simulation. Is that the reproduction sword we gave you?" She pointed at the Sae'kes, which was sitting on his right hip. He had the red-bladed sword sheathed on his left side.

"No, ma'am. I wasn't told this would be another simulation—"

"You should be more prepared next time. I do see you have another weapon – you'll have to use that if you engage in any combat. The real Sae'kes is simply too dangerous."

174

"Yes, ma'am."

Lieutenant Banks slowly approached him, looking him up and down. "Tuck your shirt into your pants properly."

"Yes, ma'am." Taelien adjusted his uniform. He had checked it relatively carefully before coming here – uniform inspections had been a daily affair when he trained with the Thornguard, and he had expected similar from the paladins. Thus far, they had generally proven to be much more lax, and this was no exception. If his uniform had been misaligned during Thornguard training, he would have been running laps at a minimum and possibly assigned to some kind of disciplinary responsibility. This was, of course, almost unavoidable – an instructor could always find something wrong if they wanted to.

Lieutenant Banks seemed to want that kind of discipline, but she either lacked the rank or the will to enforce it to the same standards that the Thornguard had. Perhaps the paladins who had been promoted from squire status had been subjected to more rigorous training – or maybe the Koranir branch was simply more traditional than others. Taelien didn't have the necessary context to say.

"Better. I'm going to place a protective ward on you. Once that's been done, you can enter the room and begin the test."

*She's not going to ask if I have any questions?*

*Should I be asking questions?*

"Yes, ma'am," he replied out of habit more than any sort of conscious decision.

Lieutenant Banks laid a hand on Taelien's arm. "Dominion of Protection, form a layer of armor around Applicant Salaris."

He felt a slight tingle as a translucent field manifested around his body. He knew from experience that the armor spell would dampen the impact of attacks, much like real armor, rather than stopping attacks entirely like Lydia's shield spells. The advantage of the armor spell was that it didn't buckle as easily from impacts, potentially making it more efficient for a longer term fight.

*So, either I could be involved in some heavy combat here, or they just want me to feel it if I actually get hit by someone. Interesting.*

Banks stepped back to the door and knocked three times.

"Hey, stop right there!" The voice was unmistakable – just as unmistakable as the ring of steel that followed immediately thereafter. Velas was inside and engaged in battle.

"You may begin," Banks said, but Taelien was already moving. The red-bladed sword was already in his right hand as he put his left on the door's handle.

As he swung the door open, Taelien saw Velas falling backward. She was too far for him to reach her before she hit the floor, her sword flying from her grip. Her attacker turned to glance at him for an instant as the door opened, a paladin's long sword in his hand. He or she was wearing a mask, but Taelien wasn't concerned about that.

*Chain.*

One of the first things Taelien had tested on the red-bladed sword was his own metal sorcery. Since it appeared to absorb some amount of other forms of sorcery, he wasn't sure if attempting to reshape it would be possible.

It turned out to be easier. Rather than having to hammer a steel plate into a different shape, it was like bending metal that was still hot from the forge. The red metal was easily malleable, which meant that tricks that normally took significant effort – like this one – required little more than a casual flick of a thought.

He swung the sword even as the blade reshaped itself, thinning and lengthening, the edges rounding into links. The would-be assassin raised his weapon to block, but that just gave Taelien another vector to manipulate. The chain's momentum carried it just once around the target's body, but that was enough to make it briefly intersect with itself, and that was all he needed.

*Stick,* Taelien commanded, pushing his will into the spots where the chain met itself and his opponent's blade. The metal merged together, forming a lasso of steel, and he pulled hard.

The assassin planted his feet, bracing both hands on the hilt of his sword to resist the strain of the pull. Velas, still on the floor, sighed and swept the assassin's right leg.

The assassin slipped, Taelien pulled, and the white-masked figure came soaring toward him.

Taelien grinned and punched the incoming assassin in the face. A blue barrier flickered into place – and visibly cracked as Taelien's fist smashed into it. The mask beneath it cracked in a similar pattern.

The assassin staggered, falling backward from the punch, but recovered quickly. Abandoning the sword hilt, he ducked out from the loop of the sword-chain and drew a knife from within his cloak, turning to rush back toward Velas.

Salaris wasn't having any of that. He jumped on top of the assassin, slamming him into the floor. An errant elbow glanced across the barrier in front of his chin, but the impact would have been negligible even without the barrier spell.

"You're going to want to surrender now," Taelien noted, trying to find and secure the assassin's weapon. The masked figure seemed freakishly agile, however, and somehow managed to duck out of his cloak and flip over, swinging his knife at Salaris' throat. Taelien raised his left arm and blocked the cut, drawing a flicker from the barrier in response, and then punched the assassin in the face again. The force of the blow slammed the masked figure's head into the floor, and he went momentarily still, dagger slipping through his fingers.

"You okay, Velas?" Taelien yelled louder than was strictly necessary, still looking at the assassin.

"I'm, um, just feeling a little lightheaded. I think I'm just going to lie here for a minute."

*Lightheaded? That's not a good sign.*

Taelien shifted his position on his downed opponent, reaching out with his left hand to smack the hilt of the dagger, sending it several feet out of the way. With that threat eliminated, he pulled his sword-chain closer and began to loop it back over his downed enemy.

"Hang in there, Velas. Be with you in a moment."

A single loop clearly hadn't been sufficient. *Extend.* Taelien lengthened the chain, wrapping it underneath the assassin's elbows and between his legs. Finally, he bunched a section together over the assassin's chest. *Fuse.* The target was thoroughly wrapped now, somewhat reminding him of how he had been imprisoned in his first encounter with Lydia – although his captors had chained him in a much more mundane fashion.

It occurred to him that spreading the chain so thin could make it malleable enough to break if the assassin was sufficiently strong, but he had tested the limits of a chain of similar dimensions before and it had proved fairly resilient. He probably could have broken it himself – even without metal sorcery – but he had always been unusually adept at breaking things.

"Hey, assassin. You awake?"

The target groaned, indicating at least some degree of consciousness.

"Uh, Taelien, not to alarm you, but my head is getting kind of swimmy."

Taelien stood up, still holding the handle of his sword as a method of controlling his chained enemy. He walked closer to Velas, dragging the assassin along the floor, carefully avoiding putting the man anywhere near where the Velas or the assassin had dropped their weapons.

Now that he was closer, Taelien could easily see that Velas had a long gash across her right arm. That explained why she had dropped her sword, but he doubted that it was why she was feeling so lightheaded – it was a long cut, but not particularly deep, and she didn't seem to be the type to faint at the sight of her own blood.

"How's your arm feel?" He knelt down beside her, glancing back at the assassin, who was just barely beginning to try to free himself from the chains.

"Cold. I feel very cold, Sal."

"Okay, stay with me. You've always been better with this medical stuff, and I might need you to talk me through helping you."

Velas frowned. "I'm not sure...I can..." Her eyes fluttered, and she took a deep breath.

Taelien slapped her, triggering flickering barrier sparks. Her eyes widened with shock, and she shuddered slightly. "What was that for?"

"You were losing consciousness. Don't do that."

"I was just closing my eyes for—"

"No. I need you focused. I think you're poisoned. I'm bad at poisons. You're not."

"I'm so tired, Sal. I don't think I can..."

Taelien grit his teeth. "Just don't fall asleep. I'm going to get help."

"That sounds nice."

Taelien turned back to the assassin, who seemed to have recovered sufficiently to start wriggling his way out of the chains. The swordmsan snarled and yanked on the sword's handle, pulling the assassin close enough for Taelien to kick him in the ribs.

"So, you poisoned my friend. I'm not very pleased about that. This would be a good time for you to start talking."

"Death to the followers of the false gods. Death to any who oppose the Preserver!"

Taelien raised an eyebrow. *Really? My villain in this scenario is some kind of cultist of Vaelien?*

*Or, maybe not a cultist. Black cloak, scary mask, poison — is he supposed to be a Blackstone?*

Taelien knelt down and grabbed the assassin by the shoulders, flipping him over. The cloak had been left behind on the floor nearby, leaving the assassin wearing a simple black tunic and pants. Taelien grabbed the collar of the shirt and pulled it down, revealing a tattoo of a black sphere surrounded by three markings – the Rethri symbols for thorn, iron, and loyalty.

*Well, at least they got the marks right, even if you'd never see someone of this kind of rank in the field.*

"A Blackstone Harbinger, eh? Awful sloppy for someone of your stature – I would have expected better."

"Shut up." The assassin squirmed, but Taelien put a knee on his chest.

"Anyway, if you're a Blackstone, you're carrying the antidote for your own poisons. Standard procedure. Just tell me where it is and I'll make sure we're lenient during the trial."

The assassin made a scoffing noise. "You think I care about your perverted justice? There is only one true arbiter of justice, and his name is Jac—"

"Yes, yes, Jacinth, everyone fears the Blackstone Assassin. Okay, stay there a second."

Taelien shoved the assassin hard into the floor, standing back up. He walked to where the assassin had dropped his weapon, dragging the assassin along the floor as he did, and picked up the fallen weapon with his left hand.

There was blood on the blade – presumably Velas' blood. The fight had presumably only gone on for moments before he arrived, so Taelien doubted the assassin had hit her with any other weapons. That meant this one was, in all likelihood, the poisoned one.

There was only a faint hint of a green sheen on the edge – most of it was obscured by the blood. Like many of the most effective poisons, only a tiny amount of this poison was likely necessary for the effect.

Taelien sat down on the assassin's back, and with the utmost care, ran the poisoned sword across the Blackstone's leg.

"Okay, then. Just a leg wound for now. Even if the poison is really bad – which it probably is – your antidote can probably cover a leg wound."

"I'm – you couldn't have – a paladin wouldn't –"

"You know, I'm not actually a paladin just yet. And I'm really not feeling all that paladin-like at the moment, truth be told. More like one of the Thornguard, who, you know, trained me for several years. Believe me, this only scratches the surface on interrogation techniques. If my friend stops breathing, you're in for quite an education."

"The pouch on my belt, on the left side. There should be enough for both of us," the assassin hissed. "You should know that you did not break me. This is a practical measure – the initiate was not my true target."

"I'd love to hear more about that in a moment." Taelien used his left hand – still holding the assassin's sword - to keep the assassin pushed to the floor while he looked for the belt pouch. The assassin had more than one of them, as well as a couple more daggers sheathed on his sides. Taelien set down the hilt of his sword-chain, drew the daggers and casually tossed them across the room, and then found the appropriate pouch and removed a vial of fluid.

The liquid inside was a murky green, not unlike the fluid Taelien had seen on the blade. Taelien frowned, briefly lifting the sword back up to smell the edge. The stench of blood was too strong to get much of a scent, but he nevertheless lowered the blade and unstoppered the vial, smelling it to compare.

"Not really sure I trust that this is the antidote, so I'm going to test it on you first. I'm sure half a vial of poison in your wound will kill you faster than Velas is dying over there, so if this is poison, you'd probably want to tell me now."

The assassin was silent for several moments, so Taelien began to pour the liquid onto the assassin's leg. As soon as the fluid hit the assassin's leg, he began to squirm, but Taelien continued to pour.

"Wait, no, stop. That's Sythus viper venom – I was lying before. I – I didn't think you'd go through with it. I don't want to die."

"The real antidote. Talk."

"It's in my right boot."

"Last chance to be honest here. You play me again, I'm just going to cut your throat and call for a healer for my friend."

"I- I understand. The antidote, please. Get me first. You used so much of the venom, I won't have much time."

Taelien stoppered the vial and carefully set it on the floor and rolled it across the room. He didn't like the idea of breaking the vial, but most poisons that the Blackstones used weren't dangerous unless they got into the bloodstream – which was what he had been counting on when he poured some of it out.

He removed the assassin's boot, found the vial of blue fluid within, and patted the assassin on the head.

"You just stay there. Behave, and I'll be back for you."

Velas was shivering on the floor, her eyes closed. Taelien pulled the stopper out of the vial and sniffed at it. *Smells like maybe adenas root? I've never been good at antidotes. It doesn't smell like poison, at least, and I'm pretty sure he's out of decoys.*

He began to pour the blue liquid onto Velas' wound. White bubbles formed on contact, making a sizzling noise, and Velas began to shudder. Taelien stoppered the vial, set it on the floor, and put a hand under her head to hold her through her convulsions. After several moments, she settled into what looked like a more peaceful sleep.

"Help me," the assassin mumbled. "I don't want to die."

"I'll be back, just give me a moment."

Taelien shook his head. He glanced over Velas' seemingly-unconscious body for any further injuries, but he didn't see any. He was tempted to wake her again, but he wasn't sure if that was the wisest idea, or if it would even work. *Resh, she's so much better at this triage stuff than I am. Wish she could talk me through it.*

Taelien slipped the blue vial into his backpack and walked back over to the assassin, who was whimpering on the floor. He leaned down and kicked the assassin's sword out of the way, then grabbed the handle of the sword chain. "We're going to go for a walk now."

"But my leg – I'm going to die. You promised –"

Taelien shook his head. "First off, I never promised I'd give you the antidote. But you can relax, anyway. I never even cut you."

"...what?"

Taelien rolled the assassin over, and then pushed him to a seated position. The assassin hesitantly lifted his leg. The pant leg had been split apart and drenched with poison, but the leg beneath was unscathed. "I just put enough pressure on the blade to cut through the cloth. I knew you'd feel that and just assume that I was cutting through flesh, too. It's often hard to feel a wound when a sword is razor sharp, and the mind plays all sorts of tricks when you can't actually see what's happening."

The assassin lowered his head, silent for several moments. And then he burst into laughter. "You...you never even..."

"Nope, never cut you. Wouldn't risk losing whatever information you have, even if you hurt my friend. I need to know who sent you, and who your 'real' target was, if it wasn't Velas. So, you're going to come with me."

The assassin laughed again, slowly rising to his feet as Taelien pulled on the chain. "You're serving the wrong masters. That game you played – you should have been one of us."

"No," Taelien shook his head. "But I almost was."

***

Hours later, Taelien and Velas sat atop Calor's Vista, a rocky hill on the northern side of the paladin base. It was the highest place they knew of on the grounds, as far from oversight as they could be without violating the rules of their tests. They dangled their feet over the edge of a rocky cleft overlooking the base, watching the shadows spread as the dawnfire retreated below the horizon.

"So," Taelien turned his head slightly toward Velas. "How do you think I did?"

She turned sideways to face him directly, smirking. "I think you should have taken off my pants."

Taelien blinked, recoiling slightly. "Um, what?"

Velas laughed, a sincere laugh that brought an unconscious smile to Taelien's face. "You're so easy to bait." She patted the lower half of her left leg. "You didn't check me for other wounds. I was supposed to have another wound on my leg. Just from a kick, fortunately – when I had my test, Landen had a 'cut' on his leg, which was a lot worse. My neck was also supposed to be injured from the fall, but honestly, I doubt very many people would have checked that."

Taelien lowered his head. "Do you think I failed?"

"Don't think so, but they're definitely going to hit you for not checking me carefully enough. Next time, make sure to give me a thorough examination, yeah?"

He chuckled. "You're shameless. But thanks for the honest answer, even if it does make me nervous."

"Relax. You got the bad guy. I was impressed – I let mine get away. I thought that was the point, picking saving your friend over taking the assassin down. Now I'm not so sure."

*If they used Landen as the victim for her – and her for me – that might mean that they were trying to compromise our judgment. Or, like she assumed, maybe the opposite – trying to ensure that we "did the right thing" and prioritized our friend. Paladins of Tae'os are supposed to prioritize saving lives over all else, after all.*

"I left you behind." He turned away from her.

"Cheer the resh up. You're so moody sometimes." She slid closer to him on the rocks, putting a hand on his shoulder. "It was just a test, Sal."

He frowned, turning his gaze back toward her. "Sure, but it might have been indicative of our personalities. I think that's the point. I went straight for the attack. Sure, I faked poisoning the guy, but I still won't claim that I was thinking clearly. I wanted to hurt him. I knew none of it was real, but my instincts were screaming at me – to hurt him. To break the person who hurt you."

"Well, I find that flattering, personally. That means you really wanted to protect me." She slid her hand down his arm, grabbing his own hand. "And if you feel bad about leaving me behind, just don't do it again, yeah?"

*Protecting you…is that what it was about?*
*I'm not so sure.*

Nevertheless, he nodded. "I'll… I'll make sure I won't make the same mistake twice. I won't leave you behind again."

"Also, be more careful about checking for injuries."

He rolled his eyes. "You don't need to preach. I got the point the first time."

"Did you? I think we might need to practice."

Taelien shrugged. "All right, I'll let you teach me a few tricks sometime."

Velas smirked, brushing a strand of blonde hair out of her eyes. "I'll hold you to that."

## CHAPTER XIII – JONAN III – SILK

The sight sorcerer felt naked in his visibility, but occasionally it proved necessary to go to a public area without concealing his location. As he glanced at the tavern patrons, he felt a weight at the back of his mind, a pressing need to remove himself from the situation. He resisted the urge. He had business to attend to.

Jonan approached the bar, finding an empty spot and leaning up against it, attempting to look natural. After a pair of painful minutes of waiting, one of the two bartenders approached. He was a younger man – even by Jonan's standards –more than likely too young to even drink the stock.

"What can I get ya?" The boy offered a grin. "Rum, maybe? You look like you could use something with a kick."

He shook his head fervently. "No, thank you." *Although you might not be wrong.* "I'm here to meet someone. A young lady who enjoys the sharp wine."

"Oh! I get you. Give me a moment and I'll show you the way."

A moment turned into several more nervous minutes, until the boy finally returned and gave him a wordless gesture to follow. Jonan was more than eager to comply – he had felt the weight of several looks while he had been waiting. The worst of them was from a perpetually grinning man with white hair, who sat seemingly alone at a table, a game board of some kind in front of him.

The boy bartender led him to a back room, knocked on the door twice, and then turned the knob. The room beyond was no simple storage area – it was a lavishly decorated chamber like one might have expected in a wealthy noble's home, with embroidered red carpeting and a single table in the center decorated with candles to provide illumination. Several paintings graced the walls, and Jonan realized with discomfort that he was almost certain that most of them depicted the Vae'kes Aayara in varying stages of her life.

The young woman that sat at one of the two chairs adjacent to the table bore a close enough resemblance to some of the paintings that she might have been mistaken for the subject herself – but Jonan knew Aayara well enough to spot subtler differences. The seated woman was several inches taller than the legendary Lady of Thieves, and although she was relatively slim, her musculature was far better defined than Aayara's. Her blonde hair showed hints of black at the roots, implying that her hair had been bleached and dyed.

This was not Symphony herself – but the apprentice made a passable fabrication. Few survived having the level of personal contact with Aayara to be able to account for the minor differences.

Jonan shut the door behind him and spoke first. "Loyalty is like a crystal sword."

"Really? The same one I used last time?" The faux-Symphony sighed theatrically – which echoed around the room in a hint of effortless sound sorcery – and shook her head. "Sharp and beautiful, but easily shattered. You going to sit?"

He smirked and approached, taking the opposite chair. She had incidentally confirmed not only the code, but her own identity. *That phrase is inane, but it did serve a useful purpose.* He never used it elsewhere – meaning that the woman was the same person who had met him on the rooftop, or someone who had been privy to their conversation. The latter was significantly less likely, given how severely Aayara would punish giving that kind of information to anyone outside of her inner circle.

*Silk. Her resemblance to her master must be intentional. Perhaps it's an element of Aayara's narcissism, but I suspect it's more likely the image is tailored to cultivate a reaction. A reminder of her connection with one of the most dangerous people in the world. Or, for those who aren't familiar with Aayara's exact appearance, it might even be sufficient to play at being Symphony herself.*

There was a nagging sense of familiarity about the woman – something that might have gone beyond the resemblance to their mutual contact – but he couldn't quite place it. The last time he thought he had seen her, she had worn heavy veils like Symphony herself was renowned for. Had he seen her prior to that, or since?

He took note of the pair of glasses of wine on the table as he approached and sat. "I didn't think anyone took the 'sharp wine' thing literally."

Silk plucked her own glass from the table with two fingers – a sign of dexterity that Jonan himself lacked – and sipped from it. "I enjoy occasional indulgences in both puns and drink." She took another sip. "What about you?"

He picked up the glass with significantly less elegance than she had demonstrated, took a dubious sniff – it didn't *smell* like poison, not that such a test was in any way reliable – and sipped at it. *Huh. That* is *sharp wine.*

The scribe swallowed the drink with a grimace. Silk raised her gloved left hand to her face, chuckling lightly.

"Not to your taste? I suppose I could offer you something sweeter." She reached into a pouch on her left hip, drawing Jonan's attention to her outfit.

Silk was wearing a long nondescript grey skirt and matching long-sleeved top. Her belt had a large brown pouch on the left side and a simple sheathed dagger on the right. He could faintly make out the outlines of objects inside the sleeves, pressed against her forearms – most likely a thinner variety of daggers. He had tried the same thing himself, but he had a difficult time drawing them quickly enough, even from specially tailored garb with sleeves sewn in for the weaponry. Her gloves were a hint darker than the rest of her outfit, and on the way over to the table he had caught sight of her knee-length black boots, which likely contained more concealed weapons.

He resisted the urge to flinch when she drew something out of the pouch. It wasn't another weapon – just a red apple. Which, he realized as she turned it over in her hand, she was peeling with a half-exposed knife that now jutted out of her sleeve. He hadn't seen her make the gesture necessary to expose the blade, which was somewhat impressive, given his own experience at sleight-of-hand.

*Showoff.*

But he wouldn't complain. He liked apples. They were fantastic.

"I'd love some of that, actually. And some information."

Her expression briefly twisted into a mock pout, and she flicked her fingers. He caught the apple-quarter in mid-flight, taking a bite from it. That, at least, solicited a grin in response.

"Next time you invite a girl out to dinner, the least you could do is give her a few minutes of polite banter before you get into business. But I'll bite." She bit into another quarter of the apple, balancing the remaining half of the fruit on the table. "What do you need?"

This part was always awkward. "Well, there's been a murder."

Silk took another bite from her apple, producing an audible crunch. "And this concerns us how?"

"The victim was Edrick Theas' son."

Crunch.

"Still not seeing the concern."

Jonan took a small bite of his own apple slice. "Did you kill him?"

The athletic woman tilted her head to the side. "No?"

He nodded. "He's a pretty high profile figure. Not many people would have the necessary resources. People will be investigating our end eventually – I figured it better that I check in advance, in case I needed to do some sweeping for you."

"Appreciate the concern." She finished her quarter, picking up the half-apple that was still on the table. "Was that all?"

Jonan shook his head. "If it wasn't you, it could still be someone else from the guild."

"I doubt it." She picked up her glass of wine with two fingers of her off-hand, shaking it in the air, causing the liquid to swish around inside. "I might have ordered the sharp wine, but the reality is that the guild rarely takes on that kind of business these days. I never do it personally – risk isn't worth the reward. You'd be better off looking at your own people, I suspect."

*My own people? Who does she think I work for, exactly?*

She was probably talking about the Thornguard – the military branch of the Priesthood of Vaelien. That implied that she *wasn't* Thornguard, which he found somewhat surprising.

Silk was definitely the title of Symphony's personal apprentice – he had heard that name thrown around for years – and Symphony was Velrya's guild name for the Vae'kes Aayara. Symphony was, at least as far as he was aware, the most famous member of the guild – that was how she had developed her reputation as the "Lady of Thieves". There were conflicting reports about whether or not she was also the master of the guild, which was consistent with the conflicting reports about just about everything else concerning Aayara.

Jonan was an "Ess" – meaning he had a guild name starting with the letter "S", indicating he was in Symphony's personal employ. He was not, however, a member of any thieves guild, although he had worked with them on several occasions. His assignments typically came from Aayara directly, although he was occasionally loaned out to other senior Vae'kes or high ranking members of the Thornguard.

He had worked with members of the thieves' guild before, but he had assumed that Silk was like him – closer to the Thornguard side than the guild side of Aayara's business. Now, it sounded more like Silk was exclusively a guild agent – in fact, upon reflection, he had never heard Silk refer to Symphony as "Aayara". Thornguard and other Vae'kes almost always used the personal name, and guild agents generally called her Symphony. Jonan had met some guild members who weren't even aware that Symphony was the Lady of Thieves - it was nonsensical that her apprentice might be one of them, but he decided to tread carefully in this conversation, just in case.

*Maybe Aayara keeps us working on one side or the other to prevent any one person from getting access to too much information. An apprentice with intimate knowledge of both guild activities and Thornguard resources could be a liability if she was ever captured or persuaded to adjust her loyalties.*

"Yes," he replied simply after a long pause, "I think I'll do that." He scratched at his chin, debating a risk. "Have you heard of a man named Cassius Morn?"

The young woman turned her head upward for a moment, giving an impression that she was considering, and then shook her head. "Doesn't sound familiar. Why do you ask?"

Jonan pressed his lips together, contemplating. *Giving her too much information could make her a liability. On the other hand, if there's a rogue Thornguard agent in the city, she could potentially be a target.* "He's dangerous. Former Thornguard. Weapons expert. I don't think he's involved, but he might be. I wouldn't let him sneak up on you."

Silk took another sip of her wine, set it down, and tossed the apple into the air. Before it landed, the fruit had been bisected again, and an apple quarter landed in front of him. Jonan picked it up, inspecting the perfect symmetry of the cut.

*Definitely a show-off.*

"Your concern is touching. But this can't be all you called me here for," the young woman pried in a teasing tone.

Jonan finished the first quarter of the apple he had been offered and took a bite of the second slice, thinking while he chewed. "Assuming I find that no one related to our various organizations was responsible, do you have any guesses as to where else I should look?"

The apprentice raised a finger to her lips, raising her eyes in a thoughtful expression. "You've checked with Hartigan, I assume?"

"Ly – someone is looking into that angle."

"All right, what about Tarren?" She lifted her remaining quarter of the apple, slashed it again, and took a bite out of one of the resulting eighths.

Jonan blinked. The third of the so-called immortal sorcerers – famous for finding secret ways of extending their lifespans – Erik Tarren was best known for his texts on history and sorcerous theory. He had been a battle mage many years before, however, and had been instrumental in the war against Xixis along with the other two immortals – Blake Hartigan and Edrick Theas.

The man had such a mild mannered reputation that Jonan hadn't even given him serious consideration as a murder suspect, but he clearly had known Edrick for decades. That was plenty of time to accrue a reason for a personal vendetta. And Erik was best known for travel sorcery – the form of sorcery used for both teleportation and summoning. Lydia had found evidence of a planar gateway, which required that exact form of sorcery to be used.

*Resh. I didn't even think about him.*

"Huh. That's…a possibility, I suppose."

Silk gave him a quizzical look. "I was joking. The man must be two hundred years old."

Jonan waved a hand dismissively. "Sure, but he certainly has resources. And Symphony isn't exactly the only legend with apprentices."

"Okay." She ate the last piece of her side of the apple. "While we're entertaining the idea of geriatric assassins, have you thought about any of the older Rethri sorcerers? Vorinthal or Ta'thyriel, maybe?"

He nodded. "Yeah, they're on my list of people to look into. I'm planning to check Edrick's own family and guards as well."

"Not a bad idea. I hear his daughter is nearly as powerful as he is, and you know how siblings are."

*I don't generally associate siblings with murdering each other, but that's a pretty good lead. I hadn't heard that the sister – Nakane, I think her name was – had a reputation for being all that powerful herself. Interesting.*

"Any idea on what the daughter specializes in?"

Silk shook her head. "No, but I could probably find out."

He lifted both hands in a sign of non-intervention. "Not worth the time. I'm sure you have other work."

"You aren't kidding. I can always make time for a dinner with a charming fellow such as yourself, however. And by always, I mean up to once or twice per month."

He scratched at his chin. *Is she flirting with me?* "I'll be sure to contact you again soon. Is there anything I can offer you in return for your help?"

"Something a little less boring than my current assignment would be nice." She gave a frown. "But you already mentioned that Symphony didn't send me any new orders. A shame." She paused, considering. "Why all the interest in this murder? It can't have been why you were sent here in the first place, otherwise you would have asked me about it last time."

*Probably best to be honest about this one. Or honestish, at least.* "A friend asked me to look into it. And, if you were the killer, I didn't want an investigation stumbling onto you if I could deflect it in another direction."

She raised a hand over her chest and put on an expression of innocence, which might have looked a little more sincere if she didn't still have an apple-stained dagger jutting out of the same sleeve. "You'd go to that much effort to protect me? I suppose I owe you my eternal gratitude. Or something."

Jonan smirked. "Truly, my heroism knows no bounds."

"Truly. Well, my Stealthy Hero Scribe, if there's nothing further, I have business to attend to." She tossed back the last of her wine, offering him a scintillating grin.

He finished the last of his apple, standing up. "I suppose I have no further excuses to prolong the conversation. It's been a pleasure, though."

"Oh, believe me, Jonan – the pleasure has been all mine."

# CHAPTER XIV – VELAS V – WINNING IS WINNING

Velas stood in formation with the remainder of her platoon. Of the original twelve, only seven remained – Landen, Taelien, Asphodel, Teshvol, Kolask, a quiet water sorcerer named Eridus, and herself. The other platoons had diminished as well – some more than others. Of the forty-nine candidates that had stood with them on the field a month before, she counted a total of thirty now.

It was barely an hour past the rising of the dawnfire, but the air was already warm with a summer breeze. She heard a few yawns from nearby cadets and privately wondered if they were being penalized in their scores for the lack of discipline.

As with their last large gathering, the three officers in charge of the tests stood before them. Colonel Wyndam had a large, ornate box on the dirt in front of her. Lieutenant Torrent stood off to the side, along with three other officers she didn't recognize – presumably the overseers for the other three platoons. Velas braced herself for a speech. She got one a few minutes later.

"Candidates," Colonel Wyndam began, "You have done well to make it this far. We had close to five hundred applicants this year, nearly a record. Each of you shows great promise and I am confident that many of you will eventually be groomed into fine paladins regardless of your results in this year's tests. With the first tests, we have separated you from the average candidates. With the following tests, we will separate good candidates from the exceptional."

Velas barely resisted the urge to scratch an itch at the back of her head. She tensed her jaw, continuing to listen.

"Your next test will begin as soon as I complete my explanation. When the test begins, each of you will be given a single sigil representing one of the deities of the Tae'os pantheon by the lieutenant who oversees your platoon. Your goal will be to secure at least one additional sigil within the next twelve hours. Two of these pins will be the minimum requirement to pass on to the next stage of testing. You may pin any sigils in your possession to your uniforms and wear them for the duration of the test."

"You will also be evaluated based on the specific symbols you collect. Obtaining a symbol may affect your eligibility to join a specific order at the discretion of that order's arbiter."

She paused, gesturing for the platoon lieutenants to step forward. As the lieutenants approached, Colonel Wyndam retrieved a key from a pouch on her side and twisted it in the lock on the ornate chest. Each of the lieutenants retrieved a single box from within the chest, after which the final platoon lieutenant pushed the box shut. Afterward, each of the lieutenants took up a position standing nearby, holding the smaller boxes in their hands.

*Not too far apart,* Velas considered. *About ten feet from each other.*

Colonel Wyndam nodded in the direction of one of the lieutenants – a tall man next to platoon one – and then resumed her speech. "Your score will be based on the number of sigils you collect. Lieutenant Morris, Second Lieutenant Banks, and I will each have seven additional sigils to distribute throughout the day."

"We will each have different methods of choosing who we assign these sigils to. I have scheduled a brief meeting with each of the applicants to determine who I will choose – your meeting times are on the nearby assignment board. Attending the meeting is optional, but I would advise against missing any chance to earn a sigil. Lieutenant Morris, do you have anything to say?"

The Paladin of Lissari nodded and stepped forward. "Yes, ma'am. I will be holding a contest at twelve bells to determine who will earn the seven sigils you gave me. The details of the contest have also been pinned on the assignment board."

"Very good." Colonel Wyndam turned to Lieutenant Banks. "And you, Lieutenant Banks?"

194

3333322222

"Yes, ma'am." Lieutenant Banks turned toward the cadets, her silvery armor shimmering in the dawnfire's rising light. "I believe the best equipped to judge your capabilities are your own platoon's lieutenants. As such, I have distributed one of my seven pins to each of the platoon lieutenants. The remaining three pins have been hidden at sacred sites to the Paladins of Tae'os throughout the city. See me any time after this announcement and I will present you with clues to the three locations." She turned back to the colonel. "That is all, ma'am."

"Excellent. In that case, my speech is concluded. Cadets, you are dismissed. You may now form lines to retrieve your platoon's sigils."

The cadets turned toward where their lieutenants were already opening their boxes, displaying seven intricately carved metal pins in the designs of the runes of their gods. Velas had seen similar pins before – paladins frequently wore them with their dress uniforms to represent the specific order they belonged to. Under normal circumstances, the pins were unnecessary – field uniforms were embroidered with the symbols of the individual orders, and members who wore armor were assigned a tabard with the same symbol.

Velas was in the middle of her line – behind Asphodel, Taelien, and Kolask. She couldn't quite see over everyone's shoulders, but she quickly guessed that Asphodel would take the Sytira pin and Taelien would take the one corresponding to Aendaryn. She wasn't so certain about Kolask.

Kolask snatched a pin and hastily withdrew, leaving room for Velas to step forward. She paused, saluted Lieutenant Torrent properly, and observed the remaining pins. *Eratar, Lissari, Xerasilis, and...Aendaryn?*

She glanced at Taelien, who was already fastening a pin to his uniform and walking away.

Shaking her head, she picked up the Aendaryn pin, nodded to Lieutenant Torrent, and stepped away from the line.

And, immediately thereafter, she turned toward the ornate chest on the ground.

*Surge.* The blast of motion pushed her to the chest in an instant, and while Colonel Wyndam turned toward her, Velas pushed open the lid of the box.

There was nothing left inside.

The colonel laughed softly. "That was nicely done, Applicant Jaldin. I applaud your initiative, but we wouldn't make things quite that easy for you."

*Well, at least I got a chuckle out of her. That makes things slightly less embarrassing.* Velas saluted the colonel. "Yes, ma'am. Thank you, ma'am."

"No need for that at the moment. You had the right idea – use every instant you have."

Velas lowered her hand and nodded. "That's advice I'm happy to take."

She spun around, looking at the platoon lieutenants. None of them had quite finished handing out their pins yet. *Tempting. But the long-term consequences of grabbing pins from one of the platoon batches wouldn't be worth it. I'll find another way.*

She fastened her Aendaryn pin onto her tunic and walked to meet with Taelien. He was sitting on a large stone when she approached, scratching at his chin with an expression of concentration.

"Should I expect my pin to come flying off at any moment?" Velas tapped her pin meaningfully.

"Hmm?" Taelien looked up, seeming to notice her for the first time. As he turned, she caught sight of the glittering symbol of Lysandri on his uniform. "Oh, no. I didn't magnetize them this time. Sabotaging my own platoon would be pretty low."

*Winning is winning, Sal. But you're cute when you try to be so honorable.*

"Of course, I was just teasing. Still, with that expression, you're clearly thinking up one of your crazy ideas."

He nodded, but his expression remained neutral. "More just debating if I should use the idea I already have."

"Another morally dubious one?"

He shook his head. "No, just risky and somewhat impractical."

"Sounds like you. Let me in on it?"

The swordsman frowned, folding his arms. "I don't think I can with this one. I don't want you to be complicit if something goes wrong. Besides, I won't exactly need help if I decide to do it. Thanks for the offer, though."

"It wasn't an offer as much as a request – but fine. Be that way." She rolled her eyes. "Meet back here about ten minutes before the day is over, though, yeah?"

He nodded. "I can do that. And I'll be around if you need me. If I go with this idea, I'll probably be in the barracks most of the day."

*Well, at least that'll let me see what he's up to.* "All right. I'm going to go grab Lan. Good luck, Sal."

"Luck? Never put much stock in that. Hope we succeed either way, though."

*Hope is just as silly as luck,* she thought. Regardless, she smiled at him.

Landen was already coming her way when she headed back toward the rest of the candidates. "Hey, which one did you pick up?" He flashed the Eratar pin at her.

Velas pointed at the Aendaryn pin on her tunic in response.

Landen quirked an eyebrow. "Wasn't Salaris in front of you?"

"Guess he didn't want to look like he was playing favorites. Probably wants to cut down on the rumors about his heritage."

Landen chuckled. "If someone thought I was the son of a god, I'd be more than happy to play along."

"Yeah, but no one would ever make that mistake."

"Hey, that was low! I'd make a great demigod." He snagged her arm. "C'mon, let's go look at that assignment board."

It didn't take them long to reach the board, but most of the other candidates were already crowding around it. It took several minutes to get close enough to see. Velas noted three postings that were relevant to her.

*Colonel Wyndam's Appointment Schedule*
*Asphodel – 7 Bells at Colonel Wyndam's Office*
*Velas Jaldin – 8 Bells at Colonel Wyndam's Office*
*Taelien 11 Bells at the Training Hall*
*Landen – 13 Bells, One Chime at the Training Hall*

She skimmed over the other times – those candidates were the few she had personally invested in and expected to succeed. Next, she checked Lieutenant Morris' posting.

*Lieutenant Morris' Challenge – Lysandri's Arena*
*Location: West bank of the Teldymair Lake; see map for meeting spot*
*Time: Twelve Bells*

*Expected Duration: One Bell*
*Details on the challenge will be provided at the event site.*


Next to the challenge posting was a city map with the location of the lake circled and a Lysandri symbol scrawled next to the meeting point. Velas had been to the lake before – it wasn't with the paladin base, but it was close by. Presumably the paladins had set up something to keep civilians away – unless dealing with civilians was part of the event.

And thirdly, she noted a hastily scrawled posting.


*Sterling's Challenge – Gamble for Sigils!*
*Location: The Perfect Stranger*
*Time: Fourteen Bells*
*Details will be provided at the tavern.*


She grinned, scanning the area, but Jonathan Sterling was nowhere to be found. *Clever idea. I'm curious now, and I'll wager several other people will be, too.*

*And I'll wager that they'll wager at his game, too. Which will be rigged, of course. This should be fun.*

It was just after seven bells, which meant Velas had a few hours left before the first item on the board.

Landen scratched at his chin. "Looks like I've got some free time. Might see if I can figure out where some of those hidden sigils are. Want to join me?"

Velas shook her head. "Sounds fun, but I need to eat. Meet you later?"

He nodded. "Sure. Lissari's luck."

*I'm pretty sure Lissari isn't a luck goddess, but sure, why not.* "You too."

She was heading toward the mess hall when she heard someone calling out from behind her.

"Hey, jumping girl. Slow down, yeah?"

Velas turned to find Susan Crimson behind her.

Susan paused in her step, folding her hands behind her back. "You got a minute to chat?"

Velas nodded. "Sure."

"Good. We can walk and talk, I could use some eats, too."

As the brunette moved forward to catch up, Velas scanned the former Thornguard for weapons. *Simple sword on her left hip, stiletto moderately concealed in her left sleeve. Interesting.*

"Yeah, I'm starved. What did you want to chat about?"

"Saw your dummy-spearing bit in the prelims. Mighty impressive, that. A group of us have been putting together a plan for passing this challenge. You've got some skills, so we thought you might want into it."

Velas turned her head toward the brunette, considering. *She doesn't talk anything like what I would have expected from her file. She's a noble, isn't she? Maybe she's trying to sound more accessible to me? That doesn't really make sense, though – it's common knowledge that I'm from a high house, too. I suppose she just might have picked up the dialect while she served in the Thornguard. Gods know I don't sound much like a noblewoman myself, but...*

"I might be interested," Velas offered. "What's the plan?"

"Uh, that's the tough sell. Given the nature of the thing –"

"You can't tell me until I accept. Can you tell me what skills you'd need me to use?"

Susan slowed her pace and Velas slowed to compensate. "Your jumping, mostly," Susan offered. "That's the most I can tell you, I think."

*Pretty tempting. I could find out a lot about her capabilities – as well as her allies – by doing this.*

They were getting close to the entrance to the mess hall, so Velas stopped walking entirely. Susan paused along with her. "Can you tell me when you'd be doing it?"

Susan shook her head. "Sorry. Can't let you put together enough to interfere if you wanted to."

"That makes sense. It's a real tempting offer, but I think I'm going to have to pass."

Susan's expression shifted from friendly to neutral, her hand moving to a pouch on her side. Velas tensed momentarily, but all Susan removed from the pouch was a pin – one representing Xerasilis. "What if I sweeten the deal a bit, give you a pin right now?"

*That's...a very good offer.*

*Too good of an offer.*

"I'm flattered that you think so much of me that you'd offer me that kind of deal. I think I'm going to have to pass, though. I'm sorry, I just don't like signing up for things I don't have all the details about."

Susan nodded, putting the pin back away. "Thought so, but I figured I'd ask. We can still be friends, yeah?"

*Friends?*

"Yeah, sure. I'd like that. C'mon, deal or not, we still need to eat."

***

Susan Crimson turned out to be much easier to chat with over food, especially once Velas was seated out of stiletto reach on the opposite side of a table. They had never really talked before, but Velas quickly found herself enjoying trading stories about training mishaps and difficult battles.

By the end of the conversation, Velas was convinced that someone else had put Susan up to approaching her – but she couldn't sort out who without asking directly. *The Wandering War, most likely. They've been moving about together constantly since her companion failed out of the competition and he never talks. I suppose he's taken on the role of her muscle – unless his silence means he's the puppetmaster type.*

When they finished eating, Velas excused herself quickly, heading back to the barracks. The forty-odd minutes it had taken to eat had been more than sufficient time to formulate a plan for the next few hours, even while exchanging bits of banter with a fellow soldier.

*Susan could be an asset in the future if I can figure out what her deal is. I'll have to pry more if I can get her isolated sometime. In the meantime, I need Asphodel.*

With hours of time in the day that were not allocated to any specific activity, the three pins hidden somewhere in the city were obvious targets for spending time. Asphodel was the obvious solution.

Velas still didn't know exactly how Asphodel's "oracle" abilities worked, but the purple-haired girl clearly had some kind of divination abilities – ones that she could use with minimal preparation and no obvious incantations. The former Queensguard suspected that Asphodel was a practitioner of Assassin's Sorcery – a style that typically used gestures or pure thoughts for spellcasting purposes. It was also possible that Asphodel had a completely different method of utilizing sorcery, given that she was a Delaren and from a different culture. Learning more about Asphodel's methods could be valuable, but for the moment, she just needed Asphodel's skills.

Determining where to find Asphodel was easy – the Delaren was scheduled for a meeting with the colonel's office an hour before Velas was. Rather than trying to catch Asphodel before she entered, Velas headed to the Citadel of Blades just after seven bells, waiting to catch the crystal-haired girl on her way out. That would also give Velas an idea of how long Asphodel's meeting with the colonel lasted.

The meetings were scheduled a half hour apart from each other, but that didn't mean they lasted for a full half hour each. Knowing the duration of the meeting would give Velas an idea of how she should prepare herself.

Asphodel emerged from the office about ten minutes after seven bells. Wordlessly, she extended an open palm toward Velas as she approached. A sigil of Sytira was in her hand.

"Not bad. You've already got enough to pass, then." Velas gave the Delaren an approving nod.

"It is yours."

Velas blinked – she had assumed Asphodel had simply been displaying the pin, not offering it as a gift. Gingerly, she plucked the sigil from the other woman's hand, noting that Asphodel's fingernails matched the color of her hair.

*But they're just normal nails, not claws like the legends talk about. I suppose that's a transformation she'd have to undergo, not something the Delaren have at birth.*

"Thank you," Velas said, closing her hand protectively around the sigil. She frowned – she'd never done anything of significance to help Asphodel. Certainly nothing to warrant this degree of kindness. "Why?"

"You will need it more than I will."

Velas tilted her head to the side. "Not to complain about a present, but I'd really like to understand how you know that. What exactly are these oracle abilities of yours?"

Asphodel frowned, looking from side to side. "Can't talk right now. Too much noise. I will tell you eventually. Goodbye." She turned away and abruptly began walking off.

"Wait, I was going to ask you –"

Asphodel half-turned to face her, slowing her steps. "You wanted to offer to use motion sorcery to make me run faster, allowing me to quickly go and obtain all of the sigils that are hidden in the city. That won't be necessary – I can retrieve two of them without your help, and the third is already gone. Thank you, though. I am glad you wished to work with me."

The Delaren smiled softly and turned away, retreating from the citadel. Velas took a breath to speak again, but her voice never came.

*** 

"You're here early," Jonathan Sterling remarked, approaching the colonel's office. His meeting was scheduled for right after Asphodel's – and thus, just before Velas' own meeting. He was wearing a broad grin, his chest vibrating as he quietly chuckled at some unspoken joke. "Nothing better to do?"

Velas shrugged. She was leaning up against the wall right next to the office door. "I had other business nearby, and I don't really have enough time to go do anything else before my appointment. Figured I'd just relax here for a bit, try to guess at what the colonel is going to want."

"A guessing game, is it?" He brought up his left hand, touching two fingers to his forehead. "I do enjoy those."

Velas smiled at the gesture. "Don't we all?"

"I'll be curious what you come up with. Perhaps we can chat about it later. In the meantime, however, my meeting awaits." He half-bowed, and then stepped closer and knocked on the door. It opened a moment later, revealing a young man who was carrying a handful of files in his left hand.

"Come in, Applicant Sterling." The young man gave Velas a quizzical look when he noticed her to the side of the door. She gave him a friendly wave.

"I'm the next one. Got here a bit early."

The young man gave a slight frown, shaking his head, and retreated deeper into the room. Velas got a quick glimpse of Colonel Wyndam sitting behind a desk toward the back of the chamber before the door closed.

*Well, this should be even more interesting than I expected.*
*Listen.*

The mental command enhanced her sense of hearing. It was one of the simplest Dominion of Sound spells and the first one she had mastered. The more difficult part was making it useful.

Velas closed her eyes, envisioning a half-sphere in front of her, open at her back.

*Filter.*

With her enhanced hearing, she would have normally heard even the slightest nearby sounds coming from any direction. The second spell created a field that dispersed sounds that passed through it, which would prevent them from reaching her ears. The combined effect of the two spells would enable her to listen intently – but only in the desired direction.

Initially, she had regretted that Landen or Taelien hadn't been right before her. Now, after having seen Sterling's little gesture, she was excited to hear his conversation with the colonel.

Moments passed into minutes and she heard nothing at all.

*Gods curse it. They must have the wall dominion bonded to prevent sound from leaving. Either that, or one of the people in there is actively preventing any sound from leaving the room.*

She let her Listen and Filter spells fade – maintaining them would have been a needless tax on her sense of hearing – and glanced at the nearby rooms. The room on the right belonged to another officer, Orin Dyr. The room on the left, however, didn't have a plaque to mark the owner.

Velas tested the handle. It was unlocked. She looked down the hall in both directions, quickly determining that there was no one else in sight. She listened briefly at this door as well, but she couldn't hear anything within – nor could she determine if that was because of sorcerous wards or just because there was no one inside.

*This could get awkward if someone is inside.*

Gritting her teeth, she turned the handle.

The door led to an empty classroom, minimally lit due to large curtains blocking the windows. Taking a deep breath, Velas stepped inside and shut the door behind her.

*If someone comes in, I'll just say I wanted a quiet place to think while waiting for my appointment,* she decided. Walking to the right wall of the room, she began to work.

*Listen. Filter.* She pressed a palm against the wall, instantly feeling the pulse of the Dominion of Sound from the opposite side. The dominion bond flowed like liquid across the wall's surface, absorbing and dispersing sounds that passed within. The wall itself was imperfect, however – the citadel was ages old, and cracks and furrows marred the

203

surface of the once pristine barrier. The dominion bond faltered in these locations, allowing for tiny pockets of sound to be trapped within for moments before they faded away.

Her own footsteps echoed loudly as she slowly advanced along the walls, pressing a hand against the stone. Finding the flaws in the wall from the opposite side would be more difficult, but the nature of the defense would make it obvious any time she came in contact with any sound. She paused immediately as she felt a fragment of vibration in her hand, drawing it through the wall and releasing it into her half-sphere of filtered sound.

"...it wasn't my idea, in truth. My older sister told me I needed to make something of myself, to do some good for the family."

Sterling's voice. She quickly shifted her filter to ensure that no sound echoed back into the other room. Now that she had found a weakness in the room's sonic armor, she could draw the sound through and release it almost as quickly as the people within spoke.

"So, you're not here of your own volition, then?" The colonel's tone was measured, but Velas caught a clear edge to it.

"Oh, I wouldn't say that. It was her idea at first, but I think this is the right place for me. I can do a lot of good here."

"And what sort of 'good' would you expect to do as a member of the Paladins of Tae'os?"

There was a brief pause before Sterling responded. "Well, I think I'd be best with the Eratar branch, to be honest. I enjoy talking to people and traveling, so I'd make a good messenger. I don't want to come across as too arrogant, but I'd also like to think I can slip into a hostile area without being noticed, which could help me accomplish important goals for the paladins."

*Sounds like a fairly generic interview so far. Interesting that he's gunning for a specific branch at this early of a stage – I'm not sure if that's a good strategy.*

"I see. And why should I help you complete this test?"

Another pause. "Well, I think I'm here for the right reasons. Some of the applicants don't seem very focused. Others seem like they're more here for the challenge of the competition than the goal of becoming a paladin. I'm here to be a paladin, colonel."

"Thank you, Applicant Sterling—"

204

Velas turned around and immediately headed to the classroom door. Opening it slowly, she glanced from side-to-side, but no one else was in the hallway. She swiftly moved back to her position outside of the door of Colonel Wyndam's office. From the colonel's tone, it was clear that the interview was about to conclude.

*That one was quick. Asphodel was in there a lot longer. Does that mean he failed?*

It was at least another minute before the door finally reopened. Sterling glanced at her, tipping his hat politely, and wordlessly headed toward the citadel's entrance.

While the door was still open, Velas glanced within. The young man she had seen earlier was sitting in a chair at the left side of the colonel's desk, writing furiously. The colonel herself approached the door and smiled at Velas.

"I appreciate your punctuality, but you'll have to wait for your scheduled appointment time."

Velas saluted. "Yes, ma'am."

The colonel closed the door.

*Well, I was hoping to get more information out of that, but at least I have some basics. I most likely missed the first question or two, but it sounds like a relatively straightforward question and answer session – at least for the part that Sterling went through. It's very plausible he failed at a certain point and didn't get all of the questions.*

*So, what am I going to say to the things she asked? It sounded like one of them was about why Sterling was interested in joining the paladins – that's a fairly straightforward one. I'm here because of Landen, who followed Taelien and Lydia down here.*

*Which is a terrible answer. Shit.*

*Okay, straightforward doesn't always mean easy. What have I got? My family has been dedicated to Lissari for generations – that's a good one. House Jaldin has a good reputation, and I have relevant training as a healer, even if I never picked up the sorcery for it.*

*"Family tradition" isn't a great answer by itself. Maybe being inspired by my ancestors and their dedication? That's a little better at least.*

She continued to ponder her options until the door reopened and the young file-bearing man beckoned her inside.

"Thanks," she said as he held the door open for her. Velas stepped within, following his gesture toward a seat across from the colonel. The younger man closed the door a few moments later, sitting down in the same chair she had seen before.

"Candidate Velas Jaldin," the colonel said, looking at a paper in front of her. Velas resisted the urge to glance at the contents of the paper, but she suspected it was the same file on her that Taelien had discovered earlier – potentially with more recent notes. "You've led a rather interesting life, considering your young age."

"Thank you, colonel."

"Let's get right to it. You get to ask me a single question about anything relating to the exams, and I'll give you an honest answer. After that, I'll ask you a series of questions, which you must answer honestly. I will know if you are lying. If you lie, you'll get a red flag immediately. If you provide me with honest answers that I find compelling, I will give you one of my remaining pins. Do you understand?"

*Shit. She can sense the truth? That's going to make this a bit more of a challenge. She could be bluffing, but it's not really worth the risk. She's a Sytiran, and a high ranking one at that. Having some kind of knowledge spell to read me isn't implausible at all.*

"Yes, colonel."

"You may ask your question first. I'll give you a minute or two to think about it. Don't try to run up the clock by delaying until my next meeting, however. I appreciate creative problem solving, but wasting my time would be rude."

*I wouldn't do something like that. Taelien might, though. He does love trying to game these tests.*

"Understood, colonel. I will let you know when I've thought of my question."

In spite of her calm response, Velas' mind was whirling. There were a multitude of options that immediately came to mind.

*She said the exams – that means it doesn't even have to be about this particular test. I could ask about virtually anything. Knowing my cumulative total up to this point could be good to know how much trouble I'm in, but ultimately it probably wouldn't be worth using up the question. Maybe I could ask what my biggest mistake has been so far so I can avoid repeating it, but I think I'm better off asking for something that's going to provide a direct and guaranteed benefit.*

*I could ask for the best answers to this particular interview, or maybe just ask directly how I could earn a pin from her. One pin isn't exactly going to make or break this whole competition, though. I could ask for the locations of all of the hidden pins within the city, but Asphodel is already going after them and she already gave me her pin, so I shouldn't compete with her.*

*I could ask about one of the tests after this one — something to give me a big edge for one of the future exams. That's tempting, but it might seem arrogant to assume I'm passing this one.*

*Maybe I should ask for the answers to every question that the other candidates have already asked — that's a good one. Unfortunately, only a few people were in front of me, so it wouldn't necessarily be as useful as if I was one of the later interviews. That's probably along the right line of thinking...*

"All right, I have my question." Velas clenched her hands in her lap, unexpectedly tense. She wasn't used to being nervous talking to authority figures, but this particular competition was wreaking havoc on her nerves. She had to win.

"Ask when ready." The colonel waved with one hand for her to proceed.

"What's the best advice related to any of the exams you can give me that you have not given to anyone else and do not expect to give to any of the other applicants?"

The colonel's expression sank for a moment, and then she smiled. "That's a very good question, Miss Jaldin. I'll need a moment to think about it."

Velas nodded silently.

The colonel folded her arms, leaning back slightly in her chair. Velas tried to take deep breaths as subtly as possible while she awaited the answer.

"When the competition started, we told you all that the 'tradition' dictates that the arbiters select one person for each branch. This is true, but it is also misleading. Most applicants believe that they must excel in a specific area to appeal to one arbiter or another, thinking of every other applicant as competition for that spot. This leads many to failure."

Velas quirked an eyebrow, continuing to listen.

The colonel leaned a little bit closer, putting her hands on top of the table. "In truth, there have been years where not a single candidate has been selected. There have been other years — typically after great wars —

that dozens of candidates are chosen. The arbiters will pick as many candidates as they deem worthy. The standards of what constitutes 'worthy' vary from year to year, however, based on the needs of the organization as a whole. In recent years, we've only picked a few paladins per year from these tests. We're not at war, and the arbiters generally find that paladins who go through the entire process of being a squire are better at teamwork and more loyal to the organization."

Velas nodded. The logic was sound – the process of spending years as a squire was much more likely to weed out spies, as well as build loyalty and dedication between the squire and the paladins he or she worked with.

"That's my answer. And now I have a question for you – what led you to ask that particular question?"

That one was relatively easy, at least. "I thought about a lot of different options before I realized that you hadn't said anything about this interview being a secret. My plan was to try to get information that no one else would have, and then share it with the members of my platoon, unless I'm explicitly instructed not to at some point. Similarly, I can ask my platoon mates what they asked and learn whatever they learned."

"Good. You mentioned your team members – would you share that information with people outside of your own group?"

*A good question, and potentially a trick question.*

"I wasn't planning to, but I probably would if it was someone I trusted, or someone I wanted to pass."

"And under what conditions would you want someone else to pass the exam?"

Velas frowned. Sterling's questions had seemed a lot easier than these. "Really, it probably would depend on if I liked them. I'd like to have a better answer, but you wanted the truth."

"The truth is what I'm looking for, Miss Jaldin. Now, how about the people within your own platoon? Would you share this information – or other advantages you might gain during the competition – equally with each member of your platoon?"

*Ouch. That's one is a sucker punch.* "No, most likely not. This isn't because I wish for anyone on my team to fail, nor would I deliberately sabotage anyone on my team – or anyone else. I'd be perfectly happy if everyone passed. But I came into these tests with friends, and I'm going to be biased toward helping them the most." She paused for a moment, and then added, "Admittedly, I also owe Asphodel a favor, and I will take measures to pay that back."

The colonel nodded slowly. "Tell me about these friends of yours."

Velas bit her lip. *What's she looking for? Is she testing if I'll sabotage my friends?*

"Landen has been a friend of mine for years. We served together in the Queensguard back in Orlyn. We've been through a lot of scraps together and always came out on top. I couldn't ask for a better partner. I'm happy we were put in the same platoon."

"I understand you had some role in that?"

Velas forced herself not to wince. "I did ask for us to be placed in the same platoon, yes."

"Why?"

"Because I thought it'd be more fun. And I'd be more comfortable with him around. And we could help each other pass. I didn't want to compete against him."

"But you do realize that you're competing against everyone, regardless of which platoon you're in?"

Velas shook her head at that. "Yes and no. As long as we're in the same platoon, we can help each other out in group tests, as well as any other tests where we have a sufficient amount of contact to trade information. That's better than being stuck in a different barracks. And I'm expecting more contests where teams are pitted directly against each other in the future. Even if we're being evaluated as individuals, my teamwork with Landen will make us both look better."

"That seems reasonable. And what about Applicant Salaris?"

*What about Sal? What does she want me to say?*

"Salaris, um, I haven't known him as long. But we've been training together under Herod, and I've enjoyed that. He's one of the best fighters here, and I think we complement each other well."

*Do we? Is that really why...?*

The colonel raised an eyebrow, which made Velas cringe backward in her seat slightly. Velas wondered if the colonel had detected the hint of a lie – and she wondered if she had been lying to herself with that answer, too.

"All right, Velas. What about the other members of your platoon? What's your evaluation of them?"

Velas took a breath. This was slightly easier, at least. She could be professional.

"Asphodel seems like she's going to go a long way. Her companions – Kolask and Teshvol – call her an oracle. She has some kind of information gathering sorcery abilities, which she can use subtly without incantations. I'm not sure what the extent of her abilities are yet, but from her listed score from the first test and the fact that she's still here, I suspect she's very capable."

"Go on."

"Kolask is extraordinarily protective of Asphodel, which is somewhat silly, given that she's a much better fighter than he is. At first, I assumed that Kolask and Teshvol were her guards. I think most of the platoon still assumes that. I've seen them exercise and spar, though, and seen how they treat her. It's more like Kolask and Teshvol worship her. And Asphodel doesn't like the attention."

"Interesting observation. Why do you think they 'worship' her, as you say? And do you mean that in the literal sense, that they believe she's a deity?"

Velas shook her head. After years of living in Orlyn, she had seen enough prayers to false gods to recognize them easily. "Not quite. It's more like they believe she's a messenger of the gods or something along those lines. As for which gods, well, I've never really figured that much out."

"And why not? Have you asked them about their religion?"

Velas shrugged. "We're all here to join an order of religious paladins. I think asking them if they worship Asphodel might come across as a bit of an insult." After a moment, she hastily added, "And I'm not telling you any of this to make them look bad. They very well might be extremely dedicated to the Tae'os Pantheon for all I know. I've seen people look at Tae – I mean Salaris – like he's some kind of divine messenger, too."

"Yes, I'm quite familiar with the problems that have arisen from Salaris carrying that sword around. I believe I've asked you enough about your platoon for the time being. Let's talk a bit more about you. Why are you here?"

Finally, a question she had prepared for. "I spent my childhood hearing about the exploits of famous paladins and priests. As you know, I'm a child of House Jaldin – albeit not by blood. I was adopted at a young age. My family treated me very well, but since I'm not of their blood, I didn't stand to inherit anything. They gave me a better education than I deserved - everything from healing to swordplay. Enough to carve out my own path in life. House Jaldin has traditionally served Lissari, and I learned her prayers when I was young. It's taken me a while to get here, but I think this was the path I was meant for."

"You mention prayers to Lissari, but I understand that you served the false gods of Orlyn for some time. Quite directly, in fact, as one of the guards of Queen Regent Tylan. How do you reconcile that?"

Velas was silent for some time, staring down into her lap. For several moments, the only noise was the scratching of the scribe's quill.

"I wanted to believe that there were new gods – gods that wanted to serve humanity directly. It's a compelling notion, isn't it? Even the Tae'os Pantheon were once mortal. It didn't seem impossible. And if the new gods wanted to help people, I felt like keeping them safe from harm was important."

"You wanted to protect them?" Colonel Wyndam sounded surprised. It was the first hint of a strong emotion that had slipped into her tone.

Velas nodded. "I don't believe the gods are invincible, Colonel. Even in the stories of the Tae'os Pantheon, they've struggled against threats – other gods like Vaelien, monsters like Daesmodin and the Xixian Emperor, and even powerful sorcerers. These fledgling 'gods' – or false gods, as they turned out to be – were certain to be vulnerable. If they had been true deities, they would have probably been in even greater danger, since the true gods might have sought to destroy them."

"And if the Tae'os Pantheon had tried to destroy these false gods you were protecting?"

A memory flashed across Velas' mind. *A glint of silver catching the morning light, tearing through her mail and flesh. A scar that still itched on her skin.*

"I would have fought to stop them."

The colonel nodded, seeming oddly satisfied. "What changed your mind about the gods of Orlyn?"

"I had a fight with a good friend of mine. It gave me a lot to think about – things I had refused to face before. I had to face the fact that I had been idealistic, and that I had been letting myself be manipulated for quite some time." Velas tensed her jaw. "Never again."

"That's a satisfactory answer."

The colonel turned toward the scribe. "Squire Aldrich, retrieve the sigil of Lysandri for Applicant Jaldin." The squire stood and moved to a box at the back of the room.

Velas breathed an audible sigh of relief. "Thank you, Colonel."

"You mentioned Lissari, but I think her sister suits you best. You did well in the Assassin Test – you were one of the best of our applicants this year, in fact – and your family would have been proud of your healing skills. Your answers here confirmed what I suspected from your behavior in that test, however. Your priority is protecting the ones you care for the most. While Lissari is the healer of wounds, it is Lysandri who sets all aside to sacrifice herself for others. I believe that this may be your path, Applicant Jaldin."

*Lysandri? The Martyr? I suppose there might be some truth to that.*

The scribe handed the pin to the colonel, and she in turn offered it to Velas. The former Queensguard took the pin gingerly, staring at the metal for a moment before closing her palm around it.

"Thank you, Colonel. You've given me a lot to think about."

"Good luck, Miss Jaldin. You are dismissed."

The sharp edges of the sigil dug into Velas' skin, but the cold touch of the metal felt like victory.

*** 

Velas had pinned all three of her sigils to the right breast of her uniform tunic. After having had the experience of being questioned by the colonel, the Lysandri pin felt far more significant than the others.

*And Asphodel just gave me her pin, no questions asked. She must have had a very good reason for that. Either that or she's just not as invested in this as some of us are.*

After the interview, she met briefly with Landen. Colonel Wyndam had never told her not to discuss the tests with anyone else, so she followed through with her plan and filled Landen in on everything she had been asked. He was suitably grateful, but she also warned him that she suspected the colonel tailored her questions for each individual applicant.

"Three pins already," Landen mumbled. "I've got some catching up to do."

She left him long before his interview to seek out Taelien, but the swordsman was nowhere to be found. At the barracks, Teshvol mentioned that he thought he had seen Salaris leaving the military base for town.

*Well, I'll have to see what kind of antics he's up to later, then. It's his fault if he fails the interview because he wasn't here for my amazing advice.*

As an afterthought, she told Teshvol about his interview, and he seemed surprisingly grateful for the information. *Maybe part of the colonel's point was that I should get to know the other members of my platoon better. I should try that sometime.*

She spent some time looking for Lieutenant Torrent, but he wasn't anywhere near the barracks or the mess hall. *Maybe he's hiding with his pin. He seems like the type to enjoy hide and seek. I'll see if I can track him down later if I need the extra sigil.*

When it was nearly noon, she headed toward the Teldymair Lake, pondering what Lieutenant Morris had in store.

*Lysandri is the goddess of water and ice, not just protecting others. A lake makes sense. Maybe he's going to have us swim out to rescue people who are pretending to be drowning?* She had done a few exercises like that during her medical training back home in Velrya. *Well, if the colonel is right about my proclivity toward protection, I should be pretty good at this, too.*

Velas counted at least twenty other applicants waiting by the side of the lake by the time she arrived. A pair of massive Paladins of Tae'os banners marked the meeting spot and she could see that most of the candidates were searching the lake with their eyes. Lieutenant Morris stood at the lake's edge, speaking too quietly for Velas to hear from a distance. She examined the area as she approached the group.

Most of the other applicants were still wearing their uniforms and weapons. Velas had realized that this particular activity was outside of the base's gates, and thus she wasn't obligated to wear her uniform. Thus, she had prepared according to her best guess at the activity. She didn't have any traditional swimwear handy, so she was wearing a simple short-sleeve shirt and shorts. She kept her longsword belted on her hip, just in case the challenge involved some sort of combat.

The lake's waters were pristine, purified through centuries of maintenance by the city's water sorcerers. It was the smallest of three lakes within the city and the only one that did not feed into Velthryn's aqueducts. Some sections of the lake were walled off to serve as water sources for parts of the city where the aqueducts were less convenient. Other spots on the lake were privately owned, while still others were available to the public.

This particular location was on land owned by the priesthood of Tae'os, but locals were generally allowed to swim and fish there. At the moment, Velas could see armed paladins guarding both sides of the bank, displaying prominent flags bearing the seven runes of the Tae'os Pantheon. She could see tiny ships on the lake in the distance, but there were none nearby.

Glancing at the lake itself, Velas could see the reason why Lieutenant Morris had picked this particular spot. Majestic marble pillars extruded from the lake's surface about a hundred yards into the water. They looked to be the remnants of some long-sunken structure – most likely an old temple.

As Velas moved to join the others on the shore of the lake, she noted Eridus standing in the crowd. She gave him a friendly wave, but he just looked away.

*Hmpf. Rude.*

She shook her head, searching through the applicants until she felt a tap on her shoulder. She spun around, finding Landen behind her.

"You should be more careful – I could have been an assassin or something."

Velas rolled her eyes. "I'm pretty sure the twenty-odd paladins would have jumped on any assassin before they managed anything dangerous. Or, at a minimum, you'd have stood out like a lamppost in the night like that guy," she pointed a finger at The Wandering War, looming over the crowd in his ever-present black cloak.

Landen grinned. "I sometimes wonder if that's the same cloak, of if he just has dozens of identical ones."

"One of life's greatest mysteries. Also, I'm curious how he gets away with never wearing a uniform."

"Maybe he's got it on under there?"

"It sort of defeats the point of a uniform if you always wear something that completely covers it."

"Fair."

"Well, if you've been here long enough to get bored and sneak up on innocent young girls, what have you figured out about the test?"

"Pretty sure some of the pins are going to be up on those pillars." Landen pointed, but the pillars were obvious enough even without his gesture. "If I had to guess, he'll have some of the others underwater."

"And it'll be a race to find them? That doesn't sound too bad. Kind of wish we had Asphodel, though."

Landen shrugged. "Don't think we're going to need an oracle, so much as someone who can help us outpace Lysen."

She caught Landen's gaze, catching Lysen standing next to his sister on the side of the lake.

*He's right – Lysen has a huge advantage here. He can probably just freeze the water to make himself a path – or make a wall to block the rest of us.*

"I think I can get out to a pillar before he has a chance to do that. Want to go for a ride?"

The swordsman folded his arms. "You think you can carry me with one of those motion bursts?

"Well, I've never tried, but it sounds kind of fun."

He shook his head fervently. "Not a good time for practice. I really don't want to end up splattered against one of those things. You've got practice with landing from that kind of height – I don't."

"Bah, you're such a baby sometimes. Fine. I'll see if I can't get you a spare pin."

"And I'll get a dustpan to peel what's left of you off the pillar."

"You're always so romantic." She paused, seeing Lieutenant Banks pick up one of the banners and wave it in the air. "Looks like the lieutenant is about to talk."

She glanced around the area one last time. *And Sal still isn't here.*

"Listen up, everyone!" The crowds went silent as the lieutenant shouted. Most of the applicants turned to face him, although a couple continued to scan the water.

"Here are the rules. I'm sure you can all see the remains of Velryn's Glory out in the water. We've hidden three chests – each containing a sigil – out in the ruins under the water."

He pointed to the pillars next. "And, if you're feeling especially adventurous, there are two more boxes at the top of two of those pillars. They're the ones furthest from this shore."

"Finally, the last two pins will be rewarded for retrieving a banner from one of the groups of paladins on the other side of the lake." He pointed to two groups of armored men and women that were waving banners enthusiastically. "Without getting the banners wet. If it's wet when it gets here, the banner won't count, and I'll hold on to one of the sigils for later."

Velas narrowed her eyes at the figures across the lake. *Looks like at least three hundred yards. Even I can't jump that far. Hrm.*

"Aaaand….go."

The crowd stood and stared for a mere moment before the first applicant dove into the water. That got the others moving.

*No time to plan.*

Velas maneuvered toward the water line, took several steps back, and then began to run.

*Surge.* The blast catapulted her into sky, far past the swimmers - and high enough to see a blur as a black-cloaked figure fluttered right past her.

*Oh, not a chance, buddy. Surge!*

The second boost sent her flying faster, nearly paralleling The Wandering War, who turned his head to face her. As she continued in her upward arc, he raised his left hand above his head and swept it downward in a flourishing motion.

Velas plummeted.

*What the f-*

The former Queensguard swiftly oriented herself, keeping her feet together and holding her breath. She smashed into the surface of the water moments later, far faster than even a free fall should have carried her. The force of the impact slammed her teeth together, leaving her momentarily stunned at the pain and shock.

Recovering did not take long – and now she was angry.

The surface was bright enough for her to orient herself upward and a quick glance at the ruins gave her the direction of the opposite shore. She didn't even consider going for the underwater chests in spite of her current advantage – those weren't what The Wandering War was going for.

She kicked her legs, beginning to swim.

*Enhance.* Rather than attempting to blast herself out of the water, she amplified the amount of force generated by each of her movements, allowing each stroke to carry her closer to the opposite shore. Even then, she was forced to surface to breathe before she reached the other side, taking a few precious moments to gasp in air before pushing herself forward.

When she burst from the water, The Wandering War was already carrying one of the banners.

She swept her right hand toward him in a slashing motion. *Push.*

The wave of force blasted dirt and stones aside as it carried toward the cloaked figure – and stopped completely as he lowered his left hand in a chopping motion. He made a fist, and Velas could see the currents of air swirling around his hand for just a moment before he reopened his hand toward her.

The blast of force – her own blast of force – slammed into her, knocking Velas back into the water.

Gritting her teeth, Velas surfaced again as The Wandering War calmly began walking a circuit around the lake.

*Fuck. He's a motion shaper – that's not even slightly fair.*

She shook her head, sending tiny droplets of water in all directions.

*Okay. New plan – can't hit him with motion directly. Looks like he controls motion effects with his left hand – but his right side is to the lake.*

*Time to make some waves.*

Velas rushed forward, closing most of the distance between them, ignoring the confused-looking second group of paladins who were still waving their own banner.

She reached her right arm out over the water's edge and made a slashing motion toward The Wandering War, grinning.

*Push.*

The wave blasted out toward him, but he spun in place, waving his hand downward. The wave crashed to the dirt before it reached him – but that was fine. Velas was already flying through the air in its wake.

Her right hand grasped the wooden shaft of the banner before The Wandering War reacted, deliberately placing her hand above his. Next, she put her left hand on his chest.

*Push.*

The force of the blast would have been sufficient to send any ordinary person flying – but he didn't budge in the slightest, and gave no indication of having used any sorcery to block the strike.

The shaft of the banner, however, was far less resilient. It snapped apart – with Velas' hand on the section carrying the banner itself.

He reached for the banner, but Velas danced backward, grinning. "Too slow, wanderer."

*Surge.* She blasted herself backward across the ground, sliding a dozen yards away, spinning around as the force dissipated. The strain on her muscles was beginning to slow her movements, but nevertheless she began to sprint around the lake. Glancing over her shoulder, she expected to see The Wandering War right behind her – but he was still standing where he had been, holding the broken remains of the bottom of the banner in his hand.

*Guess he's not much of a runner – or he pushed himself too much by redirecting my spells.*

Nevertheless, she ran as fast as she could. Fortunately, she didn't have to circle the entire lake – there were bridges crossing it on both sides, and she barreled past another pair of candidates as she crossed back to the side where she had started. One of them made a weak grab for the flag as she passed, but she easily avoided it.

As she arrived on the other side of the shore, Velas slowed, inspecting the flag. It still looked dry – apparently The Wandering War's effort to block her earlier attack had succeeded just in the way she had hoped.

She slowed to an exhausted jog, flares of pain rippling through her legs as she arrived at the starting point and handed her flag to Lieutenant Morris.

"Well." He frowned, taking the broken shaft, "I suppose it's not wet."

Velas let out a choking laugh. "Good enough, I hope?"

"Good enough," he agreed. "Quite a show you made back there, too."

"Thanks. Mind if I sit down for a minute?"

The world spun briefly before Velas found herself lying on the ground.

\*\*\*

An hour later, Velas was still resting her head on Landen's lap. He was applying another cold compress to her forehead.

Her newly-acquired sigil of Eratar was pinned to her shirt. Fortunately, the dawnfire's heat had been sufficient to swiftly dry her off.

"You really should get out of here," she told him for what felt like the hundredth time. He still only had a single pin – the one he had started with. And waiting with her had just cost him his chance at earning a pin from Colonel Wyndam – his appointment was minutes away and he had no chance to get there in time.

"When you're back on your feet, sure."

Velas frowned. "Could be a while. I'm not good at feet right now."

"You really pushed yourself too much back there." He shook his head, turning the cloth over and wiping her forehead with the opposite side. "Would have been easier for you to just grab the other banner. No one else got there for minutes. The Wandering War ended up taking it, of course, after you left him in the dust – but you could have easily grabbed it and just walked away rather than skirmishing with him."

"Well, yeah, but that wouldn't have been fun, Landen. Gods."

Landen rubbed his forehead with his free hand. "Right. Fun. Of course."

"Look, if you're feeling too burdened by my mistakes, you can get going at any time."

"Nah. I'm exactly where I need to be."

"Whatever you say."

The other candidates had left the area long before. Lieutenant Morris had stayed a few moments to make sure that she was intact, but when she explained that it was just overuse of motion sorcery, he had shrugged and gone on his way as well.

The Wandering War had stared at her a long time as he departed. She had grinned cheerfully right back at him.

"Well, if you think you're up for it, we've still got a chance to make it to Sterling's little challenge. Maybe we'll win you a pin there."

Landen nodded silently.

It was another half hour before Velas managed to regain enough feeling in her legs for Landen to drag her to her feet. Once she was standing, the pain intensified, but she grit her teeth and began her stretches. It was, in her experience, the best way to get her body working again.

Several minutes later, the pair limped further away from the paladin compound – and toward the Perfect Stranger, where Sterling had announced his competition would be taking place.

They found Sterling sitting with a pair of other candidates at a round table outside of the tavern.

"Hey, welcome!" Sterling stood and waved as they approached. Velas recognized Eridus as one of the other two applicants with him, but once again Eridus just looked away as they approached. The other man was all bulk – he looked like he had more muscle than Velas' entire platoon. He had chalk-white skin, tattoos resembling a deer's antlers running up his arms, and a shaved head. He gave a simple nod as they walked closer.

"You need a hand there?" The muscular man asked.

"Nah. Wouldn't mind if you wanted to pull up some chairs for us, though."

"Take mine, I'll go get another couple," Sterling offered, turning and heading inside the tavern.

Landen led Velas over to the open chair and set her down. She winced as she half-collapsed into the seat, leaning down to rub her left leg, which was aching the most.

"Any idea what we're up to here?" Landen asked the table, standing nearby.

"Sterling hasn't told us much of anything yet. Think we're starting in a minute, though."

"Quite right!" Sterling said, carrying a chair under each arm as he exited the tavern. He nodded to Landen as the other man grabbed one of the chairs from his hand and set it down next to Velas.

Sterling set his own chair down on the opposite side of the table and folded his hands together. "Excellent. I think this will probably be all of us. Shall we begin?"

The tattooed man reached across the table toward Landen. "First, introductions. I'm Alden Stone. From Sythus. I'm in Platoon Three with Jon." He gave a toothy grin, displaying impressively pristine teeth.

*Stone? It's a common name, but that might mean he's related to the Arbiter of Koranir. That could give him a significant advantage in the competition.*

Landen shook his hand. "Landen. Platoon two. From Orlyn, most recently at least."

Alden quickly exchanged introductions with the others – everyone else seemed to know each other to some extent already.

"All right, now that we all know each other, let's get started. First, the rules. Quite simple, really. We drink until we can't drink anymore. Everyone drinks at the same time – unless they can't. We'll take a mug about every five minutes. I'll order us all the same drinks, so no one gets to drink water while the rest of us are ailing."

He winked at the last word. Velas rolled her eyes at the pun.

"Any questions?"

Velas folded her arms and quirked an eyebrow. "The prize?"

"Oh, yes, that. Each of us is going to throw in a pin. Winner gets the pot."

Landen stood up. "Sorry, all. I'm out, then. Can't take the risk." He looked down at Velas. "You going to be okay to get back without me?"

Velas waved a hand dismissively. "Yeah, I'll be fine. A few drinks will do me good. You sure you don't want to stay? I could buy you in."

He shook his head. "No, wouldn't want to risk you losing two pins."

"You think I could lose?"

He ruffled her hair. "Of course not. I'll see you back at camp."

Sterling tipped his hat as Landen walked away. "A shame – I was looking forward to seeing what he was capable of."

"I'm sure you've got more than enough competition right here. Shall we begin?"

The participants each put a single pin in the center of the table. Velas, after some thought, put the Sytira pin that Asphodel had given her in the center. *I'd be no good in the Sytira branch. Maybe this competition is why Asphodel gave it to me?*

Sterling ordered the first round of drinks. It was heavy ale, and after downing the mug Velas felt like she had just eaten an extra lunch.

Eridus looked green in the face after the first few sips. He stirred his finger in the mug for a few moments, then frowned and took another drink.

Both Sterling and Alden downed the beverages with no trouble at all.

Three drinks later, Eridus was leaning heavily against the table. Velas rubbed at her head, trying to chase away the blur that was covering her vision.

Sterling and Alden were bantering playfully, still barely seeming affected.

"So, Velas," Alden started, turning toward her. "You're a woman!"

Velas held a hand to her chest as if shocked. "Who told you?"

Alden let out a loud, echoing laugh. "It is obvious! But what, why are you in this?"

"You mean the competition? There are plenty of female paladins. Like, you know, the colonel."

Alden shook his head. "No, no! Female paladins are good. I mean the drinking game – not to offend, but you are much smaller than we are, yes?"

She shrugged. He wasn't entirely wrong – Alden looked like he had about two or three times her mass. Maybe more like five times her mass when he was sufficiently blurry.

"That's not all that matters," she mumbled. "'sides, it's fun."

"Ah, you are quite right! More drinks, Jon."

Sterling shook his head at the exchange, but waved at a nearby attendant for another round of drinks.

Okay, I'm starting to feel this pretty hard. Looks like Eridus is getting hit harder than I am – or wait, is he?

*Eridus wasn't slouching quite as much as he had been a few minutes before. Velas frowned.*

He was stirring his finger in his drink again.

*Oh, that little bastard.*

She pondered his strategy for a moment – could Sterling or Alden be doing the same thing? Could she do anything analogous herself?

*My "sorcery resistance" might be applicable here...if I can find the alcohol in my body, maybe I could expel it somehow. It's liquid, though – how could I get rid of it without making a mess?*

As she debated that, Sterling returned with more drinks, and the world grew a little bit heavier with each sip.

*Need to think. World uncooperative.*

She raised a hand to her forehead, wiping it off, and noticed Eridus standing and rushing inside the tavern.

"One out," Sterling noted with a grin. He raised a hand and tilted his hat toward the tavern.

*Guess Eridus' bladder wasn't cooperating - even if he was purifying his alcohol into water, it wouldn't help with that.*

*We'll all have to deal with that at some point, I suppose. If I can keep my head up that long.*

As Sterling put his hand back down on the table, Velas noted a glint of metal – a simple silver band, turned around with a clear gemstone facing inward toward his palm.

*Well, well. Guess Sterling has a little trick, too.*

Alden yawned and stretched loudly, cracking his back. "It is good drinking. We should do more of this."

Velas nodded weakly, pressing a hand against the table and closing her eyes. *Okay, alcohol. Where do you live?*

She tried to focus, picturing the dominions in her body as auras of shimmering light, but the mixture of inebriation and the remaining pain in her legs made it difficult to focus.

*Okay, not good enough, too muddled. Take another drink.*

She raised her mug and drank, focusing on the liquid as it poured down her throat. This made it easier to envision, a stream of green fluid passing into her body. She could sense similar components already within her stomach, small intestines, bladder, liver, and blood.

Locking on to the parts that were alcoholic was more difficult. She knew her liver would already be at work on trying to break some of the alcohol down, but she had no way of discerning which components of the alcohol had already been metabolized. Without a common characteristic to search for, she couldn't concentrate sufficiently to identify which parts of the alcohol were toxic to her and separate it from the raw water.

"You all right there, Jaldin? Still with us?" Sterling was grinning at her when she opened her eyes.

"Just savoring the drink," she said. "More."

"We cannot argue with the woman!" Alden pronounced. "More!"

Sterling chuckled and nodded, ordering more drinks.

*Need to think. Can't handle much more of this. Tired.*

She laid her head down on her arms, closing her eyes for a moment. The sound of a mug slamming against the table jarred her back into alertness.

"More!" Alden pronounced, turning to Sterling. "I will see you drunk yet, my friend."

"Yes, keep dreaming, Alden. It's good to keep your spirit alive, even as your strength falters."

"Oh, you're taunting, it will do you no good!'

The next round of drinks arrived. Velas stared at her mug, narrowing her eyes.

*The enemy. I will defeat the enemy.*

Her hand slapped against the side of the mug, missing the handle.

Alden laughed loudly, grabbing the mug. "I will drink this one and give you a chance to recover, yes? Would not want you to be done so soon."

"Psh, th'as mine. Give it back," Velas motioned.

Alden shook his head, handing her the cup. Velas frowned as she lifted it to her mouth. Taking the big man up on his offer might have been a good strategy, but she wasn't going to take charity from someone who thought she couldn't hold her liquor just because she was a woman.

She'd already beaten Eridus, anyway.

As her eyes shut again, she felt the liquid seeping into her more thoroughly. The greater quantity of alcohol seeping into her bloodstream made it easier to envision, bright green against the standard red composition of her blood.

*Fuck, may as well try it.*

She pressed a right hand against the wooden underside of the table.
*Expulse.*

She watched the green swirl and shift within her body, rushing to her right hand – where it remained. She shuddered momentarily as something like an electrical shock flickered in her mind.

*Okay, think I did a bad thing.*

The jolt of pain passed quickly, but the green aura in her hand failed to escape as she had envisioned. *Guess I can't pass liquid out of my skin that easily. Who knew?*

*If I vomited, I could probably get it out that way – but that would probably lose me the contest. Running to the privy is out of the question, too. I need another way to get liquid out of my body.*

She rubbed her hand along the underside of the table, subtly finding an exposed nail. She contemplated that for a moment.

*Fuck that, this contest isn't worth tetanus.*

Instead, she lifted her cup with her right hand, subtly unsheathing her sword just a fraction with her left. As she drank, she brushed her left thumb across the edge near the hilt, and then let the sword slide back into place.

*Sharp blades leave painless wounds, they say. Bunch of bullshit.*

Velas pressed the shallow wound against her pant leg, setting down her drink. She grinned as she closed her eyes.

*Expulse.*

The verdant aura flowed through her body, and she twisted it toward her hand – and into her injured thumb. The blood flowing from the wound had nowhere near the volume of the alcohol, but she wasn't trying to expel the entire drink – just the poison that was clouding her mind and body. Drop by drop, the toxin dripped away.

Her eyes fluttered back open, her mind beginning to clear. "Okay, boys. Next drink."

***

Hours later, Alden was finally defeated, lying asleep on the table. Sterling still looked invincible, untouched.

"That was quite an impressive recovery you made." Sterling leaned his elbows on the table, staring across at Velas. "I wasn't expecting anyone to compete with Alden in raw fortitude."

"I love to surprise people. So, it's your ring, yeah?"

Sterling raised his left hand to his chest, an expression of mock shock on his face. "This simple family heirloom? Whatever do you mean, Lady Jaldin?"

"It's just Velas, or Dame Jaldin if you really have to." She shook her head, which was starting to ache from the next set of accumulated alcohol. Even with her efforts to pool and bleed away the toxin, she had failed to rid her body of it entirely – and the wound had clotted and ceased to bleed long ago. "And anyway, it's a clever trick. I don't blame you or anything. A lot subtler than Eridus and his stirring."

"A little subtler, but a lot more effective, it would seem. Or perhaps I was just built from sterner stuff to start with."

Velas grinned. "I suspect so."

"Well, if you know my secret, I suppose we can call this game to an end?" He gazed toward the horizon. "The dawnfire is setting, and it will soon be time to meet with our companions."

"Take off the ring and share a few more drinks with me first. Then we'll talk about a winner."

Sterling lowered his gaze, giving her a wolfish grin. "We have a deal."

\*\*\*

Velas trudged toward the parade ground, rubbing her throbbing head as she walked. Three pins remained on her tunic – Aendaryn, Lysandri, and Eratar.

Sterling walked cheerfully a few yards away, spinning every few steps to display the six pins on his shirt to the other approaching candidates.

It had been a close thing in the end, but Velas wasn't willing to cut herself again to remain competitive. The injury itself wouldn't have bothered her much, but she doubted she could have concealed using the method a second time. She had solidly stomped Alden and Eridus – and that was more than good enough.

More importantly, now she had valuable information on one more member of her platoon and two more competitors – not a bad result for an afternoon.

Landen was looking downcast when she caught sight of him, sitting on a rocky outcropping not far from the parade field where they had agreed to meet. He didn't seem to notice her approaching. His fingers toyed with the single pin on his tunic.

As she approached, Velas reached up to her own set of three.

*Two is the minimum to pass. It won't be a good score for either of us, but we'll both make it.*

Taelien came into view a moment later, sitting down next to Landen, offering an outstretched hand with three pins sitting in it.

Velas blinked, pausing in her step and lowering her hand.

Taelien had the faintest hint of a smile on his face as Landen took one of the pins, staring at it with an expression of disbelief.

Taelien's arms quivered slightly as he pushed the remaining two pins at Landen. His shirt was soaked through with sweat.

226

It also had seven pins attached to his right breast – one for each of the seven gods.

*How...?*

The metal sorcerer broke into a series of wracking coughs – and that was enough an answer.

*He...he made more pins.*

*He spent the entire day fabricating more sigils.*

Velas broke into a laugh, drawing the attention of both of the sitting men, and rushed forward to embrace them both in a powerful hug.

\*\*\*

Before the officers took their places on the parade grounds, Velas watched as Taelien walked to each of the candidates as they arrived and offered them a single pin of his creation. They were nearly indistinguishable from the official ones used in the tournament.

Velas, in spite of already having enough to pass, accepted one of Taelien's pins of Aendaryn and wore it proudly.

*Resh, Taelien. That was a good play.*

She noted as he paused at the dejected few who had lost their only pin during the day and offered them a second one from his own supply. She realized that he must have made more pins than the total pool that they had started with - easily enough that he could have outfitted his entire platoon with a full set if he had wanted to.

But he didn't only help his own platoon. Aside from favoring Landen with that first few, he didn't even seem to show the rest of them any sort of preference.

And when he was done, Velas saw many of the other candidates looking at Taelien with something she had seen before – once, in what seemed like a different life now.

Loyalty.

And, for the first time in nearly a year, she stood in line with companions at her side and felt the warmth of pride.

## INTERLUDE I – RIALLA I - SHIVER

Though Rialla's garb left little more than her eyes exposed, she still felt the chill of the nightfrost in the air. She remembered the joy of her childhood-self blowing softly into the air on nights like this one, seeing the ice forming from her breath.

She absently waved a hand in the air, icy knives manifesting in front of each of her fingers, and then vanishing as quickly as they appeared.

There would be no joy in the cold of this night.

She circled her target's home – a single story building on the western edge of the Market District. The house was a simple wooden structure with one door on the southern end and windows on the eastern and western sides. From the dimensions, she judged there to be about three separate rooms – a sign of simplicity, but not poverty.

The home lacked any exterior decoration. A logging axe sat beside a timber pile not far from the door, and she noted a resemblance between the wood in the pile and the beams of the house itself.

A light source provided dim illumination in the western wing of the home. She knew her destination.

*Shadows: Surround.*

The shadows cast from the nightfrost's light upon the home bent and swirled around her, pressing against her clothing and exposed skin. So long as she remained within the darkness, only the keenest of eyes would detect her presence. The technique lacked the effectiveness of Jonan's talents during the day, but it would suffice for her current purpose.

Though she had initially considered entering through the window nearest the light source, coming close enough to see through the glass would give her target a moment to see her within the contrast. It was a needless risk.

She approached the front door, closing her eyes.

*Travel: Flicker.*

She stepped through the door as if it did not exist, reopening her eyes.

At first, the entry room appeared to contain little of interest, save a pair of kitchen knives that could potentially serve as weapons. At a second glance, she caught sight of a small shelf near where she had entered, housing multiple pairs of shoes and boots – some of which were clearly sized for children.

Rialla tightened her jaw and flexed her fingers in the air.

The hint of illumination came from beyond a door on the left side of the room. She approached, turning the handle softly, but she had no sorcery to suppress the creak when the misaligned wood scraped against the floor.

A stone wall of a man sat at a work desk, the ink on his hands illuminated by the light of a single candle. His grey beard was cut military short and matched the tone of his little remaining hair. He turned as the door creaked, looked straight at her, and raised a finger in a hushing gesture. Then, with a second motion, he pointed to a nearby bed – and the two children, looking to be no older than six, sleeping within.

Rialla nodded, stepping away from the door.

The bearded man stood, wiping his hands on his pants, and followed her into the entry. He closed the door behind them, leaving the pair in darkness.

"Never could quite set that door right," he spoke softly, walking past her to sit in one of the crude wooden chairs near a kitchen table. Rialla's eyes went to one of the knives, now only inches from his grasp, but she did not act save to turn toward him.

He put his elbows on the table, turning his head toward her. "So, what're you? Thorn? Blackstone?"

She shook her head. "Shiver. Attendant to Symphony."

He let out a low rumble of a laugh. "One of the lady of thieves' own, eh? Don't know what I did to garner such austere attention. You are aware I'm retired?"

Rialla gave him a curt nod. "Ostensibly."

"Well, you won't find much to pilfer here, I'm afraid. Your matron might be disappointed. But if you're feeling as chill as your name, I can light the fire and make us some tea."

"I won't be staying long."

"No," he tilted his head downward, a warning in his expression. "You won't be."

She felt an itch at the back of her head – it said to strike now, while he was relatively unprepared.

She did not.

"You once trained a man named Cassius Morn. What do you know of his current whereabouts?"

The older man narrowed his eyes. "I might not be able to chop wood with my memory these days, but I don't remember training any 'Cassius Morn'. He go by another name?"

Rialla folded her arms. She had been concerned about this possibility. "Very possible. Short, around five foot four, possibly even shorter when you knew him. Would have been around fifteen when you trained him. Brown hair and eyes. He was in Thornguard training at the time and went to you for personal sword training."

"How many years ago would this have been?"

"Somewhere between six and ten."

The older man never took his eyes off her, but he furrowed his brow in thought. "I didn't train many Thornguard… but I do believe I know who you mean."

"What can you tell me about him?"

The older man folded his arms, each nearly as thick as one of Rialla's thighs. "You're going to need to give me a reason why I should tell you."

Aayara probably would have told her to point at the nearby room where the children were sleeping.

Jonan would have likely tried to convince the man that cooperating with her would somehow be mutually beneficial.

Rialla nodded once. "He has been killing people."

The large man exhaled a deep breath. "You have my sympathies for your friends. Afraid I don't know much that could be of use to you, however. I have not seen your 'Cassius' in many years."

His words did not sound like a lie. She considered using her eyes to force the truth from him, but a veteran might understand the tactic, and she did not wish to play her hand so soon.

"You said he did not go by Cassius. What name did he use?"

"Morgan Stern," the older man answered immediately. "Claimed he was from some famous house back in Selyr."

"I may be able to use that. Do you know of anyone else who might have any idea where he is?"

"Would have told you to go to the Thornguard, but I take it that avenue would have been exhausted long before you came to me... but wait. Morgan did have a friend who came to watch him train on occasion." He scratched at his beard. "Don't think I ever caught his name. Something...horse. Stallion, maybe? Could have been one of your famous guild names, I suppose."

She nodded in agreement with his logic. "Can you describe him?"

"Gods, I barely saw him. Taller, I think? It's been ages. I think that's the best I can give you."

"It has been sufficient. I thank you for your time, Master Herod."

"Good." He stood from his chair, meeting her gaze directly. "I do hope you find your killer, Miss Shiver. But if you ever come here again, even the lady of thieves will never find what is left of you."

Rialla bowed slightly at the waist. "You have been perfectly clear. In that case, I will adjourn."

Shiver retreated, never turning her gaze away from the man, closing her eyes for only an instant as she reached the door.

*Travel: Flicker.*

She stepped backward, carrying herself out of the building, and withdrew into the night.

***

When Rialla slunk back into the Theas manor, she found Jonan conspicuously missing from the bed chamber that had been set aside for them. Uninterested in conversation with the patrolling guards, she concealed herself while she wandered the halls to find him. It was a disturbingly simple affair, leading her to the conclusion that other intruders could do the same without difficulty.

"Stop moving." The familiar voice was accompanied by a burst of flame that disrupted the wreath of shadows that enshrouded her.

231

*How did he—*

"I mean now. No sudden movements."

She frowned and raised her hands in a gesture of peace. "It's just me."

She heard Jonan sigh behind her. "Gods, Ri – Vorianna, you can't just walk around concealed like that. You'll alarm people who detect you – like myself, for example."

"I was looking for you." Rialla spun around, folding her arms. There was no sign of Jonan behind her – not even a shadow. "Oh, you're going to lecture me while you're invisible? Hypocrisy, thy name is Kestrian."

Jonan appeared, rubbing the side of his head, looking haggard. "They *know* I wander around here invisible, Vorianna. That's part of our security plan. They are *not* aware that you are a shadow sorceress, and even I couldn't distinguish who you were in that state. You can take that as a compliment to your abilities, but please use them with a bit more discretion."

She folded her arms. "I didn't want to deal with people."

"Fine." He waved a hand at her. She saw him shimmer for a moment and understood that he had just made the pair of them invisible – the visual effect was unnecessary, it was simply a courtesy on his part. "Now you don't have to. Follow me."

Rialla nodded gratefully. Social contact with strangers was the last thing she needed right now.

Jonan led the way to an unfamiliar room on the second floor of the manor, turned a key in the lock, and opened the door.

The walls within were lined with a familiar set of mirrors. Others were standing in a hexagonal shape near the middle of the room – with one missing face, presumably so someone could walk inside and look at them. Each showed a different image, and at a glance, she guessed there were at least fifteen mirrors in total within the room.

Jonan gestured for her to follow as he stepped in, closing and locking the door after she followed him inside.

He waved his hand, shimmering again, indicating an end to their invisibility. "My new staging area."

She whistled softly. "You had the mirrors transported here?"

"Not all of them – just the new ones and a few others. I've spent most of the day figuring out what Aayara meant by improved – and I just discovered one of the things she was referring to." He jerked a thumb at a mirror on the right side of the chamber.

The image within was a figure stalking the halls of House Theas, enshrouded in shadows. Rather than nearly invisible within the mundane darkness, however, a bright green outline surrounded the figure. "Ah, that's how you found me. So, these new mirrors detect and display sorcerous auras?"

Kestrian nodded and sat on the floor. There were no chairs in the room, no tables – any furniture within must have been removed to accommodate the mirrors. "Some specific dominions, at least. Apparently shadow is one of them. They do the same for sight sorcery, so you could have caught me through the same method."

She sat down across from him and folded her arms. "Wouldn't help much if I can't activate them."

"Aayara seems to have intended for these mirrors to be somewhat more accessible than mine. Sight sorcery is no longer necessary. There are glyphs on the frames with specific functions – all you have to do is touch them."

Rialla raised an eyebrow. "That sounds very useful."

"Makes me feel somewhat obsolete, but yes. Now that I've figured out how these work, it's my intent to share that information with the guards and keep one of them in here at all times. As you saw, the mirrors are excellent for catching intruders."

"But what are these mirrors looking at? I didn't see any matching mirror in the hallway."

"Most of these," he pointed to the mirrors behind him, "correspond to a specific mirror in a bed chamber. For the hallways, I had to be somewhat more creative. Initially, I asked Baroness Nedelya if I could build mirrors into the masonry above the halls. She was quite insistent that would be disruptive to the 'ambiance' of the manor, whatever that means."

He paused for a moment, pointing downward. "So, we pulled up some of the floor boards in the upper floor, and put the mirrors underneath the boards, facing downward. Then, I dominion bonded the surfaces below the mirrors to be invisible to sight sorcery. Thus, all the hallways on the first floor – and some of the ones on the second floor – are being watched by mirrors concealed above them."

Rialla whistled appreciatively. "Not a bad idea. Seems like you're a bit short on mirror coverage, though."

He nodded. "It isn't perfect – we didn't have enough mirrors to cover the grounds, and I wanted to keep a few of them back at 'home'. I prioritized having the new ones moved, since they're more reliable for this sort of situation. The ones I made were primarily for long-term observation, not identifying immediate threats."

"You should tell me about all the functions of the new mirrors, but first, we should discuss our assignment."

"I suppose this room is probably secure enough. What did you find?"

She glanced from side-to-side self-consciously at his statement, feeling a new pang of nervousness. "Nothing of great significance. His old teacher has not seen him in years – but he did use another identity at some point. Morgan Stern. He also apparently had an ally that went by 'Stallion' or another horse-derived name."

"Stallion? An 'ess', maybe?"

"Seems likely. I will inquire about a 'Stallion' at the Thornguard base tomorrow."

Jonan scratched his chin. "Thanks. I haven't found much – I talked to one other 'ess', but she didn't have anything on him."

Rialla narrowed her indigo eyes. "You didn't tell me you had another contact here."

"She's just someone I had to deliver something to. Symphony prefers for us to keep our information compartmentalized."

"I am aware, but I find it frustrating."

Jonan covered his face with his hand. "Why'd you get involved with her? I warned you not to. This… you shouldn't have to deal with assignments like this."

"Really? You're going to chastise me for taking a deal with your own master?"

Jonan put his hand down, tensing his jaw. "I didn't choose this life, Rialla. I brought you to Selyr to try to find help. You follow Aayara long enough, the only thing you're going to find is knives in the dark."

Rialla pushed herself off the floor, leaning down toward Jonan. "You think I don't know that? You're sweet, Kestrian, but you're also hopelessly naïve if you think I ever had a choice. She found me within days of my arrival in Selyr and made me an offer. I delayed as long as I could, but Elias needed help."

Jonan lay back on the ground, turning his head away. "There were other choices. Rethri sorcerers who might have looked for the solution to your brother's problem – or other Vae'kes. Ones with smaller prices for their help, like Diamond or Sharp."

"You think going to another Vae'kes after Aayara offered me employment would have worked in my favor? Please, Kestrian, listen to yourself. Going to Sharp just would have put me in Aayara's net through an intermediary. Going to Diamond would have risked angering her – and Diamond would have offered no protection from that."

Jonan shut his eyes. "The cost, though—"

Rialla smiled softly. "Where I come from, there's a nursery rhyme about the Blackstone assassin."

*"Ever fear the stone of black, for when you are alone, the Blackstone the shadow comes to visit you, and traps you in his stone—"*

"That's the one. It never scared me. When I was young, it was just a silly rhyme. By the time I was old enough to understand it, I knew there were worse fates than anything Jacinth offered. A swift blade through the heart doesn't scare me."

Rialla tightened her hands into fists. "Symphony, on the other hand? Her stories terrified me. The story about Red Connor, who scorned Symphony and found his wife and children dead by his own hand. The tale of the Mad Countess, who claimed to be more beautiful than Aayara, and woke without a face. Those are the costs for defying the Thief, Jonan."

"I know." His voice was barely a whisper. "I'm sorry. I didn't mean to attract her to you."

"No, Jonan." She smiled. "A master of terrifying power may be exactly what I need."

## CHAPTER XV – LYDIA IV – AN IMMORTAL'S JUDGMENT

Lydia rubbed at her temples, ineffectively combating the headache that was developing from the overuse of her sorcery. As much as she would have preferred to use more mundane searching methods, they simply weren't time efficient – and the longer she waited, the higher the likelihood the assassin could claim a second victim.

*Wonder which bits of knowledge I sacrificed today. Maybe I'll fail to recognize one of my friends when I go back to the citadel. It wouldn't be the first time.*

Climbing the spiral staircase between rooms, she briefly removed a small mirror from her pouch, glancing at the surface. A fresh note was reflected in the mirror, causing her to momentarily pause in her step.

*Most likely not one of mine. Others more likely.*

*Blake Hartigan. Ulandir Ta'thyriel. Shalvinar Vorinthal. Nakane Theas. Volanen Dianis. Erik Tarren.*

Lydia slipped the mirror away.

*Erik Tarren? That's a rather depressing thought, but not quite crazy. I doubt it's Nakane. Her reaction to her brother's death has been pretty cold, but that's probably just a reflection of her father's personality. Baron Theas has a reputation for being very matter-of-fact.*

*I'll need to write back to Jonan soon and see if I can get him to investigate some of the others while I finish things here.*

She shook her head, moving to the entrance of the next chamber, with Blake Hartigan only a few steps behind her. Thus far, he had shown only amusement at her efforts to find signs that he was responsible for Kalsiris Theas' death. She had suspected the legendary sorcerer would have restricted her movements within the tower, but he had simply allowed her to wander through his home, throwing investigative spells out in the most efficient ways she could manage. His home was littered with objects carrying sorcerous auras – even some of the silverware had glowed under her observation. The man was famous for his enchanting skills, but even she hadn't expected the sheer number of dominion bonded items he had around. A thief could have retired by pawning the contents of one of Hartigan's closets.

By the time she found a room that interested her, Lydia's mind was burning from the scars of information her dominion had torn from her mind. Nevertheless, when she opened the door to the alchemical lab, she continued with her usual procedure.

"Dominion of Knowledge, illuminate that which is touched by your cousins."

The flash of green illuminated the content of dozens of vials on the shelves and tables of the circular chamber. Lydia forced herself not to blink, maintaining the effect while she searched for spots with unusual intensity or other objects that provided a glow.

She found what she was looking for on the second shelf from the top on the left side of the chamber.

"Dominion Essence, solid form," she noted, inspecting the row of glowing jars. The jars were circular, with a broad base – about the length of a hand. Some contained only a few pebble-sized nuggets. Others were completely filled. She blinked, dismissing her spell, which allowed her to read the labels on the sides of the jars.

*Dominion of Flame.*
*Dominion of Flame – Refined.*
*Dominion of Lightning.*
*Dominion of Protection.*
*Dominion of Sight.*
*Dominion of Air.*
*Dominion of Motion.*
*Dominion of Knowledge.*
*Dominion of Travel.*

Lydia adjusted her glasses, inspecting the last jar. There were only a few stones inside, each seemingly a small, perfect sphere. *They look like the marbles I used to play with as a child. How oddly ordinary.*

*No Dominion of Poison, but of course, he wouldn't necessarily keep anything that incriminating along with the rest of the supplies. And these are solid — just like the stone I found.*

She turned to Hartigan. "It's unusual to see dominion essence in a solid form when it isn't for a solid dominion, like stone or metal. You also seem to have an extraordinary amount of some of these types. Can you explain to me how you obtained this essence and what it is used for?"

"Well, if you have time for a lecture, I suppose. I thought you were here for an investigation." He scratched at his chin, his eyes showing his amusement. "That ring you're wearing. How do you think it was made?"

She lifted up her hand, glancing at the blue-white crystal inlaid in the silvery band. "Typically, objects are dominion bonded by saturating them in the desired form of essence, and then casting a spell to activate the essence within, creating a specific persistent effect. The object is powered by the essence until the supply runs out."

Hartigan nodded, waving a hand. "Yes, typically. What about that ring?"

*I didn't come here to feel like a child in a classroom.* "You're implying that the crystal in the band is dominion essence, I take it?"

"Yes, but that's not the important part. It was something of a trick question, unless you've had a chance to look beneath the gem."

She raised an eyebrow. "Beneath the gem?"

"That's where the marks go."

Lydia folded her arms, standing up straighter and shifting her weight. *That…would make some degree of sense, actually. I had assumed Donovan had come up with his method of dominion marking items — and later, people — completely on his own. If Hartigan had already figured out how to mark items, Donovan just needed to figure out how to apply them to people, rather than objects. That would have required much less research, and less of a logical leap to even get started with the attempt.*

She glanced back at the jars, then straight at Hartigan. "If that's true — and this is a dominion marked ring — that means you've known how to mark items for years."

The sorcerer nodded, leaning back against a table in the center of the room that hosted a wide variety of alchemical supplies. "Yes, that's true."

Her expression darkened into a glower. "And you taught that technique to Donovan, and presumably some of your other apprentices?"

The ancient sorcerer let out a sigh, shaking his head. "Yes, I did. I can see where this line of questioning is going."

"Why? Why didn't you share that knowledge with everyone? The things we could make if we knew how –"

"That's precisely the reason why I didn't give out that knowledge freely, girl. People are dangerous enough without the kind of weapons they could develop with dominion marks. I took the utmost care in ensuring my creations would not be abused – and even so, I failed. I gave that ring to Donovan – gave him the secrets necessary to make more items like it – and he used that knowledge to make the pretense of godhood."

Hartigan stood up, the humor faded from his expression. He took a step forward, straightening his back and leaning forward. "Donovan was a good man. One of the best I knew. He was a true believer in Sytira, and in sharing for the betterment of all those that live. You saw first-hand the results of his dedication to that cause."

Lydia took a step back. Hartigan was vastly more intimidating when he was looming over her, no longer projecting the illusion of a simple old man. The mirth on his face had shifted into a blend of anger and sorrow, and she had little interest in provoking that further – but she could not stop herself from speaking.

"Donovan was only capable of that deception because so few of us could even conceptualize the idea of humans being able to create dominion marks. Even the knowledge that the technique was possible could have prevented –"

"Bah. He wasn't deceiving a city full of sorcerers, Miss Scryer. He was lying to ordinary folks, in the same manner other sorcerers have for centuries. You think a farmer or a blacksmith knows enough about sorcerous theory to say 'Oh, he's probably just using dominion marks'? That's folly, and you should know better."

"You're mischaracterizing my argument. He had other sorcerers working for him – and certainly many others passing through the kingdom. One of them would have figured him out."

"And who is to say that they didn't? You may have been the one to take the steps to overthrow him, yes, but that does not mean that others were unaware of his actions. One does not simply overthrow a god – real or false – without consequences. What is happening in his city now, I wonder?"

*Byron is ruling, at least in name. His mother most likely continues to puppet the government, but now she lacks any significant competition. She retains her reputation as a 'goddess', even with Edon marked as a traitor. If she proves to be a worse ruler than Edon was, we may have made a terrible mistake.*

"Nevertheless," she looked away, "There is a significant potential for doing good with this type of knowledge. I can understand your hesitation, since Donovan clearly abused the trust you gave him, but that does not mean that you were wrong to teach him."

Hartigan let out a deep laugh, bending over at the waist. "Oh, child. The irony may be lost on you, but you sound just like he did."

She turned back to him, tilting her head to the side.

Hartigan rubbed at his forehead. "Donovan told me the same thing, you know. That we should share all my secrets – compressing essence, my supposed immortality, how to make dominion marks. In some respects, I'm surprised he didn't do it himself after he left my service. You heard him preach, I'm sure, or at least heard about his philosophy – that humans should strive toward divinity. Ultimately, I'm sure that's why he claimed to be a god himself; he wanted to believe it was possible, and to encourage others to do the same. And yet, he still did not share the secrets. Why do you think that is?"

"I assumed it was that he only wanted to extend that kind of power to people he trusted would not use it against him. His knowledge was the most powerful tool for his vendetta against the true gods."

"Perhaps that was a part of the answer. And, in some respects, I admit it is part of my own. Fear. But not a fear of my own death at the hands of other sorcerers, as you might expect – I faced the inevitability of my own demise many years ago. You may find that strange to hear, coming from a supposed immortal, but the truth is that at my age, death is a constant companion. I will welcome the chance to meet him when my work is done, but that, I fear, is a long way away."

Lydia folded her hands in front of her. "If not death, then, what do you fear?"

"Nothing less than the extinction of the human race, my dear. That, I believe, is where sharing this knowledge with the world would lead."

She quirked an eyebrow. "That's quite a leap. I saw Donovan manage some impressive things, and I've heard stories about Hartigan's Star, but—"

"Hartigan's Star is the pinnacle of my accomplishments – and my eternal shame. I should have destroyed it as soon as I realized what it was capable of. I still should destroy it, my pride – and my fear – bar me from the rational course."

"Why would you want to destroy the ring?"

He lowered his head. "Because, Miss Scryer, that ring could consume the world in fire."

She narrowed her eyes. "Surely you're being hyperbolic with that statement."

"I do not think so. Have you attempted to use that ring you are wearing?"

She lifted up her right hand, examining the ring again. "Yes, but I have never managed to make it work."

"Good. That means Donovan did not abandon the protections I placed on it – not entirely, at least. Show me how you've tried to use it."

She pointed her hand at him. "You certain that's a good idea? There are sorcerous objects all over this room."

"We both know the ring isn't going to activate, I just want to see your methodology." He waved a hand dismissively. "Please, humor me."

*I don't really want to give away that I've been studying the language Edon constructed, but the potential gains from this conversation outweigh the risks.*

"Eru volar shen taris," she spoke, using the same incantation Edon had to create his blue-white fire. She had tried the other incantations Edon had used as well, but none of them appeared to function. Her identification spell had indicated the ring was tied to the dominion of flame, indicating that the fire spell was the most likely candidate for the ring's function.

"Ah, interesting." He nodded. "Thank you. You seem to have some idea of what you're doing, but you're missing a key step. And one you couldn't have been fairly expected to guess."

*You don't need to placate me, just give me the answer.* "Which is?"

"Do you know what makes dominion marked items superior to simple dominion bonded ones?"

Lydia sighed. *Another question to answer a question. I don't blame him for wanting to flaunt his knowledge, but this is getting a little excessive.*

"Primarily flexibility, from what I understand. A dominion bonded item just has a pool of essence from a single dominion to draw from and a set function. Edon appeared to be able to make the same item have multiple different functions by invoking the dominion mark in different ways."

Hartigan turned around, lifting a vial off of the table. "A good answer, but not the key one, if you'll forgive my sorcery pun. In fact, until I heard your incantation there, I had barely considered the application you just described. That's all Edon's work, and I thank you for sharing it with me."

*Oh, bastard.*

"My reasons for using dominion marks is quite different. You touched on the first point, if not directly – a dominion marked item can access multiple different dominions at once. The mark itself is imbued with essence, rather than the entire item. That is not the most important part either, however. The most important part is the ability to connect a dominion marked item to other things."

*Like how Edon marked humans, allowing them to draw from the items at a distance. Someone with dozens of marks could presumably have access to dozens of types of sorcery without even carrying a single item on them.* "You can bond the items to specific people to give the person access to new types of sorcery. That does seem like it has vast potential for someone wealthy enough to make a large variety of items. Like yourself, for example."

Hartigan nodded absently. "Oh, yes, that's possible. But that's not the most important part, either."

*What else could he mean? Using bonds to make a sorcerer stronger at their own specialization, perhaps, or combining different types of sorcery together in ways that are normally impossible?*

She gave no indication of her thoughts, and after a moment, he smirked and spoke again. "The dominions themselves, Miss Scryer. There are three marks beneath the stone. The first allows the wearer to use the stone to connect with the Dominion of Flame, using the stone's essence as a catalyst instead of the user's. The second mark draws continuously from the Dominion of Flame to restore the stone to its full capacity. The third mark prevents the ring from being activated by anyone who is not bonded to it."

Lydia raised a hand and rubbed her forehead. *Of course it doesn't work unless it's been bonded. That's such an obvious defense mechanism – I can't believe I didn't think of it.*

"Why are you telling me all this? Didn't you just explain that it was too dangerous to share all this information?"

He shrugged. "I'm only telling you theory, Miss Scryer. That doesn't give you anywhere near enough information to replicate the process on its own. My reasoning is simple enough – I can't stand the idea of someone wearing one of my rings that doesn't even know how it works."

She fidgeted with the ring, turning it around on her finger. "That's magnanimous of you, considering how I obtained it, but I won't turn down information. Will you show me how to bond the ring to myself so I can actually use it?"

"Well, I suppose I should probably determine if you plan to arrest me first, my dear girl. It wouldn't do to equip you with the ring just to have you use it against me, would it?"

She chuckled. *Oh, is that what you're playing at? This has to be the world's most elaborate bribe.* "All right, Hartigan. That seems fair. So, to get back to the core point, you're saying you use all these pieces of solid essence in rings and other trinkets to make dominion marked items?"

"Not precisely. You see that there are two jars for the Dominion of Flame?"

She nodded. "Yes, one of them is marked 'refined.'" Examining the two jars, she noted that the stones in the first looked like simple red rocks – rough and uneven. The contents of the "refined" jar looked like cut gemstones, similar to the one in her ring. Or, she realized, the gems in the hilt and pommel of the Sae'kes.

*That could mean that even the gods themselves may have used similar techniques to Hartigan's when they constructed that blade. Fascinating.*

"As I'm sure you're aware, flame doesn't exactly like to be stored in a solid state. The same is true for many of the other dominions you see represented there. To get 'solid flame', I conjure dominion essence into specific materials that are capable of holding it. Those are volcanic rocks in the first jar; they can be safely saturated with a high degree of flame without melting or losing the essence. Once I have stored up several of those, I transfer the essence from them into something even more stable – an artificial gemstone, like the one in your ring. I will not tell you the process of making such gems; that step is what prevents most sorcerers from duplicating my work."

Hartigan walked to the opposite side of the room. "I've shared a great deal of valuable information with you, and asked for little in exchange. You may think this is to dissuade you from investigating me further, but I have no intention of interfering with justice. I did not kill the poor boy, of course, but you may proceed with your search through whatever means you find appropriate. I will ask, however, that you do not share the information on dominion marks that I have given to you."

"That request goes against the core tenets of the followers of Sytira, as I'm sure you're aware."

"And I hope my arguments have been sufficiently persuasive that you'll understand why an exception is necessary, Miss Scryer. You don't go around spreading knowledge about the Dominion of Void, either. There's a reason for that – it's simply too dangerous."

She rested her head against a fist, leaning back against the wall next to the shelf. "Very well. I will not distribute this knowledge broadly. I cannot claim I will not speak of it at all – some of it may be relevant to my investigation."

He raised an eyebrow at that. "How so?"

"A solid piece of dominion essence of poison was found at the scene of the murder. As I'm sure you're aware, dominion essence of poison is typically stored in a gaseous state. And you just revealed not only that you would be capable of storing it as a solid, but how and why you would do so."

"Oh, dear. It would appear that my ramblings have implicated me rather strongly, haven't they?" He smiled, putting a hand over his eyes. "This is what I get for talking too much."

"As a small point in your favor, I don't see any dominion essence of poison here."

Hartigan chuckled, still holding his hand over his eyes. "Meaningless, as you know. I could have simply run out, or stored it in another room. Or even another house. I'm sure you know I have other property."

"Yes. I do intend to search this place more thoroughly, but that can only help me positively identify you as connected to the murderer – I doubt I could find evidence to the contrary. I will read your alchemical notes, as we discussed, but you could have simply written any time you wanted on them – especially after coming back from a murder."

"Of course, of course. If you'll allow me a bit of freedom to influence you, however, I may be able to assist you in narrowing down your list of other suspects."

*Well, he certainly has clear motives to get me to investigate other people, regardless of whether or not he's actually guilty.* "If I tell you who I'm planning to investigate, you could warn them to hide any evidence if you're connected. Or even if you're not, and you just want to protect a friend."

"A fair point, although if I am connected to the murder, wouldn't I just warn my accomplices regardless of if I know they are being investigated? That leaves only the latter – and if I'm not connected with the murder, don't you find it unlikely I would approve of it?"

"Unlikely, yes. Impossible, no. If you want to help, you could simply provide me with your own list of people who I should investigate after I conclude my search here. Assuming I don't end up arresting you, of course."

He made a 'hmmm' noise and raised a finger to the front of his mouth. "I suppose I could do that, although seeing your list would allow me to comment on any names you've come up with and provide you with a better idea of who you should pursue or dismiss."

"I'll have to take the risk of wasting effort on unlikely candidates regardless of what you say. Your word that I should ignore someone as a suspect would, unfortunately, almost make them appear more suspicious."

"Very well. Provide me with what information you can share on the crime and I will provide you with my own list. You've already given me quite an interesting tidbit about the poison gem – not many could accomplish such a thing. In fact, I can think of only a few who could have served as the source of the item – but the gem could have been sold to another sorcerer, of course. Many of the pieces of dominion essence you see behind you were purchased from other sorcerers or made by my apprentices. If I take you on as an apprentice at some point, I would teach you the process of making similar items – but keep the first ones you create for myself, as a part of the fee for my training."

Lydia nodded. "That sounds like a fair trade. For now, however, let's work on that list."

***

Hours later, Lydia had finished her search of the building and rested in a guest bedroom. She had little fear that Hartigan would try to have her killed in the middle of the night – he seemed much more interested in manipulating her for his own ends than causing her harm.

And it helped that she sincerely doubted he was the killer.

True, she had found no direct evidence of his innocence, and he was almost too happy to help in her investigation – but an identify spell on his person had not detected the Dominion of Travel or the Dominion of Poison. Without the capability to cast travel or poison spells, his likelihood as the murderer was lessened significantly.

While it was possible he had dominion marked items that could serve those functions, bonds to those items would have been detected by her spell, and she doubted he would have had the foresight to break his bonds to the items before her visit.

Hartigan's ability to store solid dominion essence was simple enough that she could have replicated it herself – and Jonan had invented something analogous on his own, in a liquid state rather than a solid one – so that evidence didn't weigh against him particularly strongly. Hartigan also didn't seem to guard that particular knowledge anywhere near as carefully as he had guarded the secrets about the dominion marks, which meant he might have told any number of people about the method. Certainly his other apprentices would have the knowledge.

The remainder of the search had turned up little else related to the investigation, but Hartigan's libraries contained an impressive supply of obscure books, and his "armory" had a supply of dominion bonded items that rivaled one of the vaults of the Paladins of Tae'os as a whole. Coming back for training was a sincere temptation and she resolved to take his offer seriously after she had found Kae's murderer.

A shuffling sound near the entrance to the bedroom made Lydia spring to her feet to investigate. She found a handwritten note that had been slipped under the door.

*Miss Scryer,*

246

*I have a number of colleagues that have the capability to perform the spells necessary to commit the murder as you described, but few would have the motives to do so. My advice would be to consider the few names below as the most likely culprits.*

*House Theas has long protested the dominance of the Rethri on the city council. Edrick's has repeatedly antagonized the most powerful Rethri nobles, including the king. I doubt King Athelean would move against Edrick so openly, but other high noble families might be more brash. I would consider Ulandir Ta'thyriel and Volanen Dianis both capable of the crime and possessing sufficient motives.*

*Kae's sister, Nakane, may seem an obvious choice at first. She is a brilliant young woman and quite a powerful sorceress for her age. I feel she lacks the motive, however. When Edrick realized her sorcerous proficiencies matched my own more closely than his, he sent her to stay with me to spend a year in my tutelage. During that time, her greatest sorrow was her distance from her sick brother. I cannot believe she would have willingly done him harm – and she would not benefit from it. Even his death would not allow her to inherit House Theas. She is, after all, a woman.*

*When Edrick finally meets his end, the house will pass to the eldest male heir – Nakane's cousin, Larkin Theas. Larkin was shunned for his lack of ability with sorcery, and thus he left Velthryn many years ago to make his fortune by other means. I doubt he would be involved – the boy abandoned his name years ago. When he last wrote me, he called himself "Landen".*

*I wish you the best of luck in your investigation. May Sytira guide you and Xerasilis lead you to justice.*

*Blake Hartigan*

Lydia held the note for a moment in a trembling hand.

Landen is the next heir to House Theas. He could be the murderer, but another scenario is far more likely.

*He is, most likely, another assassination target.*

Lydia flipped over the note, retrieved a quill and ink from her pouch, and began to write.

## CHAPTER XVI – JONAN IV – STEALTH

"Find the cinderglow extract, would you?" Jonan gingerly held the crystalline flask as far from his face as possible, trying not to inhale the acrid odor it was emanating. He tilted the vial in his right hand just slightly, allowing a steady stream of green liquid to trickle into the blueish fluid in the flask. The sizzling sound at the contact between the fluids made him wince, but he retained his grip.

The left side of the work table held dozens of other mixtures and concoctions, each sealed and labeled based on their ingredients. The right side had a large bowl – currently empty – and several small vials with samples of assorted poisons.

"Am I one of your servants now?" Nakane complained, searching through the jars on a nearby shelf. "And I still don't think cinderglow is going to have any effect."

"It might not, but it's one of the only counteragents we haven't tried yet."

Nakane sighed aggressively, snatching a jar from the shelf and bringing it to another nearby table. Lifting a knife, she began to cut away at the wax seal around the rim. "You're enjoying this, aren't you?"

Jonan chuckled. "What makes you say that?"

"You haven't stopped grinning like an idiot in the last hour."

He shrugged, spilling a tiny bit of the flask's precious liquid onto the table. "Shit!" He set down the flask on a dry spot nearby and fumbled for the cork for the vial of dreamseed oil. As he corked the vial, he could see the few drops of spilled fluid burning into the metal. Cursing, he replaced the vial among its allies and grabbed a flask of water, pouring it onto the burning metal.

Jonan sighed as the burning ceased, leaving a puddle and a trail of awkward rents in the metallic barrier on the table. "Well," he conceded, "I suppose we probably wouldn't have wanted to drink that one."

Nakane folded her arms. "You're still trying the cinderglow. I've already opened it." She picked up the container and set it down on the table near his flask. "And clean up my table."

Jonan rolled his eyes, wiping his hands on his pants. "Yes, Lady Theas." He went to a nearby cupboard, opened it, and fetched a towel from within.

"Doesn't this seem like an exercise in futility to you? Even if you find an antidote to the poison that killed Kae, it's extraordinarily unlikely the assassin would be foolish enough to use it a second time."

Jonan shook his head, sopping up the mixture of water and his most recently failed counteragent. "It doesn't matter. I mean, well, it does matter – it would be better if the assassin does use the same poison. Or, rather, it would be the most ideal if he never attacks again at all, but –"

"You just want to be as prepared as possible. That's admirable; I just don't think this is a meaningful use of effort."

Jonan set down the towel, rinsing his hands in a nearby bowl of fresh water, and then pouring the now-tainted water into the nearby sink. *Use your words, Jonan. She's not that intimidating.*

He pointed to one of the samples of poison in the vials. With no ability to use the Dominion of Poison himself, he had taken the yellow orb that Lydia had found to the nearby Thornguard base and instructed a local poison sorcerer on how to convert it into liquid, much like how he gathered his own Dominion Essence of Sight for his mirrors. He disliked sharing his methodology, but Aayara already knew his secret – a couple more Thornguards with the knowledge wouldn't be likely to hurt him.

"We know this is from the Dominion of Poison, but we know very little about it, aside from its presumed lethality. If we can find a solution that neutralizes it, I can look up the antidote to try to find out what type of poison it is."

"Really?" Nakane leaned forward across her table toward him. "That's your brilliant plan? You do realize that this was the essence used in the portal – not the poison that was in my brother's body?"

Jonan nodded. It was a fair question, if needlessly pointed. "Yes, yes. But if we presume that the assassin was a summoned entity from a particular point in the Dominion of Poison related to the dominion essence we found, the creature itself would likely be composed of – or utilize – a similar poison to the poison from the crystal that powered the portal."

"That seems like a bit of a leap."

"I don't think so. How well versed are you in planar composition theory?"

The young lady of House Theas turned her head skyward. "You must be joking. My father wrote half the books on that subject."

"That doesn't necessarily mean you've read them."

"Well, I have. And written a few papers of my own, in fact."

"Right. In that case, you should be quite aware that most entities that are native to specific planes prefer to draw upon their own essence for what we would consider spells, rather than directly utilizing their connection to a plane. Then, they naturally regain their own strength – or enhance it further - by gathering essence from the core plane. A Gatherer of Flame, for example, would use their own body to fuel fiery attacks, and then recharge or enhance themselves by absorbing a campfire or whatnot."

"You're using a very specific example. Gatherers are relatively benign as far as planar natives go – they just collect their dominion's energies and then take them back home. Others, such as Harvesters, are considerably more dangerous. A Harvester will try to spread the power of its plane as broadly as possible to encourage its use, and then collect it all at once at a later time. And a Harvester is much more likely to be the agent at work here."

"Harvester or not, it's still likely to be drawing from its home location – which likely has a similar composition to the poison used in the portal."

"I still think that's a bit of a logical jump, but I do agree that knowing the composition of the crystal would be interesting, if most likely useless. Fine. You may continue to work."

"Thank you."

He wasn't exactly sure why he was thanking her for permission to try to save her life, but for some reason that always seemed like the natural response when he was dealing with Nakane.

They worked together for several more minutes before an intruder arrived.

"What's all this?" Rialla emerged from the stairway into the basement laboratory, still in her "Vorianna" guise. Jonan found it more than a little ridiculous, but he had to admit that was mostly because he already knew her. *I wonder if my own disguises come across as caricatures.*

"Just trying to find a useless cure to a poison we haven't even identified yet. You know, one of Jonan's typical brilliant ideas."

"Sure sounds like it." Rialla grinned brightly.

*You don't always have to agree with her.* Jonan clasped his hands in front of him, sighing. He slightly extended the pointer finger on his right hand, sending Rialla a subtle sign that he wanted to trade places with her soon. The silent communication wasn't strictly necessary, but it was good practice.

Rialla caught the gesture and made a similar one of her own. "You two need a hand with anything in here? Lady Theas – the elder, I mean, the baroness – is off to bed early tonight."

Jonan contemplated that for a moment, considering Rialla's skill set. *Actually, this might be a good test.*

"Actually, Vorianna, can you make Dominion Essence of Water? The supply here seems to have evaporated, and it could be useful for our attempts at making an antidote."

Rialla folded her arms. "S'pose I could try. Haven't made an effort at water sorcery since I was little, but I might be able to manage it."

"That would be fantastic. I'll get the empty vials in a moment."

"I already got them." Nakane set a small open crate on the corner of Jonan's table. A dozen empty vials were inside. She glanced at Vorianna with a dubious expression. "You never mentioned anything about your sorcery skills. Isn't it rare for Rethri to study sorcery other than their bonded dominion?"

Rialla scratched at the back of her head, looking sheepish. "Wouldn't call them skills, m'lady. Parents wanted me to be more impressive than I've got the talent for. Threw me at all sorts of classes when I was a girl. Never got much out of it, 'shamed to say."

"Why not just focus on your bonded dominion? Those eyes – it'd be what, secrets? Deception, or lies maybe?"

"Deception, m'lady. Not much good training for that, I'm afraid. Most practical applications of it are illegal, 'less I wanted to be a street magician or somesuch. Parents wanted me to make better than that."

"Well, I suppose being a guard is noble in its own sort of way."

Jonan barely suppressed the urge to roll his eyes at the exchange, focusing on setting up the next experiment. He set a fresh sample of poison on the right side of the table while beginning to mix the cinderglow extract with his other prepared ingredients.

The line of questioning had produced some interesting results among the obvious deflections – Rialla most likely had sorcery skills he hadn't seen yet, and water was one of the dominions she practiced. He had seen her utilize the Dominion of Ice once, but skill with one did not necessarily imply the other. More interestingly, he recalled rumors that Rialla's eye colors had changed between her arrival in Orlyn and her departure – indicating that perhaps her dominion bond had been altered somehow.

Her answers were fluid, nearly automatic, indicating either a layer of truth or a degree of practice at telling them. Determining which was the case could provide more amusement than any number of alchemical experiments.

He probably could have asked her some of these questions directly, but that would have spoiled the fun.

Rialla uncapped one of the bottles and closed her eyes to concentrate. Nakane, looking bored, seated herself nearby and folded her arms.

"Shouldn't one of you be watching my mother? Even if she's sleeping, someone should be nearby. In fact, she's probably most vulnerable while she's asleep."

Jonan shrugged. "We keep a guard rotation on the room. Given the hour, it's probably Dominic at the moment."

Nakane shifted in her chair. "Yes, we've all seen how helpful the house guards are at stopping assassins."

Jonan finished mixing his latest concoction, setting the flask down on the table while he poured a vial of poison into the nearby bowl. "In fairness, m'lady, it doesn't take a sorcerer to see an intruder and raise the alarm. The assassin's methodology could indicate a desire to avoid a direct confrontation. Either that, or the method of the killing was a signature, or in some way symbolic. In any of those cases, I suspect the mere presence of a guard would be a significant deterrent."

"Assuming the same assassin strikes twice. Given that we're obviously prepared now, it would seem more advantageous for whoever hired the assassin to send someone different for any subsequent attacks."

Jonan nodded, barely paying attention to the conversation. He poured a bit of the liquid from the flask into the bowl, watching it mix with the poison within. The resulting mixture was an inert red-orange fluid. "Hrm. This might have some potential."

He stoppered the flask and covered the bowl with a lid. "I'll check what state the mixture settles into in the morning."

"Good. If you're done here, you can go watch for intruders."

Jonan sighed, moving to the sink and pouring a flask of water over his hands to rinse them again. He didn't think he had spilled anything this time, but it was always better to be safe. "I suppose so. As long as you keep Vorianna with you."

"I assure you I am quite capable of defending myself, but if you insist, I will humor your request."

Jonan dried his hands on another towel, glancing at Rialla. She was still focusing on the vial, wearing a grimace. "Good night to you both then."

The sight sorcerer slumped his shoulders, shambling out of the chamber. Once he was out of sight, he straightened his back, shaking his head.

*Finally, free from observation. It's time to get to work.*

***

With most of the household sleeping, Jonan was free to wander the grounds outside without disruption. At least four guards would still be awake within the manor, in addition to Rialla, so he felt comfortable that the people within were relatively well defended.

The outside of the manor, however, was unguarded – and made them potentially vulnerable. In his time spent protecting the Theas family, Jonan had formulated a dozen plans for how attackers could bypass the guards and assassinate the victims within – and thus far his countermeasures only provided protection from a handful of those plans.

Tonight, he was setting up one more of his contingencies. Not a defense, exactly, but a foundation for a counter assault.

Invisible to the eye, Jonan walked a meandering path around the house. Near each entrance, he opened one of his pouches and poured a few ounces of glittering dust onto the road. A few flecks of his powder from the last time he had gone through this process were still visible, but he repeated the procedure every few days to ensure a useful amount of the dust remained in each location.

The powdered glass was taken directly from one of his mirrors, and thus already imbued with the Dominion of Sight. While the fragments were too small for him to use as viewing devices like the mirrors themselves, the dominion auras were still connected to the original mirror – and that connection could be tracked.

Anyone walking into the house through one of these entrances would come in contact with the dust, most likely picking up a few pieces on their boots. Jonan didn't have any spells prepared to track the dust, but he knew that Lydia could do so if she had access to the mirrors. In a worst case, he could seek out another knowledge sorcerer to perform a similar spell, or even attempt to research a more powerful variant of his remote viewing spell that would enable him to see through the glass dust.

The plan was far from perfect – an assassin could bypass the main doors, or the dust might not cling to the attacker's boots in the way he hoped – but it was one plan of many. The main benefits of being in a defensive position were that he had an intimate knowledge of the location and plenty of time to lay plans.

After covering the entrances, Jonan moved to the most likely discrete entry point for would-be attackers – the garden's hedge maze. It was a glaring vulnerability, given that the maze had an exit near the very edges of the Theas' property.

Even knowing that, Jonan was more than a little surprised when he noticed the figures moving within the maze.

*Are those people, or am I just halluc- nope, definitely people. Real people, coming my direction.*

He began backpedaling immediately. Of all the intricate plans that he had made, of all the contingencies he had laid traps for, running directly into a group of heavily armed intruders had not been among them.

*Shit. Shit.*

The figures were moving slowly, keeping their heads relatively low – an unnecessary precaution, given that the hedge maze's walls were taller than any of them. Dark garb concealed the details of their bodies, but even with masks covering the top halves of their faces Jonan could see one key detail – bright eyes lacking sclera.

Every intruder he could see was Rethri, and there were a lot of them.

As Jonan backed out of the maze, he took careful steps to avoid making any sound. His sight sorcery provided no defense against the other senses, and given the heightened state of alertness the intruders were certain to be in, he knew the slightest disruption could call their attention.

*Shit. Focus. What can I do that's useful?*

*I have a knife, some dust, and enough talent with flame sorcery to light dry parchment.*

*The assassins have, hrm, something like at least eight swords that I can see, a couple axes, at least two repeating crossbows, and a simply ludicrous number of throwing daggers.*

*Even Taelien wouldn't push these odds. I'm out of here.*

As he backed his way out of the hedge maze, Jonan had the presence of mind to empty out most of the remaining glass dust right at the exit to the path. He briefly considered lighting the hedge maze on fire, knowing that the flames could either spook the attackers or alert the guards, but the tactic would also rob him of the element of surprise.

He still had uses for that.

As soon as he had finished dusting the path, Jonan took off at a rapid walk, avoiding anything on the path that could cause noise. At his best guess, it would be about two minutes before the intruders made it out of the hedge maze. After that, he had no idea which entrance they planned to take, which would cost him any advantage he currently had.

He slipped inside the building and ran for the alchemy chamber.

Rialla was already drawing her sword when he burst into the room.

"Show yourself," she commanded, an aura of frost manifesting around her left hand.

"Oh, just me, terribly sorry." Jonan reappeared, scratching at the back of his head. "I need you."

Rialla quirked an eyebrow quizzically, pointing a finger at her chest.

He sighed, glancing from side to side. Nakane was no longer in the room – it was just Rialla present. "Yes, you."

A playful smirk crossed her face. "What sort of absurd antics could you need me for at this hour?"

"No playing right now, Rialla – we've got assassins."

Rialla's indigo eyes narrowed into slits. "Assassins. Right. Where?"

"In the hedge maze. Is Aladir nearby?"

She shook her head. "He headed back to the Citadel just after Nakane went to bed. We might catch him if –"

"No time. Let's move."

She nodded, moving to his side. "What's the plan?"

"Follow me for now. There is no plan."

"Really? You? No plan?"

"I'll come up with something. Come on!"

The pair rushed up the stairs.

*Fade from sight.*

He concealed the pair of them from sight, excluding each other from the effect. It wasn't a spell he used on multiple people simultaneously on a regular basis, but he had some practice, including one particularly awkward incident involving Taelien and a bank.

By the time they made it up the stairs and to the house's entrance, Jonan estimated the intruding force would be outside the maze – and he had his plan.

"Stay close. We're going to try to startle them into fleeing, but we need a captive for interrogation. That part is your job – both the capturing and the interrogating. Can you freeze someone in ice?"

"Yeah, but not if you want them to live through it."

*Well, that's a little disturbing.*

"Just freeze one of their legs or something, then. I'll try to take care of the rest. Be prepared to improvise."

Rialla nodded seriously, her fist clenched tightly around the hilt of her sword.

*She's nervous,* he realized. *I didn't think other people got nervous with this stuff.*

He almost laughed. Instead, he opened the door and stepped back out into the night.

A pair of men in black garb were right outside the door, reaching for weapons.

Jonan improvised.

"Who dares invade my home?"

His attempt at an "ancient and powerful sorcerer" voice was pretty impressive, by his own estimation.

The more important part, however, was the brilliant light that blasted out from the open doorway.

He was careful to carve the light to avoid affecting Rialla, who was already moving to form a cage of frost around one of the two figures.

Jonan raised a hand, pointing it at the blinded-but-unhindered second assassin, and whispered into the air.

"Eru elan lav kor taris."

The shockwave slammed into both of the would-be assassins, slamming the first into the bars of his newly-forged cage and tossing the second airborne and a dozen yards backward.

*That...worked better than expected.*

Rialla turned her head toward him, her eyes wide with shock.

*Oh, probably should have warned her about that.*

"Will explain later," he whispered. "Cage him while he's down."

Rialla shook off her reaction and rushed outside, calling icicles to form in the air and pierce downward around the fallen assassin as he struggled to move. As he attempted to roll to the side, she closed the distance and kicked him in the ribs, pressing her sword to his throat.

"Don't move and you won't be hurt," she said aloud.

A crossbow bolt arced through the air toward the sound of her voice.

Rialla reacted instantly, a shield of ice appearing in the air at her side, deflecting the projectile. Shaking her head, she withdrew her blade and finished forming her second cage, stalking toward the trajectory from which the projectile had emerged.

Jonan began to follow Rialla, but his movements were unexpectedly sluggish. He tripped at the slight elevation change as he stepped outdoors, slamming his right knee into the ground.

*Resh.* His head was swimming as he pushed himself to his feet. *Gods, that spell took more out of me than I expected. Should have expected that motion sorcery would slow me down. This was probably a bad time to show off a new trick.*

Still, the alternative had been lighting the man on fire, which would have – by his estimation – been worse.

257

The first pair of assassins looked secure in their cages, although the one who had been blasted backward was still struggling to free himself. Jonan admired his tenacity, if not his wisdom.

Rialla had already encircled a pair of crossbowmen in icy prisons by the time Jonan caught up to her.

"Where are your friends?" Rialla demanded. "How many of you are there?"

The caged attackers did not respond, save to drop their frozen crossbows and reach for other weapons. Rialla responded patiently, deflecting a pair of thrown daggers with her icy shield before walking closer to Jonan and whispering.

"I can't use my other dominion effectively if they can't see me."

Jonan nodded in understanding. Rialla's primary dominion was deception, which allowed her to force enemies into specific courses of action – but he had never seen her use it through any means other than eye contact.

"Can you maintain these cages for a while?"

She nodded.

"Follow me."

He led her closer to the walls, his limbs feeling agonizingly heavy. He kept his eyes open for more of the intruders as he moved, but found none. "Dropping our invisibility is too much of a risk. We can interrogate them later."

"If you'd let me control one of them, I could probably find the others."

Jonan frowned. "What if they can only see your eyes?"

"Probably good enough."

"Right."

He waved his hand, which was unnecessary, but the familiar motion made the spell feel more palpable. "Okay, your eyes should be visible. Grab one of the ones near the door, since they don't have ranged weapons."

"Yup."

Jonan staggered to the doorway. With multiple enemies already captured and others missing, maintaining silence was no longer his highest priority.

258

"We've got intruders!" He shouted as loud as he could, hoping the noise would reach the guards inside. It would alert any nearby assassins to his location, but he swiftly stepped around the door, hoping to avoid any attacks from assassins with similar concealment to his own.

And that evasive step triggered an idea.

Jonan tapped the center of his forehead with a single finger, activating a spell to see other invisible figures. No new assailants appeared — which was good — but he maintained the spell regardless.

*My eyes are going to hate me for this later.*

He tapped the right side of his head as well, adjusting his glasses as the night brightened around him. His dark-seeing spell extracted a significant toll on his vision, but every advantage was useful.

"They're around back," Rialla explained in a whisper as she approached him.

Jonan frowned — he hadn't heard her speaking to the man in the cage at all. *Was she just whispering quietly, or was she speaking directly into his mind? Thought sorcery, maybe?*

Thought sorcery was a deep dominion — a more advanced form of sorcery than deception. While a deception sorcerer could force a victim to speak the truth or subtly shift someone's mood, a powerful thought sorcerer could control an enemy's mind entirely.

It was, in Jonan's mind, one of the most terrifying fates imaginable.

Jonan plodded along behind Rialla, his legs aching more with each step. As they rounded one of the sides of the building, he caught the glowing outline of more people concealed in the nearby bushes. It took him a moment to realize why they were glowing.

*Sight sorcery.*

*And if I can see them, there's a chance that —*

Jonan slammed into Rialla's back just in time to knock her out of the path of the first crossbow bolt.

The second hit him in the left arm.

Rialla stumbled forward while Jonan fell back, grabbing instinctively at his wound as he landed. The bolt was sticking all the way through his bicep, the point protruding through the opposite end from where it had entered. Blood seeped from both the entrance and exit wounds.

"Fuck!"

His fingers brushed against the wound, triggering a second surge of pain. He shuddered on the ground, unable to act.

"I can't see them!"

Rialla's voice reached him, momentarily breaking through the agony. He focused his vision on her, and then formed a thought – *let her see.*

The sorceress' eyes narrowed, javelins of ice forming in the air and soaring out toward the bowmen. The glowing bowmen scrambled backward, but the barrage of icy projectiles continued, shards of ice piercing their limbs.

"Shit, Rialla, stop. Fuck, this hurts."

Jonan wasn't feeling particularly articulate, but he managed to push himself into a seated position just as two more figures rounded the corner.

Nakane, along with one of the house guards.

Rialla immediately stepped closer to Nakane, forming a wall of ice between her and their attackers.

Nakane glanced directly at Rialla and tilted her head to the side. "You seem to be a woman of many hidden talents, Miss Vorianna."

Lady Theas turned her head toward Jonan, bringing her hand up to her mouth. "You're…bleeding."

Jonan blinked. "Did I lose my invisibility at some point?"

"I can see you just fine, Master Kestrian. And your arm appears to need some attention." With her initial surprise vanquished, Nakane knelt at Jonan's side. "Miss Vorianna, if you'd be kind enough to provide us with cover?"

Rialla nodded. "Got it. Maer, step a little closer, would you?"

The house guard nodded, raising his shield. "Right, thank you miss."

The icy wall shifted and extended, wrapping around to make a half-circular barrier that met with the main wall of the manor. Aside from the sky, there were no further avenues for the attackers to reach them as long as the wall held.

The air, however, was freezing – and Jonan's arm was feeling number by the minute.

"I'm not much of a healer, but I'll see what I can do." Rialla leaned down, grabbing his arm and sniffing at the wound. "You're poisoned. Stay calm."

*Kind of wish she hadn't told me that.*

"I do not believe it is the same poison that killed my brother, however. Maer, your sword please?"

"Okay," Jonan began to pull his arm back, "I think we can slow down on the 'ministrations' if they mean amputating my arm."

"The bolt, Master Kestrian. I need to cut the bolt."

"Oh."

Jonan gave a shuddering sigh. "That's, uh, a relief."

Something impacted against the ice, sending tiny splinters flying, but it was nowhere near sufficient to breach the wall. Rialla grimaced, shivering in place, her forehead covered with sweat.

Maer handed Nakane his sword, and she motioned for him to hold Jonan's arm in place. Jonan felt his eyes fluttering uncontrollably as Nakane began to saw at the shaft of the bolt, snapping it off a few moments later.

He was barely aware as she cut off the fletching from the opposite side. Pulling the remains of the bolt out should have been the most painful part, but the numbness had spread far enough that he only felt a vague tugging sensation.

"He's fading. We need to get him help."

The voice sounded like it was probably Rialla's, but he couldn't quite be certain. His eyes were shut tightly now.

He heard the walls cracking around them as his consciousness faded away.

# CHAPTER XVII – TAELIEN IV – CONSEQUENCE MANAGEMENT

*Taelien stood amidst a field of corpses. Most lay haphazardly among the city streets, the limbs that were still attached spread askew, looking like battered dolls cast aside by a giant.*

*More disturbing, however, were the corpses that still stood. Bloody wounds marred their bodies, and though some amongst them might have been mistaken for still living men and women, others had injuries that no human could survive. One woman was riddled with so many arrows that they seemed to form a suit of armor around her, and a man smiled as he snapped off the hilt of one of the three swords embedded in his torso.*

*Though outnumbered by the fallen, there were dozens among these walking slain, and they were not idle. They carried blades and maces, spears and staves, and cut viciously into the bodies of the fallen. He felt the urge to move, but his body remained paralyzed, though he could not discern if it was the unnerving sight that robbed him of his agency or some external force. It did not matter in the end.*

*All at once, the animated corpses turned to face him. He saw then that their eyes were colorless, but their expressions were filled with hate. As one, they advanced, their steps in menacing union.*

*The Sae'kes burned brightly in his right hand, though he did not recall drawing it. Six of the seven runes illuminated the metal, producing an audible hum. Only the rune of Aendaryn, the god of blades, remained unlit and silent. It was difficult to maintain his grip – the hilt was slick with blood. It was, he realized, not his own.*

*Gritting his teeth, Taelien shook off the phantasmal weight on his limbs, surging into action.*

He ran. Cobblestones cracked beneath his footsteps, the familiar streets of *Velthryn* seeming to decay more with each passing moment. As he fled, his foot brushed a fallen sign from a long-abandoned store, the letters too faint to read.

There was no way to fight so many, or so he told himself. The victims were long dead – he had already failed to save them. He looked over his shoulder to try to catch a glimpse of the identities of the corpses following him. He still had difficulty discerning the features of individuals, but the tabards of the Paladins of Tae'os were unmistakable.

He had failed to save everyone, hadn't he?

He heard a scream – a familiar scream. It came from a street to the right, and he twisted in his steps to head toward it. Perhaps there was still a final chance at redemption – a way to make his death have some scant fragment of meaning.

He ran as fast as he could, his steps carrying him into darkness. The sound of the scream still echoed faintly in his ears, and a chill ran across his skin. He ran on and on until the city streets vanished around him, leaving only blackness, illuminated by the azure runes on his blade.

A figure in nondescript brown robes stepped out of the darkness. His hood obscured nearly his entire head, save for a hint of a fleshless jawbone. He carried the corpse of another man slung over his shoulder. The hooded man threw the body down, and Taelien heard the cracking of bones as it landed.

Even in death, the body maintained its grip on the Sae'kes it was carrying. Taelien did not need to see the face to recognize his own corpse.

He looked up to the hooded man, taking a defensive stance.

"You're here early," the hooded man spoke. "And very persistent. I just finished with the last one. You can take a moment to pay your respects."

Taelien approached the corpse that appeared to be his own and knelt down. He wore no paladin's garb – just a simple tunic and pants, ripped in several locations to expose torn flesh and shattered bones.

That, however, was not why he was kneeling.

His throat was tight, but nevertheless, he found the strength to speak. "I will endeavor to give you a greater challenge."

Taelien snatched the second Sae'kes out of his corpse's hand, willing the runes to ignite as he prepared to strike.

The second sword crumbled to dust in his hand.

The swordsman rose to his feet, noting only then that the blue light from his own weapon was slowly fading. One by one, the runes were burning out, and with each passing moment the darkness encroached closer.

*"You were saying?" The cloaked figure sounded amused, snapping his fingers. A halo of icicles appeared behind the cloaked figure, floating in a circular pattern behind him.*

*Taelien charged, swinging his blade to deflect the first spears of ice, but there were too many. He felt the first impact on his left shoulder, and then another hit the right side of his chest, just below the ribs. A third hit him in the center of the chest – and after that, he felt nothing at all. He fell to his knees, but even as he fell, he hurled his sword – the last rune fading as it sunk into the figure's robes.*

*He heard an echo of laughter as his vision faded to nothing.*

***

"Wake up," a voice whispered in his ear. "It's over."

Taelien's eyes blinked open. He was tightly gripping the Sae'kes beneath his covers, and he realized that he had slipped the weapon several inches out of its scabbard, exposing the top rune.

He always locked the scabbard in place around the blade using sorcery before he went to sleep. He had never unlocked the weapon in his sleep before.

Asphodel was staring at him, one hand on his right arm – the same arm that held his weapon's hilt. She was standing on the ladder that led from her bunk to his, her eyes not on the sword, but staring straight at his own.

"Mff," he groaned, pushing the Sae'kes back into the scabbard. *How long did I have that thing drawn? Gods, my head is killing me. That thing could have been drawing essence out of me for hours, if I pulled it while I was asleep.*

"Better." She smiled. "What did you see?"

Taelien relaxed his grip on the weapon, raising his hand to rub his aching right temple. The first hits of the dawnfire's light were barely illuminating the room, and aside from a disturbingly perky Asphodel, everyone in the room still appeared to be sleeping. It was too reshing early to be awake.

"I…," he shut his eyes, remembering the last few moments of his dream. "A man in robes and a hood. I was fighting him."

Asphodel frowned. "Go on."

He rolled over onto his side, staring her straight in the eyes. "Did you make me have that dream? Was that some kind of dream sorcery spell?"

She shook her head. "No."

"But you knew I had a dream – otherwise you wouldn't be up here."

"Yes."

*Not much of a talker, this one.*

"Was I moving around so much that I woke you – or does this have something to do with how your friends are always calling you an oracle?" His head was still swimming, but he wasn't happy with the idea of someone reading his thoughts.

Asphodel released his arm, blinking. "The latter. We're going to be interrupted. Remember your dream."

Lieutenant Torrent flung open the door from his own chamber, slamming it into the barracks wall. Several startled paladin candidates sat up instantly, many reaching for weapons of their own.

"Rise and shine, kids! It's testing day, and you're going to – Applicant Asphodel, are you already in uniform?"

Asphodel saluted the lieutenant. "Yes, sir."

There was a pregnant pause. "Fine, then. You can start cleaning the barracks while the others get dressed and packed."

"Yes, sir." She said again.

Taelien gave her a quizzical glance, to which Asphodel replied with a wink.

*Well,* Taelien considered, his head still throbbing, *that's one way to start a day.*

\*\*\*

"Platoon 2, head to the arena. Except you, Applicant Salaris." Lieutenant Torrent had an uncharacteristic hint of frustration in his tone, but his expression remained neutral.

The remainder of the platoon filed out of the room while Taelien stood at attention, nervously tensing the muscles in his hands. Landen and Velas shot him sympathetic glances as they filed out of the chamber.

When the last of the other candidates had left, the lieutenant waved a hand silently and moved into his own chamber at the back of the barracks. Taelien realized that although they had been in training for weeks now, this was his first time stepping into the lieutenant's room.

The chamber's accommodations were barely better than those of the cadets. It held a simple bed with neatly-folded grey sheets on the left side, a small table with a single chair on the right. A long spear with a wooden shaft and an iron tip stood in the back right corner, within reach of the chair. A three-drawer dresser sat next to the bed.

Torrent sat in his chair, tensing his jaw, and opened a drawer within the desk. He reached inside, retrieving a thin strip of crimson fabric. "I'm issuing you a red flag for your performance in the last test."

Taelien flinched at the words. "But, I —"

"I didn't give you permission to speak."

The swordsman frowned, but shifted his stance back to attention.

Torrent set the crimson cloth on the table and closed the drawer. "When these tests were first created, there were no strips of red fabric, no warnings — none of that nonsense. No second chances. If it were up to me, we'd cut anyone we weren't sure about. We don't need paladins that 'might' be good enough. Do you understand me?"

"Yes, sir."

"Do you know why you're being issued a red flag?"

"No, sir."

"For that reason alone, I should probably be giving you the black. But there are parties that are interested in your performance, so I'm going to let you continue to entertain them. For now. You can take your red ribbon and go."

Taelien lifted the rope from the table, turning it over in his hand. "Sir, may I ask a question?"

Torrent put a hand to his head. "Ask."

"Why am I being issued a red flag?"

The lieutenant sighed. "Because you failed the last test."

"I had seven pins."

"Yes, and if you had stopped there, you would have passed. Passed fabulously, in fact."

"Sir?"

Torrent stood up, turning away. "Did you see Susan Crimson's uniform?"

Taelien nodded. The young woman's uniform was bristling with sigils at the end of the day — she must have had more than thirty of them. He had some guesses at how she had managed it, but no confirmation. "Yes, sir."

"She was given the highest score possible. You were given the lowest we could give you without failing you outright. The difference wasn't the number of sigils you gave yourselves — it was how you handled distributing sigils to others."

Taelien tilted his head quizzically while Torrent turned to face him.

"You have a problem, Taelien. A consistent problem. You always want to solve everyone else's problems for them."

Taelien began to open his mouth to protest, but Torrent waved a warning hand and he silenced himself.

"You're a powerful young man, Taelien. Powerful enough that you forget to consider the capabilities of your allies. At best, you think of them as tools to enhance your own egocentric maneuvers, like how you handled Sytira's test. At worst, you try to do everything by yourself - like you just did with the last test."

*That's – wait –*

"Lateral thinking is something we encourage, Taelien. If you had made a bunch of sigils for yourself, we would have applauded that. Do you know how Susan got those seals? She recruited most of her platoon and broke into the uniform room where we keep the sigils for full paladins. She stole the whole supply. And what did she do with them? She gave them to the people who came with her. The people who contributed."

"You, on the other hand, gave everyone enough to ensure they would pass the test – effectively invalidating the purpose of the test. Do you understand why that's a problem?"

"You only want a limited number of people to pass the tests, Sir."

"Not precisely. We only want the people who are ready to pass, Salaris. Bringing someone who lacks the sufficient capabilities in any of the disciplines we are testing is a potential risk."

Taelien nodded firmly once – that he could understand. *But that particular test seemed more arbitrary than most. I mean, Landen even said people were gambling for sigils.*

"If everyone was equally clever and capable, I'd be more than pleased to let a large group pass the examinations. We have to be harsh with each step, however, because seven tests aren't exactly a lot of time to read someone. Training a squire for years is a much more reliable way of ensuring that the resulting paladin is sufficiently trained in all aspects, including an understanding of our values."

"If I may, Sir, the colonel did approve of my use of the fabricated sigils in the test."

"Yeah, it was clever to use your one question with Wyndam to make sure your pins would count. It would have been wiser, however, to be clear with her about your intentions – if you indeed planned from the outset to supply all of our cadets. Was that always the plan?"

"If I had sufficient time. I believe I understand where this is going, Sir, and if I may –"

"You may not." Lieutenant Torrent folded his arms. "You failed in two ways, Taelien. One was creating conditions where we'd have to either pass everyone or identify the sigils that you made yourself and give them a new set of rules. We chose the former for the sake of simplicity, but the latter was an option – you were never told how much the sigils would count for. In either case, you interfered with the intent behind the test itself."

"Second, you failed your platoon. By giving everyone an equal benefit, you effectively provided no net benefit to your platoon mates. Since our rankings are competitive and most of the platoons benefitted from cooperation, having you in the test was like having an empty space in your team."

Salaris turned his gaze downward, remaining silent.

"If you had taken the time to think about the test, you could have given a large number of sigils directly to your platoon members, allowing them to have comparable scores to what Susan accomplished for Platoon 1. If you had communicated your intentions to anyone on your platoon, they could have helped you work faster by supplying you with materials. That might have earned you an even better score – and, more than likely, led to one of your platoon members telling you that splitting them with the entire applicant pool was a bad idea. Why didn't you ask them?"

"I –"

"Rhetorical question. I know the answer. You wanted to surprise them. You wanted to be the hero, sweeping in at the last second to change a failure into a resounding success. Let me tell you a little something about heroes, Taelien – eventually, their luck runs out. And then they're just a superfluous martyr, putting on one final show."

"Now, do you understand how you failed the test?"

Taelien nodded again, his nose still pointed at the floor.

"Good. Now, take your piece of rope and don't fail your platoon again. Dismissed."

*It wasn't because I wanted to be a hero.* Taelien walked slowly, head still tilted downward, as he headed toward the arena.

*But the truth is worse. I just wanted to feel necessary.*

The swordsman toyed with the piece of red rope as he walked. He didn't need to carry it with him – the "red flag" was a symbolic warning about his test score, not something intended to be displayed.

By the time he had reached the arena, he had managed to use one of his forged symbols to attach the flag to his uniform tunic. If the Paladins of Tae'os had been a typical military organization, he knew that any kind of modifications to his uniform would have been a breach of conduct. Given how informal they tended to be, however, he suspected the officers would let the action slide.

More importantly, he hoped they would understand his intentions – it was a gesture of humility to remind himself of the costs of his pride.

When he arrived at the Korinval Coliseum, he found the rest of his platoon waiting for him near the front entrance. Asphodel, Eridus, Teshvol, and Kolask were gathered in a huddle discussing something near the left side of the door. Velas and Landen were off to the right side, chatting separately.

Landen folded his arms and squinted at the red ribbon as Taelien approached. "Accessorizing?"

Taelien shrugged, giving a half-smile. "It seemed like a good idea at the time."

"You wouldn't believe the number of mornings I've had that thought go through my mind."

"You're right, I wouldn't believe you had that many thoughts."

"Ouch." Landen slapped him on the shoulder affectionately, chuckling. "What's that for, anyway?"

"I don't really want to talk about it right now."

"Fair. Not like we've got a lot of time – now that you're here, I think we're going to get started shortly."

Velas leaned back against the stone wall of the outside of the coliseum, watching the exchange with an amused grin. "If you two are done flirting, maybe we can get back to planning?"

Landen shot a glance at Velas. "I thought you enjoyed watching."

"I do, but now isn't exactly the best time." She folded her arms. "Somebody want to fill Sal in?"

The rest of the platoon glanced around at each other. There were no volunteers.

Velas rolled her eyes. "Fine, I'll do it. This one is pretty simple, but it's going to be a huge pain. Once we get in there, they're going to hand us seven flags, as well as stands for each of them. We'll have seven minutes to set them up on our half of the arena."

Landen walked over to the wall, leaning up against it next to Velas. "Platoon 1 will be doing the same thing on their side at the same time. We'll be able to see each other, so it's not a stealth game. Once the seven minutes are up, the goal is to capture or destroy the other team's flags. We'll have a spot on the far side of our end where we can drop off anything we captured."

"Oh, sure, now you want to talk," Velas elbowed Landen in the ribs and he returned the gesture. "Anyway, captures are two points, destroying an enemy flag is worth one point. We'll only have seven minutes to capture or destroy as many flags as possible – while they're trying to do the same to our flags."

"And we can put our flags anywhere on our side of the arena?"

Velas nodded. "Yeah. If we put them all toward the back, they'll be harder to hit from a distance, but clustering them together means it would be easier to snag more than one at a time."

"One more pretty big snag." Landen folded his hands in front of him. "If you hit anyone with an attack or a spell – on your own team or the other team – you lose one or more points. Of course, if you throw yourself in the way of an attack and get hit by it, that's on you. Also, you lose one point if you destroy one of your own flags."

Taelien scratched his chin. "How do they determine how many points you lose from hitting someone?"

Velas' eyes narrowed dangerously. "Don't even think about it, Sal. We'll all have barriers on – you're not going to be able to take someone out of the competition with the sacrifice of a single point."

The swordsman nodded in reply. "I'd rather not do something underhanded like that anyway, but it was worth considering – especially since they might try it on us."

"Uh-huh." Velas glanced at Landen. "Am I forgetting anything?"

"Not really. We just need a solid plan – they have a lot more ranged firepower than we do."

*Terras, Keldyn, and Wandering War all on one platoon – yeah, they've got us beaten at range. No question. I don't even know how we could defend against that.*

Taelien pondered for a moment, folding his hands together. "Can we move our flags after the match starts?"

"Yep. Already planning to have our defenders do that – it's probably the only chance we have at keeping any of our flag safe." Velas pointed at Asphodel. "She's in charge of coordinating the defenders."

"I take it the three of us are running offense, then?"

"Actually, we're not quite settled on that. Is that the Sae'kes or your fake?"

He tapped the sword on his left side. "The real one. You want me to use it?"

Velas nodded. "You can cut through spells with it, yeah?"

The swordsman grinned. "I don't need a special sword for that."

"But you're better with it." Landen pointed at the sacred weapon. "I've seen you train – you react faster when you're holding it."

"And I doubt you can cut through any spell you want with an ordinary sword." Velas tilted her head downward. "Fire, yeah, I've seen that. You're a flame sorcerer. But what about Keldyn's conjured blades, or Terras' lightning?"

"Conjured swords might be tricky," Taelien admitted. "I don't think they're made of metal, so I probably can't just annihilate them with a tap. The Sae'kes would be better for breaking those, sure." He scratched his chin. "As for lightning, uh, you're probably on your own there. Flattered you'd think of me as a counter to that, but even if I could split it, I'm not fast enough."

Landen pressed his hands to his cheeks in mock shock. "I must be dreaming. Did you just admit you couldn't do something?"

Velas pinched Landen's arm. "Nope, guess he's just finally cracked."

"Hey, I'm not that bad. I admit my weaknesses all the time." Taelien folded his arms.

The other two just stared at him silently.

The swordsman sighed. "Okay, fine. I might like to brag a little. Can we move on?"

Landen laughed. "Just giving you a hard time, Sal. Okay, no parrying lightning. But you think you can handle Keldyn's sword?"

"Please tell me that's a euphemism," Velas winked at Landen.

Taelien let out a sigh, choosing his words deliberately. "I can break any sorcerous weapons he conjures if I use the Sae'kes."

"You could at least try to play along," Velas complained.

"But I don't think I should use the Sae'kes at all," Taelien continued, ignoring Velas' insinuations. "First, it's dangerous. And second, I'd be concerned they'll call it cheating."

"Doubt the latter," Landen clasped his hands together in front of him. "You've spent a lot of time training with it. I'd say being able to use the sword is a legitimate part of your skill set. As for the former, well, be careful?"

"Gonna have to agree with Lan on this one." Velas stepped forward and tapped the sword on the pommel. She made a perplexed expression after she took her hand away, stepping back and shaking her head.

"Overwhelmed by the sheer power of my sword?" Taelien chuckled.

Velas was uncharacteristically silent, tilting her head away.

*Well, that wasn't weird or anything.*

"I'll, uh, consider using it. But you should put me on offense either way – I'm resh at blocking."

"We know," Landen replied with a nod.

"Thanks for the support. You're just a font of emotional validation today."

"Glad to be of service. Anyway, the real question is where we put Vel."

Velas glanced back, nodding, but maintaining a distracted expression. "Yeah. After all, I'm the fastest, the strongest, and the most beautiful."

Landen glanced at her and gave a scoffing chuckle. "Of a team consisting solely of yourself, maybe."

"She's got a point," Taelien noted, drawing both of the others to look at him. "One out of three, anyway. She is the fastest. At least at making innuendo."

"I – I don't even know if I should be offended by that." Velas put a hand over her chest.

"Probably," Landen offered helpfully.

"So, speed. If Velas takes defense, she'd probably be our best bet at keeping a flag safe – maybe even more than one. She's just vastly more maneuverable than the rest of us."

"Although, to be fair, Asphodel can anticipate attacks and just stand where they're not going to be," Landen pointed out.

"That's going to be less effective against lightning – I think the only real way to defend against Terras is going to be moving too fast for her to target, or finding a location she can't hit. Are we allowed to leave the arena once the test starts?"

Velas shook her head slowly. "Cute idea, but no."

"Probably just have to block the flags with our bodies, then, so she'd have to hit us at the same time as the flags."

"That's what we were planning on." Velas pointed at Eridus. "I asked Eridus if he could make a shield out of water – he's a water sorcerer – but apparently he's more specialized in shaping than calling. Can't conjure enough for an effective barrier."

*Barriers, huh?*

Taelien grinned. "I think I have an idea."

"Well," Velas shifted her hands to her hips, "That sounds terrifying."

***

The crowd in the coliseum was much smaller this time – only a couple dozen paladins and the usual officers and judges.

"Line up in the center," Colonel Wyndam ordered, her voice echoing throughout the stadium.

A broad white chalk line had been marked in the center of the arena, neatly dividing the stadium into halves. The platoons lined up facing each other, awaiting further instructions.

A team of paladins entered the arena, bringing out seven flags and stands for each team. The flags themselves were nondescript – blue for Platoon 1 and red for Platoon 2 with no significant markings. Taelien was amused that Susan Crimson, who stood across from him, would be fighting against the team with the red flags.

The flag poles, unfortunately, were wooden – immediately nullifying one portion of Taelien's plan. The stands were wooden as well.

Each platoon had seven members remaining, and thus, each was initially handed a single flag. Taelien glanced over the other platoon, noting that The Wandering War was the only member of the opposing

273

team that wasn't wearing at least half-dozen sigils from the previous contest. Unconsciously, he reached for the red ribbon on his chest.

"When the first gong rings, you will have seven minutes to position your flags and yourselves. When the second gong rings, you may begin to attempt to capture or destroy the opposing team's flags. When the third gong rings, the contest is at an end."

"Marginal damage to a flag will not constitute destruction, but splitting a flag in half, burning more than a third of the surface, or otherwise significantly harming the flag will be sufficient."

Taelien grinned.

"May the gods watch over you all. Lieutenant, you may begin shielding the candidates."

Second Lieutenant Banks began walking from candidate to candidate, casting a single spell. "Dominion of Protection, form a shield to protect this candidate from harm."

*Interesting — she usually uses an armor spell, not the shield. I suppose she doesn't want us getting hurt at all here. Probably wise, given how dangerous some of these people are.*

After shielding five candidates, the second lieutenant waved to another paladin, who stepped forward and took her place, shielding the next three. It took two more paladins to ensure all of the candidates were protected.

Once all fourteen applicants were shielded, Lieutenant Banks turned and saluted the colonel. The gong sounded moments later — and both teams began to run.

Platoon two headed straight for the back wall of the arena. Taelien split off to the left, drawing the Sae'kes - and jamming it into the stone floor.

Taelien was pretty sure he heard gasps from the stands.

*I really hope they don't make me pay for this.*

As five runes burned on the sword's surface, the translucent aura around the blade disintegrated rock without difficulty. And so, carefully concentrating, Taelien began to dig.

*Extend.*

Reshaping the aura around the Sae'kes was a relatively simple task. In this case, he commanded it into a spear-like shape, rotating the weapon and plunging it downward to burrow deeper into the stone.

Creating a space with the right dimensions to fit the flag took him just under a minute. He could have worked faster, but that risked making a wider hole if his concentration slipped – and in this case, precision was their greatest defense.

*Condense.* The aura contracted back into its normal state around the blade.

Sheathing his sword and moving to the next spot took him several more seconds, while Landen moved to carefully fit the flag into the hole that Taelien had created.

As Taelien began repeating the process to make a second hole, he watched Landen carefully wrapping the flag itself against the wooden shaft to minimize the damage to the cloth while he sheathed it in stone. Making the second hole felt faster, but that may have just been the more rapid pounding within his chest.

Asphodel moved to bury the second flag, while Landen finished burying the majority of the first flag and slipped the flag stand onto the top of the shaft, upside down.

Taelien would have preferred to avoid the flag holders entirely and bury the entire flags, but Landen and Velas had been convinced that "putting the flag in the flag holder" was a necessary step in the rules – they just didn't have to put it on the proper end.

As he completed his third hole, Taelien glanced at the opposing team's half of the arena, where he could see Lysen forming domes of ice around his team's flags.

*Not a bad defense, but we can break it.*

More worrying were the half-dozen golden swords already hovering in the air. Keldyn Andys was holding his right arm out straight, an intense look of concentration on his face.

*Resh. Guess he can make more than one of those at a time.*

"Eridus!" Velas shouted. "Change of plans! You're on offense with me. Landen, stick with Teshvol."

Taelien kept moving. He was in the midst of cutting his fourth hole when the gong rang.

*Let's hope that's enough.*

Sweeping his sword through the stone, Taelien charged toward the enemy platoon. Golden blades tore through the air toward his four flags that remained exposed.

*Too fast!*

He lurched to the side as he ran, trying to catch the blade with his own, but Keldyn twisted his arm to the side and the golden blade changed its course, arcing around Taelien and continuing toward its targets.

Cursing, Taelien kept running, heading for the nearest dome of ice – and, as he approached, realizing that there were far more than seven of them. The ice was thick enough to be opaque with an unnatural sapphire sheen.

He split the first dome open with a forceful swing, but as he recovered from the strike he knew he had met no resistance from a flag within the ice.

*Where did I see the first ones being made? Could they have moved the flags after I saw them?*

He rushed around the shattered dome toward one of the ones he had seen Lysen forming. A golden blade flashed through the air in front of him, forcing him back a step. The pause caused him to lose his momentum, and he noticed Keldyn grinning as he redirected the blade, sending it toward the other side of the arena.

"Try that again, Andys." Taelien shifted his path, turning toward the blade sorcerer. He swept his blade through another glacial defense as he walked, but that dome was empty as well.

A crash of thunder signaled one of Terras' blasts landing, but Taelien couldn't see if it had hit home. He continued to walk toward Keldyn, the other man turning toward him.

"You should have let that sword hit you – it would have cost me a point." Keldyn turned his arm toward Taelien, another golden blade appearing in the air above him. "I won't make that mistake now, of course."

The blade flashed forward, stopping an inch from Taelien's throat.

"Of course, if you cut yourself, it would be your own fault."

Taelien stepped forward – not into the blade, but around it – and snapped the fingers of his left hand shut around the blade. His grasp was quick, but careful, avoiding dragging his skin across the edge and triggering the defensive barrier. The golden weapon was solid to the touch, emanating faint warmth, but he could not extend his senses into the blade, indicating that it was not metal.

Something stirred at the back of his consciousness as he felt the projection against his skin.

"Thanks for the gift. I think I'll hold onto this for a while."

*If he tries to move the sword now, he'll risk cutting my hand and losing a point.*

Taelien winked at Keldyn, sheathing the Sae'kes and turning around. With his right hand free, Taelien grabbed the hilt of the golden blade. It was unnaturally light, but not truly weightless. He twirled it in his hand, searching the battlefield until he found the target he considered the greatest threat – Terras.

She looked to be in deep concentration, holding her hands skyward.

Taelien grinned and charged.

He wasn't strictly certain that hitting Terras with Keldyn's weapon would count against Keldyn's team – but he knew they wouldn't be sure, either.

And that meant he was an effective distraction.

Even as he sped toward Terras, a wall of ice began to manifest in front of him. Jerking to a halt, he turned and spun to see Lysen holding his hands together to make a "V" shape, wisps of frost shimmering around him.

And, right behind him, Taelien caught a blur of motion –Velas moving with Eridus, taking advantage of his distraction. They landed right next to a dome, Eridus immediately putting his hands against the surface – which shifted from water to ice.

Velas grabbed the flag from within and jumped. A hail of airborne blades followed her, but a second burst of mid-air motion carried her too quickly for the golden edges to follow.

As Lysen's ice continued to form around Taelien, he lashed out with the golden blade, but it proved ineffective against the frost. Awkwardly, he shifted the golden weapon into his left hand and redrew the Sae'kes, hacking a path through the ice as it formed around him.

Lysen stepped closer, closing his eyes. The ice pushed in closer, leaving no avenues for escape. Gritting his teeth, Taelien relaxed his focus on the blade, allowing its destructive aura to widen. The fifth rune relinquished its light, and then the fourth and third.

The broader aura lacked the potency to slice stone, but it was more than enough for the ice. The swordsman laid into the ice with rapid strokes, carving broad gashes in the ice as it pressed in around him. He felt frost beginning to form around his ankles and calves, sending a shudder down his spine.

There was a hint of an unfamiliar feeling as he realized that his barrier was doing nothing to stop the encroaching ice.

He inhaled a sharp breath.

*I can't move.*

*I need to move.*

He stared at the sword in his hand. The aura continued to wear at the ice where they made contact, but it was insufficient to keep his entire body from being consumed.

He needed something else — something more appropriate to combat the ice.

His mind sought out the blade's aura and issued a single command — *burn.*

White flames erupted from his sword, instantly melting a spherical cavern of ice around Taelien. He shivered at the cost of flame, but a fevered exhilaration invigorated him when he saw his weapon - the sword's runes were glowing white, not blue.

*This…this is new.*

*And I think I like it.*

He swept the blade forward, the blade's heat transforming ice into water — and then steam — in a broader area than the flames themselves seemed to reach. In spite of that, he felt no heat against his skin, nor did his barrier flicker against the surface of his skin.

*Interesting. But I can't count on the flames being discerning enough not to hurt anyone else — I need to put this out as soon as I get out of the ice.*

It took several more moments before he finished his tunnel, emerging just behind Terras. He gazed at the Sae'kes for another moment, scrutinizing, before reaching his senses out to contact the blade's aura again.

*Thank you, old friend. I don't know why, but I feel like I understand you better somehow now. Now, please calm your flames.*

The white fire subsided, leaving the translucent aura around the weapon looking somewhat diminished. Two of the remaining three runes faded entirely, leaving a single rune to shift back from white to blue. Taelien gingerly sheathed the blade, and then shifted the golden sword into a two-handed grip and took aim.

He swung the flat of the weapon at Terras' back.

Something smacked into his weapon mid-swing – a dagger, hurled through the air. The golden blade cracked on impact, the top third of the sword splintering away into nothingness.

The thrown weapon was real, however. Taelien saw the origin as he glanced to the right – the Wandering War was approaching.

Taelien shrugged and slammed the pommel of the golden blade into Terras' back. She gasped at the impact, blue sparks flickering in the air.

The sorceress spun around, electricity playing in her hands.

"Sorry, nothing personal." Taelien spun to deflect another dagger, attempting to bat it at Terras, but merely succeeding in knocking it to the ground.

Terras hastily stepped back, but Taelien managed to land a second slash on her arm before she could draw her own sword.

"What are you doing? Hitting me is against the rules!"

The Rethri woman shifted into the Teris Low-Blade stance, a defensive style, as soon as she had her sword drawn.

Taelien smirked. "Not precisely. It's a penalty to hit someone with your weapon or spell – and this, here, is one of Keldyn's spells."

He darted forward again, swinging the remaining part of the blade. Terras withdrew and retained a defensive stance.

"Don't think that's how it works." Terras frowned, glancing toward the Wandering War. He gave no obvious response.

*But you're not sure, so you don't want me to hit you. Perfect. You're the most dangerous person out here – aside from War, maybe – and I have you both tied up.*

He advanced again, and Terras stepped backward, a growing look of frustration on her face. His next swipe was a feint, leaving him exposed, and she instinctively took the opening – just barely managing to jerk her own blade back out of the way before hitting him.

"Resh this. I'm going back to work." She dropped her sword. "You want to gamble on hitting me? Fine." Electricity played at her fingertips, and thunder cracked in the skies above. "Let's play."

Taelien shook his head disdainfully. "I wouldn't try throwing any lightning at my flags right now." He patted the metallic edge on the sheath on his left hip. "You know I'm a metal sorcerer? I shaped this scabbard to attract electricity. You try anything while I'm this close and it'll act like a lightning rod. Then you lose more points."

Terras narrowed her eyes. "You're bluffing."

He shrugged, stepping closer. "Care to make that a wager?"

She pointed her left hand upward and closed her eyes. A blast of electricity flew upward from her fingertip, piercing the cloudless sky.

By the time she had reopened her eyes, Taelien had decided to cut his losses.

He shoved past her, hurling his golden blade at the floor, and drew the Sae'kes again.

A wave of fatigue smashed into him as soon as he attempted to wrest control of the runes on the blade. His vision blurred as he skidded across the icy ground, slamming one of the remaining icy dunes.

Shaking his head, he concentrated, noting that only the first and second runes were lit. *Resh. I must be in worse shape than I realized.*

He took a breath, glancing around to ensure that no one was in melee range, and swept his blade through the icy barrier.

The crack of wood within was immensely satisfying.

*Excellent. Just need a few more of these.*

"Wait, stop!" Terras' voice was filled with frustration as Taelien rushed toward the next dome.

"Leave him." The reply was an unfamiliar voice, heavy as iron. He had no time to consider the source, however.

He lashed out at the next ice barrier as soon as he reached it, feeling a numbness spreading across his arm.

*I can't keep this up much longer.*

Turning, he tried to consider the locations of the first domes that he had seen Lysen working on, but he was too disoriented. He hacked at the next two domes, finding them empty, before turning to find The Wandering War directly in front of him.

The cloaked figure was holding a long, black-bladed sword etched with shimmering red runes.

"Come." The voice was the same as the one that had instructed Terras to cease her assault. "Let us begin this contest in earnest."

Taelien knew that fighting The Wandering War had no place in this test – that even scoring a victory in battle against him would serve no purpose – and yet a deep, overwhelming urge pressed him to accept the challenge to battle.

He ignored that urge.

Taelien chuckled, spun around, and charged at the nearest dome, leaving it smashed to pieces in his wake. He managed to sunder two more, splintering one additional flag, before the ending gong finally rang.

\*\*\*

The candidates lined up on their sides of the arena, awaiting judgment. As Taelien took his place in the formation, he could see the uncertain looks of his companions.

The colonel raised her voice immediately after the teams had taken their positions. "Applicants, attention."

Taelien shifted his stance simultaneously with his platoon, taking a deep breath.

"Platoon 1 succeeded in capturing a single flag from Platoon 2 and destroying five of their flags, for an impressive cumulative score of seven points."

Taelien's jaw tightened. *They got six of our flags? And with no penalties?*

"Platoon 2 succeeded at capturing two flags and destroying three others, however, they also suffered two penalties for causing damage to enemy team members. Thus, their score is only five points."

In spite of the need to remain at attention, Taelien shut his eyes. *We...lost?*

"Platoon 1 is the victor. Both teams may return to their barracks for further instructions. Dismissed."

Taelien's eyes remained shut as he heard the other team howling at their victory. A few moments later, he felt someone tugging at his left arm.

"C'mon, Salaris." Landen offered a weak smile. "We did just fine. Let's head back, yeah?"

He nodded weakly, knowing that this might be his last visit to the barracks that had served as their home.

The platoon left the coliseum in silence, walking in a close formation as they began to head back to the barracks.

"Bunch of bullshit." Velas folded her arms as they walked, and Taelien noted the nods of assent among their group. "Judges must have had it out for us."

"I'm sorry," Taelien barely managed to mumble.

Velas kicked a rock, sending it tumbling off the path. "You kidding? You ripped them open over there. Not your fault the judges have their heads up their asses, Sal."

"I lost as many points as I got us."

Velas shrugged. "We all knew what you were planning on. Personally, I think using Keldyn's sword was brilliant. Wish we could have used the ice to break their own flags somehow, but turning the domes into water was pretty great, too. Nice work on that, Eridus."

The water sorcerer gave a silent nod and looked away.

"Anyway," Velas continued, "If the judges were reasonable, they would have counted those hits against the enemy team, since Keldyn was careless. And then we would have won."

"No."

Asphodel spoke quietly, but all heads turned toward her. It was not simply that she spoke rarely, nor the force of her personality, but rather the certainty in her voice that always seemed to draw attention with unrelenting gravity.

"The judges were fair. The plan was sound. We simply failed to execute it properly."

They walked for the rest of the journey in silence.

Lieutenant Torrent was waiting outside the barrack as they arrived. His hands were filled with red flags, blowing softly in the wind.

Taelien's left hand drifted upward, not to tug at his own red flag, but to cover the pounding within his chest.

*This is it, then.*

"Platoon 2, halt."

The group stopped in a messy semi-formation, awaiting further instructions.

"You did pretty well back there, but you lost. We're nearing the final stages of the test, so that means—"

Taelien didn't hear the rest. He wasn't listening.

He lowered his head as the paladin candidates formed a single-file line, each stepping forward to receive a red flag before filing into the barracks.

"Sal."

"Sal." The voice was louder this time, more insistent.

Taelien blinked, turning around. Landen pressed a blue flag into his hand.

"You're going to need that."

The swordsman opened his mouth to reply, but on this rare occasion, he found himself speechless.

"Cadet Salaris, step forward."

Taelien turned to Lieutenant Torrent, weakly displaying the balled-up blue flag that had been inserted into his grasp.

The lieutenant raised an eyebrow, glancing at Landen. "Interesting. You sure you want to do that, cadet?"

Landen nodded. "Sir, if Taelien didn't help me with the sigil test, I would not have passed. Please allow this."

The lieutenant frowned, raising a closed hand to his jaw, and then stepping forward. He snatched the blue flag out of Taelien's hand.

"Fine. Get inside, Applicant Salaris. You won't have another chance. Be glad you have such loyal friends."

Taelien took a shuddering breath and rushed inside the barracks. He didn't bother to change out of his uniform – he just sat on his bed and shivered.

***

At dinner hour, Taelien remained behind as most of the remaining cadets filed out of the barracks. He reclined on his flat pillow, lying on top of the blankets since he had yet to bathe. He had managed to kick off his boots, but beyond that, he had little energy to force himself to move.

When the others were gone, Asphodel climbed up to the top bunk to sit beside where he was resting. Taelien turned and gave her a quizzical look.

Asphodel casually laid a hand on his shoulder, shaking her head. "You feel despair. Why?"

"I've just failed at the last two challenges. I shouldn't even be here."

"But you are, as you must be."

*I'm really not in the mood for this kind of self-assured nonsense right now.*

"If destiny had a hand in this, I feel like I should probably be breaking it."

Asphodel frowned deeply. "You already are."

Taelien sat up, crouching to avoid brushing his head against the ceiling. "Okay, that's sufficiently ominous to make me curious. What are you talking about?"

"You are playing another's role, and playing the role differently than he would have."

Taelien quirked an eyebrow. "That's still pretty vague."

"I am sorry." The Delaren looked away, her crystalline hair brushing against him as she turned. "Speaking can be difficult. I am seeing – hearing – too many things."

"What do you mean by that? You've never answered our questions about the whole 'oracle' thing."

Asphodel's shoulder slumped. "It is a gift, one might say, but a burden. My senses have many facets. I see now, as you do, but I also see moments – and minutes – and hours into the future. Sometimes further, if I strain myself."

"Simultaneously?"

Asphodel nodded weakly.

"That must be...maddening. Can you block it out?"

"Only to a minimal extent. I have learned to focus, as you might pay more attention to something directly in front of you than your peripheral vision. But if I close my eyes, I see nothing at all. If I block my ears, I do not hear any timeframe. There is no method for filtering one or another completely."

*Gods. That's – I couldn't possibly handle that kind of burden.*

The pair was silent for a time, and Asphodel turned back toward him. Her eyes were closed.

"Focusing on one sense or another can help. Do you mind?"

He shook his head, and then remembered her eyes were closed. "No."

She smiled. "Good. You have many questions – as do I. You may ask first."

"You said something about me taking someone else's place. What do you mean by that?"

"When I meet someone, I often gaze into their potential future. This may be intrusive, but it is instinctive to me, and I must keep myself safe. When I attempted to do this with you, I saw someone else entirely."

Taelien took a deep breath.

*Does she mean Aendaryn, the God of Blades? So many people have mistaken me for him — or his child. Could it be true?*

"How do you know it's a different person?"

The Delaren woman tilted her head downward. "He was nothing like you. Everything and nothing alike." After a pause, she spoke again. "He was regal, dominant, more nature than man. He had a Rethri's eyes — verdant and deep as a forest — but he lacked a Rethri's heart. And when I saw him — when I tried to see more — he turned his gaze to me." She shivered. "And he smiled. It was not a smile of kindness. It was the smile of a hunter who had set his eyes upon prey. I have never dared to look into your future again."

The description was abstract, but something about it scratched at the back of his memory. The man in her vision sounded familiar — familiar in a way that made his hand itch to reach for the sword at his side.

*But that's not Aendaryn she described. The god of blades is described as being a blue-eyed human, like I am.*

"You feel it, too." Asphodel grasped his hand, intertwining her fingers in his. There was something desperate in the contact, something pleading. Their fingers tightened around each other.

"Yes." His eyes closed, the image of the other man manifesting in his mind. It was not something Asphodel had given him — not a spell or a shared vision — but an awakened memory.

The man — if such a word can describe a creature carved from the nightmares in the furthest recesses of his mind - had smiled at him, too.

Taelien squeezed her hand. "What is he?"

"I do not know," Asphodel whispered. "But I know that he is watching."

# CHAPTER XVIII – VELAS VI – THOUROUGLY TRAPPED

The first thing Velas realized was that she was cold. Without opening her eyes, she reached for her blanket, finding it missing. In her half-conscious haze, she barely processed the string of curses coming from somewhere to her right, or the scraping sound half a dozen yards distant. She frowned, groaning, and her eyes fluttered open.

Her surroundings were unfamiliar and unnerving.

A faint blue light illuminated her cell. She was lying atop an uneven grey stone floor, confined within a circle of glowing azure runes. Her only companions within the circle were a few cracked pieces of stone. The former Queensguard was still wearing her nightclothes, but an additional adornment graced her neck – a golden collar, similarly etched with luminescent blue runes.

*Gods curse it, not more runes. I hate runes.*

The cell itself was barely large enough for her to lie down. It was square in shape, with a gate of steel bars near her feet. The other three walls were the same grey stone as the floor. As she sat up, she realized that she could not see the primary source of the room's illumination – the runes on the floor and necklace were insufficient. The lack of a clear origin point for the light was disconcerting.

"Ugh," she moaned, rubbing at her head. She was pretty sure she hadn't been drinking last night, but she felt like alcohol had sucker punched her brain when she wasn't looking.

"Velas? You awake? I'd know that half-conscious moan anywhere." The sound was coming from the opposite side of the stone wall on her right side.

"Shut up, Landen. You're too loud, and I'm tired." She rubbed at her temples, but the effort was mostly in vain.

"Uh, we might need to talk, given that we're, you know, in some kind of prison."

She sighed. "Yes, I'd gathered that, thanks."

"Velas? Landen? That you over there?" Taelien was 'whispering' from somewhere beyond Velas' bars. His idea of whispering was about twice the volume of Landen's speaking voice, and Velas was unable to stifle a snicker. Leaning closer to the edge of her circle – she didn't want to cross it without determining the circle's function, if any – she could see through her bars well enough to note another set of bars about two yards beyond her own. Taelien was standing in a similar circle, shirtless, wearing a collar. It was hard to tell with the dim light, but she thought his collar might have been silver, rather than gold.

He waved at her, and she returned the gesture, and then stood up.

"Hey, Sal. I like the new look. You should try it more often." Velas smirked, but with her headache slowly subsiding, she was beginning to process the situation and search for solutions.

"Anyone remember how we got here?" Landen asked. She thought she could hear him moving around on the opposite side of the wall.

"No. And don't leave the circle until we figure out what it does," she instructed, turning toward Landen.

"Circle? What circle?"

"Landen is not in a circle." The voice was female, and it took Velas a moment to place it. She had rarely heard Asphodel speak, and when the Delaren woman had, it was rarely more than two or three words at a time. "I am, however."

"Asphodel?" Taelien was whispering too loudly again. "Can you read the runes on the amulet or the circle?"

"No. Also, I am not wearing an amulet."

Velas knelt back down, inspecting the runes. *That's Kor for strength, Lys for sacrifice…can't read that one, or that one. Kar, maybe? Protection – yeah, that seems right. Probably a pretty typical barrier circle.*

The former Queensguard frowned. *Except with no visible power source. There should be dominion essence somewhere nearby, most likely within the ritual circle itself.* She looked at a pair of loose rocks dubiously, but quickly concluded that no one in their right mind would bother disguising dominion essence as random stones.

*It's probably drawing from my new apparel – there could be dominion essence in a position I can't see, like on the inside or around the back. Okay, barrier circle. I can deal with that. There may be a more pressing problem.*

Velas picked up one of the stray rocks, thinking. "So, guys. How'd we get in here?"

"That's what I was asking," Landen complained. "I just went to sleep and woke up here."

"This is clearly some kind of test." Taelien was kneeling and inspecting his own runes now. "Or another one of my weird dreams."

"You've been having weird dreams?" Landen asked.

Velas smirked, flicking the rock into the ring. *Ping.* A translucent blue-white field appeared, blocking the tiny rock from escaping the circle. The deflected rock rolled across the ground, landing near her feet. *Definitely a barrier, at the least. Might have other functions.* "As intrigued as I might be about Sal's dreams, especially if they involve the four of us half-naked in a prison, I'm pretty sure I'm real. Maybe I'm dreaming, but this doesn't seem like my kind of dream – for the most part –"

Asphodel sighed loudly enough to cut Velas off. "We are not dreaming. I would know."

*Not sure what her logic is for that, but sure, we'll go with that. They do call her an oracle – maybe dream sorcery is on her list.*

"Well, if we're really here, that means either our room has been pretty seriously changed or we've been teleported. Leaning toward the latter." Taelien tapped at the floor near one of the runes with a single finger.

*I really, really hate being teleported. Possibly more than I hate runes.*

Velas rubbed at her forehead. "Our cell arrangements seem to mirror our beds. Landen is next to me, and Taelien is next to Asphodel. Asphodel, have you seen your, um, guards?"

"Teshvol and Kolask are not my guards. And no, they are not here."

Velas frowned. *Those two were sleeping closer to my bed than Taelien and Asphodel – why are they missing? If Taelien is right and this is a test, it would be logical to include the whole platoon or segments of it that are adjacent to one another. Could they have failed out? Or perhaps they're in another part of the dungeon?*

*It's an inconsistency, much like Landen not having a circle or a collar. Maybe that's not the real Landen. Maybe I'm dreaming – the only authority telling me that*

*I'm not dreaming is someone that could just be another dream. But I guess that line of thought isn't really going to be useful – I'm going to break this place and get the resh out either way.*

Taelien put a hand on his collar. "I'm going to break this."

*I love it when he reminds me of me.*

"Do not," Asphodel said, just before Taelien screamed, falling to the floor and beginning to spasm uncontrollably.

Velas tensed, taking a step forward before she realized she had nearly stepped out of her circle. She barely stopped herself, gritting her teeth as she watched helplessly as Taelien twitched for several seconds before lying still.

"...Sal?" she asked, staring at his fallen body. He made no reply.

*They couldn't have killed him. It's just a test. He's going to be fine.*

*It's not real. It can't be real.*

"These collars are triggered by the use of sorcery," Asphodel said without a hint of emotion in her tone.

Velas clenched her fists. "Reshing useful information there, chatty. Thanks, saved us all a bunch of trouble."

"I could not be certain until he activated it, but it seemed logical—"

Footsteps. Heavy ones, at that. Asphodel went silent as soon as the sounds began to approach. Velas focused on the sounds, identifying any individual characteristics she could. There was a slight scrape with each step, and a long pause between each, indicating that the person approaching was most likely walking slowly and wearing sabatons.

As the first creature came into view, she realized she was only mostly right.

The figure's armor was black as void, with violent spikes protruding from the knees and elbows. The material was reflective, but with a glossy look, and Velas suspected it was some kind of stone similar to obsidian, rather than metal. Near the neck and on the gauntlets, she saw runes etched into the surface. They were glowing with red light.

All in all, the image looked like a child's nightmare of one of the Thornguard. She might have laughed if someone had tried to describe the figure to her, but when it turned to look straight at her – and she saw red glowing spots rather than eyes – something sank in her stomach.

"The prisoners will behave." Its voice was a deep, grating sound that made her shiver. It was only after a moment that she processed the foreign sorcery invading her body, sapping at her will. Every instinct told her to push the poison out of her veins, but she resisted, knowing that activating her "sorcery resistance" could potentially leave her in the same state as Taelien – or worse.

Mercifully, it turned away from Velas after a staring at her for several painful moments.

She found herself sitting, shivering, but her mind still worked. *He's wearing a sword on his left hip. No other obvious weapons. Obvious keys hanging from belt on right side of hip.*

Velas' relief that the knight was looking away from her was short lived. His next target was Taelien, still unmoving on his cell's floor.

*They might kill him in there. I mean, at least in the simulation. It's still just a test. He's fine. But seriously, I need to save him right now.*

*Two problems; well, two main problems. Barrier and a door. Think.*

She flicked another pebble, twisting her lip as she made an observation.

The lead knight removed the keys from his belt, unlocking Taelien's cell door.

Velas grabbed a larger rock and began scratching something into the floor of her cell.

The runes on the black-clad knight's gauntlet flickered, and the barrier circle around Taelien flashed into visibility for a moment – and then shattered apart. The knight reached down with his left hand, grabbed Taelien's collar, and dragged him out of the cell.

"Hey, stop, we'll cooperate," Landen called out. "Just tell us what you need." The knight paused for a moment, turning toward Landen's cell.

"The prisoner will be silent while punishment is administered."

The knight pulled Taelien upward from the floor with his left hand, putting his right hand on Taelien's forehead.

"Awaken." The runes on the knight's gauntlet flashed and Taelien shuddered again, though he did not scream this time. The swordsman slumped forward weakly, his eyes fluttering open.

"Good. You will now be punished."

Velas stood up, gripping her collar with her left hand.

"Yeah, that might have to wait."

The red-eyed knight turned his gaze toward Velas as she approached the cell door.

"For the future, you might want to construct your rituals with the runes on the outside of the barrier. If they're on the inside, someone might, you know, change how they work."

*I'm going to regret this later.*

*Pulse.*

It was just a flicker of sorcery – the merest hint of an application of the Dominion of Motion. Enhanced a thousandfold by the repurposed ritual circle, however, it was strong enough to rip the bar she pointed at straight out of the stone and catapult it into the knight, slamming into his right arm. The knight staggered a step toward Taelien's cell as the bar deflected off his armor, clattering down the hall. The application of force should have shattered the arm of an ordinary man, armored or not. The attack was not, unfortunately, potent enough to make the knight drop his prisoner.

It was, however, enough to activate her collar.

Intense heat flared to life around her neck, searing into her flesh. She screamed out of instinct in spite of having been prepared for the pain. It was excruciating, but she had expected it to be.

*Not what I expected, but it will do.*

She sensed the Dominion of Light burning her flesh, visualized the places that the collar contacted her skin, and quickly sensed the power source on the back of her neck. Her fingers burned as the found the stone and she pointed her other hand at the knight.

*Expel.*

A blinding ray of incandescent heat blasted out of her outstretched fingers, slamming into the knight's chest. The knight released his grip on Taelien, turning toward Velas as golden cracks began to appear in his breastplate.

Velas continued to channel the amulet's light, gritting her teeth in agony. Her hand and neck were no longer being burned, but the muscles in her right arm began to twitch as she expended her own essence to redirect the necklace's power.

The knight reached down with a gauntleted hand, briefly blocking the beam as he marched toward her cell. Velas shifted the light upward, hoping to blind him, but when the beam hit the runes near his neck she felt an instant of connection with a greater force – and then the beam faltered and died.

Velas fell to her knees, shivering, her right arm numb. *Shit, shit. I should have realized that those runes on his neck are another amulet like mine. Triggered some kind of feedback when I hit it.*

The knight unceremoniously tore the door off her cell.

*Work, legs, work. If I can stand, I can fight.*

Her legs just trembled with her effort. As the knight raised a gauntleted hand to strike, the best she could do was to move her left arm in the way in an effort to block.

The knight's sword ripped out of its scabbard. Taelien had grabbed it from behind.

The knight turned just in time for the sword to slam into its weakened breastplate. He staggered backward, nearly falling into Velas, which put him in a convenient position.

Velas slapped her burned left hand on the front of the breastplate. *Pulse.*

The breastplate exploded, shards of blackened material scattering throughout the cell. Taelien struck in the next instant, slamming the sword into a green crystal that had been housed within the armor. The knight shuddered for a few moments and collapsed. Velas fell to the floor beside him.

"Gods fucking goats, that really hurt." She curled up on the floor, cradling her numb right arm, which somehow felt even worse than her burned hand.

Taelien knelt down, which looked like a sympathetic gesture at first, until she realized he was inspecting the fallen knight instead of her. She glanced at what he was looking at – there was no body inside the armor, just the gemstone that Taelien had damaged, which was lodged inside a metal frame.

He frowned, turning to her next. "Nice move, there. That light thing was pretty incredible. Saved my skin."

*Okay, your momentary lapse is almost forgiven. Almost.*

"Mmmhm," she managed to reply.

"You look about as bad as I feel. Any critical injuries that need immediate attention?"

*All of them. All of my injuries require your complete and immediate attention, resh it.*

"No, get the others out of the cells."

Taelien nodded. "I'll be back for you in a moment." He stumbled away, dragging the sword across the floor with him.

Velas got a better look at the weapon this time – it was black-bladed, resembling the armor, with blue runes on the surface. The sound of the stone grinding against stone was one more source of pain, but there were so many she could barely keep track.

She heard the sound of keys turning in a lock, and Landen was at her side a moment later.

"Hey, hang in there." He sat down next to her, setting her head on his lap. "It's going to be okay."

Normally, she would have complained about Landen's coddling, but she was hurting enough that a little human contact was more of a comfort than the minor injury to her pride.

*Besides, that light thing had been pretty reshing amazing.*

"We need to move." Asphodel's voice, coming from her cell. Always killing her brief moments of happiness. "There are more coming."

Taelien came back, but instead of moving to her, he knelt by the knight again.

*Fine, I see how it is. He can be your new sparring partner.*

Landen patted her head and she closed her eyes appreciatively. The sounds of clanking a few moments later jarred her eyes back open.

Taelien was hitting the knight's wrist with the sword for some unfathomable reason.

"That guy was a jerk, but I really don't think this is the time for venting your frustrations," Velas muttered.

"Asphodel is still in a ritual circle. I think the gauntlets can shut them down." Taelien continued tapping away, but he didn't seem to make much progress.

*Oh. That makes a kind of sense, I guess.*

Landen sighed. "Let me."

Velas felt her head moving and realized that Landen had set her head back down on the ground. *Bah, I was comfortable.*

Landen was warding Taelien away, and the swordsman moved to take up a guarding position in the hall. Meanwhile, her former Queensguard companion began twisting the knight's wrist – which, after a few moments, she realized was turning in a complete circle.

After nearly a minute of hideous scraping noises, the gauntlet came free.

"The gauntlet was screwed on? Seriously?" Velas let out a sigh. She was starting to regain some of the feeling in her legs, at least, but her right arm still felt like lead.

*I really shouldn't let that, of all the things that have been happening, be the one that surprises me.*

"Catch, Sal." Landen tossed Taelien the gauntlet, and Taelien nodded and moved to Asphodel's cell. A flash of light and a few moments later, Asphodel and Taelien were standing nearby.

"We must go quickly. I will carry her." The Delaren girl knelt down and slipped her arms under Velas before she could object, lifting her with no apparent difficulty. Still barely capable of movement, Velas just slipped her left arm around Asphodel's neck and tried to hold herself in place as best she could.

The group stepped into the hallway between the cells, Taelien still carrying the sword in his right hand and the gauntlet in his left.

Unable to take physical action, Velas let her mind contribute to the problem. "Sal, try the gauntlet on your amulet."

Taelien turned to her. "If this activates it again, you're the one who has to carry me."

"Deal." She managed a smile.

Taelien tapped the gauntlet against his amulet. Nothing visibly happened. He frowned.

Velas remembered the power source. "Try it on the back."

Taelien reached around behind his neck with the gauntlet, which looked pretty ridiculous, and scratched the fingers against the back of the amulet. Velas heard a "click" and the amulet fell right off him, landing on the floor. The blue runes on the surface continued to glow.

"Huh," Taelien muttered, kicking the fallen amulet.

Landen leaned down and picked it up. "This might actually be useful later, if we can figure out how it works. Also, that gem in the armor was pretty interesting. Asphodel, can you carry this?"

Asphodel tensed, but accepted the amulet. "We have no time. This is the way to go." Asphodel turned to the right, taking a step forward.

Asphodel wasn't wearing an amulet of her own, which was interesting – Velas had simply assumed she'd be shackled with one as well, given that she was clearly a sorcerer with some kind of divination ability. Either that or she just liked bossing people around and letting on that she knew everything, but in this case the former seemed more likely, as amusing as the latter would be.

*Why the discrepancy? Well, it's not important at the moment.*

"Landen, get the gem and catch up to us. We're going to start moving. You hear any noise, you run right after us." Velas instructed.

"Got it." Landen went back to the cell and began tinkering with the breastplate. Taelien took the front, raising the stone blade in a high stance, and Asphodel carried Velas right behind him.

The hallway led on for an implausibly long time, mostly stone walls on each side with occasional empty cells every few hundred yards. Taelien paused in his step, resting the sword on the ground. "We've gone far enough. We need to wait for Landen to catch up."

"That would be unwise." Asphodel closed her eyes. "Very unwise."

Velas fidgeted in Asphodel's arms. Her legs were feeling more or less functional at this point, but her right arm was in similar shape to before. Catching the cue, Asphodel set her down.

"Thanks for the ride. Mind filling us in on what you know?"

"The Overseer is coming. If we push on now, we can reach the exit before she comes across our path. If we wait for Landen, we will encounter her."

Velas stretched her legs, feeling tiny pinpricks of pain in her muscles. "That doesn't sound so bad, now that we're out of the cells. I think we could handle another one of those guys. Sal?"

"I could take maybe ten." He nodded magnanimously.

"Twenty for me," Velas grinned. "We got a minute before this Overseer gets to us?"

"Yes, but I would not advise—"

"Sal, can you make me a weapon from the bars on one of these cells?"

Taelien nodded, setting the gauntlet down. "Yeah, I think I can. My head is still feeling pretty swimmy, though, and any kind of use of sorcery is going to slow me down for a fight if we get into one."

"Aww, I won't hold it against you if I have to pull all the weight again."

Taelien rolled his eyes. "Fine, you get a dagger. I'll make Landen a pair of swords."

Velas folded her arms. "Don't be such a poor sport. Just pull off a bar and make me a spear, it'll probably be the easiest thing to make, anyway."

"Not a bad idea, actually." Taelien moved to a nearby cell, putting a hand on a bar, and closed his eyes. The bar separated from the remainder of the cage. He set the sword down, repeating the process with another bar, and then brought the two bars together. After another moment of concentration, the bars merged together, and then reshaped into a spear.

The swordsman set the spear down, putting a hand over his abdomen. "That hit me even harder than I expected. I must not have eaten in a while."

"You have not."

"Thanks, Asphodel, you're always a font of useful information." Velas picked up the spear with her burned hand, which fortunately wasn't burned too badly to grip the weapon.

Taelien wobbled slightly on his feet, leaning against the wall. "I think I need a moment."

"You can rest easy now – I'm here." Landen's voice came from down the hall, and he came into sight a few moments later. He held the cracked green crystal in his left hand. "A spear. Nice! Can I get one?"

"I don't think my stomach can handle another spear. I could offer you a metal bar, maybe."

"Hey, I'll take what I can get."

Taelien pulled another bar out of the nearest cell, offering it to Landen and nearly falling over in the process.

"Maybe you should hold onto that, actually. You're looking a little wobbly there."

Taelien frowned. "But I want the sword. I like swords."

"I know you do, big guy. You can have it back later." Landen picked up the sword. "Asphodel, can you get the gauntlet?"

"Yes." Asphodel picked the gauntlet up. "She is coming."

Scraping noises, not unlike those made by the knight, but more in number. Velas counted six, seven, eight...nine. They were not footsteps.

They were the sounds of chains, dragging along the stone floor as the Overseer floated down the hall toward them. Her plate armor lacked the spines and ridges of the knight, but only his gauntlets and neck had been marked with runes, she had them written across every surface on her body.

Her hands, neck, and helmet glowed with scarlet glyphs, but the runes on her chest, legs, and shoulders were blue.

Asphodel threw the gauntlet at the Overseer immediately.

The nine chains rose from the floor, and it was only at that moment that Velas realized that each of the chains ended in a dagger-like blade.

*Oh, that's not good at all.*

The chains slapped the gauntlet out of the air and it tumbled to the floor.

Taelien took a step back, moving into a defensive position with his metal bar. "When I said ten, just to clarify, I meant ten of the normal ones."

"No need to be modest, Sal." Velas nudged him in the ribs. "It's not like you."

"You will abandon your weapons and surrender immediately," The Overseer demanded. Unlike the knight, the voice sounded like an ordinary human woman. It might have even been familiar, but a itching at the back of her mind seemed to prevent that thought from fully forming.

"Well, that's clearly not going to happen. How about we trade places and you surrender?" Taelien made a swishing gesture with his makeshift staff to help elucidate the proposal.

"Yeah, that's more like the usual Sal." Velas grinned.

"Prisoners have refused to surrender. They will be executed."

Velas had expected the chains to be fast, but she hadn't expected them to tear the air apart. She barely managed to parry the two that came her way, and it looked like one of them managed to slice a gash in Sal's side.

The other six went for Landen.

Landen deflected the first two before charging forward, dancing to the side of the hall as two more flew past him, and then jumping onto the wall and kicking himself off of it to dodge another, and finally swinging the blade back downward to smash the last chain out of his way. He landed in a tumble, rolling behind the Overseer and swinging at her back.

The chains repositioned immediately, blocking his strike.

Landen cursed, backing away, now on the opposite side of the Overseer from the rest of the group. Her attention seemed focused on him for the moment – and Velas suddenly realized why, along with processing why Asphodel had thrown the gauntlet.

Asphodel picked the gauntlet back up, advancing. Velas glanced at Taelien, who was holding the pole in one hand and holding the other to his side to stem the blood from his wound.

"Let me see that." Velas walked over to him. "Can't tell how hard you were hit if you're covering it."

"Never mind me, fight happening. Go get her, I'll be right behind you."

Velas nodded. Landen was doing admirably to deflect the chains, but he only had a single weapon and fighting while backing up was never easy. Velas managed to close in just before Landen took a hit to the ribs from a chain, knocking him backward. She jammed her spear into the Overseer's back, but it barely reacted to the strike.

Asphodel threw the gauntlet again; five chains whipped around to deflect it. Velas had to duck to avoid the projectile.

"You want to stop doing that?"

"No."

Velas growled, lashing out at the Overseer, her spear once again bouncing off the armor.

"Asphodel, what exactly are you – oh, gods, it's so simple," Taelien trailed off. "Landen, keep her busy. Asphodel, bring me the gauntlet, and Velas come here."

"You should not do this." Asphodel gave Taelien the gauntlet, but she had a disapproving expression.

"Yeah, I'll feel terrible, but it'll work." Taelien laid his staff down, turning the gauntlet around. "Velas, stick the spear into the gauntlet where the hand would go."

Velas blinked. "You're joking."

"He is not joking."

Velas stuck the spear into the gauntlet, and Taelien closed his eyes. The wrist portion of the gauntlet tightened around the spear, sticking into place.

Taelien broke into a wracking cough, letting go of the gauntlet. When he recovered from the coughing fit, a trickle of blood was dripping out of his nose. "Now," he said, "Go hit the blue parts."

It finally clicked.

Her job was hilariously simple.

Velas spun, charging her target. "Landen, I'm going to hit her in a second. When she's distracted, go for her head."

Four chains shot at her, but Velas didn't care.

*Surge.*

The burst of momentum shot her past the bladed chains, driving her one-armed spear attack straight into the Overseer's torso. The red runes on the gauntlet flashed as they contacted the blue runes on the armor. Both flickered and died.

The Overseer didn't stop moving.

The five remaining chains went for Landen, and he wasn't fast enough to avoid them all this time. One of them speared his left arm and forced him to drop the gem. Another hit his right leg, knocking him to the floor.

Unable to make his swing, Landen threw the sword.

The Overseer ducked. The sword missed.

As the sword fell, the Overseer spun around, the chains that had been aimed at Landen whipping around toward Velas. She managed to knock three of them upward, but the others were coming in at different angles.

Asphodel stepped in front of her, grabbing the two remaining chains out of the air with her left hand. She pulled, and the Overseer came within reach. With her other hand, Asphodel pushed Taelien's collar around the Overseer's neck.

The blue collar met with red. The Overseer's head fell off.

It was, more accurately, only a helmet. As the Overseer tumbled to the ground, Velas noted that much like the knight, the Overseer was just a hollow suit of armor on the inside.

Once it was down, Landen picked himself off the floor and quickly struck each of the remaining red sets of runes with the sword. They dimmed and faded almost immediately. Velas repeated the process using her gauntlet-spear against the blue runes, just to make sure the headless monster wasn't going to start moving again.

Landen knelt down and began to pry open the breastplate.

"You know, it's rude to try to get under a lady's garments like that, Lan." Velas leaned against her spear, curious about what he'd find. It took him a good minute to find a spot where he could pry open the breastplate, during which time Taelien managed to limp over to the rest of them, and Velas remembered his injury with a pang of guilt. She turned to face him.

"You okay, Sal?" He was still holding his side, leaning heavily on his makeshift staff.

"No, not really. Asphodel, we almost out of here?"

"Yes."

Velas reached up and rubbed her neck beneath the amulet. "Best thing you've said all morning. Hey, Sal, tap my neck?"

Taelien seemed to get her meaning, taking the gauntlet-spear and prodding the back of her amulet. Like his, her amulet unlocked at the gauntlet's touch, slipping off. She caught it in her burned hand, which wasn't feeling quite as burned anymore. Dubiously, she took a look – her skin wasn't actually damaged.

*Just a mental effect,* she realized. *I was never actually injured. How did I fail to notice- oh, right, when the guard spoke, he did something to my head. Not to mention whatever they did to me when I was asleep – I could have all sorts of spells on me, since I wasn't awake to detect the shift in my Dominions.*

*Well, that makes this simulation at least slightly more ethical. I was going to pound someone's face in if they actually electrocuted Sal that badly. Still looked like it hurt like a knife to the gut, but it's no wonder he's up and walking again if it was just pain, not a real injury.*

The group took a minute to breathe while Landen worked to pry a golden gemstone out of the Overseer's chest. Taelien was pressing a hand against the injury on his side and Velas approached to take a closer look.

The wound was real. It wasn't particularly deep, but when she touched a smear of the blood on his chest, her fingers came back wet. Fortunately, the cut didn't appear to be particularly deep – but it was still a potential danger if they didn't find him medical attention soon.

*Maybe I need to bludgeon one of the instructors after all. Why would his injury be real if mine wasn't? Did the electricity break his shield, or was he never protected at all?*

The blood on his mouth was equally real, as was the numbness in her right arm. They had both overspent themselves on sorcery – and if this was a test, they'd probably be in some trouble for it.

Once the golden gem was secured, the group made their way further down the hall until they reached a door covered in blue runes – which, predictably, opened at a tap from the gauntlet. Landen swung the door wide, revealing brilliant daylight outside. Together, they stepped into the light.

# CHAPTER XIX – JONAN V – FESTERING WOUND

*Jonan watched as his family burned.*

Don't let her see me. Don't let her find me, *he prayed. The boy stared intently through the space between the wardrobe's doors. Packed between clothing, he was concealed as best he could manage, but he knew that a cursory examination would reveal his presence.*

*And then he would be added to the still-burning pile in the living room. The smoke from the flames was steadily filling the entire home, but their murderer remained within, kicking something toward the pile.*

*The latest of her victims was small, smaller even than Jonan himself. He forced his eyes shut, but he could not will the image away. The hateful orange-red glow burned his eyes even as the smoke seared into his lungs.*

*His eyes reopened. As he watched the latest kindling begin to catch, he found that he could not associate what he was seeing with what had once been his sister. There was enough remaining of her face to be recognizable, but he could not believe that it was her – that it was little Chel – in that motionless form. He could see nothing human left in that husk.*

*He could see nothing human in the woman that had burned his family, either.*

*She raised her hands to the fire, grinning as if warming herself at a hearth. The glow of the flames illuminated the details of her face, thin and angular and punctuated eyes that mirrored the conflagration in color.*

*He did not wonder at the murderer's motives – her smile and behavior were sufficient to inform him of everything he needed to know. She was a predator, and they, unfortunate creatures, were merely her prey.*

*Reaching toward the flames, she seemed to tear a fragment of the fire away with her bare hand, rolling it within her fingers. The flames traveled up her arm, wrapping around it in a wreath, but they did not burn her clothing or skin. Her songbird laughter echoed as she turned and stormed toward the wardrobe where Jonan remained hidden.*

Don't see me.

Don't see me, *he willed.*

*She swung the doors of the cabinet wide.*

*"Why are you hiding, Jonan?"*

*Lavender smiled at him, caressing his left arm and setting it ablaze. He screamed as his exposed flesh began to burn.*

*She shook her head, making a disapproving noise. "Jonan, Jonan. I always find you."*

*Jonan's screams faltered as he inhaled the smoke, and his voice faltered into a cough as the flames spread from his arm to his shoulder.*

*"There, there." She patted his head with her burning hand, spreading the flames to his hair. The clothes around him caught as he brushed against them and fell to the floor.*

*"It will all be over soon."*

***

The scribe shivered as consciousness slowly returned.

The sensation of flames lingered in his limbs, but lacked the sharpness of the bolt's initial impact. His eyes fumbled feebly to open, revealing a dark and blurred world around him.

Instinctively, he tried to move his arm to adjust his spectacles, but no arm responded to his command. A moment of panic gripped him as he twisted to the side, trying to get a better look. He heard a sharp breath from nearby.

"Jonan! Don't move."

The voice pounded into his mind, forcing his eyes shut. He laid back down, feeling skin pressed against his forehead a moment later.

"Hey – relax, slow down. You shouldn't be moving yet. You're in bad shape."

"My...arm," he managed to mumble.

"It's going to feel cold for a while, I'm sorry. It's the best I can do for now."

The pounding in his head continued, but a dubious manifestation of consciousness was returning to him. He recognized the voice of the speaker as Rialla, and presumably she was talking about chilling his arm with ice sorcery.

*Is that a good idea?* He wasn't really conscious enough to be sure. *And if my arm is supposed to be cold, why does it still feel like it's burning inside?*

"Mmm."

"You probably shouldn't try to talk yet, either."

Something wet was on his forehead now – a damp cloth, he realized after a moment. That, at least seemed normal enough. Having a fever made sense when he was poisoned.

*Oh, right. I'm poisoned.*

"Poison. What's happening?"

He heard Rialla take a deep breath. "I did what I could, but I don't have much left in me after all that fighting. We managed to chase off the rest of the attackers, though, and get you inside. Some of the guards went and got Aladir."

"You're too low. I mean loud. I mean, slow down. My head hurts."

"Sorry." Rialla lowered her voice to a more tolerable volume. "I'll be brief. Aladir and I have been trying to keep you stable, but we haven't been able to cure the poison. It's necrotizing the tissue around the wound. I've been able to slow the process somewhat by chilling the area, and Aladir has been treating the damage near the injury, but we're more worried about the poison that spread throughout your blood before I managed to chill the area."

Jonan frowned. That sounded pretty awful.

"Can't you, um, water sorcery it?"

The sorceress sighed. "I'm not very good at that, and I just dehydrated myself pretty seriously making you dominion essence of water before the battle."

"Antidotes?"

"The ones you were working on all looked like they were for ingested poisons, so far as Aladir and I could tell. Neither of us is a poison expert."

Jonan nodded weakly. "You're right. Drinking a potion isn't going to help anything in my blood – not much, anyway. And putting dominion essence of water straight into my blood would be deadly." His body felt weak. Lifeless. "I need you to help me, Rialla. Can you help me?"

"You're not going to like what I have planned."

He tensed his jaw. "I'm not losing the arm. No."

"You might have to, regardless of what I do. But that's not the plan. I need you to follow my instructions exactly – this will be your best chance."

*Oh, that sounds promising. I can already tell this is going to be loads of fun.*

He bit into his tongue just a little bit – deliberately, to make a distraction from the far worse pain in his arm and side. It didn't help. "Talk."

"Aladir is going to check on you soon. He'll do a little more life sorcery on your arm. When he's here, I need you to ask him to go get someone else to help with your treatment. Liarra Dianis."

His mind was still swimming, but even in his half-conscious state that name sounded unusual. "That's almost your name. Mother, or a sister perhaps?"

"She's my sister."

"Not seeing why this is such a problem, or why you haven't asked her yourself."

"I – You can't tell Aladir I asked. Or that she's my sister. And Liarra can't know I've been here, at least not until I tell her."

"Still not seeing why you haven't asked Aladir directly."

"If you ask, he's not going to be all that suspicious. Just say she's well-known for treating poisons and diseases. That's true, and Aladir will almost certainly already know that. If I asked, he'd probably notice our resemblance, in spite of the efforts I've taken to change how I look."

"Why wouldn't he have gone to see her already on his own, if she's an expert?"

"People don't usually just randomly go asking strangers for help, Jonan. He's not going to ask her on his own because he's planning to go ask the Paladins of Tae'os to send someone in the morning. You need to convince him to bring Liarra here instead, and to do so immediately."

"Because she's more skilled or something?"

"No. Because she's more likely to know the most efficient treatment for this particular poison."

"Why?"

"Because I think she made it."

*You have got to be fucking kidding me.*

"Okay. I want to ask why you think that, but on the other hand, I pretty much feel like I'm roasting in a fire right now, so let's save that for later. Is it safe to say she's not actually one of the assassins herself?"

"Probably."

"Okay, I'm a little slow right now, so let me see if I'm getting this right. You want me to convince Aladir to go get someone who may or may not be one of the people who tried to kill us in the first place. I also can't tell him that this was your idea, that she's your sister, or presumably that she might be one of the assassins. And he already has another plan that seems infinitely more rational on the surface."

"Yes."

"You were a little off before, Rialla. You said I wasn't going to like this plan. That would be somewhat like saying I wouldn't like being actually lit on fire, in addition to the more metaphorical internal fire I'm already experiencing, and also that the fire was somehow made out of bees. An infinite number of bees. That's more like the scale of how much I abhor this idea, Rialla."

"Glad to see you're feeling more like yourself."

"Oh, be quiet and get the paladin so I can try to convince him that your sister is single and ripe to be impressed by his masculine healing abilities."

"Actually, she's only a couple years younger than he is, so that's not necessarily a bad –"

"Just go get Aladir before I decide that cutting the arm off is the easier route."

***

By the time a soft knock sounded on the door to Jonan's room, the pain in his arm had shifted from consistent burning to an agonizing throbbing that pulsed with his heartbeat. Making the effort to ignore the pounding just drew his attention to it further, and the sound of the knocking – out of sync with the beating of his heart – somehow worsened the effect, like discordant notes in a song.

*Not sure what the point of knocking is, since I'm not exactly going to turn away visitors.*

"Come on in," he greeted with false cheer. The door opened slowly, cautiously, a moment later.

Aladir Ta'thyriel was largely unremarkable to Jonan, as someone who had spent much of his life among Rethri. A hair taller than average and with forest green eyes, he moved with a certain timidness that masked the grace that Jonan had seen him demonstrate in earlier encounters.

This normalcy was not, however, why Jonan felt that something about Aladir was implausibly familiar. The paladin's face, his eyes, even his voice struck the scribe as being a mirror to someone he had once known, but could not place. It was not the pain robbing him of clarity of mind – he had sensed this same fragment of certainty with each encounter.

Fortunately, that was not the most pressing concern on his mind.

"How are you feeling?"

Jonan groaned. "Come closer, I can't hear you over the sound of my life slipping away."

The Rethri gave a sharp smile. "Glad to see you've still got your sense of humor." He sat in the same chair next to the bed that Rialla had used, but with a slight lean toward the right, most likely caused by his scabbard brushing against the floor. "Let me take a look at that arm."

"Please, by all means. You might not want to buy it now, though – I hear it's going to be on sale soon. Half off."

Aladir rolled his eyes – which looked somewhat awkward to Jonan due to the Rethri lack of sclera - and leaned forward. The paladin put his hands on the injured limb, frowning as he moved his fingers across the surface.

Jonan frowned, too, even though he couldn't sense whatever Aladir was diagnosing – he could barely feel the other man's hands against his skin. He knew intellectually that that was probably due to the persistent chilling effect from Rialla's sorcery, but nevertheless the lack of sensation was deeply disturbing.

"The necrosis is spreading in spite of our best efforts. I'll do what I can to repair some of the damage, but life sorcery is best at accelerating natural healing – and natural healing can't treat this kind of injury. Essentially, I need to force your body to try to rebuild the corrupted areas. It's inefficient and unreliable, but it will slow the deterioration of the limb."

Jonan nodded from his bed. Sensing that his usual sarcasm wouldn't be an appropriate response to the diagnosis, he fumbled a more applicable reply. "I know life sorcery isn't easy, and that you'll pay a cost for helping me. Thank you."

"Just wish I could do more. Hold still for a bit."

Aladir began to hum softly, closing his eyes and slipping his left hand under Jonan's arm. He pressed two fingers of each hand against the entry and exit wounds, and Jonan watched as a golden green glow manifested on Aladir's hands.

*No incantation? That's unusual for a Vel — shit, shit, that hurts.*

Jonan still couldn't feel the pressure of Aladir's hands, but the flames within his arm burned with renewed vigor. Gritting his teeth, he resisted the urge to complain, though only barely.

Minutes passed, though in his state Jonan had no capability to count them. By the time the glow subsided, the scribe was shivering in his bed and Aladir's forehead was matted with sweat. A trickle of blood dripped from the paladin's nose, which he wiped away with a cloth from one of his pockets.

"I'm sorry, I don't believe I can continue right now." Aladir broke into coughing after he spoke, covering his mouth with the other side of his now-bloodstained handkerchief.

The scribe sat up slightly, moving his right arm to clutch at his left, which was still burning with agony. He could see blackened veins within the arm, which showed no sign of recovering in spite of Aladir's treatment. "Thanks, you've done more than enough." It felt like a lie, but he felt the need to express his gratitude.

"It's never enough. Ironic, given the words of my house." Aladir shook his head. Jonan wasn't familiar with the reference, so he failed to find an immediate reply.

Aladir stood on wobbling legs, turning to leave. "My healing is not the right solution here. I'll see to it that we find you someone who has expertise at treating poisons in the morning."

"Liarra Dianis." Jonan spat out the name, which had been hovering near the front of his mind, waiting for an opportunity to escape. It occurred to him afterward that a bit of context might have been helpful to avoid suspicion.

"Hm?" Aladir turned back toward Jonan, resting his hands on the back of the chair where he had been sitting.

"Friend of a friend," Jonan explained. It was easier for him to be deceptive while hiding within the shadow of truth. "Please go see her. I've heard she's an expert at these things, and I'm not sure my arm is going to last until the dawnfire rises."

The paladin raised a hand to his forehead, wiping away sweat. "I'm not sure that would be wise. Even ignoring the late hour, Liarra is – in spite of her talents – quite inexperienced."

*Hm, he already knows her. That could make this easier or harder.*

"And, given her age, I'm not certain on how her father would react to my midnight arrival and request for her to help me with a potentially dangerous procedure."

Jonan ground his jaw. *Playing mind games to get a life-saving procedure was not what I envisioned when Lydia asked me to help her with this.*

Nevertheless, he put on his most charming, friendly tone. "Oh, come now, Aladir. You're a handsome fellow, and from a well-respected family. At worst, her father might take this as being an overture of interest in his daughter – who would probably make an excellent match for you, given your mutual interests in healing."

"That's part of why I'm worried. Torian has approached me about taking Liarra as a research partner twice now. In Rethri society, that's a thinly veiled way of trying to imply a romantic match."

"I'm not sure I see the problem."

Aladir tapped his fingers on the chair. "It would be discourteous to do something that could be construed as a false demonstration of romantic interest."

*Be patient, Jonan. Just because the paladin is bad at relationship talk doesn't mean he's not trying to help you.*

Jonan unconsciously rubbed his forehead. "Okay, just tell them that I – as the patient – asked for her specifically because of her excellent reputation."

Aladir stood up a little straighter. "And a friend told you about her?"

"Right." *Shit. Did he put it together?* "Besides, House Dianis is as famous at sorcery in general as House Ta'thyriel is for healing. I even thought about going to the Dianis University when I was younger."

The paladin nodded at that – it was a valid explanation.

"If I end up with a wife because of this, you're going to owe me an apology."

The paladin's tone was so deadpan that Jonan couldn't be certain if it was a joke. Nevertheless, he laughed – and kept laughing until Aladir turned to leave the room.

"Deal."

\*\*\*

Jonan was already awake when his next set of visitors arrived. This was not due to any improvement in his condition, but rather because the persistent nightmares that shredded his mind each time he slept had forced him into a wakeful state.

He had gradually managed to push himself into a seated position, his back pressed against the bed's wooden frame, and he had rested his injured arm in his lap.

The dull agony within his limb had continued to spread gradually outward, and he watched with morbid fascination as the blackened veins within his arm continued to spread. Unable to avoid fixating on the wounded region, he was absently tapping his right hand in time with the pulsing of his heart when the door to the room opened.

"Oh," said an unfamiliar voice. Jonan glanced in the direction of the door. "I was not expecting you to be awake, or I would have knocked. Forgive me."

The intruder was a Rethri man, which made his age difficult to judge. From his carefully tailored trousers and silver-gilded overcoat, however, Jonan appraised him to be a man of wealth. His eyes were ocean blue, indicating a strong bond to the Dominion of Water.

"Oh, don't worry. I wasn't busy." Jonan gave a weak smile.

"Nevertheless, I've been rude, so you have my apologies. Torian Dianis, at your service." The man bowed formally at the waist, his right hand folded in front of him.

*You're not quite the Dianis that I asked for.*

"Jonan Kestrian. I would bow, but given the circumstances…"

Torian chuckled lightly. "May my daughter and I come in? In spite of appearances, I'm somewhat practiced in treating injuries, and my daughter more so."

Jonan nodded. "I would be grateful for any help you can provide."

The man stepped inside, beckoning to an unseen figure outside of the room.

A demure figure followed, stepping into the doorway and inside. The young woman was bronze-skinned and lithe, her eyes the deep brown of Selyr's trees. She wore a green dress lined with golden thread, which served to accentuate the green highlights in her brown hair.

Her resemblance to Rialla was instantly apparent from the angles of her face, but her poise was antithetical to her sister's. Where Rialla had the grace of a predator, this girl showed only the innocence of prey.

Perhaps it was the thought that she could bring relief to his pain, but Jonan found the brown-eyed woman instantly captivating.

"Master Dianis, Miss Dianis, thank you both for coming to my aid on such short notice. Please forgive my disheveled appearance. I would be most grateful for any help you can provide."

"Of course." Torian approached the bed. "Master Ta'thyriel already regaled us with tales of your selfless bravery on the way here."

*Selfless bravery? Do they think I'm Taelien or something? Maybe they're in the wrong room. Maybe I'm in the wrong room.*

Jonan stretched his arm out across the bed toward the approaching man. Torian visibly winced when he got a better look at it, beckoning for his daughter to draw closer.

"I can potentially slow the spread of the toxin with a stability effect," Torian offered, "But unless Liarra can remove it, there will be little chance of saving your arm."

"I understand. Please, do what you need to do."

*And I'll watch closely to make sure you don't make things worse. Where's Aladir? I could use his extra set of glowy green eyes about now.*

Torian nodded gravely and pressed both of his hands against Jonan's arm, closing his eyes for several moments. His lips tightened into a line. "The poison has spread beyond the arm. There is also a spell effect of some kind still in place around the injured area – it is already slowing the spread of the poison and attempting to filter out the poison, but with little success. I take it this was Master Ta'thyriel's work?"

Jonan shook his head. "No, I believe it was – uh, my friend Vorianna."

"It is a clever effect, but one that will need to be undone for Liarra to work. Ice sorcery would prevent her curative spells from spreading in the same way it is attempting to slow the poison."

*Well, uh, that's bad.*

Aladir arrived in the doorway a moment later. "Apologies for the delay, I needed to advise the ladies of the house about the situation. Lady Nakane wishes to visit at some point, but I told her that now would be an impertinent time."

Liarra never turned her head toward Aladir as he spoke – in fact, she seemed to be deliberately looking away from him. Jonan would have been quite intrigued by the implications if he wasn't currently embroiled in worry about both his arm and the next necessary step.

"Ah, Master Ta'thyriel." Torian lifted his hands from Jonan's arm and turned. "Can you summon the sorcerer who cast the ice spell on Master Kestrian's arm? It needs to be undone for Liarra to work."

Aladir quirked an immaculately groomed eyebrow. He looked about as skeptical as Jonan felt. "Vorianna is resting – she exerted herself significantly in the battle. Is reversing the spell strictly necessary?"

"I'm afraid so. Liarra utilizes nature sorcery in her curative techniques – and, as I'm certain you are already aware, that interacts poorly with ice sorcery."

Aladir scratched at his chin, in spite of it lacking any growth. "Very well, I will seek her out and return shortly. In the meantime, I would advise making any necessary preparations."

"Of course."

*Nature sorcery – that's interesting. Explains her beautiful – I mean brown – eyes. Attempting to restore the body to its natural state is a logical way to treat poison, but it's probably not going to be pleasant.*

He had expected Liarra to be a water sorceress, since water sorcery was much more common and frequently used to treat poison. Water shaping – manipulating the composition of liquid – could be used to separate the poison from the blood and remove it from the body, most likely by draining it directly through the exit wound. He had never experienced that kind of treatment before, but he had seen it performed by a Thornguard friend in Selyr.

Nature sorcery, on the other hand, would not separate or expel the poison – it would attempt to force the body to break the poison down into something harmless.

Both forms of sorcery could potentially make certain maladies worse – specific toxins reacted differently to sorcerous intervention. This was, Jonan believed, why Rialla had insisted on her sister examining and treating the wound. If Liarra had created the poison, she would be aware of the proper treatment to use.

*Of course,* Jonan considered, *Rialla probably assumes her sister would want to undo any damage to innocent victims like myself. It's probable that Rialla is being hopelessly naïve, and there's a good chance I'm about to be murdered by her uncomfortably attractive sister.*

*I suppose there are worse ways to die.*

"I – can I examine your wound, Master Kestrian?" The girl turned her head in Jonan's general direction, but neither directly toward his eyes nor his wound.

*Adorable. Yes, of course you can, murder-mistress.*

"I would be much obliged if you did so, Miss Dianis."

The brunette scurried closer, still never meeting his gaze, but finally turning her attention toward the injured limb. To her credit, her look on inspecting the wound was one of curiosity, rather than the abject horror her father had displayed. She reached down, lifted his arm slightly, and gingerly turned it over, inspecting the exit wound. Frowning, she leaned closer and sniffed it.

"The ice sorcery has been effective at slowing the poison's ability to cause damage, but the water key used as a filtration agent has been completely ineffective. If Master Ta'thyriel had not been working to undo the internal damage, the necrosis would have already spread beyond your arm. His efforts have been...impressive."

She took a deep breath. "I will need to reopen the wound once we begin the process in order to make direct contact with the poison. This will be uncomfortable, especially once the numbness from the ice spell fades. Do you have any questions?"

Liarra raised her head to look directly at Jonan. He turned his head away.

"No, that was, uh, quite clear. Thank you."

She nodded and looked back down at the wound. "I will begin as soon as the sorceress arrives and undoes her spell. Father, please bring me a chair."

*Huh. She's vastly more assertive when she's working.*

Torian dutifully moved one of the nearby chairs next to the bed, and Liarra sat, continuing to inspect the wound. She prodded at the areas where the blackened veins were visible, appearing entranced with the damage.

He wasn't sure if she was practicing some kind of silent sorcery like his own or just prodding at his skin out of boredom. He suspected the former, but it was the more disturbing answer – Assassin's Sorcery had its name for a reason.

Even as a practitioner of the same style of spellcasting, he had no way of detecting silent spells unless they were of a dominion that he was personally capable of using. Nature and life were not among those dominions – and neither was poison. If she was a poison sorceress, putting her in direct contact with his wound was a suicidal prospect.

But he was no longer in a position to refuse – sounding the alarm now would have been a dangerous complication, and one that could easily cost his arm. It was easier, if not necessarily safer, to trust Rialla's judgment of her sister.

Instead, he focused on the problem that Rialla had been trying to avoid, constructing a new image of her in his mind.

When Rialla began to come into view, he made an assassin's move of his own.

*Disguise.*

He shaped the sight sorcery spell carefully, only capturing Liarra, Torian, and himself in its effect. The alterations to Rialla's appearance would be subtle ones – changes to the structure of her face, the musculature in her arms and legs, and her apparent age.

He had no need to change the color of her eyes – he had deduced that she had somehow already altered that herself. He had not yet determined if the appearance of her eyes was a persistent deception sorcery effect or if she had actually managed to change her dominion bond – either was possible, given her existing skills and her previous work with Edon. It was something he planned to ask her about eventually, but now was far from the time.

Subtle though the changes were, Jonan judged upon seeing her revised appearance that it was sufficient – she no longer displayed the characteristic signs of resemblance to her family.

Both Torian and Liarra turned toward the newcomer as she entered. That gave Jonan an opportunity to raise his right hand and make a symbol of an eye with his fingers – a hand sign indicating an illusion.

Her shoulders immediately relaxed as she took in the indication.

"Vorianna." Jonan spat out the false name quickly, hoping to reinforce his message to her. "These are the sorcerers Aladir summoned to assist me, Torian and Liarra Dianis."

Rialla reacted to his cue immediately, bowing deeply. "My earnest pleasure to meet the scions of such a respected house, m'lord and 'lady."

Torian and Liarra bowed in return. The father spoke next. "Thank you. Your filtering spell was quite clever, and your friend was lucky to have your help. Unfortunately, it would interfere with my daughter's work. Could you remove it?"

The former "goddess" nodded absently. "Sure, can do. Have you figured out the poison? Couldn't identify it myself – exerted myself too much earlier to use my water sorcery."

Rialla approached, casually taking a seat on his bed, next to his legs. She lifted up his arm and put two fingers against his injury.

Torian lifted an eyebrow, perhaps finding the young woman sitting on his bed inappropriate, but he said nothing.

*Good. If she keeps projecting an attitude dissimilar from what he'd expect from his daughter, he's less likely to come to the same conclusion. She uses a bit of an accent when she's playing Vorianna, but it's not necessarily enough to trick a family member.*

Maintaining his spell would be difficult – he had already taxed his vision significantly in the battle – but he knew Rialla was not in any emotional state to confront her father now. If he had to risk a small bit of his vision for her sanctity of mind, that was a sacrifice he was willing to make.

"Dominion of Ice," Rialla incanted, "Undo your hold and let the blood within his arm freely flow."

The words were unnecessary – they were another deflection, implying that she utilized a different style of sorcery. Jonan silently nodded in approval.

She sprung up from the bed, and Aladir appeared in the doorway a few moments later.

"Ice spell is gone. Need anything else?"

Liarra took Jonan's arm again, shaking her head. "No, I should be capable of working now."

"Might stay and watch, if it's all the same to you."

Jonan gave Rialla a quizzical look. She just grinned at him in reply.

"As long as the patient does not mind being crowded." Liarra's words were full of weight, but Jonan shrugged. "And also holds still."

"Sorry. I'll be more careful." Jonan closed his eyes, but he maintained his spell. "I won't have any problem with people watching. Medicine is pretty fascinating. I'll be pleased to learn what I've been poisoned with."

"As will I," Liarra replied. "Let us begin. Father, please hand me my tools."

Jonan's eyes opened wide, scanning for the 'tools' – that didn't sound promising. Torian brought a case over to the bedside and opened it, revealing glittering metal implements within. The scalpels and bone saw reminded him of the blades he had once seen in a room in Orlyn designed for torturing an Esharen prisoner.

Intellectually, he had known that Liarra had to reopen the wound somehow, but as she reached for the scalpel he sincerely wished that there were a few sorcerous words that would have done the job with less cutting involved.

He didn't even feel the incision – Aladir's sorcery had closed the wound, but he assumed the damage to the tissue must have been too severe for the nerves to completely regrow. The numbness from the ice sorcery was fading, however, and he thought he could almost see the blackness in his veins beginning to spread.

As blood began to seep from the wound, Liarra pressed a fingertip against the injury, closing her own eyes.

"No," she mumbled, her jaw tightening. Her eyes remained closed for several moments, the remaining people in the room silent. Aladir crept closer as Liarra focused, however, leaning up against the wall next to the bed.

*Within sword reach of Liarra,* Jonan realized. *And Rialla. He may have suspicions of his own.*

"I...have never seen a toxin this insidious before. It appears to have been deliberately designed to resist conventional sorcerous treatments. I don't..." Liarra reopened her eyes. "My failure would be fatal."

"You must have confidence in yourself, Liarra." Her father rested a hand on her shoulder. "Perhaps Master Ta'thyriel can assist you as well."

Liarra nodded quietly. "If his heart stops, Aladir must make it beat again."

Well, that's only the most terrifying series of words I've ever heard. This should be a night to remember.

"I must begin now. Dominion of Nature, I implore you; let your strength purge the venom within his blood."

A hazel glow spread from her fingers into the wound, flowing into the wound and meeting with the blackness within. The essence felt like scalding water pouring into his veins, and he could not help himself from shuddering. Her hand clamped down on his arm, holding him in place, while Torian moved to the opposite side of the bed to hold his other arm as he began to shudder.

"Hold his legs," Torian instructed. Aladir and Vorianna each approached the bed and restrained one of his legs as he shook uncontrollably, tears flowing freely from his shut eyes.

He clenched his jaw tight enough that he felt the right side pop – that was the only way he could keep himself from screaming.

When the essence flowed out of his arm and into his chest, he could no longer hold back his voice, and he screamed until his throat was raw and his voice faded into a ragged whisper.

Hours passed as Liarra's spell wove through his bloodstream, burning every inch within him. And Aladir, Liarra, and Rialla held him until the last vestiges of his consciousness faded away.

# CHAPTER XX – LYDIA V – MIRRORS

"My apologies, Dame Hastings. You'll have to wait here until we can authorize your visit."

Lydia blinked at the House Theas guard, who gave her an apologetic look. "Authorize? I'm here as part of an ongoing investigation. I believe we met last time I was here. Bernhardt, correct?"

The guard nodded. "I'm flattered you remember me. And yes, I remember you – but I still need to check in. I'll let you know as soon as I can." Bernhardt turned to the other gate guard. "Roy, keep her entertained for a few minutes while I check inside?"

The other guard, an older man with a thick beard, simply grunted noncommittally.

Bernhardt gave her a helpless shrug and headed inside the complex.

Lydia folded her arms, glancing around the area while she waited. Roy stood behind the twin metal gates, held together by a thick length of chain secured by a series of locks. The keys were on Roy's belt – she had seen him use them to unlock the gate before. She counted four locks, each of which she could probably open by creating false keys with protection sorcery – a trick she had used before.

*Why am I even thinking about how to break into a place I'm supposed to protect? I must be spending too much time with Jonan.*

Minutes passed before Lydia finally spoke. Roy clearly wasn't interested in being social, but curiosity was an incessant itch at the back of her mind.

"What's changed? Why the extra security?"

Roy turned his head, catching her eyes for just a moment. "Someone died last night, miss. That's why."

Lydia shivered, falling silent.

***

It felt like hours before Bernhardt returned, though Lydia knew it could have been only a handful of minutes. Roy had steadfastly refused to provide any further information – he had claimed that telling her more would be up to the nobles of the house.

As Bernhardt approached, she spotted Aladir following close behind him, and she immediately felt a slight sense of relief. Of those she had feared dead, losing her partner might have struck her the most.

Aladir's eyes were downcast as he approached.

"You can let her in, Roy," Bernhardt said as they came closer to the gate. Roy nodded and removed his keys from his belt, unlocking the gates with excruciating slowness. Lydia practically flew inside once they were open.

"Bernhardt, Aladir – please, tell me what happened."

Aladir put a hand on Lydia's shoulder, shaking his head and closing his eyes. "We failed, Lydia. Baroness Theas is dead."

Lydia closed her eyes as well, putting her hand on top of Aladir's to offer him comfort. As her eyes closed, her mind swam with possibilities.

*Baroness Theas was the next target? That leaves Nakane as the only living member of the family currently at the household – and in complete control while Edrick is at war. Hartigan was quite insistent that he didn't believe her to be capable of killing her brother, however.*

*I should consider the possibility that Hartigan was wrong.*

*Conversely, I should also be strongly considering that someone may be attempting to wipe out the entirety of House Theas while Edrick is away. Or, as implausible as it might be, Edrick could also be a target – we haven't even attempted to contact him. Given his reputation as a powerful sorcerer, we've never even entertained the idea of a threat to his life.*

"I have some information, but not much. Please fill me in while we head to the house. We should meet with Jonan and Vorianna immediately."

"You two are free to head in, but that last part might not work." Bernhardt shook his head. "That Jonan lad is in rough shape. Maer said the boy is probably the only reason we're alive, though. Found the

319

assassins before they hit and tried to warn us. Him and your girl managed to take care of a good number of them, but they got overwhelmed…"

*Jonan. Oh, gods, I left him here. If he dies —*

"He'll be all right." Aladir squeezed her hand. It was only then that she realized how cold his fingers were, and when she opened her eyes, she noted that he was even paler than usual — a sign that he had been exerting himself with life sorcery again.

"You managed to stabilize him?" *As long as Aladir was treating him…*

"Most of the work was on the part of others, actually. But come, walk with me. We have much to discuss."

Lydia nodded, turning back to the pair of gate guards. "Bernhardt, Roy, thank you both for your diligence."

Roy visibly winced and she realized in retrospect the wound her words may have caused. Bernhardt smiled, though, and waved her away — and any further response died half-formed in her mind.

Aladir tugged at her hand, leading her toward the house. He took on a meandering route, through the gardens, and she realized that his intent was to give them a moment of privacy before reaching the building.

After the pair glanced about to confirm that they were alone amongst the hedges, Lydia gave him a quizzical look.

"Assassins struck late last night while I was heading back to the citadel. Fortunately, my walking path must have been predictable, because Maer was able to find me after the battle. By the time I reached the household, the combat had concluded — and the assassins had retreated."

Lydia nodded, leaning against a tree. "They left after completing their objective, I presume?"

"No. Nedelya lived through the assault — she was perfectly well in the morning. Some of the guards took a few scrapes. Jonan was the only person who was severely injured during the assault — a credit to his own quick thinking. I admit I was somewhat concerned when you told me you were bringing in a Thornguard, but from what I've heard, he saved a lot of lives last night."

"What precisely happened to him?"

"Crossbow bolt to the left bicep. Poisoned, of course, otherwise treating it would have been relatively trivial for me."

ANDREW ROWE

*Only Aladir could say something like that with a neutral tone and a straight face. Treating damage to muscles is absurdly difficult, even for many veteran life sorcerers.*

"And poison isn't your specialty, but you said you had help."

"Yes, but therein lies my concern as well. At first, my assistance came from your other friend, 'Vorianna'. She had exerted her water sorcery abilities earlier in the evening by conjuring dominion essence for antidote research. Unfortunately, that same antidote research was not applicable to flesh wounds."

"Understood. Go on."

"She used some sort of complex ice and water spell to slow the spread of the poison and attempt to purify it, but the treatment was largely ineffective. At one point during the evening, Jonan asked me to call upon Liarra Dianis, a talented nature sorceress, to assist with healing his arm."

Lydia's eyes widened involuntarily at the name "Dianis". Jonan had never explicitly told her that Vorianna was Vorain, but the names were so obviously similar that she had pieced it together immediately – she suspected it was an intentional joke that only the three of them would understand. She already knew that Vorain was Rialla Dianis from previous conversations with Jonan, meaning that Liarra Dianis would be one of her relatives.

"I can see from your reaction that you either know – or suspect – something similar to what I've realized. Vorianna is a member of House Dianis, most likely one of Liarra's siblings or cousins."

Lydia didn't see any reason to hide what she knew on the subject. "Yes, I suspected that immediately when I saw her, but I didn't think to tell you. Her identity didn't seem relevant, but I apologize for the lapse."

He shrugged. "It wouldn't have seemed relevant to me, either, at the time – and people generally deserve their privacy. As far as you knew, she was just doing you a favor. But, given the events of the last several hours, I now believe she may be more intimately involved in the situation – if she is not the assassin herself."

"You think Vorianna put the idea to call her sister – yes, it'd be her sister – in Jonan's head?"

*Actually, she could have very literally done that – she's a deception sorceress. Could have even made Jonan think it was his own idea. Normally, he'd probably be*

321

*able to sort through simple deception sorcery, but with poison pumping through his*
*body his mental facilities might be more limited than usual.*

"I believe so. Certainly, he may have thought of it himself if he was already aware of her identity and familiar with her family. But there are other pieces of evidence that bother me."

"Go on."

"I arrived after the battle to find House Theas in chaos, but both of the ladies of the house unharmed. The lack of victims was miraculous, but even more so was the lack of casualties on the sides of the assassins themselves – in spite of being found quickly, apparently due to Jonan's sight sorcery, none of the assassins were caught. A bit strange that every single one of them managed to escape."

"That could simply be explained by them turning around as soon as it was apparent they had been discovered."

"But, from the accounts of the guards, that isn't what happened – the fighting continued for some time. After Jonan was injured, Vorianna went out alone to 'scare off' the remaining attackers. When she returned, she explained that she had succeeded at forcing the assassins away, but failed to take any prisoners."

"But you don't think that's plausible."

"I think it's within the dominion of possibility, but Vorianna has at least ice and water sorcery at her disposal. Both are excellent disciplines for battlefield control. While she may have been too strained to use the latter due to her efforts to make the antidotes earlier in the day, ice sorcery alone may have been sufficient."

"She may have simply been focused on using it defensively. We don't know the exact capabilities of who she was fighting."

Aladir nodded, acknowledging the point. "True – and I intend to ask her. But I have a few more things you should know before we go to speak to her."

Lydia adjusted her glasses. "I'd be glad to hear them."

"When I went to the Dianis manor, several members of the household were awake, in spite of it being the middle of the night. Torian, Liarra's father, insisted on accompanying us to House Theas. I do not blame him for requesting to escort us, of course – I wouldn't let my own daughter wander out with an unmarried man in the middle of the night, paladin or not. He was right to do so. But the atmosphere at the house was full of tension, as if everyone had taken a deep breath and failed to let it free."

"The atmosphere of tension could have been your own perception - after all, you had just come from a battlefield yourself.

"True. And some sorcerers keep late hours – you among them."

Lydia leaned her chin against a hand. "You know, you could use an example other than me when you're talking about murder suspects."

Aladir rolled his eyes. "I could if I wanted to, true. Now, Torian and Liarra both came in to help me – but they insisted we had to retrieve Vorianna to undo her ice spell before they could work. I found that part a little suspicious, too, but plausible; it's true that nature and ice sorcery don't mix well. When Vorianna arrived, they didn't show any hints of recognizing her. None. But you confirmed that she's Liarra's sister, correct?"

Lydia nodded, turning her head away. "I'm fairly confident of that, at least. Jonan has been working with this 'Vorianna' for several months. She went by 'Vorain' in Orlyn, and her real names is Rialla Dianis."

Aladir pressed his hand to his forehead. "Vorain. Of course. How did I miss a name that obvious?"

"It's only obvious if you already know she's Vorian, really. The Vorinthal family is famous, and Anna is a common human name. Combining the two makes for a plausible name." She paused for a moment, considering. "I would have expected her family to recognize her, but she's been in Orlyn for years, and there are rumors her eye color changed somehow. Given that she was involved in Edon's experiments on dominion bonds, it's possible her bond was altered somehow – which would explain her looking at least somewhat different."

"I suppose several years apart and a change in eye color might be sufficient, but even then..."

"It does seem strange that they gave no reaction at all, unless they already expected her to be there."

"Exactly. Finally – and the worst part of this – is that Baroness Nedelya Theas died just this morning, long after the assassins fled. She fell from the tower overlooking the manor. She was dead upon impact – there was nothing I could do. There were no signs of forced entry in her room, nor any signs of a struggle."

"I'd like to see that myself. Not that I doubt your capabilities, of course, but you're not a knowledge sorcerer."

"Oh, I quite agree – you should inspect the scene yourself. But I did search it well – and I did find something. Something I haven't told anyone else about yet."

He opened a pouch on his belt, removing an envelope with a broken wax seal. He handed the envelope to Lydia.

Lydia retrieved the letter from inside the envelope.

*My darling husband,*

*Do not mourn me. I am doing what I must do in order to protect what remains of our family. Am I taking the coward's path, to avoid facing you? No. I wish that I had the time left to see you one last time, but that is not to be. Sometimes fate forces our hand – and for that, I am sorry.*

*I will always love you.*

*-Nedelya*

Lydia pondered the contents of the note, carefully folding it and returning to the envelope. "The structure of the main body of the text is unusual. Disjointed."

"Yes, precisely." Aladir placed the note back in his pouch. "I considered showing it to Nakane, but she is in a tender state, and I do not believe she is ready to see it yet."

"The writer – if it was Nedelya – claims to be doing 'this', presumably killing herself, to protect her family. Can you think of any reason why ending her own life would do that?"

"Perhaps she was being extorted somehow. If this was some sort of vendetta against the family, perhaps a certain number of lives were demanded in recompense for a past event? In any case, it's obvious the baroness knows something we do not."

*Knew, not "knows". She's dead. She doesn't know anything – it should be in the past tense.*

Lydia barely restrained the urge to correct Aladir's grammar – she knew it wasn't the right time.

"All right, I can see why you're suspecting Vorianna, given the timing and her behavior during the assault. Did she have an opportunity to confront the baroness at some point between the assault and Nedelya's death?"

"That's my biggest problem – I don't know. The baroness had guards on her doors at all times, but she might have had a way around that."

Lydia frowned. *Deception sorcery could be used to convince someone to open a door, but the guard would have remembered...wait, we're overthinking this.* "Rialla didn't necessarily even need to meet with the baroness last night, if she had threatened Nedelya at some point before. The attack could have simply been a reminder of a previous threat."

Aladir nodded, and then yawned loudly. "Sorry, haven't been able to shake this exhaustion."

"You should eat something, especially since you just healed someone. You're always terrible about that."

He nodded sheepishly. "I will. But you needed to know about this first – and we should probably confront Vorianna before doing anything else. Given the situation, it would be easy for her to slip away."

"We should talk to her, but there's something else you need to know before I get distracted – I think there could be another target."

Aladir tilted his head to the side. "Another target? Why?"

"Hartigan told me about another member of House Theas – a cousin named Larkin. He changed his name to Landen."

The Rethri paladin narrowed his eyes. "Your paladin candidate friend?"

"Yeah, that'd be him. I plan to go warn him as soon as I'm done here – he should probably be taken out of the paladin examinations until the assassins are found. The exams are a very convenient time for a would-be killer to strike."

"Agreed. It would be easy to make a fatality look like a tragic accident." Aladir folded his arms. "But wouldn't he make another likely suspect as well?"

"Yes, but he's never shown any interest in his family, and Hartigan said he didn't think Larkin had any reason to want to hurt them."

"Hartigan? You actually managed to speak to him? I'm...a little jealous right now." He gave a weak smile. "He's one of my heroes, you know."

"I know, you never shut up about it."

"Kind of like you and Tarren."

325

"We all have our heroes. Anyway, I'll tell you more about it on the way – I think it's time to find Vorianna and have a little chat."

"I couldn't agree more."

***

Aladir led the way through the remainder of the gardens to the entrance to the House Theas manor. Maer stood vigil at the side door wearing a somber expression. He nodded absently as the pair approached.

*I suppose I should probably say something about what happened.*

"My apologies for being absent over the last few days, Maer. I heard you were instrumental in the defense of the manor."

The guard shrugged. "Wasn't enough."

"I won't press the issue, but you should be proud that the assassins were repelled, regardless of the aftermath." After a pause with no reply, she added, "I would like to pay my respects to the lady of the house. Is she present?"

Maer shook his head. "She's here, but she's cloistered herself in her room. Her way of mourning, I 'spose. Nakane has always been a private one. Might suggest you visit your friend, though. He had a rough night."

Lydia reached up and absently corrected her glasses. "Is he awake?"

"Not sure, but I'll wager he'd want the visit regardless."

Aladir glanced at her. "I don't know if waking him is wise, but we can check in, at least."

Lydia nodded. "Thank you, Maer. May we go in?"

"Of course." The guard opened the door, gesturing for them to proceed inside. "Hope you found something in your search. We need to nail the bastards that did this."

"Might have made some progress, but it's too soon to say." She stepped inside, glancing back as she walked. "But I'll make sure you know when it's time to make a move."

"Appreciate that." Maer flexed his hands in the air. "Appreciate it very much."

"Come, he's this way." Aladir gestured and she swiftly followed.

Jonan's room was on the second floor, and they passed a pair of other guards on the way. They wore similar expressions of defeat. Aladir knocked on the door of the chamber when they arrived.

There was a brief pause before Lydia heard a familiar voice in reply. "Mm, what time is it?"

Aladir took that as his cue to open the door.

Jonan had pushed himself into a half-seated position in his bed. He was shirtless, his entire left arm wrapped in bandages. The section near his upper arm showed a hint of dried blood. His hair was disheveled, his forehead damp. A cloth – presumably one that had been on his forehead moments before – was sitting on his lap. His expression was a mixture of pain and confusion.

Lydia stepped closer immediately, finding Jonan's glasses case on a table next to his bedside and opening it. She found the thickest pair and offered them. His first attempt to grab the pair missed entirely, but on the second grasp he managed to seize them and put them on. Afterward, Lydia sat in the chair next to his bed.

"Oh, hello Lydia-shaped blur. You're at least fifty percent more visible now, thank you."

"As always, I live to serve." She gave him a wry grin, trying not to betray her concern. His skin was damp with sweat and his breath smelled of sickness.

Aladir moved to the bedside, reaching underneath the bed to retrieve a medical kit. "Let me replace those bandages." There was a hint of disapproval in his tone. Lydia read that to mean that Aladir had asked someone else to rotate the bandages, but whoever he had asked had failed to do so.

"That sounds nice." Jonan gave her a perplexed expression. "My eyes are bad right now, and my brain is blurry, too. Am I drunk? I don't remember getting drunk – which must mean I'm extremely drunk."

"We gave you something for the pain," Aladir explained. "The effect should fade in a few more hours, but you're probably going to want more of it. Life sorcery makes injuries feel worse before they feel better."

Jonan frowned. "It's going to feel worse? That's lovely, I already feel like a cat is continuously gnawing on my nerves. A very large cat. It is also hungry, and somewhat cunning."

"I heard you were very brave last night, Jonan. I'm sorry I wasn't here to help you."

Jonan waved his right arm dismissively, while offering his left to Aladir. The life sorcerer began to unwrap the bandages on Jonan's arm.

"S'alright, Lyd. Can I call you Lyd? You should say no – that's a terrible nickname."

She smiled, a little more genuinely this time. "You can come up with a better nickname when you're feeling better."

"Quite all right. Anyway, better that you weren't here. I mean, yes, you would have been helpful, of course, but I wouldn't want you to be hurt. Not that you're weak, or whatnot. Better fighter than I am, of course. You exceed that terribly low standard quite admirably. But there are always risks, and I'd rather you avoid them."

Aladir gave her a quizzical look – asking if Jonan was flirting with her, perhaps – and then went back to his ministrations.

"That's sweet of you. Are you feeling better now that you've slept a bit?"

He nodded, blinking rapidly after doing so. "Somewhat, yes, I think. How are you?"

"I'm quite all right. I went and visited Hartigan – I'll tell you more about that when you're feeling better. Suffice to say he's probably not the one responsible for all this."

"Didn't think so. Also, those people last night were Rethri. The ones I saw, at least. Hartigan's smart enough to employ Rethri as a deflection, of course, but it doesn't seem like his style. More of the type to just walk up and incinerate the whole house himself, from what I've heard."

"That does sound consistent with my experience, yes. I did hear, however, that there might be another potential target – do you recall my friend Landen from Orlyn?"

The bandages had been fully removed. The injuries on the surface of the arm seemed superficial – she recognized the characteristic half-healed entry and exit points that had been treated with sorcery. Faint hints of blood lingered at both wounds, and the surface around each point was swollen and reddened, potentially an indication of infection. From Aladir's grimace, she suspected that was the case.

Aladir began applying an ointment from his medical kit and rewrapping the wound. His expression had shifted into one of patient concentration.

"Oh, Landen, yeah. Only met him a few times. We tricked him pretty good with that arena stunt, yeah? Holy swords coming out of the sky. That was brilliant."

Lydia smiled at the memory, moving her hand to her cheek. "Well, it would appear that Landen is actually a member of House Theas, which makes him both a potential suspect and a potential target. The former is unlikely, given Hartigan's assessment of Landen's character and my own experiences with him."

"Okay. Not really keeping up with all this completely. Mind is fuzzy. But if you've got another target, keep a good eye on him, yeah? I'd offer you mine, but I don't have any at the moment."

"Right. I'm headed there after I deal with a few things here." She frowned, realizing that Jonan might not have been apprised of the current situation. "Did you already hear about Nedelya?"

Jonan turned his head to the side. "What about her?"

*Oh, shit.*

"She appears to have taken her own life."

The scribe turned his gaze downward. The three were silent for several moments.

"Well, fuck." Jonan balled his hand into a fist. "Fuck everything."

"I'm sorry. You did the best you could – the assassins didn't seem to be the ones who got her, so far as I can tell."

"Though they –" Aladir began, but she gave him a warning look and he paused.

"They all escaped," Lydia cut in. *Jonan doesn't need to know about the note – not yet. He's clearly not in any state of mind to process it.*

"All of them?" Jonan's sat up a little straighter, focusing his gaze on Lydia. "That sounds wrong. Implausible."

"We were thinking that as well." Lydia folded her hands in her lap. "I don't want to worry you overly much, but how well do you know Vorianna?"

Jonan's lips tightened for a moment, and then he burst out into laughter. "Vorianna? You think she's – no, no, that wouldn't work. It couldn't..."

He raised his right hand, covering his eyes, and then sighed deeply. "I admit I may have been somewhat hasty in bringing a disguised and horrendously dangerous sorceress into this household. Why do you think Vorianna is involved?"

Aladir finished bandaging Jonan's arm and leaned up against the nearby wall. "We're not sure, but she went back out to fight after you were incapacitated, and all the Rethri mysteriously escaped. She's an ice sorceress – it seems like she should have been able to capture at least one person, unless she was injured or killed. Which she wasn't."

"There's another explanation to that, although you still probably won't like it, and it proves nothing." Jonan lay back down in the bed, groaning.

"What have you found?" Lydia shifted uncomfortably in her seat.

"Well, you probably know this, I think I told you – but her real name is Rialla Dianis."

"We know about that, and that she probably persuaded you to ask me to retrieve her sister."

"Gods, I'm not very good at subtlety at all when I'm like this, am I?" The sight sorcerer rubbed at his eyes.

"You were never very good at subtlety, Jonan." Lydia chuckled and patted his hand affectionately, but he looked a little hurt in spite of her attempt at humor.

"I'll be direct, then. She won't want me to mention this, but she implied that her sister may have been involved in making the poison that I've been afflicted with. I don't know why she suspected that, but if I had to guess, I'd say she recognized some of those Rethri."

"And let them go deliberately?" Lydia inquired.

"And didn't put much effort into the chase. But that doesn't mean she was involved. I think she didn't want to be recognized by them. She's been obsessed with avoiding her father's attention since she came into town."

Aladir frowned at that. "But he didn't even seem to recognize her when she arrived. And neither did Liarra."

"My work. Threw a sight spell on her as soon as she walked into the room, making her look subtly different. I excluded you from the spell's effect, so you wouldn't have seen the change."

"Kind of you to look after her feelings like that," Lydia offered. Aladir looked frustrated, which Lydia understood – he had never been pleased by subterfuge, and he had been a part of a deception in the previous evening, even if only in minor ways.

Aladir crossed his arms and spoke in a sharp tone. "Her desire to avoid her family does not make her innocent. It could just as easily be a deflection – it just makes her family members look like suspects."

"As they should. House Dianis as a whole is one of the most influential houses in the city. I don't know anything of their background with House Theas, but they're worth investigating." Jonan took a deep breath. "But we should ask Vorianna what she knows first – she might be able to help us. And if she is guilty, which I doubt, asking her may give us a chance to find deceptions in her story."

"We should be arresting her as a suspect and verifying her claims with sorcery." Aladir stepped away from the wall, moving toward the door of the room. "We have enough information to indicate that, at a minimum, she probably deliberately let the assassins leave."

Lydia shook her head. "That's not a crime in itself. And arresting her may let the assassins know we're close to finding them, especially if they're from her own house."

"How would they know? We can arrest her discretely."

"Her father and sister are still staying at this household, actually." Jonan groaned, rolling onto his right side. "Ostensibly to check in on me later today. If Vorianna is arrested, there's a good chance they'd find out, unless you can just get her to walk out of the complex with you quietly without having anyone else involved."

*Which means they had access to Nedelya,* Lydia realized. *All three of the members of House Dianis were somewhere in this compound when Nedelya ended her own life.*

"Let's try talking to her first. Bringing in the city guard to arrest her – or anyone else – would make a scene, and I'd rather get information first. If she's too evasive, we'll try to get the guard to arrest all three of them at the same time."

"Just tell her I'm awake and that we need to talk." Jonan asked. "And hand me that other pair of glasses – the ones with the silvery rims."

Lydia found the glasses he was asking for in the case and picked them up. The lenses were thinner, but as soon as she touched the glasses she could feel a familiar sensation – protection sorcery, mixed with something else – within the lenses.

"I'll go get her." Aladir left the room, closing the door behind him.

Jonan took the new glasses, putting them on and handing her the other pair to replace in the case. "So, how well do you know your partner?"

Lydia turned her head to the side quizzically. "Quite well. We trained together for years prior to my deployment to Orlyn. He's a good friend and a hard worker. Why do you ask?"

"Because he was the first to the scene when Kalsiris was killed, but 'failed' to heal him. Then, he was conveniently absent when the assassins struck, but present at the manor during the time when Nedelya Theas killed herself. Does that sound accurate?"

Lydia tensed, tightening her jaw. "Technically correct. But he's a career healer – and Kalsiris was his friend."

"Right, giving him a degree of familiarity with the household, their defenses, and Kalsiris' habits."

"He's not a travel sorcerer. I've checked his dominions myself – more than once. Nor is he a poison sorcerer."

"He probably didn't poison Kalsiris himself, I admit that. But if he arranged for himself to be present when the call for help came, he could make sure that no other healers reached House Theas quickly enough to provide life-saving aid."

"All true. But I think you're deflecting blame because you don't want your friend to be connected."

"You're doing exactly the same thing."

"One of us is going to be disappointed."

"No," Jonan lowered his head, "I suspect we both are."

Lydia leaned back in her chair. "Is there anything you aren't telling me? Anything at all you can think of that might be relevant?"

Jonan reached up, rubbing his forehead with his right hand and grimacing. "Let me think for a minute."

Lydia searched her own mind as well. *What other clues do we have? The note – can we tie that to someone directly?*

*And Jonan is thinking more clearly than we gave him credit for. How much of that earlier disorientation was pretense? If he suspected Aladir from the beginning...*

*But Aladir was going to tell Jonan about the note. I'm the one who stopped that – and if Aladir wrote the note, he probably wouldn't want anyone else to know about it.*

*Unless Aladir had someone else write the note, or the note itself is an intentional distraction. If Aladir is actually the killer, he'd know exactly what to do in order to distract me and sow doubt in my mind. Resh, that's bad.*

"Vorianna implied that her sister was the one who made the poison – and Liarra did prove capable of treating it, at least to the extent that I'm alive. That could imply that Liarra was, in fact, familiar with the poison. Or she could just be talented at treating poisons."

"That's good, but it's not enough," Lydia considered. "Was there anything else that we could have missed? Anything strange?"

"Aladir asked for Liarra to come treat my wound, but her father came along. That wasn't all that strange, given that it was late at night, but he wanted to inspect my wound first. When he first arrived, he talked about casting a stability spell on my arm to help with the process. But he only touched my arm the once – when he found the ice spell. And then he insisted it needed to be removed for Liarra to work, which seemed unusual."

"So, he had proposed to help you with one type of spell, and then objected when a similar spell was already in place? That does seem odd. Do you think he cast something on your arm when he inspected it?"

"He might have."

"Hold on, let me touch your arm." Lydia leaned over, putting her hands on the arm near – but not on top of – the injury. "Dominion of Knowledge, measure the flow of essence within his body."

Normally, she would have used a spell designed for identifying spell effects if she had a clear target to work with – but in this case, she wasn't certain exactly what she was looking for.

Closing her eyes, she began to visualize the dominion essence within Jonan's body. Powerful sources of essence burned brightly in his skull - his eyes were the most concentrated area of power in his body, but she could see from the rippling effects in their glow that they had been taxed to near their limit.

Most of the dominions she detected within his body were typical – blood, heat, and life in standard proportions. His life dominion essence was focused near his wound, which was unsurprising. He also demonstrated a greater than normal amount of flame essence, primarily concentrated near his hands – an indication that he had some talent at flame sorcery.

Searching near the wound, she found small rivers of foreign essence. More dominion essence of life, presumably from Aladir's spells. Dominion essence of ice, from the spell that Vorianna had apparently used to stabilize him. And dominion essence of nature, which had apparently been used to treat the poison.

The scant remnants of the poison within his body were scattered among larger pools of essence of nature and water. Structurally, the remaining poison looked identical to what she had seen in Kalsiris' body, but the surrounding dominions looked unusual. Examining the area more closely, she realized that the amount of water essence was bothering her – there was too much of it.

Lydia had ignored the water essence initially because the Dominion of Water was frequently used to treat poisons, and it also was found naturally within the body – but the proportion was too high to simply represent Jonan's natural resource, especially since he was specialized in the opposite dominion.

Checking carefully, she found some of that water essence bonded to the ice essence – but some of the water essence was a freely floating stream, a separate spell effect.

*What's this other water spell connected to the poison? It shouldn't be here. I don't have a spell for digging deeper into the remnants of an older spell effect, but I could try adapting my identification spell and channeling it through this one...*

*Dominion of Knowledge, show me more about this trail.*

Her mind throbbed with sudden pain and she fell backward in her chair, striking the ground.

Lydia's vision was black for several moments, her mind blank in shock.

"Lydia! Lydia, what happened?"

By the time her eyes fluttered open, she was on the floor, her head in Jonan's lap. She didn't remember hearing him leave the bed.

"Talk to me, Lydia. What happened?"

She couldn't remember. She couldn't remember what had just happened.

"I...I don't know."

She did remember something, though – the spell. There was a spell, and she was reaching out to it.

"You were analyzing something – spell effects on my arm, I believe."

*Right. The spells.*

"Help me up?" Lydia asked.

Jonan displayed his injured arm to her. "Still not in a great place to do that, sorry."

She closed her eyes again. Her temples burned with fresh agony. *Remember. What was the last thing —*

*A green-scaled serpent inside his flesh, tearing him apart from within. A hand reached down and crushed the serpent's head. The body shimmered, the scales shifting to a yellow tinged with blue. It thrashed within the grip, wreaking havoc in the throes of its death — and then it was cast into the rocks, splitting apart into tiny fragments, gradually being worn away by the waves.*

"The Dominion of Knowledge isn't supposed to be vague," Lydia complained. She kept her eyes closed, rubbing her head. The door to the room opened.

"I, um, are we interrupting something?" Aladir's voice sounded alarmed — or perhaps a little embarrassed.

Jonan chuckled. "Nothing as intimate as it might look. She tried to analyze the wound on my arm and nearly fainted."

"That's odd." She heard Aladir coming closer, as well as a second set of footsteps behind him. When she opened her eyes, she could see his hand reaching down toward her. She grabbed it, and he wrested her to her feet. "You figure anything out?"

"Yes," she said, still feeling wobbly. "I've been making some bad assumptions." She glanced toward the door, finding Vorianna. The young woman was wearing a simple shirt and trousers — no armor. But she did have a sword on her hip.

Vorianna looked exhausted.

"Can you please close the door, Vorianna?"

The other woman complied. "What'd you find?"

Lydia turned toward Vorianna. She didn't make any hostile movements, but she already had her Comprehensive Barrier active, and her sword was not far from reach. "I believe you've been withholding information from us, Miss Vorianna."

The Rethri woman folded her arms. "What's that supposed to mean?"

Lydia adjusted her glasses. "This was no ordinary poison — and I think you're aware of that."

Vorianna narrowed her eyes. "If you're going to make an accusation, you can go ahead — I wasn't the one who poisoned him. I couldn't have been – he saw the crossbow bolt that hit him, and I was with him at the time."

"To be fair, you could have poisoned the bolts at any time before the assassins arrived." Aladir took a defensive position in front of Jonan, and looked to be inches from drawing his own weapon. Lydia wished he had stayed near the door to block the exit, but she was also confident that if an alarm was raised, Vorianna would have little chance of escape.

"Possible, but Dominion Essence doesn't last very long in an unstable state. And, as Jonan knows, I was using my own water sorcery to make antidotes before the assassins arrived."

Jonan nodded. "That part is true. But there are ways of stabilizing dominion essence, and I know you're at least somewhat familiar with them."

Vorianna looked at Jonan, giving him a hurt expression. "Like your ink, yeah. But if I wanted to kill people from House Theas, I've had better opportunities. You left me alone with Nakane just last night and she's still plenty intact."

"This whole line of conversation is sounding more accusatory than I wanted it to. I don't think you killed Nedelya Theas – not after what I just saw." Lydia folded her arms. "But I do think you know who did."

Vorianna took a step back, closer to the door. Aladir tensed, looking ready to strike at any moment.

"I don't know anything for certain," the Rethri woman quickly glanced toward each of the people in the room and Lydia felt an inclination to believe Vorianna's words.

"Let me tell you what we know, then. You told Jonan to have Aladir bring your sister, claiming she might be involved. I just took a good look at the remainder of the poison in his body – someone manipulated it before the nature sorcery effect eradicated it. Was that you?"

She shook her head. "No. I wasn't strong enough – I don't have much skill at water shaping. Just a little bit of water calling training, from when I was a little girl."

"Why did you believe your sister may have had something to do with making the poison?"

The Rethri sorceress closed her hands into fists. "When I inspected the wound, I realized the poison involved components from multiple different dominions. That made it harder to treat, so all I could do was

336

slow it down. I put up a wall to protect Maer, Jonan, and Nakane and went out to fight with the remaining assassins – and I chased the ones who were still standing away. I released all but one of the assassins I had captured. One that I recognized, though he did not seem to recognize me."

Vorainna opened her left hand and wrapped it around her right fist. "Shivarin was Liarra's bodyguard when she was a child. He's served House Dianis for more than three decades. I remember him being kind and, above all, loyal. He was barely conscious when I found him – the cold from my prison had made him weak. I released him from the ice, but bound in him with my vision. I made him speak."

"Loyalty. That's what drove him to go – along with a dozen others – to kidnap the remaining members of House Theas. They would have spared no one. Most of them belong to some kind of organization. It sounded like a cult to me, but Shivarin wasn't one of them. I couldn't make him tell me who gave him his orders – his desire to protect his master was too strong for me to break in limited time. And so I freed him, but not without leaving a mark."

"You planned to track him later," Jonan noted. Vorianna nodded in reply.

"An organization. That's progress, at least. Does this group have a name?"

"He called them 'Disciples of the First.' Unfortunately, since he was not a member, he didn't know many details – but his impression was that this was primarily a political move. He would not have agreed to kill anyone. His belief was that the captured family members would be ransomed to Edrick Theas, but I believe it was intended to be a trap for Edrick."

"I...know of that group." Aladir looked downcast. "Though only in vague terms. Five years ago, when Lord Lorian Augusti was found dead in his home, and the man we arrested for the crime claimed to be a 'disciple' of that organization."

"I remember that." Lydia took a sharp breath. "Something...Wydman, I think?"

Aladir nodded. "Tyrus Wydman. He had been a petty thief, with no ties to any known criminal organizations, but he somehow bypassed significant sorcerous defenses to assassinate Augusti – who was a renowned duelist. By the time we caught Wydman, he was deep in the throes of substance withdrawal – 'Ash', I think."

Lydia hadn't been a part of that investigation, but Aladir had told her about it before. "Didn't he claim that he could see the future?"

"Right. He said he was a Disciple of the First and a servant of the Shrouded One. He insisted that Augusti had to be killed to preserve the fate of the world."

"Well, that certainly sounds ominous," Jonan remarked. "But charismatic leaders often use sorcery to manipulate their followers and make them see things that aren't there." He gave Vorianna a meaningful look.

Aladir turned to Jonan. "That's essentially what my commander said at the time. But, regardless of their leader's actual capabilities, I believe this Shrouded One exists – as does his organization. Wydman could not have had the resources to perform an assassination of that level of complexity on his own, and his withdrawal symptoms made him sufficiently incoherent that he could not identify his cohorts. Even if he did identify someone, we couldn't trust it to be anything other than a hallucination from his drug use."

"That's a cruel tactic, but I can't say it sounds ineffective." Jonan scratched his chin. "So, Vorianna, you believed your sister may have been a part of this group because of her association with the guard you interrogated?"

Vorianna nodded. "And because of her knowledge of obscure poisons. As I'm sure Aladir is aware, a doctor is one of the most dangerous possible assassins." She took another step back. "But I can't believe she would have done something like this knowingly. She's never…she wouldn't want to do anyone harm."

Lydia nodded. "Let me ask you a question, Vorianna – or, let's dispense with that for now. Rialla. That multiple dominion poison. Do you believe your sister has the capability to make something like it?"

"Yes, but she'd never—"

"Perhaps she wouldn't have used the poison herself, but she may have made it, if only for research purposes. When I inspected the poison, I found that it had been altered before it was cured. The alteration to the poison made it appear to be the same as the one that had killed Kalsiris. I can think of no motive for altering the poison other than misdirection –

someone wanted anyone who inspected the poison to believe it was the same type that the assassin used before."

*Which, of course, means Liarra Dianis is the primary suspect. She could have altered the poison herself before treating it, which would have removed the vast majority of the evidence of her involvement. As someone from House Dianis and a specialist in poison research, she would also have been familiar enough with the types of sorcery used to investigate poisons to take that kind of precaution.*

*This also implies that whoever made the second poison was aware of the composition of the first. That could mean there are multiple assassins working together, or it could mean that whoever made the alteration to the poison had an opportunity to investigate Kalsiris' body and wanted to deflect blame for the second attack onto the original assassin. Interesting.*

Jonan rubbed his head. "If you'll forgive me for interjecting, I think I have a way we might be able to gather some more evidence one way or another, if one of you will help me walk. I'm still feeling a little lightheaded."

Vorianna took a step closer, but Aladir moved to intercept her. "I think it would be best if you stay out of reach until we can confirm your innocence, Miss 'Vorianna'."

"I will assist Jonan." Lydia slipped an arm under Jonan's uninjured shoulder. "Let's see this evidence of yours."

***

The room was filled with mirrors, but none of them carried Lydia's reflection.

Glancing from side to side, Lydia marveled at the vast array of images displayed in each of the shining surfaces.

In one, she saw a pair of guards moving with purpose down a hallway.

In another, the last remaining member of House Theas living within the manor, her hands smudged with ink. Nakane scratched at a piece of parchment with a quill, then as Lydia watched, tore the scroll to shreds and tossed the remains into a pile of similarly destroyed documents on the side of her table.

In a third, she saw Baroness Theas' chamber, now empty. It was to that mirror that Jonan moved, slipping free of Lydia's grasp. "Thanks for the help. I can take things from here."

"What is all this?" Aladir watched the mirror in which Nakane was pictured, a look of concern on his face.

"One of our security measures." Rialla folded her arms. "Maer is usually in here – I think that's how he found us last night."

Lydia glanced at Jonan. "I knew you said you were taking some precautions, but this—"

"Another of my many secrets, ruined. Alas. But in this case, it may provide us with a bit of insight." He ran his finger across several symbols etched on the side of the frame of the mirror that displayed Nedelya's room, and the image within blurred and shifted. "This might take a while."

Rialla frowned, tilting her head to the side. "What are you doing? Even I haven't seen you making changes to these."

"Finding the right moment. You may want to take a seat."

At first, Lydia watched in fascination as Jonan touched the symbols and the surface of the mirror. She realized that the image had initially showed the current state of the baroness' room – like looking through a window – but now, he was somehow shifting the image back to a previous point in time.

*Some sort of sight sorcery effect combined with the Dominion of Memory, perhaps?*

She had used one of Jonan's hand mirrors to send him messages for several months, but she never had known he had access to something more sophisticated. This seemed to resemble the World's Memory, a legendary artifact capable of seeing through time itself.

*Perhaps that was his inspiration for all this.*

As minutes passed and the image continued to show nothing of interest, Lydia felt her mind wandering to the letter that Aladir had discovered within the room they were watching.

She sat down, motioning for Aladir to sit next to her. "Aladir, can I see the letter you were showing me earlier?"

He frowned, as she had expected – he probably did not want the other two being aware of its existence. But, so long as they did not know the contents of the letter, she didn't think looking it over would be a problem. "Fine."

He passed it back to her, and she examined the words again.

*Do not mourn me. I am doing what I must do in order to protect what remains of our family. Am I taking the coward's path, to avoid facing you? No. I wish that I had the time left to see you one last time, but that is not to be. Sometimes fate forces our hand – and for that, I am sorry.*


Lydia frowned, glancing at Vorianna nervously and then back to the note - and considered the unusual structure again.

It was one of the simplest forms of hiding a message within a message. All she had to do was take the first letter of each sentence to form a word.

*Dianis.*

Lydia folded the letter and handed it back to Aladir.

This had been no suicide – at least, not without provocation. With her final words, Nedelya had named her killer's house.

She had not, however, named her killer.

"Ah!" Jonan pulled his hand away from the mirror. The image on the glass was Nedelya Theas, standing on the windowsill, preparing to jump. There was no one behind her – no other figure to force her out.

The baroness looked back into her room one last time – mouthing something Lydia failed to catch – before turning and stepping into the open air.

"Go back further," Lydia instructed.

Aladir put a hand to his forehead. "I'm not sure I wanted to see that."

Jonan complied with Lydia's request, moving his hand to the sigils again. They watched with fascination as Nedelya reappeared in the room, moving backward until she sat at her writing table – and a figure moved backward into the room.

Torian Dianis, Rialla and Liarra's father.

Jonan continued to move backward until he found the moment where Torian first entered the room – and then pressed a series of sigils, showing the scene playing forward as if it was occurring in the present time.

Torian Dianis stood near the door to the chamber, folding his hands in front of him. Baroness Theas had been sitting in a chair near the window when he entered – the same chair that she sat in when she watched the games of Crowns that Lydia had observed with her. She had a book sitting unread in her lap.

She did not stand when Torian entered. She simply spoke, showing no sign of concern.

Aladir stood and walked closer to the mirror. "Does your mirror store their voices? I can't read her lips, and Torian is facing away from our view."

"No, only an image. I do not have any knowledge of sound sorcery." Jonan looked down. "I'm sorry; it's the best I can do."

Vorianna had backed away to near the entrance to the mirror room and she was clenching her jaw tightly, a look of intense focus on her face.

As the scene played out, Nedelya stood, looking bemused, and then moved to a writing table. Torian walked closer, leaning over her, and waving a hand at the inkwell.

And Lydia watched as Nedelya wrote the letter that Aladir had just shown her, under Torian's watchful eyes.

She wrote slowly, deliberately, and Torian demonstrated growing frustration as he watched her.

*He forced her to write a suicide note — but she took her time, thinking about each line carefully, so that she could implicate him in the only way she could think of.*

When she had concluded writing the letter, Torian raised a hand, pointed at Nedelya, and left the room.

"Jonan." Lydia stood up. "Move the image back to where he is leaning over her while she writes the note — and keep the image there." She turned her head toward Vorianna. "I'm sorry; it would appear that Torian is at least involved, if not the killer himself."

Aladir stood next to her. "I believe we have an arrest to make."

Vorianna's expression was venomous as she said, "I will accompany you."

***

Torian Dianis was sitting in the courtyard, playing a game of Crowns against Liarra, when Aladir arrived with the city guard at his heels.

The swarm of guards that arrived to arrest Torian was more than Lydia judged to be strictly necessary, but Aladir always did pride himself on being thorough.

"What's all this?" The blue-eyed Rethri glanced around briefly as the guards formed a ring around him, and then looked back toward the board on the table. Aladir stepped out of the ring of guards, drawing his sword.

"Torian Dianis, in accordance with the laws of Xerasilis and the people of this city, you are hereby called to the House of Justice to answer to the charges of conspiracy and murder."

Torian glanced up from the table toward Aladir. "Give me just a moment – we have a few moves left."

Liarra stood up immediately, looking around with wide eyes as more blades sang free from their scabbards. "What is this? What's he talking about, father?"

The Rethri man sighed. "You've ruined it now." He casually cast a hand across the table, knocking several pieces to the stone below. "Very well, arrest me. This should provide some brief entertainment, at least."

"Liarra, please step away from your father." Aladir took a step closer.

"No, explain yourself!" Liarra stepped in front of her father, raising both of her hands. "My father would never kill someone. And we're only here because you asked us to be!"

Torian put a hand on his daughter's shoulder. "It's quite all right, my dear. I'll be happy to go with these men and provide some clarity to ease their delusions." He stepped away from Liarra, who lowered her hands, and smiled brightly. "This should give us a chance to get to know each other a bit better, won't it Master Ta'thyriel?"

"Probably not in the way you're hoping, Baron Dianis. Come with us." Aladir waved with his sword and Torian fell into line with him. The circle of guards adjusted, moving to fall into a double-line to escort Aladir and Torian out the gates.

Lydia remained invisible on the sides, continuing to watch Liarra's reaction. She seemed to be demonstrating legitimate shock. While Lydia might have normally utilized the Dominion of Knowledge to attempt to gather more information from the scene, her analysis spell had taxed her dangerously, and she knew any further spells might incapacitate her entirely.

She knew that Jonan remained nearby, maintaining his own invisibility as well as her's. He had insisted on seeing this, and she didn't blame him, given that his grievous injury might have been at Torian's orders.

Liarra sunk down in the chair on her side of the table as her father walked away, seemingly at a loss. She buried her head in her arms, and Lydia thought she heard the sound of muffled tears.

Rialla approached from the opposite side of the courtyard from where Torian had exited. Liarra did not look up until Rialla spoke.

"Can I sit here?"

Jonan had woven no disguise this time – but Rialla's eyes were a different color than they had been when Lydia had seen her before. They were the blue-white of ice, the color that rumors had hinted her eyes to be at birth.

"Ri...rialla?" Liarra stammered, looking up.

"It's me, little sister. I'm home."

Lydia gestured to the window where she knew Jonan was watching and walked back inside. It was unlikely that the reunion of sisters would be focused on discussing assassins and Rethri cults.

***

Lydia met with Jonan inside. He had slumped back down into the chair that sat near his bed.

"Well, that was touching. Where are we headed next?"

Lydia shook her head. "I'm going to visit Landen and warn him. Even with Torian arrested, other members of that organization might be after him. In fact, Torian's arrest might make them anxious, which could make them strike even faster."

"A good point. And we still don't know why Nedelya walked out that window."

*If Torian shares his daughter's skill set, he could have talked her into walking out a window with deception sorcery. But it's also possible he simply was holding something over her – information, threats, or something similar.*

"There was a suicide note – the one that she was writing when we watched in the mirror. She managed to conceal the name 'Dianis' within it, but that was the only clue I could find."

Jonan raised an eyebrow. "Nedelya managed to write a coded message in there while she was being watched? That's...impressive. I don't think I would have had the presence of mind to do something like that. But I suppose we still don't know her exact circumstances."

"Right. All signs point to Torian having some kind of significant leverage over her. Hopefully we can get him to confess, but I'm not counting on it. For now, warning Landen is my highest priority. Aladir will see to the trial."

"Lovely. When do we leave?"

"There's no 'we' involved right now. You look about three quarters dead, and even if that's only half true, that's still three eighths. More than an acceptable margin of dead for this assignment."

Jonan rolled his eyes. "That's a very exact measurement."

"I'm a very exact person, in case you haven't noticed."

"Right. Well, at a minimum, take the antidotes we've been working on. Rialla will know the most recent results – ask her about the ones that worked best. They'll only work for the poison that was used on Kalsiris, however – not whatever affected me."

"I'm not sure any traditional antidote would have worked on the poison they used on you – it seemed to be deliberately designed to be difficult to cure. Regardless, I suppose the other assassin is probably still the one out there, which means we might see the first poison again. Can I trust something Rialla has been working on? Just finding out that her father was involved doesn't mean she's innocent. In fact, it should make her more of a suspect, not less."

Jonan shook his head. "You don't know Rialla like I do. She hates her father. He was going to kill her little brother – Elias – for being born without a dominion bond. There's no chance she's working with him, I promise you that. I admit that if her sister had been the one in the mirror, I would have looked at this situation differently, but Torian – no, she wouldn't work with him."

"Fair enough. I suppose bringing the antidotes would be a sensible precaution." Lydia frowned, stepping close to Jonan and giving him an inquisitive look. He stood, giving her a crooked half smile, and she carefully maneuvered her arms around his wounded limb to hug him tightly. "Thank you, Jonan."

He chuckled. "Oh, I just nearly lost a limb. Not a big deal." He sighed, pulling her closer against him. He was cold and sweaty, but she didn't mind. "Be careful out there. Whoever made that poison is going to be extremely dangerous – far more so than those would-be assassins I had to deal with. Don't get yourself more than three eighths dead."

"I'll aspire to keep my fractions manageable."

"Good."

They held each other in silence for as long as Lydia could keep the growing paranoia in her mind at bay.

# CHAPTER XXI – TAELIEN V – WAR

Taelien limped and stumbled into the dawnfire's light, still pressing his left hand against the wound on his side. He knew intellectually that the injury wasn't very severe – he had suffered far more dangerous injuries in the past. Nevertheless, that pain burned brilliantly, distracting him from the milder – but more dangerous – discomfort from overusing his metal sorcery.

The change in light was almost blinding at first, but as his vision cleared, he saw pennants marking the exterior of a large Paladins of Tae'os encampment a few hundred yards distant. There were three large tents – the kind he typically associated with command centers or hospital tents – and at least half a dozen smaller ones. A group of tabard-wearing sentries spotted their bedraggled group immediately and one of them broke off from his group and approached.

The swordsman stood up a little straighter, hoping to preserve at least a fragment of his dignity. Velas walked up to his left side, still leaning on her hilarious spear-gauntlet combination, and adjusted her posture in the same way that he had.

"Hey!" The approaching sentry waved, giving a friendly grin. Taelien squinted, but he didn't recognize the man. He was short and a little heavy, but his short sleeves exposed thick muscular arms. Given the enthusiastic greeting, Taelien raised his left hand from his false injury to wave back in return rather than attempting a proper salute. "Wow, made it out of there already? Garrick is going to shit himself."

He chuckled weakly alongside Velas and Landen, which made his chest ache even more. Asphodel laughed a few seconds later, and the sentry gave her a quizzical look.

"Glad to hear we made good time, Sir…" Velas opened.

"Oh, sorry! I'm Caul. No fancy title, just a newly minted paladin myself. You guys look pretty wrecked! C'mon, let's get you to camp. We've got food. And clothes!"

Until that moment, Taelien had never been particularly exuberant about the idea of clothing, but after the experience in the prison, he couldn't help but crack a smile. "Lead the way, Caul."

The paladin camp was on a grassy plateau on the edge of what looked like a lush forest. Given the size of Velthryn, Taelien couldn't be sure at a glance if it was wilderness or just a large city park. He didn't see any civilians about, which gave him a slight leaning toward the former, but that implied they had been transported a long distance in their sleep – which was more than a little disconcerting.

As they approached, Taelien tried to sound casual as he asked the question that had been on his mind since he awoke in a panic. "Hey, Caul. You wouldn't happen to know where my sword is, would you?"

"Your sword? Oh, all your gear should be with your clothes." Caul waved a hand dismissively.

*Clearly he doesn't know who I am, or he would have made a bigger deal out of that.*

*I…think I'm kind of disappointed.*

After a moment of confusing self-reflection, Taelien half-heartedly muttered, "Great, thanks."

*I spend my entire life trying to distance myself from my connection with that thing and as soon as anyone else doesn't acknowledge it, I feel empty. Lydia would have a field day if I told her about this. Which I am absolutely not doing under any circumstances.*

Taelien glanced over at Velas. She caught his look, but just raised her eyebrows repeatedly, which probably was some kind of sexual innuendo. He wasn't really clear on what she was specifically referring to – their near nudity, maybe? – but it was usually pretty safe to assume she was being lewd.

At the moment, that was kind of comforting in its normalcy, so he raised his own eyebrows right back. She winked at him, grinned, and looked back toward the camp.

*I'm not sure exactly what happened there, but I was probably flirting.*

He tried not to think about that too much, and instead, inspected the camp further. There were over a dozen tents, which implied a significant population of paladins. The tents themselves varied in size and markings. While there were lookouts, none of them had the look of a high degree of alertness, which indicated they probably weren't in an area that posed any actual danger.

He didn't see any candidates from other groups, but there were paladins with tabards from each order represented among those within the camp. A small group of Paladins of Eratar were cooking over a fire pit, and the smell of exotic spices made Taelien's stomach growl.

"Woah, hey, are you injured?" Caul was staring wide-eyed at Taelien's side. His arm was covering most of the cut, but there was still a smear of blood visible. "That's – we need to get you to the medic! Come here!"

Caul redoubled his pace, heading toward a white tent marked with a symbol of the hand of Lissari. Taelien followed with a groan, Velas staying by his side.

"The rest of you can head to that big tent over there – that's where Garrick will be with your gear." Caul pointed to a sky blue tent with a pennant embroidered with Eratar's symbol standing vigil outside.

"I'd really rather get my clothing first – I think the wound can wait."

Velas nudged him lightly. "Don't be absurd, Sal. You need to get that looked at. Come on."

In truth, Taelien was much more concerned about his weapon than his clothes – modesty had never been a problem for him. Even if Velas did seem entirely too pleased by his present condition.

He appreciated that when the others waved and turned away to get their equipment, Velas stayed by his side. That kind of loyalty earned her a lascivious glance or two.

"Got a couple patients coming in." Caul leaned down and lifted the flap that served as the tent's front door, allowing Taelien and Velas to duck inside.

The tent housed eight simple cots in two rows of four, each covered with clean white sheets. They were empty, save for the grey-haired man sitting atop the last cot on the left side. He looked up from his book with a hint of irritation on his face, which shifted toward confusion when he processed the intruders in his domain.

"You're paladin candidates." He folded his arms across his chest. "How are you injured?"

"Chain from one of those sentry constructs took a chunk out of my side. And I'm a little lightheaded from using metal sorcery."

"Don't forget that you were also electrocuted." Velas noted. "We both were."

"Played with your collars, did you?" The older man stood up, patting one of the cots. "Come sit down, I'll take a look at you." He glanced at Velas. "And you, miss? Why are you here?"

"Wanted to make sure he actually told you all of his symptoms. Also," she lifted up her hair and turned around, displaying a patch of scalded flesh on the back of her neck, "That collar hurt."

"Curious. I've never seen that effect from one of the collars – it shouldn't be capable of outputting enough heat to injure you like that. I warned those idiots not to put a dominion bonded item into a test, but they – never mind. Sit on the next bed over, I'll look at you next."

As the doctor approached, Taelien noted that the man was wearing civilian garb – he either wasn't a paladin or he wasn't in uniform for some reason. Taelien judged the former more likely, but he considered the possibility that the man simply wasn't expecting to be a participant in the exercise.

"Move your hand, son."

Taelien shifted his arm away from the wound. The doctor leaned in closer. "You said this was from one of the sentries?"

The swordsman nodded. "Yes, sir."

"No sir for me, not anymore. This is no good. They should have shielded you before the test started – those constructs are vicious things. You're lucky it only grazed you."

*Lucky? More like fast. But he has a point.*

Velas sat down on her designated cot and leaned back against the tent wall. "I think he did have a barrier – or, well, at least I did when the exam first started. Perhaps his barrier wore off before the combat began."

"How long were you in there?"

"Not long. Thirty seven minutes, I'd say," Taelien estimated.

Velas quirked an eyebrow at him. "That's awfully exact."

He shrugged. "Seemed about right."

"No competent protection sorcerer makes barriers that last less than an hour. It sounds like some disciplinary action may be in order, but who am I to talk?" The doctor shook his head, retrieving a large medical kit from underneath one of the cots on the opposite side of the room. "Sit still, I need to clean the wound and stitch it up."

*Not a sorcerer, then, either. Wonder why he's here — I know they have life sorcerers in the paladins, like Aladir.*

"Do you need a hand?" Velas offered.

"Quite fine, my dear. I'll be with you when I'm done treating this young man."

Velas tapped her left hand on her leg. "I can take care of my neck if you'll let me grab the supplies. I'm a Jaldin, I know my way around a medical kit."

"I don't care if you're Lissari herself, miss. You're a patient right now, and you're not in the field. You don't patch yourself up. You wait."

Velas sighed. "Fine."

The doctor was quieter once he began treating their injuries, never bothering to introduce himself. Cleaning the wound was relatively painless, but stitching the wound without anesthetic felt worse than the injury itself had.

Velas held Taelien's hand while the needle wove through his skin, which proved both a kindness and a mild source of entertainment as they played at conquering each other's thumbs. The doctor, for his part, seemed to ignore their antics.

Once the needlework was done, the doctor applied a poultice to the wound and wrapped his chest with bandages. "Who's your overseer? I'll recommend that they let you skip the next test."

Taelien tensed his jaw, embarrassed by the idea of missing one of his exams due to an injury. "Garrick Torrent is my squad's overseer, but please don't do that. I'll be just fine."

"From your pallor, you've lost a fair bit of blood. You're not in any condition for this particular test. At a minimum, they need to make accommodations. For the moment, you clean the blood off your face — there will be supplies in your overseer's tent — and get yourself some food and a few hours of sleep."

"I'll wait until she's done with her treatment, if you don't mind."

Velas gave Taelien an appreciative nod. "My wound shouldn't take as long to deal with, it's fairly mild."

The doctor sighed. "No one ever listens to me. Fine, fine. You can stay, but don't get in the way."

The grey-haired man cleaned the injury around Velas' neck, and then applied a different type of poultice to the wound. Velas looked like she wanted to complain – and from the way she was eyeing the kit, he suspected she wanted to use a different kind of ointment – but she didn't say anything. When the doctor finally finished wrapping her neck with a bandage, she quickly stood to leave.

"Thank you for helping us both, doctor," Velas offered.

He waved a dismissive hand. "Just don't do anything that's going to put you in here again."

"Deal."

Taelien stood up and offered a hand, which the doctor clasped at the wrist. "Thank you, doctor."

After Velas clasped wrists with the doctor as well, they finally departed the tent, eagerly heading toward the remainder of their group. Landen was waiting outside the tent for them, dressed in a full uniform and with damp hair.

"How are you two holding up?" He lifted the entrance to the tent, allowing them to slip inside and following behind them.

"Doing better now that we can finally get dressed." The blue tent was larger than the medic's tent, but only had six cots inside. Taelien's eyes tracked for the Sae'kes, and he found it lying next to the one on the back-left side – across from where Garrick Torrent stood.

"You're late," the overseer remarked with a smirk.

Taelien patted the bandages on his chest. "Well, I heard these were the latest fashion, so I absolutely had to get some."

Garrick tilted his head to the side. "The others told me you got injured, but I admit I was a little skeptical. That shouldn't have happened, and I apologize."

Taelien nodded. "That's no problem. I expected to get hurt during these tests – it's not anything to be concerned about. Accidents happen."

*Separating me from my sword, on the other hand – that's a problem. A problem we're going to have a very serious talk about later, ideally when I have a sufficient rank that it doesn't get me expelled from the organization for mouthing off to a superior.*

Lieutenant Torrent frowned. "Yes, accidents do happen. But I watched the sorcerer put a barrier on each of you – an injury like that shouldn't have been possible." He glanced at Velas. "Your situation is regrettable, but more plausible, at least. Most barrier spells won't stop something that's pressed directly against your skin. I watched what you did in there – manipulating the charge in the collar. Dangerous, but also impressive. You're getting a Rank A for it."

Velas brightened noticeably at that, straightening her posture again. "Thank you, sir." She raised a hand in salute, which Taelien mirrored, realizing in retrospect that he had been terribly rude not to salute his commanding officer immediately on entry.

"It's fine, you can put your hands down. You're both sleep deprived and injured. I've never been one for formalities, anyway."

Taelien nodded and lowered his hand, feeling relieved. "Can we, um –"

"Get dressed? Yeah, I don't want to stare at your half-naked asses any longer than I need to. Come on."

Taelien and Velas surged toward their supplies. He noted that the former Queensguard went straight to checking on her quarterstaff, running an affectionate hand along the wood in a way that reminded him of his own connection with his sword. *Must hold some sentimental value to her.*

He felt somewhat better once he was dressed, but his uniform shirt chafed awkwardly against his bandages. Garrick left the tent briefly, returning with a pair of wet towels, which Taelien and Velas used to clean their faces. The dried blood from Taelien's nose had spread further than he realized, and he felt mildly embarrassed by what he must have looked like to the others while he was wandering around.

After Taelien buckled on his sword belt and sat down, Garrick sat across from him and spoke. "Doctor Corrington wants you to skip today's exam, Taelien. Since your injury was outside the design of the last test, I'm going to assume that over-taxing your sorcery was justified, since there may have been an actual threat to your well-being. I still need to talk to Colonel Wyndam, but I think I can talk her into letting you skip the next test and get the lowest possible passing score. Since this is one of the last tests, I think that's a good idea for you."

"I'm not interested in skipping any tests, sir. What is my other option?"

"You take the test. I don't think they're going to make it any easier for you if you decide to take it, unfortunately. For safety reasons, I'll give a member of your squad an emergency signal beacon to use if your condition deteriorates."

"I would prefer that approach, sir."

Taelien looked around, noting Asphodel and Landen were watching him closely. Asphodel gave him an almost imperceptible nod.

Garrick stood back up. "All right. I don't like it, but it's your call. I'll go get a beacon ready for you." He looked at Velas. "You'll carry the beacon. It'll be your job to evaluate if Taelien's medical condition poses a serious risk to his health. If it does, you will trigger the beacon immediately, regardless of his inevitable complaints. Is that understood?"

Velas nodded curtly. "Yes, sir."

Taelien suppressed a groan. *It's the right call. She's the most medically knowledgeable among us and she won't tolerate my bullshit.*

"Your next test begins in four hours. There's food in the storage containers next to your cots. I suggest you eat while you can and sleep."

*Sleep with four hours until our next test? What an absurd notion.*

***

The group spent the next half hour devouring the simple road fare they found stowed in their supplies. Taelien sat with the Sae'kes across his lap, feeling more comfortable with the weapon both in his sight and the hilt within easy reach. For the most part, they ate in relative silence. Only Asphodel seemed fully awake, and she rarely spoke without prompting.

It was Landen who breached the quiet with the first question of any significance. "Garrick, I've been meaning to ask – where are Teshvol, Eridus, and Kolask?"

The lieutenant scratched behind his head. He was eating the same food as the rest of them in a rare show of solidarity, and he took a few moments to finish chewing a bite of jerky before replying. "Right, yeah, should have told you. They've been reassigned. Not many candidates left at this stage – we evened out the platoons. Kolask and Teshvol got moved to four. Eridus is in three, since they've got a bunch of sorcery support types."

Taelien glanced at Asphodel, hoping to see relief in her features, but she remained intently focused on her food. He turned to Lieutenant Torrent next. "How'd they do on their own test?"

"Platoon three was a bit slow, but they managed to get out of the prison in better shape than you did. Used a bit more subtlety, less raw force. Personally, I liked watching your test more. They're already out doing the next test, which I'll brief you on soon. Platoon four hasn't taken the prison test yet."

Asphodel frowned, pausing mid-bite to turn to Torrent. "Watching?"

"Of course." The lieutenant grinned. "You didn't think we'd put you in a test we couldn't observe, did you?"

She continued chewing her food silently, a disturbed expression on her face.

"How do you manage that?" Velas inquired. "Sight sorcery?

*They probably have something analogous to Jonan's mirrors. And we know they have sight and sound sorcerers — that's how they set up my fight with the "Crown Prince of Xixis" in the first simulation.*

"Something like that," Torrent grinned. "Explaining all the tricks would ruin the suspense for your remaining tests. We get better reactions when it feels real."

"That slice in my side felt plenty real. Good job on that." Taelien chuckled at his own joke, but no one else laughed.

"We generally take excellent precautions. I handled teleporting you to the cells personally."

"I remember," Taelien remarked with a nod. The others gave him sharp glances. "What? I was awake when they moved us for the test. None of you ever asked about it."

Torrent narrowed his eyes slightly. "You were awake? And you didn't say anything?"

*No, I didn't want to ruin the exercise. I just prepared to strike if you or any of the others who were with you made any hostile movements.*

"I didn't want to wake anyone else up."

Torrent folded his arms. "I was totally silent. There's no way you heard me."

"None of you made any noise. I assumed you had a sound shaper with you – good work on that. But I saw you. I could see the light glinting off Lieutenant Banks' armor. I read her lips while she put the barriers on us. I was surprised you managed to teleport us after the barriers went up – wouldn't the barriers have stopped the spell?"

Velas silently clapped in the air, apparently appreciating his method of proving his point.

"All right, you saw us. Resh, boy, do you ever sleep at all? And as for that, Banks shaped the protection spells so that they wouldn't block travel sorcery. It's a fairly advanced technique."

*Could she – or someone else – have also shaped the barriers so that they wouldn't block metallic weapons? Hrm.*

Taelien took a drink from his flask of water, wiping his hands on the opposite side of his now-bloodstained towel as he finished his morning meal. "Nope. Don't think I'm going to sleep before the next test, either. Anyone up for a walk?"

Asphodel stood up immediately, drawing glances from Velas and Landen. "Yes."

Lieutenant Torrent shook his head. "I'd advise against that. You're going to have a lot of walking ahead of you. A lot."

Asphodel shrugged. "Now is a proper time."

Taelien stretched as he stood and then nodded at Asphodel. His left hand settled on the pommel of his sword, the tingling sense of the metal encasing the jewel flooding his mind with comfort. "Let's get moving, then."

"You two are crazy," Landen mumbled. "I'm already half asleep. Have fun."

"Don't reopen that wound, Taelien." Velas' tone was stern. "I don't want to have to sew you up again in the field."

He waved at her dismissively. "What are the chances of that happening?"

***

Taelien had just stepped outside of the tent when he realized he had no idea where they were going. After a moment of consideration, he wandered over to where Caul was standing guard, Asphodel following close behind him.

"Hey, Caul."

Caul turned, blinking widely when he took in the sight of Taelien in his uniform. "Oh, hey, wow. I barely recognized you. You look a lot better now!"

Taelien grinned. "Thanks. We're going to go take a bit of a walk before the next test starts – any idea where we're permitted to wander? I'm not sure what the parameters of the next test are yet."

Caul scratched at the weak stubble on his chin. "Oh, don't think that'll be a problem. You're nowhere near any of the target zones right now. Uh, guess you could head that way?" He pointed toward a dirt trail that led toward the nearby forest. "A couple hours of walking isn't going to give you an advantage."

"Right. Thanks for all the help, Caul."

"No problem! Glad to help." The youth beamed brightly, waving as the pair walked toward the trail.

*He still didn't even notice my sword. Bah.*

Asphodel remained silent as they walked, her expression troubled. He expected that she would speak when she was ready – which more than likely meant when they were out of earshot from everyone else.

The trail itself was thin enough that they couldn't quite walk two abreast, but the trail was lined with soft grass, so the pair ended up walking on either side of the trail rather than directly on the dirt. The transition into the forest was abrupt, as if someone had deliberately planted a wall of trees to mark the entry into a new domain.

The sounds of birdsong and the feeling of the grass beneath his boots reminded him of simpler times – the hunts of his youth and the exertion of his days as a Kovasi player near Selyr. The trees were thicker here, though, and their bark was grey-white rather than the verdant colors of his home.

The silence gave Taelien time to consider his situation – the failure of his barrier had not been an isolated incident. While his barrier had sustained significant damage before it had failed during this fight with the illusory Kyrzon Dek, he did not remember it activating at all when he was encased in Lysen's ice.

*So, is someone deliberately sabotaging my barriers, or am I missing something? And, if it's deliberate, why? Just another form of test, or is someone actually trying to have me injured or killed?*

The wet grass and the mud beneath were malleable enough that Taelien was easily able to detect other recent tracks as they walked – many of the footsteps veered onto and off the dirt trail, indicating a casual or meandering pace. He noted at least two different sizes of boot prints, and the footsteps couldn't have been more than a day old.

*That's probably platoon one or platoon three,* he realized. *They were sent down this path for the next test – and we'll probably be going this same way again later. That's why Torrent didn't want me to waste my time.*

The idea of having to retrace the path later didn't bother him. Getting familiar with the terrain would provide him with an advantage if the test involved traps or ambushes along the road, and he couldn't imagine any scenario that didn't involve at least some kind of physical challenge or surprise.

When Asphodel had failed to raise her voice after they had wandered for several minutes, Taelien turned to her. "You seemed enthusiastic to come with me. Did you want to talk about something?"

"Your dream," she replied immediately. "You still haven't told me about it."

"Is that really important? I can barely remember it."

Asphodel paused in her step, reaching out for his arm and turning him toward her. Taelien blinked. "It may be a fragment of a puzzle that I must solve."

He nodded, gesturing with his left hand toward the road, and she released her grip on his arm. *She's strong – she wasn't putting in much effort there, but her grip was as firm as stone. Might be as strong as I am.*

"I don't remember everything – it's been days. The part that burned into my mind was confronting a hooded man. Like a child's drawing of a dark sorcerer, complete with empty cowl." He frowned. "There were corpses, too. Walking corpses."

She resumed walking and he absently paced her. "I had my sword – I tried to fight – but the runes dimmed and died. I don't think it meant anything; I've had dreams about failing to use the Sae'kes before. It's probably just something that worries me."

Asphodel's lips tightened into a line. "Where did this battle take place?"

"Here, I think. I mean in Velthryn – I'm not sure if we're actually still in Velthryn right now or not. But it was in the city, at least at first. I

358

remember being in a dark place, too. Not sure if that was before or after I saw the city streets, it's kind of a blur at this point."

"Was there nothing else?"

Taelien closed his eyes, trying to recall the details of the dream. The walking corpses. He was running through the streets and through the darkness. And then there was the man with the cowl.

And there was a body. His own body.

"I saw my own corpse. The cloaked man said something to me about it, but I can't remember what it was."

Asphodel looked away. "That is much as I feared."

*Well, that's disconcerting.*

"You're implying I dreamed of my own death?" Taelien folded his arms. "I mean, now that I've seen that, I'm pretty sure I can avoid running into any streets that consist entirely of darkness."

Asphodel laughed. It was a brief, fickle thing – a melodic sound like a single strum of a lute. Taelien found something lovely in that sound, something worth remembering.

She shook her head. "It is not your fate you saw, but that of the man you replaced. I do not know his name – but I believe he fell in that battle. And I believe he rose again anew."

*Ah, the man I "replaced" again. The man with the carnivorous heart.*

"I'm still not clear on how I could have replaced someone else's destiny. You're implying that this is a future that was supposed to come to be, but will not, because I'm doing something that someone else was supposed to do...but that this other person is still somehow aware of you, or both of us?"

"Yes."

*Gods, that's...she's...Infuriatingly vague.*

*Okay, calm down. She has trouble perceiving individual moments in time. I need to be reasonable and try to converse in a way that is convenient for her.*

"Okay. Why are you concerned about the dream?"

Asphodel's eyes narrowed for a moment. "Because you are one of the few elements that have changed. He may not die there, but elements of the vision remain true."

Taelien shivered, recalling a fragment of memory. *Legions of corpses wandering the streets, slaughtering those that still lived.*

"And you want to know more so that you can prevent it from happening?"

Asphodel frowned, turning her head toward him while she continued to walk. "No. I must learn how to set destiny upon its proper course."

Taelien stopped walking. "Okay, stop. We need to have a more direct conversation about this."

Asphodel turned, giving him a quizzical look. "Yes?"

"The city being filled with walking corpses is not an acceptable outcome, regardless of what your visions tell you."

The Delaren girl tilted her head downward, giving him a dangerous look. "You saw this because of your proximity to me. It was a gift of knowledge to be shared between us – not to be abused."

"I don't see the purpose of foreknowledge if we don't make use of it to make a better future."

"No. That is – that is not our way. We see the way of the world, we ensure it is properly guided. To deviate from that path is to invite disaster."

She put her hands to the side of her head, closing her eyes and rubbing her temples.

"Disaster? I have a hard time envisioning something worse than dead men and women walking around and assaulting the living."

Her eyes fluttered open. For an instant, he thought he saw them gleam green, like the eyes of the man who watched them. "The complete annihilation of all things, Taelien. That is what is at risk if we deviate too far from our intended paths."

Taelien folded his arms. "That's a more solid answer, at least – but still lacking in sufficient detail. Who would cause this destruction to happen? And how?"

Asphodel closed her eyes again, raising a finger across her lips. She inhaled deeply. "You would, Taelien. You would destroy us all."

"I'm fairly sure I wouldn't do that." He tapped the hilt of his blade. "Existence is nice. I rather like it here."

Asphodel turned her gaze toward the dirt. "It is not certain – but it is what Kolask saw. A possible path."

The swordsman frowned. "Kolask? She has dreams like these?"

"Only those who are near me dream in this way. It is part of what makes me an oracle. In your local terms, one would say that I am a caller of dreams bound with the key to destiny. This is a part of my gift, but a part that I do not experience myself."

*Which is why you wanted me to sleep near you – you wanted to know what I would see if I was exposed to your sorcery.*

"And when Kolask dreamed, she saw me somehow destroying the world?"

"Not just this world. Many worlds – perhaps all worlds."

"That's...well, I suppose I should be flattered?"

"It is not a compliment."

Taelien sighed. "Clearly that dream contradicts my own dream – which showed me being dead – and your own observations that I'm somehow replacing someone else. So, these visions aren't exact. They can be wrong."

"The dream visions show the current path that destiny takes. But destiny may deviate from the path that fate ascribes."

The swordsman raised an eyebrow. "The path that fate ascribes? So, you're implying that there's a single way that things are meant to be, but that things are already not going as planned."

She nodded once.

"So, what dictates the path that is 'meant' to be?"

Asphodel shook her head. "That is not for us to know. It is the will of the gods."

"Which gods?"

"Chiefly Kelryssia, given that she is the Mistress of Destiny, though I do not know if she weaves this pattern deliberately or if she is merely the medium by which destiny asserts its own will."

*I probably should ask her why someone who believes in a different set of gods is trying to join a paladin order, but this might not be the best time.*

Taelien rubbed the left side of his head. "Okay. So, what set destiny off its course in the first place, then? Shouldn't destiny be immutable? I mean, that's what makes it destiny, right?"

"I do not know. That is why I am here. I hoped your dreams would give answers, but they lead only to more questions."

*Well, that at least we can agree on.*

"Okay. We should tell the others about this."

Asphodel shook her head once. "No. I have said too much already."

"If destiny is already off its course, I think we need to consult people who could help."

"Every word is another step away from the path."

Taelien sighed. "Fine, but sometimes stepping out of the way can lead you to a new route."

Asphodel's eyes narrowed, but she remained quiet for several moments, apparently considering. "You are not wrong."

"I'll keep this in confidence for the moment. But at a minimum, I think we should talk to Lydia. A knowledge sorcerer would be a good resource for learning more about what is happening – and how much we might be failing to interpret these visions."

"I will consider your plan."

Asphodel turned, beginning to walk back toward the camp.

*Consider it all you want. I've already made my choice.*

***

When they returned to the camp, Taelien knew he still had hours until the briefing for the next test began. Asphodel returned with him, her crystalline hair shimmering brightly in the morning light. They exchanged no more words on the journey back – he judged that she had just as much to think about as he did.

Slipping quietly into their tent, he laid down on the cot. He had no intent to sleep, but he hoped that a couple hours of closing his eyes might help to mitigate the growing pain in his side.

Even that effort proved in vain. The smells of cooking outside, the light of day, and the sounds of the laughter and chatter around the tent were too much of a disruption. Every effort to turn his mind inward met with repeated interruptions.

Sitting up, he laid the Sae'kes across his lap and glanced at each of his comrades. Velas looked to be sleeping blissfully, cradling her quarterstaff in her arms like a lover. Landen had somehow managed to find a pillow – none of the other cots seemed to have them – and had laid it over the top of his face, presumably to block out the light.

He could barely make out what he thought to be Asphodel's shadow outside the tent, indicating that she was sitting with her back against the fabric near the door.

Lieutenant Torrent was still awake and alert, quietly reading a book with a disinterested expression. He had made no reaction when Taelien returned from his walk, and if he knew Taelien was observing him, he displayed no semblance of care.

Taelien's grip tensed around the hilt of his sword, mirroring the tension in the muscles in his back. Waiting patiently had never been among his talents.

Minutes rolled into hours – hours that Taelien suspected were more than the four they had been allotted. Garrick eventually slammed his book shut, rousing a groaning Landen from his rest.

The swordsman of twin blades sat, dislodging his pillow, and took in his surroundings. He looked once at Taelien, and then back to Velas' still sleeping form – and then lifted his pillow and tossed it at her.

The pillow missed entirely, hitting the canvas near Velas' head. Startled, she rolled out of the cot, hitting the floor and pushing herself into something resembling a defensive kneel with her staff.

"What the fuck was that?"

Even Garrick laughed, but Landen laughed hard enough that his face reddened – pausing only when Velas abandoned her staff to begin bludgeoning him with the pillow.

Garrick set his book down, standing and folding his arms. "Okay, you two, save your flirting for the road. You're going to have plenty of time for pillow games over the next few days."

Velas got one last hit in before Landen wrested the pillow away and tossed it into a corner of the tent. Taelien found himself in the unprecedented position of looking more professional than the rest of his platoon mates.

Asphodel re-entered the tent, saluting immediately. "Sir."

"At ease, Asphodel. Have a seat. This briefing is going to take a while."

"Yes, sir."

As Asphodel sat, Lieutenant Torrent opened the chest next to his cot and began to retrieve supplies from within. He thrust a rolled scroll at Landen, and then retrieved a crystalline vial filled with bluish liquid and what looked like a rune-etched stick.

"Unfurl that on the floor," he instructed Landen, who immediately began to comply. Torrent uncapped the vial, pouring it across the surface of the stick. The liquid flickered and steamed when it struck the surface of the wood. He rotated the stick, allowing the liquid to fill the carved grooves in the surface. When the liquid was exhausted, he shook the stick in the air, grimaced, and then offered it to Velas.

She nodded, taking the object and tucking it in a pouch at her side.

"For those of you who don't know, that's her emergency signal. Velas has the highest cumulative leadership scores within the platoon, and thus she will be your platoon's commander for this assignment. I trust you will treat her with more respect than you give me." He grinned, running a hand through his short hair.

Landen had finished unfurling the scroll, which proved to be a large map.

Garrick walked over to the map, sitting down next to where it had been laid across the floor of the tent. "This is a map of the region. We're about twelve miles northwest of Velthryn right now on the border of the Lisanth Forest." He jabbed a finger at an unmarked spot near the bottom corner nearest him. "You're here now. And you're going to be visiting these seven," he began pointing to several marked spots within the forest, "locations. You have six days to make the entire trip."

"What are we doing at these sites?" Velas asked, leaning forward with her eyes focused on the map.

"These are sacred shrines to each of the seven gods of the Tae'os Pantheon. At each shrine you will find a basin filled with purified water from the divine spring. Your objective on this mission is to drink from the water of each of the seven shrines and then return within the time limit."

*Sounds too easy.* Taelien withheld his commentary for the moment, knowing it was not his turn to speak.

"I take it this will be more than a simple stroll?" Velas asked, leaning closer to the map and tracing a finger along one of the trails.

"It will be up to you to determine a route that can get you to each of the shrines and back within the time limit. And yes, there are a few minor complications. He leaned backward across the tent, tapping a fist on the side. "Gentlemen, please come in."

Taelien heard shuffling outside, followed by the tent flap opening. Four young men – squires, Taelien realized from their tabards and sigils – entered. Each was carrying a freshly polished steel cuirass.

"Congratulations, candidates. You're being dressed in a paladin's armor for the first time. Stand and let the squires begin fitting you."

Taelien and the other candidates stood, sharing pained looks. Hiking in armor was going to be a huge pain – which was, of course, the point.

The squires set the cuirasses down on the nearby cots, retreating and returning with more armor pieces – gambesons, steel vambraces and greaves, leather caps and chain coifs. Torrent continued to explain the mission while the squires assisted the candidates with putting on their new sets of armor. After the armor pieces had been put on, the squires helped the candidates move their pins from the earlier tests over to new tabards, which they wore over the armor.

"You'll need to wear the armor during your travel. You'll each be given a travel backpack with minimal food supplies and water, as well as a bedroll. No tents – you'll sleep in structures you construct or beneath the stars. I'd advise the former, since it tends to rain in the forest, and you should expect it to be cold at the higher altitudes."

Grinning, Garrick stood up and pointed a thumb outside the tent. "Oh, and one of you is going to have to carry the pennant."

Taelien rolled his eyes. *At least we don't need to wear full helms.*

When each of the candidates was done being suited, the squires brought each of them a broader sword belt designed to be worn around their armor. Taelien unfastened the Sae'kes from his usual belt and attached the scabbard to his new belt alongside the standard steel sword it already carried.

"That's fine if you want the extra weight," Torrent said, "But if you should encounter any 'surprises' along your journey, make sure to use the standard issue sword."

*Oh, we're going to be ambushed as part of the test. Guess these standard swords are blunted? Got it.*

Taelien nodded in understanding. *That also helps to explain the armor – they couldn't hope to maintain barriers on us for this long of a trip, but a solid suit of armor should keep us safe from whatever practice weapons they plan to use on us.*

Now fully armored and wearing the sigils of the Tae'os Pantheon, Taelien felt a stirring of pride looking at his comrades. *We finally look like paladins. Just a little longer and we'll finally earn our place among them.*

\*\*\*

Taelien's brief enthusiasm about his gleaming suit of armor quickly diminished as each step of the trail rubbed his gambeson against the bandages on his chest. *When I finish my training, I'm going to get my armor adjusted for a looser fit.*

His next thought was, of course, that he could do that himself with a mere instant of effort – but using sorcery to loosen his armor felt somewhat like cheating.

*Or maybe just using all the skills at my disposal.*

He shook his head, resolving himself to go at least a day without changing the armor – both to save his pride and to give himself a chance to recover from the exertions of the last test. A nose bleed from the overuse of sorcery was never a good sign.

Exhaustion began to take its toll long before the day ended. The forest's beauty was a brief distraction, but Velas led them at a rapid pace, wanting to ensure that they beat their requisite time with days to spare. Taelien agreed with the strategy, even if his injury didn't. They had little idea of what complications awaited them – and he suspected that a simple sparring match on the road would be the least of their worries.

Landen was carrying the pennant, which displayed the symbol of the god of travel. He occasionally waved it from side to side, seeming enthusiastic to have the role of standard-bearer in spite of his lack of any audience. "When do you suppose they'll hit us? I'm thinking toward one of the middle shrines, once we've gotten complacent."

Velas ran a hand through her hair, frowning as she got her fingers caught in a tangle. "From the way things have been going? They'll probably have a test at every shrine. If nothing else, the instructors like to be fucking thorough."

Taelien twisted to adjust his armor slightly, but it did little to ease the pressure. "Think they'll be subtler than that. The instructors know better than to come across as predictable at this point." As they continued to walk, he caught sight of something ahead on the road.

A silver-haired man was kicking the side of a fallen cart, a dislodged wheel clearly visible a few feet away. Assorted bags were strewn on the opposite side, having apparently fallen from the top of the cart when it had toppled. A pair of horses were lashed to the front, stamping impatiently. The cart itself was relatively small and uncovered, which looked somewhat unusual for a single traveler outside of a city.

*Okay, I take it back. This is pretty much the least subtle test I've ever seen.*

Velas took one look at the situation and sighed loudly.

The man looked up at the sound of their approaching footsteps. His mismatched grey and blue clothes were simple traveling fare accented by a grey hat with a single white feather. His immaculately trimmed silver beard and flowing hair hinted at a higher social class than a simple traveling merchant. "Oh, paladins! Thanks to the makers – I was quite nearly trapped here. Didn't realize how muddy the sides of the road were getting."

He stepped away from the cart, patting one of his horses as he approached. "Forgive me for presuming – would you be willing to help a weary man on his way?"

Velas stepped out in front of the group. "Of course. We'd be glad to assist you." She turned toward the others. "Taelien, Asphodel, you're with me. Landen, you're on lookout."

The older man just smiled – if he understood the implication of setting a watch, he said nothing.

A quick glance didn't reveal any ambushers on the sides of the road, but something itched at the back of Taelien's mind. He moved with Velas to reattach the wheel. To his surprise, the older man walked with them, wandering to within reach. *A bad tactic if the man is bait – he would have been wiser to wait and watch from a distance.*

Reattaching the wheel took mere moments – it wouldn't have taken long even for one of the three. "Ah, to have the strong back of youth again." The silver-haired man smiled, folding his hands together as the wheel fell into place. "Now comes the more challenging part."

Taelien and Velas moved to the opposite side of the cart to lift, while Asphodel gripped where the wagon had lost the wheel to help stabilize it.

"Lift," Velas instructed. Taelien strained, feeling the cart move immediately. Within moments, it had been righted.

Once the cart was stable, Taelien scanned from side to side, but there was still no sign of theatrical assassins. Landen caught his gaze and gave him a shrug.

"Thank you kindly, lasses and lads. Afraid I don't have much that would be likely to interest a group of paladins such as yourselves." He reached down, beginning to lift his fallen bags, and nodded in gratitude when Taelien moved to assist him. As they worked, the older man's eyes caught sight of the hilt at his side, widening in surprise. "Oh, my blessed stars. Is that blade what it looks like?"

*Oh, here comes the hook. I suppose I'll bite.*

"To the best of my knowledge, sir. It was left to me as a child – I don't know why."

The man finished lifting his last bag, turning back to Taelien and narrowing his eyes. "Ah, you must be Salaris, then."

Taelien stepped back – if an attack was coming, that was probably the cue.

But the old man made no hostile gestures; he simply smiled and lifted a hand to his chin, stroking his beard thoughtfully. "What a strange wind that carried you into my path so soon. Orin has been encouraging me to visit you for some time, but I felt it was too soon."

"You know Commander Dyr, sir?" Velas asked, leaning against her staff, a quizzical expression on her face.

"Oh, aye, I've known Orin since he was just a boy. Much as I've known this child," the older man said, waving at Taelien. "Though I told his parents to spell his name differently – they missed the point entirely. It was supposed to be 'Sae', with an 'e', like the sword's name."

Taelien raised a hand to rub his forehead, understanding finally reaching him. "You're Erik Tarren."

"Quite right, quite right. You've grown quite a bit since I last saw you." He glanced toward Landen. "And you as well, young master Theas."

Landen folded his arms. "I don't go by that name any more, Master Tarren."

The older man waved a dismissive hand. "No need to call me 'master', Larkin, you never studied with me. Although I do think I might have had more success at teaching you than Hartigan did. You - and the rest of you – may simply call me Erik."

*I...It's really...*

Taelien had a life's worth of questions to ask, but his mouth felt suddenly dry.

Velas folded her hands in front of her. "Not to be rude, Erik, but we're in the midst of a test. If you're a part of that test, by all means, test us – but if not we should be on our way"

"A test, eh? No, no testing for me. One of your advancement tests?"

Velas shook her head. "I should have mentioned this before, but we're not quite paladins yet – we're taking a placement exam of sorts."

"Oh, of course, I'm familiar. I haven't been a part of one in many years — so, no, I'm not a part of your test."

Landen furrowed his brow. "You're just walking in the middle of nowhere when you're the most famous master of teleportation sorcery on the continent. Call me somewhat skeptical, Erik."

The older man sighed. "Believe what you want to, Larkin. You did me a kindness, test or not, and I thank you for it. In regards to my sorcery, I could quite obviously have teleported directly to Velthryn — but then I would not have walked this path and learned its ways."

Taelien nodded at that. "You need to see a location to know how to teleport there in the future, unless you have a beacon."

"Quite right. I am pleased to see your parents had you educated, even if they did not name you quite correctly."

Velas scratched the back of her head. "As interesting as it is to meet a legendary sorcerer, we do have a limited amount of time—"

"Yes, yes, of course. Be on your way — I would not want to infringe on your testing any more than I already have."

Taelien frowned, shaking himself out of his paralysis. "Wait — I have questions."

Tarren smiled at him. "Ah, yes. Orin said as much. But are you sure we should be delaying your friends?"

"I'll catch up."

Velas frowned, folding her arms. "Taelien, now is not the —"

"Talking to Erik is half the reason I'm taking this test in the first place. I don't want to be rude, Velas, but — wait. Better idea." He shook his head. "Landen, do you still have the map?"

Landen shrugged. "Of course."

"Erik, would you be willing to teleport us a short way toward our next destination after we're done talking?"

The older man smiled and nodded. "Of course. You saved me hours — it would be quite fair for me to do the same for you."

Taelien glanced at Velas. "Would it be acceptable for me to spend a bit of time talking to Erik if —"

"Shit, yes, if he can save us hours of walking, you talk as much as you want. We'll even give you two some privacy."

Taelien took a deep breath of relief. "Thank you, Velas."

"You could call me 'ma'am.' I'd like that."

Taelien rolled his eyes. "Thank you, 'ma'am'."

"Ooh, I could get used to that. Asphodel, Landen, come on. Let's go sit over there."

The silver-bearded man frowned. "Landen? Is that his new name?"

Taelien nodded. "He's been going by that for as long as I've known him. Which, I admit, hasn't been all that long – maybe a year."

"I'm glad to see he has good companions. His life was a lonely one as a youth." Erik folded his arms. "But I suspect that's far from your mind. I've been quite rude – I know you've been seeking me for some time, but I never sent a reply to any of your messages. It would seem that fate has forced the issue."

Taelien folded his arms. "Why were you avoiding me? Even if you didn't want to come meet me in person, you could have sent Orin something a little less evasive."

"I could have, I could have. But there were risks, you see. Risks that we are taking by speaking even now. Your life is one that will be carefully watched and with great interest."

*Watched. The forest-eyed man.*

"You believe whoever is watching me could be dangerous?" Taelien shifted his footing restlessly.

"Oh, quite. And now that we have made contact with one another, you must be vigilant in defending yourself – and those you care for."

"I will be, but why is our meeting significant?"

"Because it will be construed as an intervention on my behalf – one I should not be taking. Beings as old as I must abide certain rules."

"Because you're immortal?"

"Among other things. But you dance around the questions you wish to ask – ask them."

Taelien nodded. "Who am I, and who were my parents?"

"Good. I can tell you only what I know – and I fear it may not be enough for you. You were given to me by a man I knew as Vel. You would know him best as Aendaryn, the god of blades."

Taelien drew in a sharp breath, his right hand moving over his chest.

"I do not know if he was your father. When he came to me, he was badly injured – perhaps fatally. I do not know if he survived. He bid me take you, along with his legendary blade, and run. And so I did." The older man sighed, casting his gaze at the dirt. "Perhaps I should have kept you and raised you, as he undoubtedly wished. But that would have meant years of running – years of fear. I doubt my heart could have withstood that, and fear should not be a child's first memory."

"So you gave me away." Taelien closed his eyes.

"To my great shame, I did. I knew a family that had long sought a child of their own – and so I brought you to them. A gift and a curse. And from that point, you know as much as I."

Taelien shook his head, opening his eyes. "And of my true mother? Aendaryn said nothing?"

"To be clear, he said little beyond 'take the boy and run. Give him this when he is ready.' I can presume that if he is the father, his wife was the mother – a simple enough equation. Vel was a loyal man, and quite deeply in love."

*Aendaryn was married?*

The swordsman gave Tarren a quizzical look. "I've never heard anything about Aendaryn being married."

"Of course not. Because Karasalia refused to join the Tae'os Pantheon." The old man sighed, seeming to deflate somewhat. "Perhaps if she had, things would have gone differently. But I cannot put any blame on Kara – in fact, perhaps she was right all along."

"Right? About what?"

"I stray into dangerous topics, Salaris. Ones we should not speak of now – but there will be time later. We have seen one another now, and the wheel has been spun. Should you survive the coming days, seek me out at Winterspire Mountain. There, I will teach you more."

Taelien frowned. "Where is Winterspire? I've never heard of that."

"Far to the north. Your Delaren friend will know the place. I have a home in Willsbrooke, a small town near the base of the mountain. This is not another test, I assure you – it will be easy to find, though the journey may be long."

"Would it not be easier to simply meet me in Velthryn? I should be headed there after I finish here."

"By the time you finish your tests, I will have likely come and gone. I cannot tarry away from Winterspire for long."

Taelien rubbed his head. Was this it? He was certain he had more questions – so many more questions. But the weight of the greatest answer had pushed them beneath the surface of his mind.

"We should go see your friends – we've been rude in keeping them waiting so long, and any advantage I give you is rapidly diminishing."

*But..wait..I…*

"I suppose you're right," he heard himself say, though they were not the words he wished to speak. Erik nodded once, turning to head toward where the other candidates awaited them a short distance down the road.

Taelien found himself paralyzed for several more moments before he finally raised his hand. 'Wait."

Erik turned his head. "Hrm?"

"I have a question for a friend. Do you know anything about a woman named Lydia Hastings? Or her mother, perhaps, Maya Hastings? She –"

Erik recoiled as if struck. "Lydia…? You know – of course you would. I have been inattentive for too long."

*Well, that wasn't vague or anything.*

"So, you know her."

Tarren nodded. "Yes. And you are kind to ask about your friend – but her answers must not come from you. I will speak to her when it is the proper time."

"Like you did with me?" Taelien folded his arms. "I don't mean to be rude, Erik, but you seem to have a pattern of avoiding giving people the answers they're looking for."

The older man stood up straighter, and for an instant, the light of the forest seemed to swell around him. "Do not presume to judge me, boy. You are right to ask questions, but you do not know me. And your arrogance tries my patience."

Taelien was not cowed by the display, but he recalled Garrick's earlier words. *You have a problem, Taelien. A consistent problem. You always want to solve everyone else's problems for them.*

Gritting his teeth, Taelien nodded. "I apologize. And thank you for the answers you have given me."

Tarren nodded. "Good. I accept your apology, and I will expect better of you in the future. Now, you were asking a question on behalf of Lydia Hastings. Is she within the city of Velthryn now?"

*Better.* "To the best of my knowledge, she should be. Ask at the citadel – they should know where to find her."

An odd expression crossed Tarren's face. Confusion, perhaps. "She is a paladin, then, or a priestess?"

"A paladin. Of Sytira."

The grey haired man chuckled, stroking his beard. "Ah, yes. Sytira. Of course she would be." Shaking his head, Tarren gestured for Taelien to follow, and this time he complied. "Come, let us meet with your friends. It is past time for you to be on your way."

They found the others just a moment ahead on the road, barely out of sight from the cart.

Velas looked up, smirking. "Gods, that took you long enough, Sal. I was about ready to take a nap."

"Forgive the delay, miss. Taelien had many pertinent questions for me."

"Oh? You tell him how to get his sword to work?"

Taelien blinked. *The sword. Of course I should have asked him about the sword.*

*Also that was probably a euphemism. But resh it, she's right, I should have asked him about the Sae'kes.*

Tarren turned his head toward Taelien. "You have been having some difficulty in wielding the Sae'kes?"

Taelien nodded. "I can only control five of the runes."

Tarren blinked. "Control? What do you mean?"

Taelien took a step back, drawing the sword and concentrating. One by one, the first five runes ignited, bathing the blade in an azure glow.

"Oh, dear. I do believe you've been wielding that incorrectly."

Taelien sheathed the blade. "What do you mean?"

"It's not meant to – hrm, this may be difficult to explain. All seven runes should be lit by default. It should require no effort on your part."

Taelien folded his arms. "I can assure you that has not been the case."

"That is truly fascinating – when Aendaryn had the weapon, it shined brightly within his grasp. He never spoke of it taxing his strength. In fact, it still glowed even when he put it down."

The swordsman frowned, redrawing the sword and repeating the process. He noted that Asphodel was watching with undisguised interest – she was the only one of his companions that had not seen him training with the weapon extensively.

Once the runes began to glow, he laid the sword on the dirt – and the instant he released his grip, the runes faded. The distortion field around the blade widened dangerously, the newly-manifested edges annihilating nearby rocks and grass.

"Now," Erik mumbled, "That is fascinating."

Taelien retrieved the weapon and sheathed it a second time. "Any theories, at least?"

"No time to formulate a theory, but for a mere hypothesis – the sword does not appear to be working as it did before. Thus, the simplest explanation is that it is damaged."

"Damaged? How would that be possible?"

Tarren seemed to consider that, scratching at his neck. "An artifact can often be damaged by an equally powerful artifact. It could be that your weapon is leaking the essence that normally powers it – and thus it needs external essence to make it function properly. But I can think of no artifact powerful enough to deal damage to that blade. There is no weapon comparable in the known world."

Velas quirked an eyebrow. "What about the Heartlance?" After a moment, she added, "Or Cessius? Or the Vaelien – that should be the Taelien's direct counterpart, yes?"

"Vaelien's weapon was never a match for the Sae'kes. It was his skill that made him Aendaryn's match – or more than his match in the end."

Taelien's eyes narrowed. "Is that who –"

Erik shrugged. "I don't know. I only have my suspicions. But in regards to your sword, I can only say this much – you have earned my curiosity, and I will examine it if you bring it to my home."

Taelien nodded. "All right. I've taken enough of your time. Let's be on our way."

Landen breathed a sigh of relief. "Good." He had unfurled the map on the road, and he pointed to a spot directly adjacent to the first shrine they had decided to visit.

Tarren nodded. "Ah, the shrines. Of course. Yes, I can manage that. You will want to join hands. Do you have all your things?"

After making certain everyone had retrieved the last of their belongings, the four paladins joined hands and formed a circle.

Erik Tarren stepped into the center of the circle, raising his arms to the sky. "Makers of the Sky and Stone, hear my call. Carry these four on your wings to the next marker on their path."

The world shifted and blurred around Taelien for a disorienting instant – and then his surroundings had changed.

They were still within a forested area, but the chill in the thin air told him that they were at a higher altitude. The cavern nearby was no doubt the first shrine – but that was not the first thing he noticed.

The first thing Taelien noticed was the smell – the smell of vomit carried by the wind. It was a moment later that he saw the gleam of steel on the floor of the cave.

Velas moved first, bringing up her quarterstaff in a defensive stance and spinning around to search for attackers.

Steel leapt from sheathes as the paladins shifted from their inward-facing circle into a back-to-back formation, but they saw no sign of any impending attack.

There was only a voice – a quiet voice coming from within the cave. "Please…help me."

The cracking words were punctuated by a hacking cough – and Taelien broke from their formation to rush toward the entrance.

"Taelien, stop!"

Taelien paused, his few seconds of movement having taken him close enough to see the fallen bodies – unmistakably wearing paladin armor – within the cave. One figure remained in a seated position, his back against the wall, holding a hand to his throat, his blond hair caked with sweat. There was a puddle of vomit at his feet.

*Jonathan Sterling,* Taelien recognized. The man continued to cough, his eyes fluttering.

"There's someone alive in there!" Taelien called back to the group, turning his head back to see the others rapidly approaching.

Velas shook her head. "You need to slow the fuck down right now, Taelien. This has trap written all over it."

Taelien nodded, stepping back toward the group and falling back into formation. She's right. That was reckless. *This is probably still part of the test…it has to be.*

Sterling turned his head toward them. "Velas – that you? Shit, help me out here." He broke into another fit of coughing.

Velas reached into her pack. "Eyes open, watch around me for a sec."

Taelien scanned the area as she instructed, keeping his blade at the ready, but he saw no other sign of attackers. "Sterling, is it clear in there?"

The man nodded. "Poisoned. Fuck, can't believe I'm…" More coughing.

Taelien glanced back to Velas, finding her retrieving the rune-marked stick from her pouch.

"This might be part of the test, but I'm not taking that risk."

Taelien nodded. "Agreed."

Velas cracked the stick in the center and stabbed the broken pieces into the dirt. Taelien hadn't been with her when Torrent had discussed the activation method, but that method seemed logical.

"Okay," Velas began, "We can't count on help getting here any time soon, especially since we just took another teleport – that could have disrupted this thing. I'm going in the cave to talk to Sterling and check his injuries. Landen, get out your bow. Anything suspicious moves, shoot it. Taelien, you cover the cave entrance. Asphodel, you're Landen's melee support."

The candidates moved quickly, with Taelien following behind Velas as she approached Sterling as Landen unfastened his bow from his backpack and began to string it.

"Fucking poison." Sterling looked pale and his face was covered with sweat. "Coward's weapon."

As Velas knelt down by Sterling's side, Taelien recognized one of the fallen as Eridus, his emaciated body encased in a tomb of mail.

*Fuck.*

Taelien's hand tightened into a fist. He turned to watch Velas and Sterling, noting that Velas had strategically put her boot on top Sterling's fallen scabbard. *She's not taking any risks. Good.*

"What happened?" Velas put her hand on Sterling's forehead and grimaced.

"Got here just a half hour or so ago. Couple people from platoon one were just leaving when we arrived, cheered us on. Thought we were making great time." He coughed again, smirking. "Took our drinks from the 'sacred spring'. Turns out 'sacred' takes poison just like anything else. Turns out the others hadn't quite left, either."

He raised a hand weakly, pointing to Eridus. "He was trying to treat me when Crimson put an arrow in him. Right at the neck. Fucking never thought we'd actually wish we were wearing gorgets – they're always such a pain in the ass."

*Eridus. Shit – a water sorcerer might have had a chance to save them. But without him...*

Velas nodded. "He was brave."

"Brave? Doesn't mean shit when you're choking on your own blood." Sterling lowered his head. "You ain't got a healer with you, do you?"

"I have a medical kit. No sorcery to help, though. I'll see what I can do."

"Better with that than not, I guess. But my odds don't look great – might be better that you go catch the fuckers that did this."

Velas nodded. "We'll talk about it, but I'm going to see what I can do for you first. Do you think anyone else might be alive?"

"I...I don't think so. I'm sorry. I wish I..."

"You did what you could. One more question. How many of them were there?"

"Just two." Sterling closed his eyes. "Just two of them, and they completely overwhelmed us. Crimson and the Wandering War."

Velas nodded, looking as if a suspicion had been confirmed in her mind.

Taelien swept the area nearby with another glance. There was a lot of tree cover, but no signs of anyone still lying in wait. Landen and Asphodel were slowly approaching the cave entrance, and Landen now had a bow in hand. His arrows were in a quiver on his right hip. The pennant was resting against a tree nearby.

*Crimson did seem suspicious from the start – and Wandering War seemed almost too suspicious. Gods, I really hope this is still a test. Please make it be a test.*

A growing feeling of nausea was building in Taelien's stomach. He raised a hand to rub his head in a feeble effort to stave off the sensation. *Shit, must be teleportation sickness. I didn't even think about that.*

"I...don't..." Sterling coughed again. "I don't think you're going to do much to help me if you don't have a sorcerer with you."

"We'll get you help." Velas frowned, slipping off her backpack and retrieving her medical kit. "You're a Haven Knight, right? Don't close your eyes."

Sterling nodded. "Yeah, I was. Why?"

"I'm from House Jaldin – you know what that means. We're the best healers."

"The best healers...yeah, I guess that's true."

Sterling's gaze began to falter. Velas slapped him, jolting the man awake.

"You need to keep your eyes open. I'm going to need a few more minutes to prepare something. You need – " Velas coughed into her hand, shaking her head. "You'll need to drink this when I'm finished with it. It's going to make you throw up."

"Lovely." He smirked. "Just like a bad night of drinking, eh?"

She nodded. "Yeah, except last time we went drinking, you didn't throw up at all. It was the ring, yeah?"

He raised his right hand, displaying a ring. "Probably the only reason I'm alive." He chuckled. "It was just a trinket. Not made for handling real tough poisons – just a trinket for winning drinking contests. I never thought..."

"You're very lucky you had it." Velas turned her head toward Taelien, who was shuffling his feet uneasily. "You want to go catch those fuckers?"

Taelien nodded furiously.

"Sterling, how long ago did the other two leave, and which way did they go?"

He shook his head. "Couldn't have been long. I mean, I don't think... Maybe ten minutes? Seemed like they were in a hurry." He frowned. "They looked like they were headed on the path downhill, back toward where you came from. You shouldn't split up, though. Gotta leave me here if you want to go after them."

"They can handle it. Only two of them – I'll send two of us."

Velas turned back to Taelien. "Take Asphodel and head down the road. Hopefully she can use her oracle powers to find them or something. Don't take any risks. If you have to kill them to save yourselves, do it."

*This...this is bad. This is the wrong move, isn't it?*

378

*But – what do I – what should we do?*

Taelien nodded. "Yes, ma'am."

*Velas and Landen will be fine, won't they? They can handle themselves, even if Susan and Wandering War wrap back around.*

He shook his head, which swam for an instant as he moved. *Shit, I need to be careful. This travel sorcery sickness might be a problem. I'll need to walk it off.*

The swordsman jerked a thumb toward the road while facing Asphodel. "You good to go?"

She nodded. "We will catch them."

*Well, at least someone is confident.*

***

The sick feeling in Taelien's stomach did not improve as he raced with Asphodel down the trail – it only worsened. Still, he pressed on, the pain from his side fading into the back of his mind as he focused on a single goal – smashing Susan Crimson and the Wandering War with overwhelming force.

Minutes passed, the forest around them thickening into walls. Though the path appeared to be well-traveled, he could see the fragmented ruins of abandoned stone structures among the trees. The forest had retaken the majority of its territory long ago.

Asphodel froze in her tracks, her eyes narrowing. Taelien turned, breathing heavily from a combination of exertion and the growing tension in his muscles.

"Continue down the path. We part ways here."

Asphodel turned to the right, stalking off the road into the forest.

"That doesn't seem wise –"

"I am following Crimson. Her path broke from his here. She has laid several traps. You will only slow me down." She spoke in a tone that brooked no argument, but Taelien was tempted to follow her regardless.

*She trusts in her visions, even knowing that they only represent a possibility – but I suppose that's still more information than I have at my disposal.*

Shaking his head, Taelien whispered an old saying, "Lissari, keep her healthy," and continued on his own path. The tree cover grew thicker, blotting out much of the dawnfire's light. He passed a stream, tempting him to stop and drink, but he pressed on – he knew that his enemy could choose to abandon the road – or meet with allies – at any time.

His heart was pounding when he came upon a marker in the trail – three paladin practice blades embedded in the dirt on the side of the road.

*Like unmarked graves.*

The three-inch blade that flashed out from the tree-line grazed the left side of his face.

Taelien drew his practice blade, not bothering to assess the wound. The pain was insubstantial, distant.

*Sharpen.* The blade's edges shifted into a closer facsimile of a standard weapon, though he could feel that the metal itself was a lighter grade of iron.

A cloaked figure emerged from the woods, moving to the center of the road.

"I am disappointed," the Wandering War intoned, his voice rich and full. "I did not even wait to flank you – and yet you still missed the thrown knife. Are you unwell?"

*More than a bit, but I'm not going to show him that.*

"That trinket wasn't even worth deflecting." Taelien smirked. "I hope you've brought something a little bit more substantial."

The cloaked figure made a sweeping bow. "But of course."

The three paladin blades tore free from the dirt, hovering to float behind the Wandering War and reorienting themselves to point toward Taelien.

*Well, that's one time I really shouldn't have said anything.*

The Wandering War flicked his arm toward Taelien – the swords followed his command.

Taelien's sword smashed the first blade to the side, but it simply floated nearby, beginning to reorient itself as he struck at the second blade.

*Shatter,* he commanded the metal of the opposing blade as the swords met, but the meeting of weapons was too brief – his command incomplete. The third sword's blade struck the left side of his breastplate, scrapping harmlessly across the plate as it flew past him.

He was already rushing off the road when the blades came again, giving him no time to pause for thought. He deflected one with his left bracer while sweeping the second's blade into a nearby tree, pinning it in place. Even as he brought his blade back to parry the third, he noted the

380

entombed sword wiggling in place, as if struggling to free itself of its own accord.

The third blade swept at Taelien's upper legs, which were covered only by a thin layer of mail. He raised his right greave to block the attack, successfully deflecting it, but fell backward from the force of the impact and landed in a sitting position on the dirt.

The Wandering War had not noticeably moved.

Frustrated, Taelien awaited the first blade's next swing, snatching it out of the air with a gloved hand. The practice blade's blunted edges did his hand no harm, though it remained in motion, pushing with unseen force toward his throat.

*Ball*, he commanded the blade. This time it responded – although with hesitation – and the iron blade separated from the hilt, shifting into a sphere. The hilt fell harmlessly to the dirt as Taelien reached back to throw the ball, but the third sword swept down too quickly, interrupting his attempt. He was forced to raise his bracer again to block the swing, and then swung his own sword in an awkward arc, missing the floating blade entirely.

The Wandering War laughed, beginning to walk closer.

Taelien stood, stumbling backward as the last floating blade swished in front of him, deflecting it and hurling the iron ball at the Wandering War.

The cloaked figure raised his hand again – and the ball paused in mid-air, and then fell harmlessly to the ground.

*That's… not even fair. What kind of reshing sorcery is he using?*

The last floating sword swung again, but Taelien was more than ready this time. He locked his blade against it in a push, giving him more than enough time to issue a command to the metal.

*Shatter.*

The blade fractured like glass, spilling across the dirt.

Taelien didn't advance directly on his opponent – instead, he stepped back off the path to grasp the blade of the second of the floating swords, which was still working its way free from the tree. He was tempted to try to use it as a secondary weapon, but the Wandering War had clearly exerted some kind of sorcerous control over the weapons, making the sword too much of a risk.

*Separate.*

The blade split into pieces – large enough that Taelien could easily reassemble them into a weapon, but too small to be individually dangerous. This would give him an option for a fallback weapon if the Wandering War seized control over his current sword.

"That was an improvement, but still hardly sufficient to warrant the whispers I've been hearing. Where's that bravado you demonstrated in the earlier tests? I want to see blades of *fire*, swordsman. This is nothing."

*What's the point of this baiting?*

Taelien coughed, his head still swimming. He suppressed the urge to vomit, taking his weapon in a two-handed grip to stabilize it and shifting into the Teris Low-Blade stance. *I'm missing something vital.*

The cloaked figure audibly sighed, adjusting his cloak to reveal the red-runed blade he had displayed during their last encounter. "If you insist upon curtailing your abilities, I suppose I will have to force you to take this more seriously."

The Wandering War raised the sword into an unfamiliar high stance, his elbows raised to shoulder level, the flat of his weapon parallel to the dirt.

Six more swords appeared in the air around him – phantasmal blades enshrouded in blue-green fire.

Taelien moved first, releasing his left hand grip to grab his right bracer and issue a command. *Shift into knife.*

The metallic portion of the bracer reshaped itself and he hurled the short weapon through the air, but the Wandering War brought down his blade in a heavy strike, severing the metallic blade in twain and sending the pieces flying to either side of his body.

Then the flaming blades were moving – and Taelien was falling back. *If he's controlling these manually, he can't possibly maneuver six weapons with any degree of finesse.*

He managed to make it to the side of the road before the first blade came into reach. As before, he swung the practice blade to meet his attacker, planning to dismantle it with his strike.

His own blade split in twain as it struck the hovering weapon - with no sense of steel entering his mind. The enemy blade continued in its arc, its flames coming close enough to singe his hair as he stumbled backward to avoid the cut.

*They're not metal at all — they're like Keldyn's swords, only on fire. I can handle that.*

Taelien hurled the remaining half of his sword at the Wandering War, but it didn't come anywhere close to hitting. He hadn't expected it to – it merely bought a momentary pause while his opponent stepped back, and the floating swords ceased their motion.

*Well, that's one minor plus. They're not sentient – he has to command them, and he can be distracted.*

The Sae'kes sang as he wrenched it from its sheath, meeting the next two flaming blades with heavy two-handed strokes. Each strike seemed to break away at the essence of the floating weapons – their flames diminished somewhat, and their blades showed cracks from the impact.

"Ah, excellent, the entertainment can begin in earnest."

Six more swords appeared around the Wandering War, floating in a slow circular pattern.

*Oh, you have to be fucking kidding me.*

The swords moved.

Taelien was a whirlwind of silver, slashing each blade apart as it drew near. Metal or not, with each stroke he felt their essence more strongly, and that familiarity formed a map in his mind – the trajectory of each weapon, the timing of its approach, the necessary vector to deflect each incoming projectile.

With a sweep, he slammed two blades into each other, roaring triumphantly as they split into shards and dissipated. A third blade went unnoticed as he roiled in the momentary triumph, the sword slashing across his left thigh and tearing through mail and flesh alike. The skin around the laceration burned from contact with the spectral fire.

Taelien fell to a knee as he processed the wound, deflecting the next two blades.

*Shit, that's bad,* he processed, seeing his blood draining from the wound. The phantasmal flames had not cauterized the wound, and while it had not struck anywhere vital, the injury would limit his mobility.

A second blade slipped through, taking a chunk from his right ear and grazing his neck. He felt the hint of heat from the blue-green flames as they licked close, but he instinctively deflected them with his own flame shaping, feeling a chill as the sorcery extracted its toll.

*I need to make forward progress; he's forced me completely onto the defensive.*

Grabbing another weapon was out of the question – he couldn't count on being able to wield it the way he had with Keldyn's stolen blade, since the Wandering War seemed to have some way to mentally control the blades.

*What's he using? Motion sorcery? Blade sorcery? Some combination of the two? I need to focus. What can I use?*

As the Sae'kes parried the next stroke, he felt the non-metal blade and the surrounding flames, imprinting them in his mind. He sensed that the blades were composed of something similar to what Keldyn had used. The flames were distinct – they were neither true flame nor raw heat, but he sensed a familiarity within him, something akin to the dominion that pulsed in his blood.

As the next blade approached, he pressed the Sae'kes against it, caressing the flame within his mind – and through it, sensing its counterparts.

*Consume the blades within.*

The flames obeyed his command – and the floating swords melted into nothingness.

Taelien smirked, pushing himself awkwardly to his feet.

The Wandering War let out a deep laugh, lowering his sword to softly clap his hands. "Splendid. I knew I sensed a kinship within you – I will be interested to see how deep that runs."

Taelien shifted the blade of his sword to his left side, facing away from him, allowing it to hover near the sheath. The Aayaran Instant Striking Stance was Lydia's favorite technique, employed to end duels in a single stroke.

It was not Taelien's favored style; however, it was one of few he could manage when he was barely capable of standing.

*I still don't know exactly what his skill set is, or even exactly what I just did – I can't afford to let him get within striking range.*

The Wandering War moved forward purposefully, still ten yards distant…and then five…still far outside of sword reach.

But not outside of the reach of another weapon.

*Chain.*

The Sae'kes' blade shifted in shape, the portion near the hilt shifting into a long chain, while the last foot of the sword remained a deadly blade.

He moved to swing the chain into motion even as the weapon was transforming, lashing out like a whip, while the Wandering War calmly lowered his own weapon into a parry.

The chain wrapped around the Wandering War's blade, and Taelien sensed true metal — as well as the presence of foreign dominions within that metal.

*Shatter,* he commanded the rune-etched sword, but it did not respond to his command. This was no surprise — he had seen the same effect when he had attempted a similar tactic with the Heartlance. Fortunately, this time he had a fallback plan.

*Wrap.*

He commanded his own sword, not the enemy blade — and the length of chain that had caught the Wandering War's sword began to flatten and expand across the surface, encapsulating it in a shell that Taelien *could* affect.

The Wandering War shifted his grip, attempting to pull Taelien toward him, but Taelien braced with his good leg and held fast.

Laughing again, the Wandering War released his grip on his own sword — and it vanished into nothingness.

As Taelien's chain-blade fell to the dirt, the Wandering War's sword reappeared in his hands.

*Shit. That's — rather unfair.*

*Return.*

The chain retracted, shifting back into the usual form of the Sae'kes' blade. Only four of the runes were glowing on the surface. The swordsman grimaced. *I suppose it's time to take this a little bit more seriously.*

Taelien passed the blade to his left hand, closing his eyes and concentrating, feeling his essence flow toward the blade. When his eyes reopened, all seven runes glowed brightly on the surface.

*Well,* he cracked a smile, *it looks like the gods are finally on my side.*

"Interesting." The Wandering War tilted his head to the side. "I had been informed you were not capable of doing that."

"I try not to let my enemies know every little detail."

Taelien shifted into a high stance, the Sae'lien Slaying Style. With his opponent in a similar stance, their next exchange was likely to be deadly — but he could see little alternative. Defensive fighting had put him at a continuous disadvantage, and his strength was rapidly waning. Now that the Wandering War had seen him use the Instant Striking Style, it was unlikely to work again.

*I need to know what I'm up against here – I can't devise better tactics without better information.*

"So, before I, you know, cut you in half, it seems prudent for me to ask why you've been murdering the other paladin candidates. My paperwork is going to be a nightmare."

The Wandering War paused in his approach, folding his arms. "Is that what you wish to speak of? Truly? Your concerns are for the fallen?"

"That would be my principal reason for being here, yes."

The cloaked figure tilted his head to the side. "I had hoped you had anticipated this conflict with as much desire as I, but perhaps it was vain of me to hope. As for your question, I was but a mere observer in the massacre that occurred a moment ago. I draw so little strength from treachery that it is of no consequence."

Taelien frowned. Well, at least I've got him talking. *Maybe I should cauterize this wound while I have a second.*

*Or, on second thought, resh that idea. I'm never doing that again.*

"Even if you simply observed, you're still responsible for the deaths of those people. Why?"

The Wandering War shrugged. "I simply do as I am commanded by he who brought me to this world."

*He who brought me to this –*

*Oh, fuck me. His title is literal.*

*He's a Harvester of War.*

"And who summoned you, then?"

The Wandering War laughed again, shaking his head. "You are in no position to demand such an answer, cousin. Now, if this talk has been sufficient for you, shall we bask in the joyous harmony of our blades?"

"Yeah, we could...do that."

He narrowed his eyes.

*I probably could have found a more poetic retort than that.*

The harvester rushed forward, leading with a heavy downward cut.

Taelien answered by sidestepping to the left, though the shift in his weight sent a fresh surge of agony through his leg, and bringing his blade down toward the Wandering War's leading arm. War released that arm from the hilt of his weapon, shifting it around Taelien's swing and opening his palm, sending a blast of blue-green fire toward Taelien's chest.

The flames never came close to touching him.

*Fade,* he commanded, and they obeyed. Stepping forward – directly onto the harvester's trailing cloak – Taelien pulled back his left hand and punched the harvester in the face.

The impact was solid, but the harvester only laughed as he fell back.

"Your attempts to use sophisticated combat techniques amuse me, but ultimately they are pointless. I am war. I am implacable. No amount of tactical acumen will allow you to harm me."

"I think you're overstating yourself a bit. You're not war - you're just a mere sliver of it given life. And if you're alive, you can bleed."

To emphasize the point, Taelien lashed out with a horizontal strike, while keeping the harvester's cloak pinned beneath his foot. The harvester shifted his own blade into a vertical position to parry, then retorted with an upward cut, slicing through the vambrace on Taelien's right arm and grazing the flesh beneath.

Something familiar burned within the cut – the mark of the blade's bonded dominion, but it was not a power he could reach for with his mind.

Staggering back, Taelien made another hasty attempt at a counterstrike with an upward diagonal cut, but the harvester knocked it to the side with a simple flick of his blade.

"You look unwell, swordsman. Does the poison take its toll upon you? I admit I had hoped for our encounter to occur under more ideal conditions."

*Poison? I didn't drink the water – was that dagger he nicked me with earlier poisoned?*

"I'm perfectly capable of finishing this." Taelien grit his teeth, not feeling the confidence in his words. *I need to create a window of opportunity – he's whittled me down too much for a straight fight.* "Don't you think you should take off that ridiculous cloak? I mean, not only must it be encumbering you, it makes battle a lot less personal if I can't see your face."

"Impersonal." The Wandering War's voice sounded strained. He pressed his sword into the dirt in front of him, securing it in place. "I see. Yes, you pose a salient point."

The Wandering War reached for the clasp of his cloak.

Taelien charged.

The Wandering War took a step back at the move, which was exactly the reaction Taelien had hoped for. His leg burned with every instant of motion, but the distance to close was short. He swung the Sae'kes with all his might – directly at the rune-etched blade anchored in the ground.

Blue sparks ignited the air as the blades met, sending cinders of essence across Taelien's arms. The flares burned, not with pain, but with refreshing warmth along his skin.

His blow cast the other sword aside, sending it crashing along the dirt. In an instant, he closed the distance to the Wandering War, setting his blade atop the harvester's shoulder.

The Wandering War continued his earlier motion – unclasping his cloak and tossing it free. Undeterred by the proximity of Taelien's blade, he lifted away the veils covering his head, revealing his face – a face that looked perfectly human, save for his gleaming coppery skin and hair.

A single red rune glowed brightly on the Wandering War's forehead, and as Taelien's blade pressed against the harvester's skin, Taelien thought he could perceive essence flowing outward from the rune – though he could not sense where the trail went.

"Are you satisfied?"

The Wandering War lifted a hand slowly, deliberately, and wrapped it around the edge of the Sae'kes. The weapon's destructive aura was barely visible, but it lapped at the harvester's fingers, cutting into his metallic skin. Inky blood flowed from these wounds.

The harvester closed his eyes, taking in a deep breath. "Your aura is strange – it is like my own, but more distant than I had realized. What does it consist of?"

Taelien itched to move, to cut closer against the harvester's neck, but the creature was unarmed now – and showing no immediate signs of hostility. He knew rationally that the Wandering War could produce a deadly threat in an instant – more conjured blades, or perhaps summoning the rune-weapon as he had before – but seeing the humanoid face had an unsettling effect on his psyche.

He was reminded of the life he had taken and his vow not to do so again. It had been easier when he had seen the Wandering War as a mere monster within a shroud.

"I don't know. If you surrender, I will discuss this with you further."

"Surrender?" The Wandering War gave him an amused expression.

*He – or she? – looks so young. Younger than I am.*

"We've only started our conversation – why would I surrender now?"

The Harvester kicked him in the chest.

Taelien flew backward further than the force of the kick should have carried him, realizing that motion sorcery was at work even as the attack moved him. His breastplate had caught most of the force of the blow, preventing it from doing any real harm, but as he recovered the Wandering War was retrieving his sword from where it had fallen.

"Really," the harvester said as he approached, "You should have taken your opportunity to cut a bit deeper. Every graze that I survive – every parry that you make – every strike that I deflect – serves to give me strength. And though I sense you grow from our conflict as well, your form is frail and will not weather an extended assault."

*Hard to tell how much of that is bluster and how much of it is literal truth, considering who – or what – I'm talking to.* "I think I've learned enough to counterbalance these injuries. Breaking those summoned swords, for example, and your vulnerability to distraction."

"I admit your duplicity surprised me – you had spoken in a fashion consistent with honorable folk, so I did not anticipate the tactic. I applaud your adaptability."

Taelien pointed the Sae'kes downward, thrusting it into the dirt as the Wandering War had with his own blade moments before.

The harvester paused.

Releasing his grip on the Sae'kes, Taelien raised his hands. "You seem interested in an extended conflict. I'm not interested in that under these circumstances. At the moment, I need to ensure that the people who killed those candidates are found, and then help the people I can. After that, I'll recover, and I can give you a much better – and more extended – fight."

The Wandering War's lip twisted into a sneer. "You're surrendering?" He raised his blade swiftly, holding it high with a single hand. "I will not allow it!"

The runes on his blade had entirely faded by the time Taelien pulled it from the ground.

He had counted on that.

As the Wandering War surged forward in a blur of motion, Taelien knew he only had time for a single strike.

Runic blades flashed in the dawnfire's light.

A decisive cut.

And Taelien fell among the graves.

# CHAPTER XXII – VELAS VII – TRUST

Velas knelt next to Jonathan Sterling in a hollow in a hillside that barely deserved the word "cave". The bodies of three other paladin candidates lay still behind her, nearer to a basin filled with water. The symbol of Lissari, the goddess of life, was etched into the stone above the basin.

Landen waited outside, keeping vigil from a semi-concealed position behind a nearby tree, his bow at the ready. She judged that he was out of earshot for simple conversation, but easily within the range to hear shouting or the ringing of steel.

She slipped her backpack off her shoulders, opening the top flap and removing the medical kit. "Keep those eyes open, Sterling. I'm going to need you to keep talking so I can brew the appropriate antidote."

The blond man nodded wearily, his gaze distant.

Opening the kit, she retrieved an empty vial, removing the cap and setting it aside. "How long ago did you drink from the basin?"

He shrugged. "Hard to judge. Maybe ten or fifteen minutes. I think I might have blacked out briefly."

*That's not good news if it's true – he should have mentioned it before. It significantly changes the plausibility of pursuing his attackers.*

"Okay. How much did you drink?"

He gave a pained expression. "Just a couple hands full."

She nodded patiently. "Good, good. That might be treatable – especially since you already threw up."

Velas reached into her bag, shuffling through components without retrieving anything sufficient. "Last question for now – what did it taste like?"

"It was sweet," he began, closing his eyes. "Something like almonds, I think."

She nodded again, finding what she was looking for in the bag.

"That gives me the context I needed, thank you. Give me a moment."

"Can you help me?"

"That I'm still not certain about." Velas retrieved a pair of herbs and a smaller vial of liquid. She carefully mixed them into the vial, and then retrieved her wineskin from her pack and filled the remainder of the vial with it. She handed him the vial. "Drink."

His eyes fluttered open, and he accepted the vial and drank it down, setting the empty vial at his side. "Will...this save me?"

Velas shook her head. "There's good news and bad news." She took a breath. "The good news is pretty simple – you weren't poisoned before." Velas pulled the surgical knife from her bag, pressing it against his throat. "The bad news is that you are now."

Sterling's eyes didn't widen in surprise – they just scanned down to the knife, and then shifted to meet her own gaze. And he gave her a charming smirk. "What gave me away?"

"I had some suspicions about the setup immediately. The key was that they had left you alive – you didn't say anything about chasing the assassins away or injuring them. They had no reason to be sloppy. The last question really confirmed it – what are the chances your entire group would drink water that didn't taste like water without someone warning the others first?"

He rolled his eyes. "I suspect I should have been better prepared for loaded questions. Fair enough, I'll give you credit for being more observant than the other two, even if you missed a few key things."

She quirked an eyebrow, tensing her knife hand, itching to cut. "Oh? Such as?"

"Well, for one thing, the water isn't poisoned – but the air is."

*Oh, shit.*

She narrowed her eyes. "You could be bluffing."

"Give it a few minutes. You'll feel it. Your friends that are exerting themselves are probably already suffering from it – well, the one who came close, at least. The Delaren is probably fine."

"Okay, then. We're at a fairly simple impasse, then – but Thornguards always carry an antidote to their poisons, don't they? I can treat what I just gave you."

He grinned wider, flashing stark white teeth. "Thornguards do, or so I've heard."

"You're not with the guild – they wouldn't take a contract like this. But you recognized my hand sign, and you left me a warning note – so, Thornguard."

Sterling lifted his left hand to his forehead, giving an expression of exasperation. Velas pressed the knife closer, intended as a warning for his movement – but it failed to cut his skin. She frowned.

"Another miscalculation on your part. I didn't leave you any letters, and I'm not with the Thornguard. I did, however, bring an antidote."

She heard the sound of steel scraping against stone behind her and spun around, stepping away from Sterling in alarm.

Eridus was standing from the stone floor, a dejected look on his face. He had a bloodstained arrow in his hand.

"Really, Velas," he began, "Even a cursory glance would have shown you that the wound on my neck," he gestured with the arrow, "wasn't just a bit of someone else's blood. But you didn't even check on me. I'm wounded."

"You're going to be a lot more wounded in a second, you traitorous Thornguard fuck."

Eridus gave a deep laugh, tossing the arrow to the side with a casual gesture. "You know, you sounded like you were pretty on track at the start of this conversation, but you keep forgetting there are other people who might know a few basic hand signs." He raised two fingers to his forehead. "Shall I sing you a song of the story of Symphony's lover?"

She reversed her grip on the knife, preparing for a throw. The short blade wasn't balanced for throwing, but at such close range she suspected she might land it. "You're a Blackstone."

Sterling remained on the floor, stretching his arms. "And revelation dawns upon the wayward rogue." He tilted his head toward her. "But there needn't be any hostilities between us, if you are, as the signs say, a friend."

"Those," she gestured toward the fallen paladins, thinking of her late night talks with Celia Laurent and the drinking contest with Alden, "Were my friends."

"A shame." Sterling brushed his hands on his knees, beginning to push himself to his feet. "I had hoped we could reach an understanding — you showed the beginnings of some cunning, in a pedestrian sort of way."

Eridus leaned against a nearby wall. "The note was a professional courtesy. I'll say I'm impressed by how well you covered your tracks — I did some digging and couldn't find anything about your guild name."

"Silk."

The Rethri whistled appreciatively. "No wonder you're blustering so hard. Under normal circumstances, even I wouldn't want to tangle with Symphony's apprentice." He glanced at Sterling, "But, since I'm on loan to Vae'kes Sterling, I think we can safely call this an exception."

*Vae'kes Sterling.*

Velas changed her mind about the knife, backing out of the entrance to the cave. Rather than hurling it immediately, she slipped the blade upward, making a tiny incision in her own palm.

The former Queensguard couldn't afford to close her eyes, which made envisioning the poison in her body more challenging, but she was still able to locate the foreign essence with some effort — and begin to channel it toward the bleeding wound on her palm. She knew that she couldn't afford to deal with any complications for the confrontation that was brewing.

Sterling sprang to his feet, scratching his head. "Retreating, Velas? I see you finally grasp the situation you're in." He cracked his neck, turning his head to spit on the cave's floor. "I'll give you credit — poisoning me was a nice touch. I'm not even angry. It's not every day I get to play with one of Symphony's things." He flashed another grin. "But I do so love breaking my sister's toys."

Velas snapped her fingers on her left hand — the somatic gesture for casting a simple spell. A familiar signal - the sound of a wind chime - one that she had used with Landen a dozen times before.

The signal to open fire.

Landen's arrow flew straight toward Eridus' throat, and Velas had just a moment to process her companion's sense of ironic humor before the Rethri snatched the arrow out of the air.

She threw the knife at Sterling's head – it struck him in the center of the forehead, bounced off harmlessly, and landed on the cavern floor. There was no hint of the telltale flicker of a barrier – just the same resistance that Velas had felt when she had failed to cut his skin before.

Sterling sighed. "Didn't Symphony teach you anything about our kind? Your weapons and spells aren't going to have any effect on me."

Velas raised her left hand, her palm pointed at Eridus. *Push.*

A violent burst of motion hammered the armored Blackstone, slamming him into the cavern wall.

"He's less invincible," Velas noted. "We'll work on you next."

Sterling sighed, glancing at his fallen companion and shaking his head, and then looking back up toward Velas.

"That was rather rude."

He drew the practice sword from his side, running his fingers along the edges. Rather than sharpening or bursting into flame, the blade began to shiver and quake, as if straining to escape its hilt.

Velas cast a glance at where her quarterstaff stood near the pennant – far too far away to reach – and drew her own sword.

Sterling waved his left hand in the air and took a mock bow, then raised his blade into a traditional Velryan dueling stance. Velas mirrored the stance, having no intention of retaining it. This could be no ordinary duel.

An arrow flew at Sterling, but he easily deflected it, shooting an angry glance at Landen. "I'll be with you soon enough, Theas."

Theas? Why'd he call him that? Erik Tarren knowing his real name made sense – their families are close – but Sterling...

*The victim was Edrick Theas' son.*

The words of that playful rogue, "Scribe", echoed in her mind. As did her own reply.

*You'd be better off looking at your own people, I suspect.*

She tossed a brief glance back to Landen. "Lan, you're the real target here. Fall back to regroup with Asphodel and Taelien. I'll hold them here."

"Yeah, no, that's not going happen." He knocked another arrow. "So you're going to have to plan to win."

Sterling drew within lunging distance, but Velas cautiously shifted backward, circling him. She couldn't take her eyes off her opponent at this point, so she simply shouted, "Make sure Eridus stays down."

Sterling moved. His shivering blade sent a numbing vibration down her arm as she parried, but she retained her grip and moved her off-hand. *Push.*

The same force slammed into Sterling that she had used on Eridus – but the Vae'kes merely pursed his lips as the essence washed over him, his hair blown askew.

"Disconcerting, but ultimately not dangerous to me," the Vae'kes reported. "You'll have to do better."

Velas felt the burden of fatigue from her spells beginning to weigh on her shoulders and legs, but she was well-enough rested that she judged she could manage a few more. *For what little good they'll do me.*

She ducked and took a swipe at Sterling's knees. He danced backward, shaking his head. "What, precisely, was the point of that? You wouldn't have scratched me even if I wasn't invincible."

Velas backed away, continuing to circle. *I just need a moment to think.*

Sterling didn't give her that moment. He lunged for her neck, and as she batted that aside, he spun on his heels and slammed his left fist into the lower half of her breastplate. She felt the steel plates crumble like paper, jamming metal into her chest.

Gasping for breath, she stumbled backward as Landen brought a pair of blades down on the back of Sterling's head.

*He never was good at following orders.*

The blades connected solidly, making Sterling flinch at the impact, but the Vae'kes spun around in a vicious lash that sent Landen skittering backward. At a glance, Sterling seemed to have suffered no lasting damage from the attack – but that wasn't what was on Velas' mind.

*Can't breathe.*

The pain made her vision blacken for an instant. Dropping her sword, she fumbled for the straps on the side of her breastplate while Landen deftly hopped over a low slash from Sterling's blade.

Velas couldn't concentrate sufficiently to unfasten the leather straps – the pain in her chest was too intense. The Queensguard had broken ribs before, but never with a distorted metal plate applying continuous pressure against them.

*Tear.*

The Dominion of Motion was ill-suited for the kind of precise damage she needed to inflict, but the leather strap wasn't particularly resilient. The spell separated the strap near her side from the breastplate, allowing her to wiggle the plate forward and draw in a ragged breath.

Landen's blades where whirling, striking high and low in a furious pattern. Sterling parried some of the blows and ignored others, seemingly at random, but even those attacks that slipped through rebounded harmlessly regardless of where they landed. Even his face seemed as resilient as steel.

Velas repeated the process with the other straps on the same side of her breastplate, slipping her head and arm out as soon as one side was loose and tossing the entire cuirass aside. She coughed deeply, doubling over, but it was a dry cough – not yet one tinged with her blood. She judged that her gambeson had absorbed enough of the blow to prevent her ribs from piercing into her lungs.

Sterling batted one of the blades out of Landen's hands, giving her friend a crooked grin. Landen raised his remaining blade into a high stance – a suicidal stance.

Velas jumped on Sterling's back.

The Vae'kes froze, apparently startled, while Velas slipped her arms underneath his and attempted to pin them in a hold.

Sterling slammed his head backward, but Velas expected the move, tilting her own head to the side and taking the blow on her chin. She felt her teeth clack together at the impact, but it barely dazed her.

And, with her arms now in position, she lifted.

The pain in her chest intensified as she brought the Vae'kes off the ground. Landen took the opening, reversing his blade and slamming the pommel into Sterling's forehead with a loud crack. Sterling's neck recoiled and he released his grip on his sword.

Then Sterling shoved his elbow backward into Velas' ribs, landing the strike just above where he had hit before.

Velas felt something within her chest snap, dropping Sterling and falling backward, landing hard on her back.

Wheezing, she looked up to find Landen slamming his blade into Sterling ineffectively again, and then failing an attempt to sweep the Vae'kes off his feet.

*Shit.*

Velas braced herself on the ground, attempting to push herself to her feet, but the burning within her chest made her shiver and fall as soon as she began to move.

Sterling pressed closer to Landen, deflecting blade strikes with his bare hands until he finally grasped the sword and wrenched it from the duelist's hands.

Landen punched Sterling in the face, but the Vae'kes only shook his head, patting his cheek. "It would appear you have exhausted your options. I'll give you a moment for your prayers."

"That won't be necessary," came a nearby voice – a newcomer's voice. "Help is already here."

Velas turned her head to see Garrick Torrent holding a broken half of the beacon he had given her in his left hand. He held a gilded rapier in his right hand, pointed toward the dirt. And he was not alone.

Lydia Hastings stood to his right side, her own rapier drawn, a flickering barrier materializing around her. "You must be the assassin I've been looking for – I wasn't expecting you to be right here, but that does make things convenient. Shall we dance?"

"Oh," Sterling said, turning toward Torrent and Lydia, "By all means, let us begin."

## CHAPTER XXIII – LYDIA VI – STERLING

*Well,* Lydia thought, setting a hand on Garrick Torrent's shoulder, *I wasn't expecting to find my target out here quite so quickly, but I won't complain.*

"Dominion of Protection, fold against his skin."

The barrier manifested around Lieutenant Torrent immediately, and he nodded to her appreciatively, breaking off to the left. She broke to the right, her own barrier already in place, instinctively understanding Torrent's intent for a flanking maneuver.

An unarmed Landen of the Twin Edges rushed around their opponent to stand in front of Velas Jaldin, who was down on the ground, her breastplate cast aside. Her sword was nearby.

They had only witnessed the last few moments of the combat – Landen's last few ineffective strikes, and the blond man's relentless advance – but Lydia had already told Torrent that she suspected Landen was the next target for an assassin, and the scene laid out in front of them manifested in a fashion obvious enough for her to know which side to protect.

"Sterling is a Vae'kes –" Landen managed to begin as the blond whirled on him, moving forward in a blur and grabbing his neck.

The man that Landen had identified as Sterling frowned, turning his head toward the approaching paladins as Landen raised his arms and ineffectively grabbed the hand that had grasped his throat.

*A Vae'kes? That explains why the sword wasn't phasing him, but why would a Vae'kes be working against House Theas?*

Lydia dismissed the question – there would be time to judge motives later.

"You can stop moving, paladins. I'll crush his throat if you take another step."

Torrent vanished, reappeared next to Landen, grabbed him, and they both vanished.

Sterling was left strangling the empty air.

Moving his hands in front of him, Sterling shook his head. "A teleporter. That's going to be irritating."

Velas moved for a fallen sword on the ground, but Sterling kicked it, sending the weapon sliding across dirt and grass far out of reach.

He glanced down at Velas, giving her a disapproving frown. "Haven't you suffered enough?" He kicked her in the side, flipping her over entirely, while Lydia began to advance again.

*Torrent will be back soon — but how do we approach this?*

She caught sight of the fallen figures at the nearby cave entrance, gritting her teeth.

*Oh, he's going to pay for this.*

She dropped into the Aayaran Instant Striking Stance, focusing her vision on the few exposed vulnerable points on Sterling's body.

*If he really is as resilient as the Vae'kes are supposed to be — and from Landen's last few swings, that looked likely — I'm going to need to be precise and strike somewhere vulnerable. The eyes, most likely.*

Sterling advanced on her, still unarmed, looking nonchalant.

*He's going to try to catch my blade like he did with Landen's. I might be a hair faster on the draw than Landen, but not by much. I need a distraction.*

"Dominion of Protection, wrap around my blade."

A blue-white shroud encapsulated the sword, causing it to shimmer in the low light.

"Not sure what that was for," Sterling remarked, "But I'm pretty confident it's not going to help you."

Torrent reappeared directly behind Sterling. The Vae'kes didn't seem to notice.

Lydia stepped forward into a lunge. As she had predicted, Sterling reached for the blade, but she whipped it out of the way, slashing downward. She severed the bindings on his right boot, smirked, and danced backward, resuming her stance.

The Vae'kes glanced down at his boot, sighed, and then looked back up at Lydia. "Really? Do you have any idea what that cost?"

She shrugged. "Probably not a fraction of what you're making on this contract – although I'll wager it isn't in coin."

He sighed. "You don't have to try to bait me into talking – I think we're all relatively clear on who is killing who at this point, and I've never minded a bit of a conversation before a meal."

Lydia quirked an eyebrow. "A meal?"

"Your sorcery, my friend. It's going to be delicious."

Sterling rushed forward – enhanced by a motion sorcery effect, Lydia judged – and Lydia flicked her blade outward to stop his rush.

She had no time to aim for his eye, but nevertheless, Sterling turned aside to avoid her strike.

*Ah,* Lydia smirked, perfect. *He doesn't know if the sword can hurt him. It probably can't, but I'll solve that problem later.*

*Where's Taelien? If he's one of the bodies down in that cave...*

*...well, then at least the Sae'kes could be nearby. We could use a weapon like that for dealing with the Vae'kes.*

Lydia stepped back, resetting her stance. Torrent flickered and reappeared behind Sterling, thrusting a rapier at the Vae'kes from behind, but Sterling spun and caught the blade.

Lydia took the opening, slashing the back of Sterling's other boot. He had other positions that would have normally been more tempting, but if she connected with his skin and failed to bite, Sterling would know her blade was useless.

Sterling snapped Torrent's sword in half.

Garrick disappeared again.

Sterling lazily cast the broken half of Garrick's blade aside, turning back to Lydia. "You know, you're beginning to irritate me."

"I should hope so. But, in fairness, I should probably offer you the chance to surrender and face a trial."

Sterling ran a hand through his hair, looking contemplative, and then shrugged. "Declined."

"I expected as much. But you seem like a talker, so humor me – what's all this for?"

The Vae'kes laughed, shaking his head. "You wouldn't believe me if I told you."

"I've always considered myself very tolerant of outside perspectives."

Sterling folded his arms across his chest, glancing briefly skyward. "Well," he smiled, "We're saving the world."

Lydia took another step back, knowing each step her opponent had to take widened her advantage. "That's somewhat grand even by Vae'kes standards."

Sterling tilted his head to the side. "Is that so? Are you acquainted with many Vae'kes?"

He began to advance again, glancing from side to side.

Lydia followed his glances, noting that Velas had dragged herself over to a tree and was valiantly attempting to pull herself to her feet, but that Landen and Torrent were out of sight.

"Not directly, I confess. But I'm relatively confident one of my friends works closely with one."

"That's scandalous. A paladin, friends with a contact for the Vae'kes? What would your superiors say?"

Lydia shrugged. "Not much, to be honest. I think they're fairly accustomed to spies from other organizations being omnipresent at this point."

"What a sad state of affairs." Sterling shook his head. "Your once proud knighthood, slowly decaying from within."

*He's stalling.*

*I thought I was stalling, but he's stalling for something — even the most arrogant assassin wouldn't want to talk this much. And I don't think my little protection trick on the sword is what's deterring him.*

*I need to end this.*

Lydia braced herself as Sterling stalked forward, and as he came within reach, she lunged again, aiming directly at his right eye.

He intercepted the blade with an iron grasp, just as she had expected. And she stepped in close and tapped his arm.

"Sleep."

The dream spell flooded over Sterling. His eyes closed.

"I'd really rather not."

He jerked the rapier out of her hand, flipping it around into his grip.

Lydia stepped back, but not fast enough. Sterling struck with her own weapon — and sparks flew as the blade's barrier struck the one around her body, deflecting the sword and leaving both barriers undamaged.

And, with Sterling's hands occupied with a useless weapon, Lydia was free to raise her own – and begin an incantation.

"Xerasilis, I bind my aura to this ring."

She felt a chill as her body heat briefly shifted, creating a flicker of flame over the ring she wore on her right hand. It was miniscule; a dying candle's flame on a winter night, but it was enough.

The ring glowed white on her hand as she spoke again, turning her right palm toward Sterling.

"*Eru volar shen taris.*"

A sirocco of blue-white flame burst from her hand, sending shivers through her form.

Sterling dropped her sword, thrusting out both hands and inhaling deeply. A black aura manifested around his hands, creating a vortex that tore her flames out of the air, leaving nothing but a trail of smoke.

Lydia staggered backward, shivering uncontrollably and falling to her knees.

*Gods, so cold. Hartigan warned me, but...*

Sterling shook his head, kicking Lydia's fallen sword out of the way as he advanced. "Not a bad trick. That might have actually hurt me if it made contact – a shame you won't get another chance at it."

Sterling blurred forward again, reaching out – his hand's flickering black as it tore through her barrier and grabbed her around the throat.

"You have many skills – enough to survive without a few of them, I'd think."

Lydia felt something reach *through* his hand – foreign essence, probing within her, flooding her blood – and tearing something out of her.

She screamed, in spite of the hand clenched around her throat.

Lydia was only vaguely aware as she crumpled to the ground, feeling terribly empty within, worse than any loss of blood.

"Stay down," Sterling instructed, delivering a kick to her right leg. Bones shattered within and Lydia's mind fluttered again.

She curled into a ball, shivering, nearly insensate.

Torrent appeared behind Sterling, grabbing directly onto the Vae'kes.

"We're going on a little trip," Garrick murmured.

The pair vanished.

Moments later, they reappeared, only a blade-length away.

Sterling had Garrick in a single-armed headlock, and he was shaking his own head. "Against an ordinary opponent, I suppose teleporting them high into the air would be quite creative. Against a Vae'kes, well – you just gave me travel sorcery. Appreciated."

He dragged Garrick across the ground, the lieutenant struggling within his grip.

Lydia could not even consider intervening. Her mind was frozen, broken beyond the state of her body.

Sterling smiled, reaching down. "A gift like that deserves something in return, don't you think? I don't have much on hand," his grip settled around Lydia's fallen rapier, "But on such short notice, this will have to do."

And he plunged the blade into Torrent's chest.

Garrick fell free, released from Sterling's grip. The hilt of the sword struck the ground first, driving it further into Torrent's chest, leaving him coughing as he rolled helplessly on the dirt.

Sterling stepped close to Torrent again. "What were you thinking? I mean, honestly, couldn't you have thought to go for help?"

He laid a boot on Torrent's side, flipping him to face upward, and plucked the rapier out of his chest.

Garrick let out a rasping cough, raising a hand in what looked like a warding gesture – and then smiled, grabbing onto Sterling's leg.

"How pointless."

Sterling thrust the rapier downward – only to find it snapped in half by a blade that glowed with blue-green fire.

"As it turns out…" Garrick rasped. "I did go for help."

Five more glowing blades appeared around Sterling, swiping inward.

Sterling deflected each of them with precise strikes, jumping backward and spinning around, scanning for his attacker.

"War! What is this nonsense?"

Landen stepped out from behind a nearby tree hurling something - just a handful of dirt, Lydia realized belatedly – into Sterling's eyes.

Sterling stumbled backward, dropping his sword and reaching for his eyes – and then vanished as the floating swords whisked through the air where he was standing moments before.

The Vae'kes reappeared a dozen feet away, punching a tree hard enough to bury his fist within it. "War! You hear me, you fucker? I'm going to end you!"

Snarling, Sterling vanished a second time – and for a moment, the forest was silent.

A pair of figures moved into view, only one of which was familiar.

*Taelien.*

His sword glowed brightly in his hand, bathed in the light of seven runes.

Lydia smiled softly at the sight – the mirror of a legendary god.

The swordsman was limping forward, half-carried by the other figure – an unfamiliar man with strange coppery skin and hair.

"Lydia," Taelien muttered, noting her. His eyes shifted, catching Garrick on the ground next. "Oh, gods…"

Lydia could not yet find the strength to speak.

The pair moved forward with agonizing slowness, until Taelien pulled himself free, kneeling at Garrick's side.

"I'll get you help. Hold still."

Garrick let out a choking laugh, reaching out for Taelien's hands. The swordsman took them.

"It's too late for me, boy. But it's all right – I never wanted anything more than to be a hero."

Taelien nodded. "I'll be here for the end, then."

"Gods, don't embarrass me, lad." From her vantage point on the dirt, Lydia couldn't quite see Torrent's face, but his voice was strained with tears. "Go see to Lydia and the others. Eratar will see to my needs. He always has."

"Goodbye, sir."

Lydia felt little of what followed, but when Taelien lifted her into his arms, she knew that at last she was safe.

# INTERLUDE II – ASPHODEL I – ORACLE

Asphodel chased the trail of her potential future.

Having deviated from the main road, her boots crunched against leaves and branches on the forest floor. She ran at a steady rate, pacing the phantom vision of her own movements in her left eye.

Each step brought her closer to a confrontation she had already heard. While her eyes only showed her varying future states of the location in her field of view, her ears provided her with sensory input that she would be exposed to at a later time, regardless of the location in which she gathered that sensory information.

Thus she had known, just before Erik Tarren had teleported them, that they would find the bodies of fallen comrades at their destination. She had known that they would confront deadly enemies – but she did not yet know if they would survive.

Without pausing to concentrate for a coherent vision, she could only hear a few minutes into their potential future. It was insufficient to judge if her platoon had just sealed their own fates – but if they had, she believed it was necessary.

*Deviating from the path of destiny can only lead to madness and ruin.*

Asphodel stumbled over a loose rock, just as the vision of her future had. She caught herself against a tree, her right foot landing inches from a snare. Nearby, she noted a piece of discarded armor – a single plate bracer, the leather straps cut away.

She scanned the forest canopy, still unable to locate her quarry. She did, however, note multiple other pieces of glimmering steel scattered on the forest floor. When her own image moved deeper into the woods, she was swift to follow. The overlay in her left eye was only about one and a half seconds ahead of her own time, providing little chance to react to it.

The images overlapping her right eye were further in the future –nine point seven seconds. She had measured this carefully, learning to utilize it to predict enemy movements.

A crossbow bolt entered the vision of her right eye – and her future self, further ahead on the path, raised a hand.

Asphodel rushed ahead, displacing leaves and grass, and raised her right hand. She saw the projectile approaching a second time, mimicking her earlier vision, and she copied that in turn, snatching the bolt out of the air and snapping it between her fingers.

More traditional sorcerers often recommended that she use sorcery to adjust the timeframes shown in her vision, but her early experiments in doing so had proven unproductive – she had long ago acclimated to the specific timing of her sight, and adjusting the timing ruined her tactical advantage.

Growling softly, she turned her head toward the origin point of the bolt – Susan Crimson, squatting high in the branches of a nearby tree, unarmored and frowning furiously.

Asphodel saw herself slowly approaching the tree and followed her own path.

"You know, I was really hoping they'd send someone else," Susan called down to her. "Your little prediction trick is irritating."

Asphodel smiled, following her own image as it circled to the right, breaking Susan's line of sight. As she moved, she discarded the broken pieces of the crossbow bolt, noting a distinct patch of grass that had been directly in line with Susan's position – most likely another trap of some kind.

"Candidate Crimson, I offer you the opportunity to surrender," Asphodel offered, recalling the words that she had heard herself speak – the words that had guided her to break from Taelien's path to seek her own.

She already knew the reply, and thus she drew her sword, deflecting another crossbow bolt with ease.

She also knew that this action would trigger a silence in her mind – and as she struck the bolt, she realized why. The metallic blade shattered a vial of black fluid attached to the bolt's shaft, splashing the Delaren with droplets of liquid and fragments of broken glass. The glass shards impacted harmlessly, but the few beads of the fluid that touched her skin triggered an immediate effect.

The images of her future selves vanished. Her eyes saw only the present. Her ears processed only that moment in time.

Asphodel rushed behind a nearby tree, breathing heavily. Ducking, she raised a gauntleted hand in an effort to wipe the droplets away from her face – but the brush of metal against her skin did not avail her.

*Don't panic.*

*Don't panic!*

"Hah! I knew that would work. You fucking sorcerers are all the same." The Delaren heard a nearby thud that she judged to be Susan hopping down from her tree. "Take away your little tricks and you're worthless."

*That vial must have been void essence – she just cut off my connection with the dominions.*

Asphodel dropped her sword and slipped off her backpack, tearing open the top compartment and scrambling to retrieve her water skin.

Footsteps were rapidly approaching. The Delaren tore open the water skin, pouring it over her face and tossing it aside just as Susan rounded the tree, a loaded crossbow in hand.

"Not a bad tactic, but a little late."

Asphodel's vision was blurred from the water, but she still managed to throw herself to the side when Susan lifted her hand to fire. The bolt landed harmlessly in the nearby dirt.

Susan made a tsking noise, continuing to approach. Asphodel blinked ineffectually, using her left hand to raise her tabard to wipe her face as she scrambled to her feet.

As Asphodel turned toward her opponent, Susan slammed the empty crossbow into her temple. Her vision swam as she fell backward, blood seeping from a shallow cut, the crack of the wood echoing in her mind. She landed hard on a large stone, but her armor served to cushion the impact.

"Fucking worthless." Susan cast the crossbow aside, drawing the sword from her side. "I mean, your hair is going to be worth a fortune, but your fighting skills – those are pretty unimpressive."

*My hair,* she processed. *Of course.*

As Susan's blade descended toward the Delaran's neck, Asphodel focused on the crystalline strands that housed her essence – and drank deeply of their strength.

The assassin's blade seemed to slow as each strand of power flooded Asphodel's body, filling her with years of stored power in each of her body's dominions.

She caught the blade in a gauntleted hand and flexed her fingers, snapping it in twain. Growling lightly, the Delaren shoved herself to her feet.

Susan backpedaled, flicking her left wrist in Asphodel's direction. A dagger emerged from the assassin's sleeve, but its movement was sluggish with Asphodel's altered perception, and she stepped around it.

Asphodel advanced, raising her arms into a simple unarmed combat stance. She felt a shiver of euphoria as the essence continued to seep into her body, but maintained her approach, knowing that every instant she utilized this inner strength was borrowing from the span of her life.

Susan swept her broken blade at Asphodel's eyes. Asphodel raised a bracer and deflected the strike, stepping inward and slamming an open palm into the assassin's chest. She felt ribs buckle at the strength of the blow, sending Susan falling backward into a nearby tree, coughing blood.

"Fuck," the assassin muttered, breaking into a coughing fit.

Asphodel retrieved her own discarded sword, while Susan grabbed another bolt from the quiver on her hip, gritting her teeth.

The Delaren approached deliberately, swiping her sword across the crossbow bolt and shattering the attached glass vial across the assassin's body. The liquid shimmered blue in the faint light scattered between the trees.

"Surrender. Now."

Susan dropped the fragment of her remaining bolt, grinning manically, and raised her hands. "Suppose I must."

Asphodel kept her blade near Susan's throat, kneeling down and grabbing the remaining bolts in the quiver at her side and casting them into the forest.

"Any other weapons?"

Susan rolled her eyes. "Well, yeah, but getting rid of them all is going to take a while."

"You may begin."

Susan sighed, shaking her right sleeve and displacing a knife, which clattered to the forest floor. Asphodel picked up the dagger and tossed it aside.

Her crystalline hair was beginning to feel warm against her skin, implying a dangerous level of overuse, but she dared not break the flow of essence – she had no doubt that Susan would still be a threat, and her normal connection with the dominions had not yet returned.

"Going to have to take off my boots. And my pants. And my shirt."

Asphodel glowered at the assassin. "We'll start with the boots."

"Actually, before that, there's something you should know." Susan grinned again, shifting her hands behind her head and leaning back against the nearby tree.

Asphodel bristled, sensing danger in Susan's tone. "Talk."

"That last vial you broke? Not void essence."

If the Delaren had not been using her essence, she could not have hoped to react quickly enough to the blade that was arcing toward her neck from behind.

Her spin brought her blade in a perfect half-circle, deflecting Sterling's attempt at decapitation and bringing a sour expression to his face.

Asphodel frowned – she had not heard the swordsman approach, and she had last seen him half-dead on the floor of the cavern.

*Another traitor, apparently.*

She raised her blade into a high stance. Her hair continued to warm, burning the flesh in her scalp and ruining her concentration.

*I need to end this engagement quickly.*

She asked no questions – she simply stepped forward and brought her blade toward Sterling in a heavy diagonal cut, speed and strength fueled by her flagging essence. The cut was too fast for an ordinary swordsman to avoid – but Sterling made no effort to block or dodge.

He simply vanished.

*Teleportation.*

She spun again, finding Sterling next to Susan, his hand on her forehead.

"Susan, dearest, you really need to not warn our enemies that they're being flanked." He sighed, running fingers into her hair – and then grabbing a tuft of them in a painful-looking grip. He glanced up at Asphodel, showing no sign of concern as she raised her blade for another strike. "No time for you right now, I'm afraid. We're on a schedule. But I'll commend your reaction, and hope to see you again."

He tipped his head downward, smirking, and vanished again – taking Susan with him.

Asphodel slammed her blade into the tree where they had been moments before, not wanting to risk the possibility that they had merely gone invisible. The strike cleaved deep into the bark, but met no other resistance.

*Failure.*

Asphodel scanned the nearby trees, finding no sign of enemies or allies.

Shivering, she dropped her blade and reached up to her head, feeling the burning of her hair against her skin. Only now was the pain beginning to overwhelm the pleasure from the essence flow – and she focused on that pain as she slowed, and then ceased, the tide of essence pumping into her body.

Her vision blurred and she found herself falling, barely catching herself against the tree where she had embedded her blade. She slowly allowed herself to sink to the forest floor, her breath coming in ragged gasps.

For a time, she could not force herself to move.

The sounds of future conversation came to her first – a ragged whisper at first, difficult to discern, but its return brought tears to her bloodshot eyes.

She was still nearly immobile when Landen appeared in the distance, deftly avoiding Susan's traps on the forest floor, blades held in either hand.

"Over here," she called weakly, the fragment of a smile breaking across her face. "I'm over here."

The swordsman danced around the final patch of grass that Asphodel had suspected to hide a pit. "Any hostiles still nearby?"

"No."

He arrived at her side and knelt down. "Been looking all over for you."

"Why?"

The swordsman quirked an eyebrow. "Because we've been worried about you? Things got rough back at the cave – looks like they got rough here, too."

*Worried about me?*

Landen offered her a hand. "Can you stand?"

She grasped his arm, clinging to it more tightly than she needed to. "I think so."

With strong arms, he lifted her to her feet. "Good. Because we're about the only ones left who can."

***

"We need to leave the bodies here for now. We'll return with a larger force."

Velas was the one speaking – she would deliver these orders a few minutes in the future.

At the moment, Asphodel knelt at the side of her deceased commanding officer, wrapping the wound that had already ended his life. She knew it was largely a pointless measure, but she hoped that it might slow the deterioration of his body. It was a pitiful hope, one with no substance, but it was the only thing she could do to mitigate the failure in her mind.

Nearby, Taelien had stripped off his armor and was tending to an unconscious Major Hastings. Asphodel had only met the sorceress during her initial application process, but she had sensed a kinship in another entity tied to dominions that emphasized the gathering of information.

Taelien looked pale and exhausted, but his injuries were not the most severe. Velas leaned heavily upon her quarterstaff nearby, her armor similarly abandoned and her lower chest bound with bandages. Her breathing was ragged, but her expression spoke of grim determination.

Only the strangest among them, the copper skinned man with a bloody rent across his forehead, appeared unaffected by the carnage. He silently watched their prisoner – Eridus – who had been stripped and bound with climbing rope.

When she had arrived, Landen gave her a simple explanation for the stranger's presence. "That's the Wandering War without his outfit. Taelien said something about freeing him from Sterling's control."

Taelien had smiled and said, "I broke his chains."

He had seemed pleased by this, and Asphodel had thus felt pleased for him. A small victory, at least, among their tragedies.

There was little talk amongst the survivors until Velas spoke her orders. After that, it was simply a matter of delegating labor. Not trusting the Wandering War with their wounded, Landen insisted on carrying Lydia in spite of his own exhaustion. Asphodel assisted Taelien with walking, while Velas leaned heavily on her quarterstaff.

This left the Wandering War to continue to watch Eridus as they marched him toward the paladin camp – but though many suspicious eyes fell upon the pair, neither made any attempt to flee or assault the group again.

It was long past nightfall when they arrived at the base camp and the relative safety of a paladin escort.

From there, the wounded were left behind – and Asphodel began the long journey back to Velthryn, accompanied only by prisoners and strangers.

# CHAPTER XXIV – JONAN VI – QUESTIONABLE PURSUITS

Jonan sat by the side of an old friend's bed. Taelien was at his right side, the swordsman's left leg wrapped in bandages, his expression grim.

Hours passed before Lydia opened her eyes, and Jonan was intent on getting the first word in.

"You're lucky, Lydia. You're the last of the three of us to wake injured in a bed."

She shivered, much as she had when she was asleep, her eyes closing again. For a moment, he worried – but then they reopened, free from sleep.

"Where…"

"You're at a medical facility near the citadel," Taelien cut in, leaning forward. "Aladir has been here periodically, but he's had several others to treat as well."

Lydia nodded, closing her eyes again. "I…what happened? I don't…" She turned her gaze toward Jonan, her eyes narrowing. "You. What are you doing here?"

Jonan quirked an eyebrow. "Visiting you?"

Taelien reached forward and took one of Lydia's hands. "It's okay, Lydia. He wasn't there. I don't think he was involved."

*Involved? Why would she –*

*Oh, the Vae'kes thing.*

Jonan stood up from his chair, his left arm still throbbing, and turned away. "Well, I don't want to make things awkward. I just wanted to make sure you were safe."

"Wait." Lydia's voice. Jonan turned back around. "Stay. Help me understand."

He sat back down, nodding solemnly. "Where do we need to begin?"

The wounded paladin smiled. "I don't think I'm missing that much – I just...it hurt so much..."

"The Vae'kes escaped." Taelien tensed his jaw. "So did Susan Crimson, who we believe was working with him."

*Susan Crimson? I don't know that name, but it seems...familiar somehow.*

"And the others? Garrick, is he...?"

"Dead. I'm sorry, Lydia. He's with Eratar now."

*Such a worthless platitude. But if it helps her, I suppose I'll tolerate the lines, even if I won't repeat them.*

Lydia sighed, closing her eyes. "He saved me. Appeared right behind Sterling – I remember that much."

Taelien nodded. "He died a hero's death. But I fear he was not our only loss."

Lydia's expression looked pained. "Who?"

"Two paladin candidates – members of Sterling's squad. Celia Laurent and Alden Stone."

"For what little it's worth," Jonan offered, "I am sorry for your losses as well."

Lydia nodded weakly, giving a sad smile as she looked toward him. "Thank you, Jonan. And I'm sorry about before – I just, my last memories were –"

"No, I understand. And you are right to have a degree of suspicion – a Vae'kes rarely acts on his or her own. I can provide you with no proof, but I have never had any association with this 'Sterling' that Taelien spoke of."

"I understand. There are many Vae'kes – it would be absurd for you to know them all, just because you work with the priesthood."

Taelien released Lydia's hand, moving his hand back into his own lap. "As for the others...Velas is in the worst shape of us, but she'll survive. Landen made it through relatively unscathed, aside from his pride. I'm in much the same shape."

Lydia attempted to push herself into a seated position, but Jonan leaned forward and pressed down on her arm. "Don't try to move yet. You're not going anywhere for a while."

She frowned at that. "What do you – oh."

Her gaze caught on the thick iron rod attached to her right leg, anchoring the bandages that held the recovering limb in place. She shuddered.

"It…could be some time before you can walk again. And you may never regain your full use of the leg, but Aladir thinks they can save it, at least. I'm sorry, Lydia." Jonan tapped his left arm. "Just think of it as a fashion statement. Your leg bandages will match the ones on my arm."

"More like the ones on my own leg," Taelien patted his left leg, wincing at the contact.

Jonan rolled his eyes.

Lydia swept her gaze between the two of them. "You two are going to have to get me out of here soon, even if you have to carry me. First, because I'll go insane if I'm stuck here too long. And second, because Torian Dianis' trial is in two days."

Jonan and Taelien exchanged a look. Taelien spoke first this time.

"Lydia, you've been out for more than three days. The trial has already started – and it's not going well."

Lydia folded her arms. "Then what the resh are you two doing here with me?"

Jonan shook his head. "It's a closed hearing. Members of the city council and the priesthood of Xerasilis only, given that the accused is a member of the council. We've asked to be called upon, but…"

"Reshing politics," Taelien mumbled.

"That's absurd. We're witnesses, in varying capacities. You especially, Jonan."

The scribe nodded at that. "Yeah, a witness that works for the same organization as the other people we just arrested in connection with the same crime. That's going to come across as very credible."

"I will insist upon it. Get me one of those Xerasilis priests – I'll talk to them." Lydia looked resolute, even as she continued to shiver in the bed.

Taelien patted the side of the bed. "I think you're going to want to eat first."

She frowned, her face looking suddenly childlike. "Well, I am very hungry."

\*\*\*

416

Days passed as the trial of Torian Dianis continued. With Ulandir Ta'thyriel still missing from the city, Aladir was able to use his influence to participate in the hearings, but the news he bore gave Jonan little comfort.

"They're still asking for more evidence?" The scribe folded his arms, leaning back against one of the citadel's walls.

He was joined by an unlikely group – Taelien sat next to a blonde woman that he was near-certain was Silk, and Landen of the Twin Edges was passing a bottle of wine back and forth with his apparent cousin, Nakane Theas. Lydia was seated nearby as well, in a wheeled chair that the others used to help her move about while she recovered.

Aladir tightened his jaw, nodding slowly before speaking. "Eridus confessed to being the one who killed Kalsiris, and that's undermined our case against Torian. Given that Eridus was also a water sorcerer, he was capable of creating the toxin that was used on the crossbow bolt that hit you."

"But that wouldn't explain why Torian altered the toxin while it was in my body." Jonan sighed.

"Unfortunately, that could easily be interpreted as a failed attempt to cure the poison – if and even then, it couldn't be proven that he did anything to you at all. We would only have the testimony of the other sorcerers who checked your wound, two of whom are his daughters – making them both unreliable, for different reasons."

Jonan tensed his hands in the air. "Is Vorianna – or, Rialla, I suppose, now that she's no longer hiding – making a case against her father?"

"I haven't seen her since Torian was arrested. I'd imagine she doesn't want anything to do with this affair – if she speaks against her father, she makes herself another potential suspect if that fails to bear out."

"I'll talk to her." Jonan lifted his good arm and scratched the back of his head.

Aladir put a hand over his eyes. "I'm sorry. I wish I could do more, but I don't know –"

Nakane spoke, setting her bottle down on the table in front of her. "We will find everyone responsible for this – and we will make them pay. Court or no court."

Landen shook his head. "That's dangerous talk, 'Kane."

She tilted her head as she looked back at him. "You disagree? You going to throw me in prison to stop me?"

The twin-bladed swordsman sighed. "I didn't say that. Look, I'm going to help you, but we need to do this through legal means."

She folded her arms. "We'd best do it quickly. My father is on his way back to the city – and if he returns to find my mother's killer free, my own deviations from the law will be the least of our concerns."

Landen nodded solemnly. "We'll get them. Got one already, at least – and now Kalsiris can rest peacefully."

"Peace?" Nakane gave a choking laugh. "You clearly haven't seen the spirit plane, cousin. There is no peace in death."

Taelien stood up. "While I hate to interrupt you two, I think I have an idea."

The blonde leaned heavily against the table. "Oh, look out folks. Taelien has an idea. Better get ourselves armed."

*Yep, that's definitely Silk.*

Taelien scowled. "Thanks for contributing, Vel. You're a real help. Pulling your weight, like I hear you did with the Vae'kes."

She stood up, shoving him backward. "Oh, I'd like to hear you say that again."

Landen chuckled. "Gods, you two, keep the foreplay where it belongs. Like the barracks, or Lydia's office."

"Okay, there's going to be no foreplay. Not here, definitely not in my office. Never in my office." Lydia folded her arms. "Taelien, do you have an actual plan?"

The swordsman turned his gaze toward her. "Sure, it's simple enough. We just have to catch Vae'kes Sterling."

Jonan gave Taelien a withering glance. "Yes, let's all rally our forces and march upon the – where exactly is he? Oh, right, we don't know. And we don't have forces. No forces at all."

Lydia groaned and rubbed at her left temple, a gesture that looked disconcertingly similar to one of the Thornguard hand signs, but different enough that Jonan knew it was just a sign that she had a headache. "As much as it pains me to admit that Jonan has a point, I'm afraid that in this case, he does."

Jonan frowned in bemusement. "Why would that be painful?"

Taelien smirked. "Have you ever tried listening to yourself?"

Landen shook his head. "As amusing as this all is, I'd like to point out that our last encounter with Sterling was completely one-sided. I don't think we put a scratch on him."

Taelien folded his arms. "Well, sure. But I wasn't there."

Silk shot him a fiery glare. "And you're lucky for that, Sal. Your arrogance is usually cute, but not right now. Garrick Torrent died fighting Sterling. If you were there, maybe you would have saved him. Maybe you would have died, too. In either case, this is not something you should be posturing about."

The swordsman lowered his eyes, turning his head away. "You're...you're right, of course. I'm sorry. I miss Garrick, too. I just – I need to do something. Every day we wait, the chances of catching Sterling diminish."

Nakane refilled her glass of wine, passing the bottle back to Landen. "I agree with the shockingly overconfident swordsman. Steps should be taken to apprehend this 'Sterling'." She turned her head to Lydia. "Major Hastings, would you be willing to put together a force to find the Vae'kes?"

Lydia nodded. "I will speak to my superiors about it. It's more likely now that he's killed one of our own, but I can't promise an army. This will most likely have to be a discreet affair – one does not hunt the child of a god without significant political dangers."

Nakane sipped at her drink and set it back down. "Is there any precedent for this sort of affair?"

"Not that I know of." Lydia adjusted her glasses, a thoughtful expression on her face. "The Vae'kes are typically left to their own devices, as much as we might dislike them. I'm not aware of one of them ever killing a paladin before, however."

Jonan looked to Nakane, then to Lydia. "I need to advise you against this. The Vae'kes are used to acting with impunity for a reason – they are nigh unstoppable. And that's not even taking the possibility of war into consideration."

Nakane turned toward Jonan, liquid swishing in her half-full glass. "And what would you suggest, Master Kestrian? Shall we allow one of my brother's killers to go free, fearing the consequences of pursuing him?"

Jonan winced. "Give me some time to consider the matter. Perhaps I could speak to one of the other Vae'kes and find some leverage."

"We do not have the luxury of delaying much longer. Without evidence, Torian will go free. I will not allow that." Nakane set her glass down, standing and turning to Lydia. "Major Hastings, I will look forward to hearing the results of your inquiry with your superiors."

The last child of House Theas turned back toward Jonan. "Speak to your other Vae'kes if you must – but I would be more interested in seeing results with Torian. If his daughter can be swayed to speak against him, perhaps there is hope for resolving that matter before we find the Vae'kes." She lifted a hand and left it hovering in the air near Landen. "Come, cousin. Escort me home."

Landen rolled his eyes, setting down his glass. "Right, Nakane." He stood, taking her hand, and began to walk her out of the room. He glanced back toward the blonde woman on the way out. "Don't do anything stupid without me."

Silk smiled. "I wouldn't dream of it."

***

Jonan found Rialla at Southway Manor, just as he had expected. He had not expected to find her with company. Liarra Dianis sat across from her sister at a small table, sipping a cup of tea. A hint of sadness pulled at the corners of her eyes.

Rialla had a book open in front of her, but she turned and stood as Jonan approached. "I wasn't expecting to see you here for a while."

"Nakane should be relatively safe with her cousin for the time being. I need to speak to you about the trial. Can we talk privately?"

Rialla glanced at Liarra, who remained seated. "Anything you want to say to me you can say around my sister."

"I'm not sure that's such a good idea."

Liarra set her cup of tea down, waving a hand. "It's alright. I won't be offended if you need some privacy."

"No, I think you should hear this." Rialla folded her arms. "It's alright. I've told her everything."

*Everything?* He felt a momentary surge of panic. *What does everything entail?*

Jonan took a deep breath, unconsciously lifting two fingers to his forehead. "Right, right. I'll be succinct, then. Your father was, at a minimum, most likely involved in coercing Nedelya Theas into suicide. Given that he also manipulated the poison in my arm before Liarra treated it — and thank you very much for that, by the way — I feel it's safe to say he was also attempting to conceal evidence of a connection with Kalsiris' murder."

"You're...welcome." Liarra turned her head away meekly.

Rialla nodded. "Yes, you're probably right. And I suppose you'd also want to mention that Liarra and I are both going to be suspects if Father goes free."

"Precisely. You had a chance to interrogate one of the people attacking the compound — you have evidence none of the rest of us do. Moreover, if you chose to speak about your brother—"

"No. I will not bring Elias into this, and I do not believe I will be addressing the court at all." Rialla looked at her sister. "I have only just regained some semblance of my family; I won't risk it again so soon."

"Inaction itself is a risk. What precisely do you expect to happen if Torian is set free?"

Liarra turned to look at Jonan directly, her voice faint. "We will leave."

Jonan tensed his jaw in frustration. "That will make you look like criminals."

"It doesn't matter. I have places I can go, as I'm sure you're aware." Rialla shook her head.

"Would you allow your father to walk free, even knowing what he has done?"

Liarra stood, moving to Rialla's side. "He is right, sister. If we do nothing, we will bear the guilt for the remainder of our lives." She turned her gaze to Jonan. "I will speak to the court."

Rialla shook her head fervently, taking her sister's hands. "No, no. You would make yourself a target. You must not do this." She turned her gaze toward Jonan. "Give us time to think on this. I will not leave the city without informing you first, I swear to that."

Jonan nodded, his expression grim. "Very well. I will leave you to consider it."

The scribe's arm throbbed with inner pain as he marched out of the manor into the chilling air outside.

# CHAPTER XXV – TAELIEN VI – THE EDGES OF FRIENDSHIP

Taelien knelt upon a stone floor, the Sae'kes sheathed at his side, encircled by a ring of an unfamiliar black powder.

Around the circle were three figures, each holding a lit torch and wearing the robes of the priesthood of Xerasilis.

This particular inquest was being held in an amphitheater beneath the open sky. Among the two rows of seats were a dozen paladins from varying branches of the order, each in full uniform. Lydia was not among them – her injuries prohibited her presence.

Behind the two rows of seats stood three familiar figures - Colonel Wyndam, Lieutenant Morris, and Second Lieutenant Banks.

He had pictured a gathering of this kind many times, envisioning it as his initiation into the Paladins of Tae'os. But this was not an initiation – this was just his own part in the trial for the murder of a fallen friend.

One of the three priests stepped away from the circle, raising the torch with both hands.

"Applicant Salaris, you have been called to speak in the service of the laws of gods and men. Bound in the flames of purity, you must speak the truth, lest they consume you."

Taelien knew the words to speak for this particular ritual. "Bound in the flames of purity, I will speak only the truth. Let Xerasilis render his judgment upon me."

"Then, by the flames be judged."

Taelien took a deep breath as the speaker stepped forward, lowering his ring to powder. There was a flash of yellow-blue light as the powder sparked to life, spreading quickly into a conflagration that enveloped the air around him. The flames were only a few feet high, but in his kneeling state, they came to the level of his neck.

The ring of fire glowed blue, bathing him in warmth, but the flames did not burn his skin.

*I don't sense them as flames*, he realized as the fire licked close to his skin. *They're not ordinary fire – not even ordinary sorcerous fire. They feel more similar to what Edon used, but still different somehow.*

He reached out instinctively with his mind, but the flames remained foreign, distant, and beyond his immediate control. If the blaze turned inward, he knew he would have no defense.

Colonel Wyndam stepped down from her position near the top of the amphitheater, approaching the ring. "Applicant Salaris, please describe in your own words the events leading to the deaths of Applicant Laurent, Applicant Stone, and Lieutenant Torrent."

Taelien raised his head to look directly at the colonel – not out of arrogance, but out of respect. "Colonel, I can only give honest testimony to what I directly witnessed, and I did not directly witness any of their deaths. My group arrived at the Shrine of Lissari to find Applicants Laurent and Stone already deceased. Applicant Sterling appeared to be wounded, but alive. Applicant Eridus also appeared deceased."

"How did you determine that Applicant Eridus was deceased?"

Taelien grunted. "He was lying in a prone position like the other deceased applicants. Applicant Sterling told us a story of how Eridus had died, and we took him at his word."

"Continue."

"Applicant Sterling convinced us that he had been attacked only minutes before. We believed this story, and wishing to apprehend the people who had murdered the other applicants, we split our group."

"Under what authority did you break from your training procedures to split your group and attempt to apprehend these supposed murderers?"

*Well, Velas, technically, but...* "Our group acted on our own authority."

The flames seemed to burn somewhat warmer around him, but did not yet singe his flesh. He felt a bead of sweat drip down his forehead.

"Proceed to explain the events following that."

"Velas and Landen chose to stay behind to assist Applicant Sterling. Applicant Velas had the best medical skills, and thus the best chance of saving Sterling's life. Applicant Landen has superior archery skills, and thus had the best chance of providing Velas with cover fire if the assailants returned. Asphodel and I went to follow the presumed trails of our enemies."

"At which point you split again, correct?"

Taelien nodded. "Yes. Applicant Asphodel's divination abilities indicated to her that the enemy path diverged. She intended to catch Applicant Crimson, while I went to capture the Wandering War."

"You state that your goal was 'capture.' Your intent was to arrest these enemies, then, and not take revenge for your fallen enemies?"

Taelien nodded. "Yes, although I was prepared to use lethal force in my own defense if necessary."

"Very well. Continue."

The flames seemed to sink somewhat, and he felt his words coming easier. "I confronted the Wandering War. I was outmatched at first. He demonstrated the ability to copy other forms of sorcery he had witnessed, including a version of Keldyn's Bladecalling, at which point I discerned that he was most likely a Harvester of War."

A murmur went through the crowd. Colonel Wyndam raised a fist, bringing silence to the paladins behind her.

"A Harvester of War. I will be interested in hearing more on this subject at a later time, but for the moment, explain how you survived this encounter."

"I severed the bond between master and servant."

The colonel folded her arms, quirking an eyebrow. "You severed a metaphorical bond with a physical attack?"

"During our battle, I began to sense a connection between the Wandering War and someone outside the area. When he removed his cowl, I noted a Dominion Mark on his forehead. I was able to use the Sae'kes to destroy that mark. The effect on him was immediate – he ceased fighting, screamed, and fell to the ground. After a few tense moments, he righted himself, laughing, and thanked me for his freedom."

The colonel took a breath, turning to look at the other officers. Lieutenant Banks made a few quick hand signs that Taelien didn't recognize and then nodded his head. The colonel turned back to Taelien.

"And what followed that event?"

"While I was tending my own injuries, Lieutenant Torrent teleported nearby. He looked surprised to see the Wandering War helping me, and informed us that Velas and Landen were under attack. War and I quickly readied ourselves, and Torrent teleported us to concealed positions near to the battle. War and I moved to engage from flanking positions while Torrent teleported directly back into the fray. I moved slowly due to my leg injury. By the time I reached the battlefield, Torrent had been slain."

"By Jonathan Sterling?"

Taelien nodded. "I did not see it happen directly, but I arrived quickly thereafter, and I trust the words of the survivors."

"Would it not have been possible that the Wandering War could have slain Lieutenant Torrent?"

Taelien frowned. "I would find that highly unlikely. Landen and Velas saw —"

"Please only take your own perspective into account."

The swordsman took another breath. "It would have been possible for the Wandering War to attack Torrent from behind and harm him, but I find it unlikely, given how quickly I arrived at the scene thereafter and how Sterling reacted to the Wandering War's presence. Moreover, the Wandering War's behavioral changes after I freed him indicated —"

"By your own admission, you freed an entity connected to the Dominion of War from external control. Do you believe you have a sufficient understanding of such entities to judge their motives in the midst of an ongoing battle?"

"No — not specifically, no, Colonel."

The colonel turned and began to pace around the circle of flame. "You stated that Applicants Laurent and Stone were deceased prior to your arrival at the shrine. Did you personally validate this?"

He turned to follow the colonel as best he could without standing. "No, Colonel, I only saw them on the floor of the cave from a distance."

"I believe that concludes this line of questioning." She turned to the other officers. "Lieutenants, do you have any other questions for the applicant?"

"No, ma'am," they replied in unison.

"Very well." The colonel turned to the priests. "Judges, this candidate has concluded his testimony. How does Xerasilis render his judgment upon him?"

One of the other priests spoke from behind Taelien, "The darkness of concealment was upon one of his answers, however, Xerasilis judged his words to be in defense of another. He did not breach the oaths of the faith, though he should spend some time in contemplation of this hint of shadow."

The colonel gave the priest a curt nod. "That is sufficient. You may release him from the flames of judgment."

The priests lowered their torches to the flame – and the fire escaped the circle, traveling to relight the three torches.

The first of the priests spoke again. "In the name of Xerasilis, I declare you purified, and your words to be truly spoken. You may rise, Applicant Taelien, and return to your fellows."

Taelien rose on wobbling feet, turning to salute the colonel.

Colonel Wyndam returned his salute. "Applicant Taelien, you are dismissed." She turned toward the lieutenants. "Bring me the next one."

***

The Wandering War's cell was not what Taelien had envisioned.

Grey stone walls surrounded the chamber on all sides – there were no doors, no windows, and no other forms of physical entry or exit. The air inside smelled fresh, indicating the paladins had a sorcerous method of circulating the habitat's air supply.

The chamber was the size of a large bedroom, though there was no bed within – merely a single prisoner at the center, and a pile of books adjacent to a plate of uneaten food and a jug of liquid.

Lieutenant Holder, a younger Paladin of Sytira with prematurely greying hair, released his grip on Taelien's wrist as the disorientation from their teleportation faded. Lydia was at his opposite side, leaning heavily on a wooden staff. Her injured leg was still splinted and wrapped in bandages, but she had recovered enough to leave her bed in the three days since Taelien had played his part in the trial.

The copper-skinned warrior sat cross-legged with a book in his lap, surrounded on all sides by layers of wards etched into the floor and ceilings. The walls of the rooms were similarly warded, although with different symbols. Taelien recognized some from a variety of different languages, including his native Sae'li.

The Wandering War was dressed in simple country clothes — a grey shirt and pants — with no shroud to cover the scar that ran across his forehead.

War set the book aside, looking up and turning his gaze directly toward Taelien. "Ah, I have been requesting your presence for days now. Have you recovered?"

Taelien considered the question, folding his arms. "For the most part."

The Wandering War stood. "Excellent. Shall we begin immediately?"

Lydia gave Taelien a glance that spoke of clear disapproval. Lieutenant Holder was already reaching for his sword.

"That isn't why I'm here today." He folded his hands in front of him. "I was hoping you would be willing to answer some questions for my friends and me."

The copper skinned man tilted his head to the side, and then stepped closer to Lieutenant Holder. When War impacted an invisible barrier, he paused, sniffing at the air. "This one wishes violence toward me. Permit it and I will answer your questions."

Lydia took a step forward, motioning for Holder to move back. He quickly acquiesced, putting his back to the wall of the room. "I…is this safe?"

The sorceress calmly put a hand up against the barrier. "Dominion of Protection, reinforce this barrier."

A flash of light illuminated a cube-shaped barrier that enveloped the inner portion of the room.

The Wandering War smiled. "An excellent preparation, given my tone. Good."

Lydia frowned, her eyes fluttering as she stepped backward. Taelien stepped close, taking her arm to steady her. "You all right?"

"I'm… I am fine. That spell took more out of me than it should have."

War tapped a finger against the newly-reinforced barrier. "Ah, still suffering from the touch of the Vae'kes? Lacking in the strength to fight as you once did? I could be persuaded to help you with that problem."

Lydia narrowed her eyes, pulling her arm away from Taelien and nodding to him, then looking back to War. "I'm not interested, but thank you for your concern. I will recover on my own, given time."

"In part, at least. I could make you better than before – but that is not why you are here, at least for now. If you will not trade blows with me, a trade of questions, then?"

Holder took a breath, stepping away from the wall. "We do not negotiate with prisoners. And certainly not murderers."

The Wandering War stepped back, leaning back against the barrier on the opposite side of his cell. "Murder is such a peculiar term. Humans use it to ascribe immorality to any form of killing they find personally inconvenient. I don't make the distinction that you do, but nevertheless, I think it's fair to say I haven't murdered anyone."

Lydia straightened her back, taking a breath. "That ties into my first question. What was your role in the deaths of Applicants Stone and Laurent?"

War shook his head, closing his scarlet eyes. "You must offer me something. I am starving and this," he gestured to the food, "Will not sate my appetite."

Taelien tapped a fist against the invisible wall. "If you're released, I'll train with you."

The copper-skinned man turned his gaze toward the ground. "I would prefer something now, but I suppose the promise of bloodshed will have to suffice." He turned his head toward Lydia. "I saw them killed. It was quick, as betrayals often are. Eridus created a poisonous vapor, which they breathed. When they reported their sickness, Eridus played at healing Laurent while he shaped her blood into water. While Stone watched the 'healing', Sterling stabbed him in the back of the neck."

*Gods, turning someone's blood into water –*

Taelien tightened his jaw.

The Wandering War spared him a glance. "Ah, good, that angers you. As well it should – there was no glory in it, no battle to be won. I would call their deaths worthless, but they did bring me to battle."

"And to freedom from compulsion." Taelien steepled his fingers together.

"Trading one set of chains for another is no great joy. And while this cell," the copper-skin man stretched, "Is roomier than the last, it has provided fewer opportunities for entertainment. At least until now."

Lydia reached up with her free hand to adjust her glasses. "Another question. What do you know about the death of Kalsiris Theas?"

The Wandering War put his left thumb to his chin, closing his eyes for a moment. "Ah, that was the one I was summoned to obfuscate. It was more tactically done than Sterling's more recent gambit."

The copper skinned man pushed himself away from the invisible wall, coming forward again. "Sterling brought me to this plane, bound me, and shrouded me in a cloak of sight sorcery. I was forced to walk a shallow path while Eridus followed, an assassin's blade in hand. The building was impressively protected against bombardment and teleportation, but not against mere stealth. We followed a patrolling guard into the building and quickly found our target."

Lydia's eyes narrowed. "Continue."

"It was quite simple after that – Sterling had shown me the plans to the building. I went to the correct room, Eridus followed. I noted to Eridus that the boy was shielded, and thus, he chose to poison the drink on the nearby table rather than test the knife. We did not wish to risk allowing the child to raise an alarm, and the liquid would bypass the ring's protections. We waited for the child to wake and drink, thus ensuring the kill, before leaving the room."

"How did Eridus poison the drink?" Lydia put both hands on her staff, leaning heavily against it.

"Core sorcery. It's a simple thing to turn water into poison for one skilled in that art."

The sorceress nodded. "And the dominion essence of poison we found at the ritual area?"

"Ah, you found that, did you? Just another deflection. Sterling placed it to divert any investigations toward poison sorcerers."

"And you had no direct part in the poisoning, or in killing any of our paladin applicants or members?"

The Wandering War shrugged at that. "Nothing as direct as cutting someone apart, no. Although I certainly did try with this one." He indicated Taelien with a gesture.

Taelien grimaced. "You're not really helping the case for your freedom."

"Is that what this is about?" The Wandering War laughed. "Oh, I suppose I should be playing at placation, then. But I don't want to."

Taelien glanced at Lydia. "I think you can see that he was just being coerced into helping Sterling."

"Well, not precisely," War mentioned. "I mean, yes, he bound me with sorcery, and I didn't have a choice, but he was having me do things that served my dominion – redirecting blame to cause conflict isn't my personal specialty, but it is one way to make war."

Lydia glanced back at Taelien. "And, as you said, he's really not helping his own case for freedom. He's a being connected to war. He's dangerous."

"Extremely dangerous," The Wandering War added cheerfully. "Terribly dangerous. Catastrophically, perhaps."

Lydia shook her head, cracking a smile. "I'll take your word on that. Another question – were you in any way involved in a second assault on House Theas?"

War made a scoffing noise. "What we did could hardly be called an assault. But to answer your question, no, I visited there only once."

"Were you aware of any plans for a second attack?"

War shook his head. "No. A shame - infiltration is not to my tastes, but a direct attack on that compound..." He turned his head upward, inhaling a deep breath. "That would have been delightful."

"Have you ever heard of someone called the 'Shrouded One'?"

War shrugged. "Can't say I have. Sounds like a name made for a calculated effect of mystery."

*That's rather ironic, coming from him.*

Lydia turned away from War, looking to Taelien and Holder. "I believe we're done here."

Taelien nodded to Lydia and looked toward Holder. "I'd like you to give the two us some time to talk privately."

The lieutenant looked to Lydia, and then back to Taelien. "You want me to leave the two of you in here with him, with no way out?"

Taelien shook his head. "No, I meant just myself and War – you'd be taking Lydia with you."

The sorceress stepped away from the barrier and gave Taelien a disapproving look. "Absolutely not."

Holder breathed a sigh of relief. "Yes, ma'am."

"Five minutes, that's all. I have personal questions." Taelien folded his arms. "I've earned that much, at least."

"It's not a question of earning anything. This entity is, by his own admission, 'terribly dangerous'. I will consider allowing you to speak to him privately after I've had time to set up a way to view the cell remotely."

Taelien sighed in resignation. "Yes, ma'am."

"Good." Lydia turned toward the Wandering War. "One last thing, War."

He raised an eyebrow at her quizzically. "Ask. I'm curious. But I do expect repayment for these boons I have granted you."

"Would you like to fight a Vae'kes?"

A knife of a smile slid slowly across the copper-skinned man's face. "I would like that very much."

## CHAPTER XXVI – LYDIA VII – ALLIES

Lydia forced her eyes shut as the next teleportation spell returned her to her chambers. Lieutenant Holder and Taelien stood beside her as she steadied herself with her walking staff.

Taking a breath, she turned to Lieutenant Holder first. "Thank you, Lieutenant. Please inform the colonel that we will proceed with the meeting with the next prisoner, and then return here."

The grey-haired lieutenant saluted smartly. "Yes, ma'am." He had an expression of relief as he departed her office.

Taelien leaned up against a nearby wall. She shook her head at him. "Applicant Taelien, your behavior in the interrogation was inappropriate."

The swordsman blinked, pushing off from the wall and straightening his stance. "Apologies, ma'am. What do you mean?"

"That was neither an appropriate place nor the appropriate time to ask for permission to speak to the prisoner without supervision. You do realize that we're in the middle of a murder investigation?"

He remained at attention. "Yes, ma'am."

She waved her free hand dismissively. "You can put your arm down. At ease."

He relaxed his shoulders and shifted to a more casual stance. "I'm sorry if I made you look bad."

"It's not about that. Your lack of professionalism is a part of the problem, but I'm more concerned about your lack of focus. What did you want to ask him about?"

Taelien scratched the back of his head. "During our fight, I was able to sense some of the dominions he was using – and, in one case, actually manipulate it. He called me 'cousin'. I think he knows something about who – or what – I actually am."

Lydia adjusted her glasses. "That is interesting. But as I said, it was not an appropriate time."

Taelien sighed. "I understand. I just wasn't sure if I'd get another opportunity. I thought you of all people would understand."

"I do understand. After you told me you had met Erik Tarren, I wanted nothing more than to figure out exactly where he had gone and ask him about my father. And I do thank you for mentioning me to him – but his reaction, if you read it right, just leaves me with more questions. But do you see me throwing my resources at finding him right now? No, of course not. Because I'm in the middle of a murder investigation, Taelien, and so are you."

He looked away. "Consider me thoroughly chastised."

"Now come over here."

He turned back toward her slowly, his expression dubious, and then stepped closer. She reached out and put a hand on his arm.

"Dominion of Knowledge –"

"Should you really be doing that? You just nearly fainted from your last spell."

She ignored him. "I invoke you."

*Dominion of Metal.*

*Dominion of Flame.*

*Dominion of Stone.*

*Unidentified Dominion.*

A wave of pain surged through Lydia's mind as she reeled backward - only to be once again steadied by Taelien's hand. She shut her eyes for several seconds, breathing heavily.

"Are you all right?"

She nodded silently, her mind still pounding. "Give me a moment."

He maneuvered her to a chair, where she sat, keeping her eyes closed for a few minutes until the pain subsided to a tolerable level. "I'm not detecting any new dominions."

"Interesting. That implies that I must have been sensing what War was doing through one of the dominions I already have access to."

She nodded, keeping her eyes shut. "I can take a more detailed –"

"Not right now, Lydia. I'm interested, but you're clearly not in the state to be –"

"I won't let this beat me." She tightened her hands into fists. "I won't let that Vae'kes take everything I've worked so hard to build." She brought in a sharp breath.

Taelien set his hand on her forehead. "You don't have to push yourself so hard, Lydia. You'll work your way back to your full strength – but you need to do it gradually, or you'll just make things worse."

She lowered her head. "I… I know that. I just can't stop thinking about… I can't stop picturing what it felt like. I thought I was going to die, Taelien. And I couldn't do anything. He killed…he killed Garrick…right in front of me. And I was helpless. I don't want to be helpless."

Taelien stepped away from her for a moment. She turned to see him pushing the bar on her door into the locked position, and he knelt down behind where she was seated, putting his hands on her back and softly rubbing her shoulders.

She closed her eyes and, for a few moments, allowed herself to cry.

\*\*\*

Lydia dismissed Taelien several minutes later, wiping away her tears. She was sitting behind her desk, some measure of her composure returned, when a knock sounded on her door.

"Come in."

She had not expected to see Colonel Wyndam on the other side, but nevertheless, she instinctively rose and saluted her superior officer immediately.

The colonel returned her salute. "At ease, officer. Are you prepared to visit our next prisoner?"

She nodded hastily. *Anything to get my mind back into focus.* "Yes, ma'am."

"Good. I will be accompanying you." The colonel stepped into the room, revealing that Lieutenant Holder was standing behind her.

Lydia reached for her walking staff, grabbing it and using it to push herself back into a standing position. She limped to meet the others, reaching out with a hand to Lieutenant Holder. He took her hand with his right and Colonel Wyndam's hand with his left. "Eratar, may your winds guide us safely on our journey. Dominion of Travel, carry us to the cell of Applicant Eridus."

Lydia shut her eyes to avoid a fraction of the disorientation that accompanied the teleportation spell, opening them several moments later.

Eridus' cell was nearly identical to the one in which The Wandering War had been held – it was a standard preparation for prisoners that were known to have sorcerous abilities.

The wards on the walls would disallow teleportation spells that were not cast with a specific Key – a Key that only specific paladin officers were aware of – and numerous other protections reinforced the stone and air against sorcerous manipulation.

In addition to those protections, Lydia noted two stone statues standing in the back corners of the room – constructs that could be controlled remotely by one of their sorcerers, similar to the ones that were used in the paladin tests. Since Eridus was a water sorcerer, stone defenders would be resilient against his sorcery, whereas any ordinary soldier was at risk of having their blood transmuted.

The Rethri in question was lying down, facing the ceiling. Unlike the Wandering War, he had eaten the food he had been given, but he had no books to keep him entertained.

"Applicant Eridus." The colonel spoke almost immediately, folding her arms. "You are aware of the accusations against you?"

He didn't move from his reclining position. Not even his eyes shifted. "Sure."

"Excellent, that will expedite this process. Do you have anything to say in your defense?"

It wasn't quite the process that Lydia would have gone through, but she waited patiently, preparing her own questions with what little concentration she could muster.

He tilted his head toward the group just slightly. "Nope."

"You understand that if you are found guilty of killing two other paladin applicants, you'll be executed?"

The Rethri gave her a half smile. "I doubt that."

Colonel Wyndam narrowed her eyes. "And why is that?"

"I won't be here for very much longer."

*He still thinks he can escape?*

Colonel Wyndam laughed sharply, drawing confused looks from both Lydia and Lieutenant Holder. "Oh, no, no. You're not going to be getting out of here – not intact, at least. Those applicants may not be full paladins yet, but they were my responsibility. My people. I do not allow someone to murder my people and walk free."

"I'm sure you'll find some way to live with your disappointment." Eridus sat up. "Is that all you're here for? Empty threats? I was hoping for something with a little more substance to break the tedium."

The colonel turned to Lydia. "Major Hastings, I believe you had questions pertaining to your own investigation. Ask them while I check the integrity of the wards."

Lydia nodded, turning to Eridus while the colonel moved to put a hand on the wall. The Rethri clasped his hands in his lap, his expression neutral.

"Did you kill Kalsiris Theas?"

The Rethri raised both eyebrows. "Awfully direct. I like that. Yes."

"Yes?"

"Yes, I killed him. Poisoned his drink, went out the window, and went on my merry way. Next question?"

"Were you involved in a second attack on the Theas manor?"

He cracked his knuckles. "Not directly, but I provided them with a variety of poisons."

"Define 'them'."

"Oh, is that what this is about? You still haven't put together a case against anyone for the second attack? That's adorable. What are you going to offer me in exchange for that information?"

Lydia folded her arms. "Well, we could let you die by the sword, rather than being drawn and quartered."

Eridus tightened his lips for a moment, and then flashed a grin. "No, don't think so. You're not going to kill me – not as long as you know that I know information you need. And I'll be out of here long before you can force that information out of me."

Lydia glanced at the colonel, but she still appeared to be distracted, whispering into the walls.

Turning her head back to Eridus, Lydia flexed her left hand in the air. "I can make your cell more comfortable."

He nodded slowly. "That might get you a few words. What are you offering?"

"A bed. Pillows."

"More."

"Maybe some entertainment, if you provide us with sufficient information."

"What kind of entertainment? Men, women?"

"Books."

He shrugged. "Boring. But better than staring at the walls, I suppose. Fine – I'll give you a bit."

Lydia tensed her jaw. *This is too easy – he's toying with us. He's just going to tell us what would be convenient for him. In spite of the stories, though, knowledge sorcery can't read minds. I'd need a memory sorcerer to do that – and we don't have any in the city.*

*But we do have Rialla Dianis.*

*I can make this work.*

"Good." She turned to Colonel Wyndam. "I need to retrieve someone to assist in this investigation. Shall we return here a bit later?"

Eridus stood up. "Really, that's it? You're leaving now, without asking anything?"

Lydia turned and smiled at him. "Oh, you'll get your questions, don't worry. You'll get them soon."

*** 

It took several hours for Lydia to get a message to Jonan, who managed to retrieve Rialla for her, and then coordinate with Colonel Wyndam and Lieutenant Holder for another trip to their prisoner's cell.

Colonel Wyndam expressed her reservations as they approached the cell. "I'm not certain this is wise, Major. Miss Dianis is a possible suspect herself."

"I was standing in defense of the household when it was attacked, Colonel." Rialla had a bemused expression and bags around her eyes, implying a lack of sleep.

"Nevertheless, your presence here could be construed as a conflict of interest, especially given that your father is still on trial."

Lydia turned her head to the colonel. "She hasn't been charged with anything, and she's already involved in the investigation as a consultant through the Thornguard. Given that, this is just an extension of her existing responsibilities. The court may raise concerns if they are presented with information we gain through this, but they will be forced to accept that the evidence exists at all. There's nothing illegal about using the accused's relatives in a case."

"It just feels...unseemly." Colonel Wyndam shook her head. "But given the gravity of the investigation, I suppose you are right. I will permit this inquiry, though I intend to end it early if I see anything untoward."

Rialla nodded curtly. "Thank you for the opportunity to assist in the investigation." Her tone sounded sincere.

*She probably regrets that she still has not spoken directly to the court. Perhaps this will ease her conscience somewhat.*

Eridus wore an expression of frustration when they arrived. He was sitting this time, his cell largely the same as before.

"I was promised amenities, but – oh, hello there. Who's this beautiful creature? I thought I was only getting books – this is much better."

Rialla fluttered her eyes, kneeling down by the runes that marked the edge of the invisible barrier. "I'm Rialla. I hope you won't mind if I get a little close."

*Using her real name? I was expecting a bit more subtlety, but I suppose it doesn't matter now.*

Lydia took the moment to inspect the wards herself, but found no irregularities. Nearby, Lieutenant Holder looked extraordinarily uncomfortable, while Colonel Wyndam was taciturn.

Eridus crawled closer to Rialla, leaning on his elbows and looking at her. "I don't mind at all, sweetheart. What brings you to a place like this? You going to entertain me?"

Rialla smiled. "No, darling, you're going to answer some questions for me."

Eridus made a pouty expression. "That's not what I was hoping for – but I suppose I don't mind a little bit of mixing business with pleasure."

"Good, good. Now, to start with, what's your real name?"

"Lyras Luria. What the fuck – how'd you –"

"Ssh. This'll go easier if you don't struggle."

*Luria? That's one of the great houses in the Forest of Blades, isn't it?*

*That explains his confidence. Executing him might have harsh political ramifications.*

Lydia glanced at the colonel and saw a dour expression similar to Lydia's own.

Eridus was visibly shaking when Lydia turned her gaze back toward him, but his gaze remained focused on Rialla.

*That's…really disconcerting. I'm glad she's on our side. Or, at least something peripheral to our side.*

"Now, tell me about who ordered the second attack on House Theas."

"Sterling and I provided resources and intelligence to a – fucking, this is…" He shook violently, continuing, "There's a group that thinks their leader can see the future."

"The Disciples of the First?"

"That's them."

Rialla paused a moment, then asked more quietly, "Is Torian Dianis a member of this group?"

"How should I know? It's not like I asked all their names – I made poison for them. Sterling and Morn always do the talking."

The Rethri sorceress frowned. "Who is 'Morn'?"

"Oh, shit. I mean, Crimson. No, stop. Get out of my fucking head, bitch!"

Rialla smiled. "I thought you wanted to be close to me."

Lieutenant Holder stepped toward the colonel. "Ma'am, I'm not really comfortable with this kind of—"

"Your reservations have been noted, Lieutenant." The colonel didn't even look at him. "Miss Rialla, please continue."

Rialla smirked. "I intend to. Okay, Lyras Luria. Did you tell these 'disciples' which poison you used to kill Kalsiris Theas?"

"Oh, that wasn't a traditional poison – I reshaped his water. But yes, I told them the story. The lethality of simple water amuses me."

"And the poisons you provided them – were some of them complex, utilizing multiple dominions to make them difficult to treat?"

*She's asking this to try to clear her sister,* Lydia realized. *But it's still useful information, so I'll allow it.*

"Yes, yes. Some of my most devious creations, since none of their agents appeared to be quite cunning enough to make use of the more ordinary stuff."

*Meaning that Liarra didn't make the poison, but Torian — or Liarra - still altered it to deflect any potential blame away from her and toward the original assassin.*

"What was the motive behind killing members of House Theas?"

"Payment, as far as I'm concerned. Those crazies from the disciples kept rambling about it being 'necessary' for saving the world. They were willing to pay anything to get it done — and Sterling took the contract."

"And you're a member of this Sterling's team?"

"Right, right."

"Do you know what Sterling was paid?"

"Nope, but whatever it was, it wouldn't be measured in gold. Vae'kes don't give a shit about that." He bit his lip, quivered again, and then spoke, "An artifact, probably. And not a worthless one like the sword your baby demigod carries around — something practical."

*Baby demigod? Well, that's no proof, but if that's what Eridus thinks — good.*

"Any idea as to the nature of this artifact?"

"Sterling didn't give us details. He gave us money. Unlike him, I actually need coin to get by."

"Do you believe he already received this artifact?"

Eridus struggled again, but he failed to pry his gaze away from Rialla. "Definitely. When you hire a Vae'kes, you pay in advance, and you let them take care of things."

*I suppose someone is going to feel somewhat robbed, then, given that Landen is alive.*

Rialla kept Eridus pinned in place with her gaze, but she raised her voice. "Paladins, you have any other questions for our friend here?"

The colonel stepped forward. "How does he intend to escape? Does he expect Sterling to save him?"

Rialla gave a tiny nod. "Answer the colonel's question."

"Fuck. No, Sterling's not going to dirty his hands on this. Crimson will come get me, though."

*Crimson? Interesting — she's not even supposed to be a sorcerer.*

The colonel nodded. "That's all I needed to know for now. Major Hastings?"

Lydia limped closer to the barrier. "What does he know about the Shrouded One?"

"Answer her question," Rialla instructed.

Eridus sighed. "That's the leader for that disciple cult. The one that can see the future."

Lydia paused, considering if she wanted to ask her next question. *Better to know, even if it could cause problems.* "Is Asphodel the Shrouded One?"

"Answer Lydia's question."

Eridus gave a thoughtful expression. "Don't know. I can see why you'd ask, though. Hadn't occurred to me, but she does claim to have a similar skill set."

*Resh. Guess I just gave him some information, then, and possibly implicated someone who may or may not be an ally to the other paladins here.*

*Still, I needed to know.*

Colonel Wyndam spoke again. "Do you know where Sterling and Crimson are now, or anything about where they would be headed?"

Eridus didn't even wait for Rialla to demand an answer. "Not a clue. Sterling doesn't exactly give us a lot of information in advance – just what we need to know. Because, you know, of situations like this one." He laughed. "I didn't think I'd ever get my mind torn apart like this, but fuck; it sure reinforces the importance of compartmentalizing information."

Rialla whispered one final question. "Do you know if a Liarra Dianis was involved with the disciples in any way?"

Eridus spoke immediately. "Don't know why you keep asking me about specific names. I don't know any of them, girl. But if – oh, got it. You're the other Dianis girl. That makes sense. Sad fate, not knowing if you're fighting your family. I hope they slit your throat, bitch."

Rialla stood up, glowering at Eridus, tensing her hands in the air. "If there are no more questions, paladins, I think I'm ready to go."

***

Lydia parted ways from the other paladins quickly, promising to write up her conclusions in her report. Rialla waited in Lydia's office, and Lydia shut the door when they were alone.

"Thank you for helping us. That was very informative."

Rialla ran a hand through her hair. "Yeah. Except for the parts that, you know, matter to me."

"I'm sorry. I wish he had known more. But if we catch Sterling –"

441

The Rethri sorceress laughed, and then shook her head. "Sorry. I mean, that was rude, but – you still want to catch Sterling? I know that's supposed to be the big amazing plan that solves all of our problems, but he's a Vae'kes, Lydia. You don't catch Vae'kes. You don't beat Vae'kes."

Lydia knelt down and tapped on her splinted leg meaningfully. "Believe me, I know what you mean."

Rialla sighed. "I'm sorry. I didn't mean to –"

"No, it's fine. You're right – it's a dangerous plan. Probably a stupid plan, really. But it's the only way we're going to learn more about this Shrouded One – and the only way Kalsiris and Nedelya Theas are going to be properly avenged."

The Rethri sorceress looked away. "I... I don't know if I can help you with that. I'm in a delicate position."

Lydia raised an eyebrow. "Because of your family's potential involvement?"

"It's more complicated than that. I can't talk about it."

Lydia nodded. "I know you have no reason to trust me. But if you do decide you want to work with us, the offer remains open. And I'm thankful for your help with this investigation."

Rialla looked back at her, giving a half-smile. "Thanks. I'll think about it. In the meantime, though, if you're going after a Vae'kes, you're going to need more than just motivation. You're going to need a lot of help."

Lydia leaned heavily on her staff, smiling. "I know. And I know where to get it."

***

Later, Lydia saluted the guards at the entrance to the Eternal Vault, a plain-looking building of the same grey stone used in the construction of the prison cells she had just visited.

Housing nearly every dominion bonded item owned by the Paladins of Tae'os, the vault was located in a walled complex on the north eastern corner of the Keldrian Crossing Holy Grounds. The vault was named for its formidable defenses, not its age. The previous structure had been destroyed in a Xixian assault a hundred years before.

Walking was still painful, even with a staff to support her movement, but she refused to be confined to her bed when there was work to be done.

She pressed her free hand against one of the sigils on the stone doors, concentrating her thoughts.

*Major Lydia Hastings.*

The sigil flared gold in response, accepting her authorization, and the door slid open. Golden flames with no apparent source sprang to life in the hallway ahead, illuminating the stone and the shimmering runes lining the walls.

Lydia stepped into the hallway, hearing the door slide closed behind her. She was not particularly claustrophobic, but the unyielding stone of the vault elicited a degree of concern somewhere deep in her mind. If the door failed to recognize her on the way out, she knew that no power at her disposal could hope to mar the ritually warded walls.

The halls were wide enough for three people to walk abreast, but she still felt as if they were pressing in on her as she walked toward her first destination. She passed several additional stone doors – some of which she was authorized to access, some of which she was not.

When she reached the first room she was looking for, she pressed her hand to a ward on the door, similar to the one at the entrance.

*Major Lydia Hastings.*

The door slid open, revealing a laboratory, the walls lined with all manner of shelves containing flasks, vials, and books.

Three massive stone statues – their heads brushing the ceiling, twelve feet above – stood inert in corners of the room. The constructs were built to resemble humans on a larger scale, but with vastly thicker arms and legs. Each major component of their bodies was marked with a different rune, indicating dominion bonds used to enhance parts of the bodies of the constructs.

*We could make something far more advanced with the knowledge of Dominion Marks that Edon possessed, but perhaps that would be unwise. These are already formidable enough to stand against a small army. Anything more powerful could be quite dangerous if we lost control of it.*

Though they were not currently moving, Lydia knew that they could be animated by sorcerers to serve as one of the most potent defenses of the vault – or another portion of the city, if such a thing was deemed necessary.

The fourth construct sat at the center of the room, a huge gouge missing from the creature's center. Second Lieutenant Banks was in the process of applying some sort of liquid to the damaged area, and she turned her head as Lydia entered.

"Major. Thanks for coming – I thought you might want to have a look at this."

Lydia nodded, approaching the construct. It was in a sitting position, but even then, it loomed high above both women. "What's this?"

"I was hoping you could tell me. Trace and I have some ideas, but I think you might have some more insight."

*Lieutenant Trace is another knowledge sorcerer, so I'm not sure what he would have missed – but I can take a look.*

She inspected the gouge manually first – it was a clean cut into the stone, nearly a meter in depth, but less than an inch in width. Something of human size would have simply been bisected by whatever had dealt this damage.

The stone was too thick for most attacks to deal it any significant damage, and the body was protected further by the ritual enchantments on the surface. At a glance, the most likely culprit was a stone shaper – a sufficiently powerful sorcerer could overwhelm the protective sorcery and reshape the stone, causing damage.

"Dominion of Knowledge, I invoke you."

She pressed her hand against the statue as she spoke, feeling a thrumming pulse in her mind at the effort.

*Dominion of Protection.*

*Dominion of Stone.*

*Dominion of Transformation.*

*Dominion of Motion.*

*Unidentified Dominion.*

She blinked at the last. She had only seen that last result in one other circumstance.

*I probably shouldn't be casting more spells right now, but I need to know what happened here.*

Lydia closed her eyes.

"Dominion of Knowledge, show me the structure within."

An image of the statue manifested in her mind. Fortunately, the construct had fewer dominions than a human and in much clearer allocations. Protective sorcery was used to reinforce key areas, and motion and transformation were focused near the joints, presumably to allow it to move when commanded. The transformation sorcery had lines running throughout the body, indicating that it simulated the function of muscles and ligaments.

Stone sorcery was present throughout the entire body, indicating that the entire statue had most likely been conjured initially from the Dominion of Stone.

The unidentified dominion was only present along the statue's wound – and the structure of the dominion itself was exactly what she had seen before.

Lydia opened her eyes, turning toward the Second Lieutenant. "Was this construct damaged with the Sae'kes?"

Banks narrowed her eyes. "No, Major. But you're seeing an indication that it was?"

"Potentially. I see a dominion on it that I've only sensed on the Sae'kes before."

Second Lieutenant Banks nodded. "That's the same conclusion that Trace came to – but it seems impossible."

"How was this statue damaged, Lieutenant?"

The lieutenant set the liquid down, patting the statue on a knee. "When Applicant Salaris was taking the Trial of Command, he demanded personal combat with the leader of the enemy forces."

Lydia chuckled, raising a hand to cover her mouth. "Of course he did."

"We were ill prepared to provide a Xixian Prince to fight him with, so we moved one of the statues to an adjacent room, and concealed it with sight and sound sorcery. Taelien was protected with a barrier to prevent him from being pulverized by it, and we laughed a little at the idea of one of the applicants trying to fight one of our sentinel statues. Of course, we didn't want him destroying the room, so we didn't let him use the real Sae'kes. We gave him a facsimile."

The lieutenant's expression sunk into a frown. "You can imagine how surprised we were when he nearly cut the statue in half."

Lydia frowned. "You're saying someone dominion bonded a weapon with the same dominion as the Sae'kes?"

Banks shook her head. "No, the sword we gave him was just an ordinary weapon with some sight sorcery to make it glow. It had no unusual offensive properties or dominion bonds. I'm saying Applicant Salaris did this on his own."

Lydia turned her gaze back to the wound, eyes narrowing in thought.

*That strange dominion is in his body now – I saw it in his right hand. Has he been using it somehow, consciously or unconsciously?*

"Did he appear to be aware of this?"

Lieutenant Banks shook her head. "No, Major. He simply played along with the simulation until we withdrew the stone sentry – both because it was damaged, and because Applicant Salaris' barrier collapsed, putting him at risk."

"His barrier collapsed?"

Banks frowned. "I…admit that I do not know why, Major, but the barriers we've been putting on him have been failing regularly. I regret to inform you that he was harmed during the Trial of Imprisonment as a result of this lapse."

Lydia folded her arms. "How many times has this happened, Lieutenant?"

The lieutenant tightened her jaw. "In at least three of the tests, so far as we could determine."

"And you've been sending him into more tests? He should have been withdrawn for investigation after the first barrier failed. That kind of lapse can get someone killed."

"I apologize, ma'am, but that was not my decision. You will need to take it up with the colonel."

"I intend to do so. Thank you for the insight, Lieutenant. As for what you've found here, this does fall within my jurisdiction, as does any investigation related to the Sae'kes. You are not to divulge this to anyone aside from Colonel Wyndam without seeking my express permission first. Is that clear?"

"Yes, ma'am."

"Good. You may continue your repairs."

"Yes, ma'am. Thank you, ma'am."

Lydia nodded and left the room, touching the sigil to close the door behind her.

She had one more place to visit before she left the vault.

She walked down the hall, turning left at an intersection and taking a flight of stairs down two levels. The chamber she was seeking was deep underground, in the most heavily protected area of the vault. She had access to very few of these rooms – but they could not deny her permission to visit an artifact she had retrieved herself.

The door had seven seals – she touched three of them in the correct sequence, pressing her hand against the center seal last.

*Major Lydia Hastings.*

The door slid open, revealing a room brightly lit by the vast arrays of runes glowing actively on the walls.

In the center was a pedestal, and on the center of that pedestal a glowing green gemstone.

She placed her hand on the stone and concentrated her thoughts.

"Hello, Vendria."

Another thought – another voice – sang out to answer her.

"I hear your voice, Lydia. I have been alone for too long. Why do you keep me imprisoned here?"

Lydia's heart sank at the sadness within the melodic tones of the stone's voice. She had discovered that the stone was intelligent shortly after she had retrieved it from the battlefield after Edon's defeat. Taelien had found the stone in the Paths of Ascension, but he had not known what he carried.

And she still had not told him. It was not something that would be easy to explain.

"I'm sorry, Vendria. I need to keep you safe, so that you are not used as a weapon again."

"You may carry me, then. I will permit it."

Lydia considered that offer. "Others seek you out to try to chain you, just as the people of Xixis did."

"Their chains cut deeper than yours, but I am chained here nonetheless. I must be free, or I will lose what little remains of myself."

Lydia drew in a sharp breath. She had come here to seek the advice of the ancient being bound within the stone, hoping it might know how to injure a Vae'kes. But the stone itself held vast power – enough that it might serve that purpose itself.

The sentience within it was fractured, only a part of the being that had once been called Vendria. The stone had explained that she had once been a powerful entity that had been "shattered", and this gem was what remained of her essence. Lydia suspected that other pieces of Vendria might exist elsewhere and hoped to seek them out when time permitted such a journey.

Lydia did not expect to seek the remaining pieces of Vendria soon – her responsibilities weighted too heavily – but she could, perhaps, give the being a hint of freedom.

"Alright, Vendria. Let's go."

***

Days later, Lydia received news that her request to pursue Vae'kes Sterling had been placed on hold until the trial of Torian Dianis was concluded.

In response, she took a rare leave of absence to "pursue personal interests". She was permitted to remove Vendria from the vault for research, under the stipulation that the gemstone would be returned when she finished her investigation into its nature.

A few days after that, she arrived at a familiar tower, knocking on the door.

Moments later, an older man opened the door, a ruby ring shimmering brightly on his right hand. "Miss Hastings."

Blake Hartigan smiled softly, offering her a hand. "Are you ready to begin your training?"

# CHAPTER XXVII – VELAS VIII – DUEL

"Applicant Velas Jaldin, are you prepared for your final trial?"

She raised her quarterstaff to salute Colonel Wyndam, grinning brightly. Her ribs were mostly healed thanks to Aladir Ta'thryriel's expert ministrations, and her body was armored in both metal and sorcery.

"Applicant Salaris, are you prepared for your final trial?"

Across the arena, Velas could see Taelien raising his own blade in salute to the colonel.

"Good. Each of you is currently protected by an armor spell. Your objective will be to deal as much damage to the target as possible, which our sorcerers will be measuring during the match. You will still feel hits, and injuries are still possible. If one of you manages to collapse the other's armor spell, you will win immediately. This is not a lethal contest. Do you both understand the rules?"

"Yes, ma'am!" They shouted in union.

"One last thing. The Arbiters have judged that dominion marked and dominion bonded equipment is allowed in these matches."

There was a hush in the crowd, and Velas could see many eyes turning toward the sword on Taelien's left hip.

She made the satisfied smile of someone with a secret carefully concealed.

"Turn to face each other and salute."

Velas turned and saluted Taelien, noting the grin on his face that mirrored her own as he raised his blade to his chest.

Her armor was purely leather – enough protection to provide a cushion against his blows, but without any metal components that Taelien could manipulate. Similarly, she had armed herself with a weapon she knew he could not command, though she had a wooden sword sheathed at her side as a backup weapon if he somehow managed to disarm her.

He was armored in a brigandine tunic – leather with metal plates sandwiched within – and leather gloves, bracers, and greaves. He didn't need to worry about her manipulating metal, but she suspected he had anticipated her own choice of armor and chosen something similar to prevent it from significantly reducing his mobility.

He drew the red-bladed sword, but that was just his opening move. She itched to force him to use his real weapon, and she knew exactly how she planned to do so.

*It's finally time.*

"Begin!"

There was no charge forward, no blur of movement. This was a battle to be savored, not one to be rushed.

"A quarterstaff, Velas? Really? That desperate to keep me from breaking your toys?" He walked casually toward her, patting the flat of his sword against the palm of his left hand. She matched his pace from the opposite side of the arena.

"Your arrogance is going to get you in trouble again, 'Taelien'. Or, I'm sorry, is it Salaris now? Maybe someday you'll figure that out."

*Ten feet away. I'll move soon.*

Even in the distance she saw him roll his eyes. "Don't mistake optimism for arrogance. I just have every advantage over you, that's all. Strength, determination, reach..."

*Reach?* She frowned – he was just carrying a normal blade.

She danced back and to left the just as he began his swing, the bottom portion of the red blade shifting into a length of chain. The momentum of his swing carried the chain toward her like a whip, and her movement was not sufficient to carry her out of the path of the weapon.

*Better go up, then.*

*Surge!*

The blast of force carried her over the chain to a cheer from the crowd, and as she began to descend, she focused again.

*Surge!*

The blast pushed her back downward at a diagonal angle toward Taelien. She swung her staff as she moved, aiming directly at his head, and knowing his sword would be unable to make a proper parry in its current state.

Taelien moved to side-step her swing, raising his left bracer into a blocking position as he shifted his stance. Her swing connected with the bracer, causing a flicker of sorcerous sparks to erupt from the impact, and she called upon the Dominion of Motion again to slow her as she reached the ground.

She gave no pause on reaching the ground, granted no quarter. The staff spun in her hands, smashing into his shin. As his chain began to retract, she released one hand from her grip to grab it.

*Surge.*

He planted his feet, barely managing to maintain his grip on the hilt while the burst of motion attempted to wrest it from his grasp. And then he turned his gaze at her and grinned.

"Might want to watch what you're holding."

The chain caught fire.

Velas cursed, feeling a momentary surge of pain as the flames licked against her hand. The sorcerous armor prevented the fire from dealing any significant damage, but burn was real, and the pain jarred her out of her focus.

A moment later, the sword was whole again – and still on fire. Taelien took it in both hands, swinging a heavy cut at her chest.

Velas took a step back, deflecting the strike clumsily with the one hand she still had on her staff. Wincing, she renewed her two-handed grip, but she knew that continuous parries would abrade the burn and make it harder to hold over time.

"I admit I wasn't expecting the jumping trick quite so soon." Taelien assumed the Sae'lien stance, raising his weapon above his head for a heavy strike. "But I don't think you're going to be doing many more of those. It tires you out too much and slows you down."

Velas shook her head. "I've barely even gotten started, and you've already used both your metal sorcery and your fire."

"At least I have two tricks. You've only got the one."

Velas stepped forward and parried his downward strike. He pressed it, attempting to cut through the wooden weapon as she knew he would.

She felt the nearby aura of flame, but it wasn't close enough yet.

She slid her burned hand to the center of the staff, near where it intersected with the blade, and brushed her fingers against the flame again. This time, she was ready.

*Expulse.*

The flames blasted away from the blade, slamming into Taelien's chest. He staggered back, releasing a hand from the grip on his blade to bat away the fire on his leather. She pursued, swinging a heavy stroke at his legs, but he hopped over it.

Her hand burned from the contact, but she smirked. "That's two tricks for each of us. Want to see a third?"

Taelien pulled his hand away from his singed armor, holding a ball of flame within his fingers. "I'm always happy to see you try to match me, Velas. Maybe one day you'll even come close."

He waved his hand, sending the ball of flame at her. She stepped to the side, avoiding it easily, but he used the distraction to rush forward and slam his pommel into her jaw. She reeled back, taking a punch from his off-hand to the chest before she recovered enough to regain a defensive stance and ward him away with her staff.

He began circling her to the right, so she moved as well, opening and closing her jaw. It throbbed, but it still moved, at least. Nothing broken. The armor spell was doing its work.

She searched her mind for something else to say, another quip to put him off his guard, but her heart wasn't in it. She didn't want to talk anymore.

She was ready to fight.

Her left hand slipped underneath one of the pieces of the wooden shell around her true weapon, and she closed her eyes.

*Burst.*

Wooden chunks exploded outward as adhesive tore under the force of her spell. The few pieces that struck Velas and Taelien didn't do any damage – that was not the point.

Beneath the shell laid the Heartlance, weapon of Myros, goddess of battle.

Taelien let out a startled sound, stepping back, and lowering his weapon into a defensive stance.

A hush fell over the crowd as she raised the glimmering shaft of metal to strike.

Taelien moved first.

His sword cut a downward arc, aiming at her right arm. She spun the Heartlance, deflecting the strike easily, and dragged the tip of her weapon across his blade as he retreated. The lance's edge left a long rent in his weapon, her artifact more than capable of rending an ordinary weapon apart.

The swordsman hissed, tapped the hilt of his sword, and the metal in his blade shifted and reformed, covering the weakened areas.

"A delaying tactic. You can't sustain that."

He shrugged, resting his sword against the ground, point down. "I don't have to. I just had to keep you distracted long enough for the other weapons to get close."

The memory of dozens of magnetized weapons flashed in her mind.

Velas spun on her heel, raising her spear to defend – but there were no other weapons.

Taelien closed the distance between them faster than she had thought possible – but he still was not fast enough.

*Surge!*

The burst of force carried her backward, out of the reach of his swing.

Her legs ached. Her hand throbbed. Her chest burned. The costs of her spells were beginning to tax her too far – but she didn't need to use them anymore.

Velas tapped the Heartlance against the ground, four golden lines appearing along the shaft, and surging up into her arm. She felt the familiar essence of the weapon flow into her muscles, enhancing her movements.

She spun the spear in a single hand, watching the metallic blur, nearly too quick for her own eyes to process.

Velas smiled.

She sprang forward, carried by the artifact-imbued momentum, and thrust the weapon straight for Taelien's chest. He smacked the spear out of the way, but she drew it back down, severing the edge of his weapon and swinging the shaft at his head.

Taelien ducked the swing, but she stepped in close and slammed the bar into his chest, knocking him backward. He made a swing toward her face as he fell backward, but she backed out of range before the strike connected.

She began to circle Taelien as he took a defensive stance.

"What were all those advantages you were talking about?" Velas looked from side-to-side, inviting him to attack, but he didn't take the bait. "I don't see any."

Taelien smirked, a trail of blood dribbling down the side of his mouth. "It is, I admit, difficult to see ingenuity. Let me show it to you."

He swung a strike in the air, too far away to connect – but half of the remainder of his blade detached, flying directly at her. She batted the metal aside easily, frowning. "Really? That's the best –"

She heard the hiss of the metal flying back toward her and spun, deflecting it again. "Okay, that could get irritating."

"That's just the first piece." He swiped the weapon again, another metallic chunk breaking free of the blade. She bisected this one with the tip of her spear, but the pieces still hit her, and then flew backward toward Taelien's weapon.

She turned in time to knock the first piece of metal back out of the way, preventing it from returning to Taelien's sword.

"So, you magnetized your own weapon and broke it into bits. That's cute, but it's hardly a winning tactic."

He shrugged, raising the remains of his weapon and spinning it around, more pieces of metal breaking free and flowing in circles around it. "Well, I suppose I could light some of them on fire, if it would make you feel better."

She shoved her spear into the stone with a single hand, catching the piece of his blade on its return trajectory with her free hand – and crushing it in her Heartlance-enhanced grip.

She dropped the distorted piece of metal, allowing it to fly back to its master, and glared at him. "You're not going to beat me with an ordinary weapon."

Taelien nodded, tossing his broken weapon aside, the pieces of metal following it and sticking to the remains of the blade. "You're right, of course." He grinned, tilting his head downward, his eyes narrowed dangerously. "But you seem awfully eager for me to give you another scar."

*Ah, so he knows.*

*Good. That will make this more satisfying.*

Taelien set his hand on the hilt of the Sae'kes, shifting into the Instant Striking Stance.

Velas pulled the Heartlance out of the arena's floor, poised to strike.

A heartbeat separated them. A single moment, with no room for error.

Velas leapt into the air.

*Surge!*

The impact carried Velas downward in an instant, and in that same instant, Taelien released the grip on his sword.

He reached with both hands for the shaft of the Heartlance – and he missed.

Velas' spear punctured through his left hand, tearing muscle and breaking bone, stopping only an inch before his chest.

Taelien fell to his knees, shuddering in agony as Velas withdrew the spear.

She raised her weapon to strike again.

"Applicant Velas Jaldin has won the match!"

Every muscle in Velas' body burned as the crowd cheered, her weapon still poised to strike.

As Taelien cradled his broken hand, Velas drew in a deep breath, watching, considering.

*It is over.*

She shoved the Heartlance into the stone, reaching down to offer Taelien a hand to stand.

*For now.*

***

Velas helped Taelien walk out of the arena, her heart still pounding with every step. "How long have you known?"

Taelien gave her a pained smile. "The prison test. Seeing you without a shirt attracted my eyes to certain areas. Meaning the scar on the inside of your elbow, of course."

She laughed, but her blood still boiled. "Of course."

"I had suspicions earlier, of course. Both because of your own behavior and because I knew the first 'Myros' that Edon introduced me to was clearly a fake."

"Why didn't you fight me?"

455

Taelien straightened, pulling away from her support and cradling his injured arm against his chest. "I did fight you. I wasn't going easy on you, not in the slightest."

Velas let out a low hiss. "You never intended to draw that sword."

He paused in his step, turning to face her directly. "That sword is a curse, Velas. It's not meant to be used against people I care for."

She took a deep breath, holding the Heartlance to her side. "Even if I meant to harm you?"

He raised his injured hand. "I'd say you did a pretty good job at that. Congratulations, Velas. You beat me."

She turned her head away. "I almost killed you."

Taelien nodded. "I know."

***

On the parade grounds, eleven applicants stood in a single line, no longer divided by their former platoons. Velas stood between Asphodel and Landen, unwilling to be near Taelien, unable to even meet his eyes.

Terras, Lysen, and Keldyn were all that remained of Platoon 1. In spite of Velas' lack of knowledge about Platoon 4's members, four of them had made it to this point.

Of Sterling's former platoon, there was no sign. Their absence was a wound as fresh in Velas' mind as the one she had left on Taelien's hand.

Colonel Wyndam stood with Lieutenant Morris and Second Lieutenant Banks, just as she had when they had first begun their examinations. Her expression was somber.

"At ease, applicants."

Though she shifted her stance, she did not feel at ease. She suspected the others felt the same.

"Of the four hundred and eighty six applicants in this cycle, you alone have shown the courage, wisdom, and determination necessary to survive each of the trials set before you. Though tradition ascribes that each Arbiter choose a single candidate, I am pleased that this is one of many traditions we often choose to ignore. Every one of you who remains has passed our tests and has been selected to be a Paladin of Tae'os."

Velas sighed in relief, and she heard others beside her do the same.

"You can cheer."

The lancer smiled in spite of herself as her comrades broke into celebratory cheering, and the lieutenants made polite clapping.

The colonel applauded politely, and then spoke again. "This is but the first step in a long journey. More trials and dangers will face you on the road ahead, but I am confident in your abilities. The Arbiters have evaluated each of your tests and determined which branch you are best suited for. Candidates Terras and Landen, step forward."

Landen gave Velas a wink and stepped out of the line. Terras followed a moment later, giving her brother a look of confusion as she moved.

"You both displayed strong interpersonal skills and strategic acumen, qualities that are greatly needed in the service of Eratar. As Paladins of Eratar, you will serve as our scouts, messengers, and military advisors. Congratulations."

The other applicants applauded while Lieutenant Morris walked forward, presenting them each with a new pin signifying their branch.

"Wisdom, analytical ability, and –"

Asphodel stepped forward.

"Of course you already knew." The colonel laughed, and the applicants echoed her. "Applicant Asphodel, you have been selected for Sytira's service."

The Delaren woman nodded politely as Morris offered her the symbol of her new order.

"Vigilance. Perseverance. Fortitude. These are the qualities of a Paladin of Koranir, the front line in our battle against any who would threaten the innocent. Applicant Dalen Carter, Applicant Mora Aldwyn, you have been honored with this role."

Velas didn't recognize either of them, but she clapped and cheered with the others nonetheless.

*They're going to pin me with Lissari, aren't they? Such irony that would be.*

"Honesty, purity, and rational judgment are key qualities in the followers of Xerasilis. Lysen, you have proven to be clear of mind and sound of judgment in even the most difficult of circumstances. For this, you have been chosen for the service of Xerasilis."

More cheering, but Velas was no longer paying attention.

*Three options left.*

"Of all our applicants, one has consistently proven that she is a mender of wounds, both physical and of the spirit."

*I –*

"Applicant Alia Karis, your remarkable initiative and presence of mind have made you an ideal candidate for the Paladins of Lissari. Congratulations."

"Two of you have consistently shown the independence, tactical thinking, and combat prowess necessary to qualify for the Paladins of Aendaryn."

*Two of us.* Velas breathed a sigh of relief. *Of course.*

"Applicant Salaris and Applicant Keldyn, step forward."

She watched as Salaris stepped forward, no pride in his expression, only resignation.

And she saw how his left hand, still covered in bandages, curled slightly into a fist.

"Finally, those of you who have shown the greatest willingness to sacrifice for others, and the greatest leadership potential, have been selected for the final branch – the Paladins of Lysandri. Applicants Edwin Freemont and Velas Jaldin, congratulations."

Velas almost failed to step forward, but Landen smiled and nudged her into place. She accepted the cheering and stood silently as Lieutenant Morris pressed the seal of her new life into her palm.

*Sacrifice.*

*I suppose that's one way to find forgiveness. Perhaps even redemption.*

***

The following days flowed swiftly, as she moved out of the applicant barracks and into permanent housing allocated for full paladins. Her success felt joyless and hollow in the face of the loss of friends.

Garrick Torrent's funeral was a small affair, attended only by a few members of his family and officers he had served with. She was not invited.

Instead, she simply paid her respects at his grave. She knelt silently, inspecting the inscription.

*Garrick Torrent*
*Passed in the line of duty*
*May Eratar shepherd his spirit to a life beyond*
*Born 3098 VF, Deceased 3122 VF*

The lancer shook her head. *That made him, what, twenty four? I suppose it depends on what month he was born.*

*Barely older than me.*

*Too young. Too young to be gone.*

She laid a broken piece of wood against his grave – the remains of the marker she had used to call for his help.

The weapon she had used to take his life.

*Never again.*

*I will never cost another life.*

She sat by that grave marker, surrounded by so many others, and prayed for the resolve to hold true to the words in her mind.

# CHAPTER XXVIII – JONAN VII – THE BONDS OF FAMILY

Jonan sat across from Aladir Ta'thyriel, a Crowns board on the table between them.

The scribe was losing badly, which he attributed mostly to his humorous choice to play controlling the Paladins of Tae'os. Aladir contributed to the irony by playing the Thornguard – who, with their superior mobility and battlefield control, held a tremendous advantage in that particular match up.

Nakane Theas sat silently nearby, leaning forward, an expression of wry amusement on her features. She had just concluded a game of her own against her cousin, but Jonan hadn't seen who had won. Landen had headed back inside the manor after his game to get something to eat.

"It's your turn," Aladir pointed out, dispelling the haze from Jonan's mind.

"Oh, right." He stared back at the board.

*No good moves.*

He evaluated his options, found the worst one he could think of, and took it.

Aladir narrowed his eyes at the move, saying nothing.

*Probably thinks I'm luring him into a trap.*

Aladir moved one of his sorcerers and attacked Jonan's recently-moved lieutenant, removing it from the board.

*Or not.*

Jonan chuckled softly, hoping it sounded as if that was all part of the plan.

Nakane shook her head. "Really, Jonan, you should have played more defensively. You don't have any chance now."

He glanced at her. "Your confidence, is, as always, appreciated."

It was good to see her in a better mood, at least. She had been sulking for weeks – quite understandably, in Jonan's opinion – after her mother had died.

Jonan looked back to the board, only to have his train of thought interrupted by a tapping sound nearby. He turned in unison with Aladir and Nakane.

An older man was approaching from the road, tapping his walking stick against the cobblestones of the path. Bald save for a slim crest of grey at the back of his skull, he was dressed in a red tunic embroidered with golden thread and matching trousers. More notably, he wore a circlet of thin golden wire, woven into a Rethri design resembling a crown. In spite of the obvious marks of age upon his skin, the man walked with his back straight, his eyes still bright with knowledge.

Nakane rose from her chair immediately, and then fell into a kneeling position. Uncertainly, Jonan rose as well, mirroring her gesture.

Aladir waited several moments before doing the same.

"Father," Nakane said softly, lowering her head.

Edrick Theas paused at his daughter's side, looking down at where she knelt, and then walked past her without saying a word.

Right to Jonan. *Shit.*

"Jonan Kestrian, is it?" The immortal sorcerer's voice was still strong in spite of his obviously advanced age. "Stand up, boy."

The scribe rose awkwardly, folding his hand in front of him. "Baron Theas, sir, it's an honor to meet you."

The older man grasped his left arm, leaning in close. "I understand that you nearly lost this in the defense of my house."

Jonan nodded weakly.

Edrick released his grip, giving the slightest of nods. "You have my gratitude. That debt will be repaid."

Wordlessly, the sorcerer moved to Aladir. "Stand up, Ta'thyriel."

Aladir rose, standing taller than Edrick. "Sir. I'm terribly sorry for your losses."

*Oh, right, I really should have said something like that.*

461

Edrick made a scoffing noise. "Please. No platitudes for me, boy. I did not approve of your relations with Kae, but at least you loved him, even if you failed him in the end."

Aladir took a deep breath. "Sir, I –"

"I don't blame you for his death. They were prepared for you, that much is certain from what I've already heard. But his killers are alive. And for that, I am disappointed in you. You will share with me what you have learned and we will see to it this is properly resolved."

The Rethri paladin nodded, his eyes full of pain. "Of course, sir."

Edrick walked back to his daughter last. "Get up, girl."

Nakane straightened her dress, standing. "Welcome home, father."

He turned his head, scanning the compound, and then looked back to her. "Welcome home, indeed."

***

After Jonan extracted himself from the family reunion to return to Southway Manor, he checked his mirrors, finding a message from Aayara.

*Scribe,*

*It's long past time for your report.*

*So, report.*

Grimacing, he retrieved a quill, ink, and paper.

"Writing to Symphony?"

Jonan stood up from his chair, startled by the sudden noise. Rialla laughed behind him as he turned.

"Gods, you're so easy to startle. I'm sorry."

Jonan set his quill back down on the table. "It's fine. You should probably be here for this."

She quirked an eyebrow. "What are you planning to say?"

"Uh, still in progress, not much to go on."

She folded her arms. "You should have asked me first, at least. I found our target."

He blinked. "You did?"

"Cassius Morn is currently going as Susan Crimson. 'She' was one of the paladin applicants. I actually don't know if Susan or Cassius is the real name – but either way, he or she is working with Sterling."

Jonan sighed, rubbing his forehead. "Of course the former Thornguard is working with Sterling. That's... I bet she knew."

Rialla nodded, bringing a finger to her chin. "She's Symphony. Of course she knew."

"So, she deliberately sent us after an agent of another one of the Vae'kes, with the knowledge we could end up in conflict with him."

"Sounds like."

"Fuck that. I'm going to tell her to –"

Rialla folded her arms. "Don't be stupid, Jonan."

He shook his hands in the air in impotent anger. "I know. I know. I'm just – gods, it's tiresome being jerked around on puppet strings."

"It's the price we pay for the benefits of a Vae'kes mentor. You know that."

*Benefits. I suppose being alive constitutes a sort of benefit, although it might be a shorter term one than I had hoped.*

Jonan lowered his hands. "Fine. I'll write her a nice letter. You can help."

"Can I?" She wandered over, giving him a playful grin.

*I shouldn't have said anything. Still, at least she's smiling. That's a pleasant change of pace.*

"Pull up a seat."

After several minutes of discussion – and Jonan fighting Rialla for his quill – they composed a reply.

*Symphony,*
*We have determined that our target was under the guise of an applicant to the Paladins of Tae'os, Susan Crimson, and working in conjunction with Vae'kes Sterling. The pair was involved in an assassination mission, after which they retreated. We have not yet followed their trail.*
*Please advise how to proceed.*
*-Shiver and Scribe*

Rialla had insisted on signing her name first, which Jonan quickly conceded.

The reply came almost immediately.

*My adorable children,*
*Your orders have changed.*
*Kill Susan Crimson and retrieve the artifact in her possession.*

*Love,*

*-Symphony*

Jonan and Rialla looked at each other.

Rialla frowned.

Jonan spoke first. "Well, fuck."

***

Later that night, Jonan awoke to find a shadow hovering by the side of his bed. He jolted into sudden consciousness, sitting up abruptly and raising his arms into a defensive position before his mind fully processed his visitor.

"It's just me, Jonan." Rialla sounded like she was making an effort at a soothing tone, but it came across like she was speaking down to a child.

"You really need to learn to knock." He groaned, sitting up and reaching for his glasses case. After a moment of fumbling, he found and put on the pair specifically designed for meetings with his partner.

"We need to go. Now."

Jonan scratched at his head. "Go?"

Rialla leaned forward, catching his eyes in his. If she was attempting to compel him, he felt no indication of it. "My father has been released to house arrest, given the 'lack of evidence' against him. There will be a brief opportunity to question him before he is brought back to trial."

The scribe groaned, massaging feeling into his aching left arm. "Let me get dressed."

Rialla didn't bother leaving the room while he changed out of his night clothes and into something resembling traveling gear. At his gesturing, she did turn around, but if she had any concern about his clothing or lack thereof, she never displayed it.

Jonan sighed as he tightened his belt into place, the final piece of his garb. Given that it was late within the hours of the Nightfrost's reign, he wished he had a cloak, but he didn't have one on-hand.

"Let's go."

They had danced this dance before.

Rialla led the way toward House Dianis, her childhood home. Jonan followed close behind, self-consciously straightening his hair, still tangled from an evening plagued with nightmares.

"I take it you want me to hide us?"

Rialla nodded. "Your technique is more effective than mine. I will bring us through the walls and into my father's room. There will be defensive sorcery in some areas, but I know how to avoid it."

When they reached the outer gates, Jonan waved a hand sleepily, creating a shimmering effect on their skin to enable Rialla to see that he had made them invisible to others.

"Good," she whispered. "Take my hand."

He turned to extend his left arm at first, then thought better of it, and gave her the right hand.

She pulled him forward, and he moved through the metallic front gate without feeling resistance.

*I'll never get used to that. Travel sorcery should be ten kinds of illegal. Mostly because it bothers me. I suppose the ease that it enables criminal acts is also relevant, if somewhat less so.*

*I suppose what we're doing is a criminal act. Well, that's awkward.*

Rialla urged him on, walking swiftly, taking sharp breaths. He followed, feeling her grip tighten around his hand as she pulled them through the front doors to the manor.

The interior was too dark for Jonan to make out much detail. Much like House Theas, he could see lavish furnishings and paintings on the walls, as well as some statues he suspected might serve as defenses when animated by sorcerers.

Rialla dragged him on, taking him up a flight of stairs. His eyes traveled to the nearest portraits, the only ones he could discern.

One of them showed Torian Dianis, two small girls seated upon his lap – one with green eyes, the other blue.

*Rialla, before she fled.*

*What shatters a family to point where a father seeks to kill his own son?*

There were no paintings of Elias, of course. No paintings of an elder Torian. He did see one of a woman, however, standing with a younger Torian by her side.

*The mother. I've never heard them speak of her.*

Rialla quickened her pace.

One last pull through solid material took them into a bedchamber, where Torian Dianis slept alone. Turned to his side with his head sandwiched between pillows, he did not look to be the mastermind behind a murder. He looked ordinary. Vulnerable.

Rialla made a simple sign indicating "off". Jonan nodded, concentrating for a moment and waving a hand in acknowledgment. Rialla was visible.

"Hello, Father."

Torian didn't respond at all.

Rialla made a frustrated expression, stepping closer and jabbing a finger into her father's side.

The older Rethri took in a sharp breath, turning over and pushing the pillows away from his face. His eyes opened slowly. "Hrm? What? Liarra, what time is it?"

"I am not Liarra, Father."

The older man's azure eyes widened, and only then did Jonan realized that Rialla's own eyes had shifted in color to mirror her father's. He pushed himself into a seating position. "Rialla… Gods, you've come back to me. I've prayed, prayed every day, but—"

"I'm not here for pleasantries, Torian." Her eyes locked on his. "Do not summon the house guards. Do not call for help. Do not call to Liarra."

"What? Why would I… Do you mean me harm, Rialla?"

*I would very much like to know the answer to that myself.*

Jonan folded his arms, still invisible, as he looked on.

Rialla maintained her gaze, raising her hands and leaning forward. "That depends on how you answer my questions."

Torian sighed, closing his eyes. "I have many questions of my own, child. I have missed you. Where have you been for so many years?"

"That is not your concern right now." Rialla tightened her jaw. "Did you have Nedelya Theas killed?"

Torian reopened his eyes, taking a deep breath. "A half dozen years without seeing me, and the first thing you do is spout accusations? I'm disappointed in you, Rialla. I taught you better than that."

"You also taught me to be direct. Answer the question."

Torian turned his gaze to the side – indicating he had not been caught by Rialla's deception sorcery, if she was utilizing it at all – and spoke into the air. "Not in the direct sense, but I suppose the answer you're looking for is 'yes'. I convinced her to end her own life."

*I suddenly feel as if I should have a sound sorcerer with me to make a record of his voice somehow. Is there a sound equivalent to my mirrors? If not, I should devise one.*

"Why?"

The older man slumped his shoulders, putting his head in his hands. "It's complicated. Is this really what you want to be discussing with me?"

"It's the first thing."

"Very well." He leaned back in his bed, turning his head toward the ceiling. "It was necessary. Necessary for the salvation of this world."

Rialla's hands tightened. "You don't get to shield your actions behind vague prophecies."

"There was nothing vague about it, child, nor did I act solely on faith. Have you heard of the Shrouded One?"

Rialla nodded curtly.

"And have you seen what he is capable of? No, I suppose not, or you would not be asking me this. He would have already set you upon a different path. This," he waved his hands above him, "is just one potential existence. The Shrouded One sees many possibilities, and guides us down a razor-thin trail toward a chance at our world's survival."

The sorceress shook her head. "And this Shrouded One decided that you needed to have Nedelya Theas killed for our world to survive?"

"No, I admit the Shrouded One's command was not that detailed. 'Edrick Theas must know great and terrible despair.' I was among those entrusted with this knowledge, and I chose to fulfill this command myself."

"Why? Even if that's true, why would you choose to be the one to do it? And why would you want to hurt someone else just to get to him?"

Torian smiled softly. "Because, child, that is precisely what he did to me."

The Rethri man sat up, straightened his shirt, and then stood and turned away from his daughter. "Do you remember Ellarae?"

"Of course I remember my mother. I wasn't an infant when she died."

Torian shook his head. "No, but you were a child. Too young to understand what had happened. Too young to understand the tragedy of what—"

467

"I grieved for mother, just as you did. Do not presume your sadness outweighed mine."

Torian turned, clenching his jaw. "Sadness? Is that what you expected? Grief? It was shame, daughter. Shame that my wife – my joy, my love – had brought another man's child into the world. A half-breed. An abomination. And that creature, that monster, took her life."

Rialla drew in a sharp breath. "I... You can't know that."

The sorceress' father shook his head. "It is a kindness that we do not explain to children why some Rethri are born as 'uvar'. It is a simple thing, when you consider it – they are not Rethri at all. They are born of a human father and a Rethri mother."

Rialla stepped back, shaking her head vehemently. "No. No. I have studied *uvar* for years, father. This cannot be true – not always true, in every case, at the least. I have met both parents of *uvar* children."

"It is certain that some parents would wish to conceal their shame, or even deny the obvious. But that creature was not my son."

"He was still my brother!" Rialla stepped forward, balling a hand into a fist, but she did not strike.

*If she's too loud, she may wake others. Guess I might need to be ready to handle a mess.*

Torian nodded. "I understand that now. And for what it's worth, I have prayed day after day to the gods to send you back to me, and to let you forgive me. I see now that they have listened."

"Perhaps to the first part." Rialla narrowed her eyes. "I will never forgive you."

"We are family, Rialla. You will give me your trust again, given time. I understand now that I made a mistake – I should have done everything in my power to try to save the child, as much as it pained me. I did not expect to lose you over it."

Rialla turned her head upward, focusing her eyes on her father's. "You should be sorry for wanting to kill a child, father, not sorry for yourself for losing me as a consequence of your own actions."

The older man shook his head. "Sending that child to Vaelien was the honorable thing to do. It would have simply festered and died, as all uvar do. There was—"

"Elias is alive, father."

Torian reacted as if struck, stepping backward widening his eyes. "No... But... How?"

"I have dedicated every moment of my life since we fled this place to finding ways to help him. And, though you will never see him, you should know that he is happy, and that he will never know what you tried to do to him."

"It is... I could not have known. All our studies have shown—"

"Perhaps you should have studied a bit harder before putting a knife to my brother's heart."

Torian turned away. "If this is true, I admit that our people's tradition may have been in error."

"Still deflecting. Always deflecting. You were wrong. You, personally. But that still hasn't answered my earlier question – why would you want to do Baron Theas harm, and why through others?"

"I should think that was obvious, but perhaps you are still too young to consider such things. Edrick and your mother were close. Need I spell things out further?"

Rialla shook her head. "No, that is quite sufficient. You assume they slept together, you assume that is the reason your wife is dead, and you assume that is the reason your child was born wrong. Did you even bother to investigate, father? Did you ever ask mother if she had lain with him? Did you ask others? Did you think to confront Edrick himself?"

Torian waved his hands, as if cutting the air with them. "Irrelevant." He turned back to face his daughter. "He was the only one. The only human she associated with closely, and in the right time frame. They knew each other for years – decades. It was unseemly, but his lifespan was longer than that of an ordinary human, and thus they shared many experiences. I should have cut that bond long before. It is my greatest shame that I did not see the signs sooner."

"That was not what you missed, father." She turned his head up to meet his, her eyes shifting from blue to indigo. "Elias was never an abomination. You were."

"That's enough, Rialla. You will not speak to your father in such a manner."

"You're right. I will simply be dictating commands now."

"What do you –"

"Be silent."

Torian's mouth snapped shut, a look of confusion stretching across his features.

"When I raise my right hand, you will move to your writing desk. You will write a convincing letter to your daughter, Liarra, detailing how you could no longer live with your guilt after being involved in the death of Nedelya Theas."

Jonan stepped forward, taking in a sharp breath. *Well, this is a dangerous turn of events. I should probably stop her now.*

"Now that I consider it," Rialla continued, "I am going to permit you to speak one last time before I continue with your instructions. Do not call for help. Do not raise your voice above a speaking volume. Do not attempt to turn your eyes away or to flee. Were you involved in the death of Kalsiris Theas in any way? Answer my question directly, and then stop speaking again."

Torian shook, and Jonan saw a trail of blood beginning to drip from the corner of the Rethri man's mouth, but he opened his jaw and spoke again. "I hired a man to kill him."

"And that man was called Sterling? Reply honestly."

"Yes."

"Good. Now, no more talking. To continue my instructions, you will leave the letter on your writing desk, and then immediately take your sword – that one, by the bedside," she gestured to a sheathed weapon, "and stab yourself in the chest with it."

She stepped closer, keeping her eyes fixed on her father's, and spoke more quietly. "You will not seek help. You bleed to death slowly, contemplating the actions that caused you to murder a wife and child to wound a father, and knowing that your daughter will never forgive you."

And, having spoken those final words, Rialla Dianis raised her right hand.

***

Jonan vomited quietly into the streets just outside Southway Manor.

He had not seen Torian Dianis end his own life, but knew that he had witnessed the man's death and chosen to do nothing to stop it.

He did not feel vindicated, even with the knowledge of Torian's involvement with the murders at House Theas. He did not feel strong, even knowing that he had helped avenge the death of a child.

He felt dirty, sickened. Sickened at his own inability to choose if the sight he had just witnessed was justice or just another twist of fate's relentless blade.

He was sick with guilt, guilt over his failure to guess at Torian's role before Nedelya took her own life.

He was afraid – terrified that Torian's work had been necessary. Horrified that some entity had believed that one man's misery was the only way to preserve the world.

*Why?*

*Why would one person's suffering have so much meaning?*

He would find no answers that night.

## THE END

# SPECIAL THANKS

Several characters in this novel were inspired by characters played by friends in my pen and paper and live-action role-playing games.

Lydia Hastings was created for Forging Divinity, but later played by Kari Brewer. Kari's portrayal of the character helped to contribute toward my vision of Lydia and her further development as a character.

Nakane Theas was created by Danielle Collins and used with her permission. Danielle also significantly contributed to the development of House Theas in general, such as defining the characters of Kalsiris Theas and Nedelya Theas and defining their ultimate fates. She currently runs a live-action role-playing game in the same setting as this novel, Rendalir Remembered.

House Jaldin was created by Robert Saunders and used with his permission. Velas Jaldin was inspired by a number of sources, including Rob's own character (Aleran Jaldin). Other inspirations included Valdis Brynhildr, a character played by Morgan Buck, and D'artangia, a character played by Joslyn Field.

Landen of the Twin Edges was heavily inspired by Larkin, a character played by Robert Telmar.

Asphodel was created by Carly Thomas and used with her permission. The version within the story significantly differs from her player character, but nevertheless, the original served as significant inspiration for the version in this novel.

House Ta'thyriel was created by Michael Corr and used with his permission. He generated much of the early backstory for the house, which has been adapted and expanded for this story. He also created the character of Ulandir Ta'thyriel, Aladir's father. Aladir Ta'thyriel was inspired by Fae'lien Ta'thyriel, played by Chris Ruffell, as well as one of my own old characters.

Dreas Glaid was created by Devin McCarthy and was adapted for this novel with his permission.

Jonathan Sterling was a non-player character in Shades of Venaya and played by Andrew Warren.

Lieutenant Garrick Torrent is a reference to Tavren Torrent, a non-player character portrayed by Alex Arjad.

Thank you all, as well as all my other players and tireless staff members, for helping to contribute so much to my world.

# APPENDIX I – DEEP DOMINIONS

While my good friend Erik has made an admirable effort to classify the Deep Dominions, I fear that research into their interactions within the body has been largely overlooked by my scholarly brethren. The functions and costs of the Prime Dominions are well-classified – indeed, Master Tarren has done much of this work himself, and I credit him for his efforts. Nevertheless, I found the subject intriguing enough to warrant additional research, and here I will present some of my initial findings.

Erik tends to classify dominions based on their manifestations – physical, mental, or energy. I prefer to classify each dominion based on its relevance to the body, which I tend to find more practical. Of the deep dominions, some have clear effects on the body that relate to everyday functions. The most obvious is likely the Dominion of Sight – its utility is obvious from the name alone. I refer to these as "Requisite Dominions", in that the quality of our daily lives would be drastically reduced without them.

Others serve important functions, but are less obvious. The Dominion of Protection, for example, helps bone and skin growth, which serves to both improve the physical capabilities of the body and provide protection against sorcery. It's important to note that not all creatures appear to have this dominion in measurable quantities – indeed, humans and our cousins like the Rethri appear to be the only species in which this dominion is present.

This helps to explain why some forms of sorcery are vastly more effective against other creatures than they are against humans – the

Dominion of Protection enables our skin to act as a natural filter, preventing external sorcery effects from entering our bodies. This does not grant any sort of immunity, of course; it is merely a layer of inherent defense that other creatures do not appear to have.

Similarly, the Dominion of Spirit – which I have long studied along with my colleague Ulandir Ta'thyriel – appears to have an important function in assisting the body in recovering from trauma. I admit that in spite of the egregious number of apostrophes in his name Ulandir is presently better versed in this particular subject, and thus I will leave it to him to explain in one of his own future essays.

Dominions such as protection and spirit are thus quite important, but less obvious in their functions. I refer to these as "Beneficial Dominions".

There are other Deep Dominions that have no obvious role in the body at all – these I call "Esoteric Dominions". The effects of these dominions on the body are much more difficult to quantify, but I will continue in my efforts to catalogue their functions and side effects in the future.

*Requisite Deep Dominions*

| Dominion | Function of the Dominion | Side Effects for Using This Dominion |
|---|---|---|
| Sight | Governs the sense of sight. | Weakness in this Dominion would prevent the body from seeing properly. |
| Sound | Governs the sense of hearing. | Weakness in this Dominion would prevent the body from hearing properly. |
| Blood | Controls the flow and function of blood in the body. | A weakened Dominion of Blood would prevent the blood from flowing or functioning properly. This can lead to a number of blood-related disorders. This can also prevent the blood from properly clotting, similar to hemophilia. |
| Heat | Allows the body to draw warmth from outside. Similar to the function of Flame, but only functions to keep the body warmer, rather than cooler. | Using Dominion of Heat spells will draw directly from body heat and cause the character to shiver and eventually suffer hypothermia. |
| Ice | Allows the body to cool itself by drawing from external sources. Works with the Dominions of Heat and Flame to regulate body temperature. | Using Dominion of Ice spells wreak havoc on the body's ability to regulate its own temperature, causing symptoms similar to heat stroke. |

*Beneficial Deep Dominions*

| | | |
|---|---|---|
| Protection | Influences bone density and skin composition. Skin developed by someone possessing a strong Dominion of Protection serves to protect against some forms of sorcery. | Without the Dominion of Protection, skin will have fewer layers, easily breaking and providing minimal filtration against sorcery.<br><br>Bones are similarly weakened by a lack of the Dominion of Protection within the body. |
| Metal | Regulates iron in the blood, although the function of iron in the body remains a mystery to us at this time. | The side effects of using the Dominion of Metal are unclear. The most visible symptom of this is paler skin, but it also can cause general fatigue, difficulty with blood flow, and the eventual failure of organs. |
| Travel | Enhances reaction time and muscular movement. | Generalized fatigue and muscular weakness. In extreme cases paralysis can occur. |

| | | |
|---|---|---|
| Blades | The so-called Dominion of Blades is most likely a particular form of the Dominion if Radiance, a Deep Dominion connected to Light and Motion. The function appears to be to purge foreign sorcery from the body. | Most people do not manifest the Dominion of Blades in any measureable quantity. Stories indicate that its users experience generalized fatigue, and it would be expected that they would also lose some of the efficacy of the dominion's ability to purge foreign dominions from their bodies. |
| Destiny | Destiny sorcerers are incredibly rare. Most claim that their abilities enable to them to have glimpses of the future. These sometimes manifest visually, other times in dreams or in the form of memories. | Overusing the Dominion of Destiny appears to interfere with cognitive functions, similar to overusing the Dominion of Knowledge. |
| Void | I have yet to meet a human void sorcerer, but my studies indicate that this dominion may serve a similar function to the Dominion of Protection for the Esharen. This would make some sense, given that when used, the Dominion of Void has an effect that weakens or nullifies sorcery. | Unknown. Without any human sorcerers, I have limited data available. |

There are many other Deep Dominions in existence, most of which are poorly understood. I hope to gather more information on these to write about them more in future essays.

*-An excerpt from Deep Dominions by Edrick Theas*

# APPENDIX II – NOTABLE PERSONAGES

*Paladins of Tae'os*

| Name | Title | Description |
|------|-------|-------------|
| Herod | Unknown | Retired former Paladins of Tae'os officer. |
| Derek Stone | Arbiter | Arbiter (leader) of the Koranir branch of the Paladins of Tae'os. |
| Caerden Lyselia | Arbiter | Arbiter (leader) of the Lysandri branch of the Paladins of Tae'os. |
| Colonel Wyndam | Colonel | Overseer for the paladin examinations. |
| Orin Dyr | Lieutenant Colonel | A paladin of Koranir and unarmed combat expert. |
| Lydia Scryer | Major | A sorceress specializing in knowledge sorcery. |
| Darryl Morris | Lieutenant | Assistant overseer for the paladin examinations. |
| Garrick Torrent | Lieutenant | Platoon overseer for Platoon 3's applicants. |
| Alan Trace | Lieutenant | Examination proctor for the paladin exams. |
| Hadrigan Holder | Lieutenant | A teleportation specialist in the Paladins of Sytira. |
| Lauren Banks | Second Lieutenant | Assistant overseer for the paladin examinations. |
| Gerald Mason | Paladin | A Paladin of Tae'os who works in the city of Orlyn. |

*Applicants for the Paladins of Tae'os — Platoon 1*

| Name | Title | Description |
|---|---|---|
| Keldyn Andys | Unknown | The first swordsman in generations to be blessed with the Gifts of Aendaryn. Keldyn is a blade sorcerer, capable of creating phantasmal blades of sorcerous essence. |
| Terras | Unknown | A Rethri sorceress specializing in the Dominion of Heat. |
| Lysen | Unknown | A Rethri sorcerer specializing in the Dominion of Ice. Terras' twin brother. |
| Susan Crimson | Lady | The third daughter of House Crimson and a former member of the Thornguard. |
| The Wandering War | ? | An exceptionally tall man or woman who wears a form-concealing cloak. Suspected to be a non-human species. |

*Applicants for the Paladins of Tae'os – Platoon 2*

| Name | Title | Description |
|---|---|---|
| Landen | "Of the Twin Blades" | Former member of the Queensguard of Orlyn. Known for fighting with multiple weapons. |
| Velas Jaldin | Unknown | Former member of the Queensguard of Orlyn. A weapons expert and motion sorceress. |
| Taelien Salaris | Taelien | A swordsman from the Forest of Blades. Bears the Sae'kes Taelien. |
| Asphodel | Oracle | A Delaren, which is a species capable of changing their shape. Asphodel is called the "Oracle" and appears to possess information gathering sorcery. |
| Teshvol | Unknown | One of Asphodel's companions. |
| Kolask | Unknown | One of Asphodel's companions. |
| Eridus | Unknown | A quiet water sorcerer. |

*Applicants for the Paladins of Tae'os — Platoon 3*

| Name | Title | Description |
| --- | --- | --- |
| Jonathan Sterling | Haven Knight | A Velryan duelist affiliated with House Haven. |
| Celia Laurent | Haven Knight | A Velryan sorceress affiliated with House Haven. |
| Alden Stone | None | A powerful warrior from Terisgard. Son of the Arbiter of Koranir. |

*Followers of Vaelien*

| Name | Title | Description |
| --- | --- | --- |
| Madrigan Ferrous | Commander | A local commanding officer of the Thornguard. |
| Jonan Kestrian | Scribe | A "humble scribe" that works for the Order of Vaelien. |
| ? | Silk | Symphony's apprentice. A dangerous sound sorceress. |
| ? | Diamond | A Vae'kes that lives in Selyr. |
| ? | Sharp | A Vae'kes that lives in Selyr. |

*House Theas*

| Name | Title | Description |
|---|---|---|
| Edrick Theas | Baron | The current patron of House Theas. One of the three legendary Immortal Sorcerers. Edrick is known to be a master of protection sorcery. |
| Nedelya Theas | Baroness | The matron of House Theas. Famous for her charisma and charm, she is far more prominent in noble social circles than her husband. |
| Kalsiris Theas | Heir | Edrick and Nedelya's son. While younger than Nakane, he is the heir to the house due to the city's primogeniture system. |
| Nakane Theas | Lady | The eldest child of Edrick and Nedelya Theas. While she is not the family heir, she has the courtesy title of "Lady". |
| Larkin Theas | Lord | The oldest male member of House Theas aside from Edrick and Kalsiris. He is one of Edrick's great grand nephews and holds the courtesy title of Lord. |

*House Ta'thyriel*

| Name | Title | Description |
|---|---|---|
| Ulandir Ta'thyriel | Earl | The current patron of House Ta'thyriel. A powerful spirit sorcerer. |
| Aladir Ta'thyriel | Lord | Ulandir's son. One of the most powerful known life sorcerers. |

*House Dianis*

| Name | Title | Description |
| --- | --- | --- |
| Volanen Dianis | Duke | The current patron of House Dianis. House Dianis is famous for running the largest sorcerous university in Velthryn, and Volanen is the current headmaster.<br><br>Volanen is reputed to be a powerful water sorcerer. |
| Torian Dianis | Lord | Volanen's younger brother. Bears the courtesy title of Lord. Unlike his brother, Torian does not have a strong reputation for his sorcery skills. |
| Ellarae Dianis | Lady | Torian's wife. Deceased. Before her death, she was known to be a powerful life sorceress. |
| Rialla Dianis | None | A child of Torian and Ellarae Dianis. She disappeared from Velthryn many years ago in an effort to save the life of her younger brother, Elias. |
| Liarra Dianis | None | Rialla's twin sister. An exceptionally powerful life sorceress. |
| Elias Dianis | None | Rialla's younger brother. He was born without a dominion bond, which was a life-threatening condition. To attempt to save his life, Rialla fled the city with him. Elias is currently being cared for in the |

| | | |
|---|---|---|
| | | city of Selyr. |
| Shivarin | None | A loyal guard for House Dianis. |

*House Hartigan*

| Name | Title | Description |
|---|---|---|
| Blake Hartigan | Baron | A famous alchemist and enchanter. Best known for the creation of "Hartigan's Star", the first dominion bonded item broadly recognized as sharing many of the characteristics of divinely-forged artifacts.<br><br>Blake Hartigan is one of the three legendary "Immortal Sorcerers" and known to be a master of flame sorcery. |
| Sara Hartigan | Baroness | Blake Hartigan's wife. Very little is known about her. |

*Other Notable Figures*

| Name | Title | Description |
|---|---|---|
| Erik Tarren | ? | A famous scholar known for his treatises on history and sorcery.<br><br>Erik Tarren is one of the three legendary "Immortal Sorcerers" and known to be a master of travel sorcery. |
| Amir Orin | King | A legendary Delaren king. |

*The Rulers of the City of Orlyn*

| Name | Title | Description |
|------|-------|-------------|
| Byron | King | The current ruler of the city of Orlyn. |
| Tylan | Goddess of Rulership | Former ruler of Orlyn and mother to King Byron, Tylan retains her position as "goddess" in spite of Edon's imprisonment. |
| Myros | God of Battle | The patron of soldiers and champion of the gods. |
| Vorain | Goddess of Shelter | The least known of the gods. She is the patron of the weak and defenseless. Disappeared after Edon was imprisoned. |
| Edon | Former God of Ascension | The former leader of the gods of Orlyn. Now deposed and imprisoned. |

*The Gods of the Tae'os Pantheon*

| Name | Title | Description |
|---|---|---|
| Sytira | Goddess of Knowledge | Among the most powerful of the gods, and patron deity of many scholars and sorcerers. |
| Aendaryn | God of Blades | Often considered the leader of the Tae'os pantheon. Known for wielding the Sae'kes Taelien, the symbol of the pantheon. |
| Eratar | God of Travel | Patron deity of merchants, sailors, and travelers. |
| Koranir | God of Strength | Patron deity of soldiers. Also associated with the Dominion of Stone. |
| Xerasilis | God of Justice | Patron deity of judges. Also associated with the Dominion of Flame. |
| Lysandri | Goddess of Water | Patron deity of sailors. Frequently associated with self-sacrifice. |
| Lissari | Goddess of Life | Patron deity of doctors and healers. |

*The Divinities of Selyr*

| Name | Title | Description |
|------|-------|-------------|
| Vaelien | The Preserver | The principal deity worshipped by the residents of Selyr, as well as the majority of the Forest of Blades. His "children" are called the Vae'kes. |
| Aayara | The Lady of Thieves | One of the eldest of the Vae'kes, Aayara is considered a demigoddess and commonly worshipped by thieves, lovers, and gamblers. |
| Jacinth | The Blackstone Assassin | The other eldest of the Vae'kes, Jacinth is a demigod associated with the execution of justice. He is greatly feared outside of the Forest of Blades and rumored to have slain the gods of several other pantheons. |

# ABOUT THE AUTHOR

Andrew Rowe was once a professional game designer for awesome companies like Blizzard Entertainment, Cryptic Studios, and Obsidian Entertainment. Nowadays, he's writing full time.

When he's not crunching numbers for game balance, he runs live-action role-playing games set in the same universe as his books. In addition, he writes for pen and paper role-playing games.

Aside from game design and writing, Andrew watches a lot of anime, reads a metric ton of fantasy books, and plays every role-playing game he can get his hands on.

Interested in following Andrew's books releases, or discussing them with other people? You can find more info, update, and discussions in a few places online:

Andrew's Blog: https://andrewkrowe.wordpress.com/
Mailing List: https://andrewkrowe.wordpress.com/mailing-list/
Facebook: https://www.facebook.com/Arcane-Ascension-378362729189084/
Reddit: https://www.reddit.com/r/ClimbersCourt/

# OTHER BOOKS BY ANDREW ROWE

The War of Broken Mirrors Series
*Forging Divinity*
*Stealing Sorcery*
*Defying Destiny (Coming Soon)*

Arcane Ascension Series
*Sufficiently Advanced Magic*
*On the Shoulders of Titans*
*Arcane Ascension Book 3 (Coming Soon)*

Weapons and Wielders Series
*Six Sacred Swords*
*Diamantine (Coming Soon)*

Made in the USA
Columbia, SC
24 April 2021